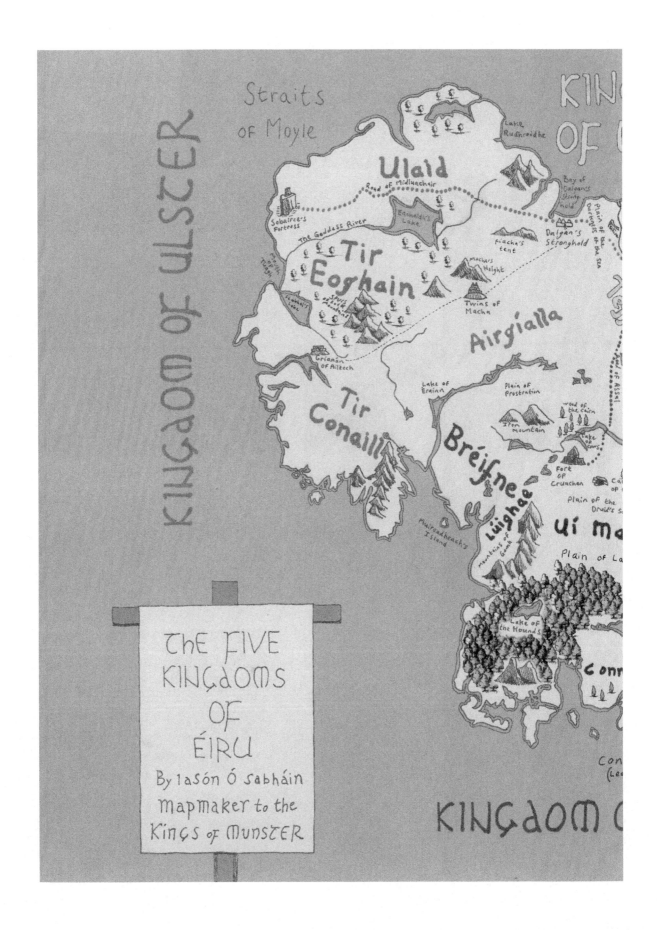

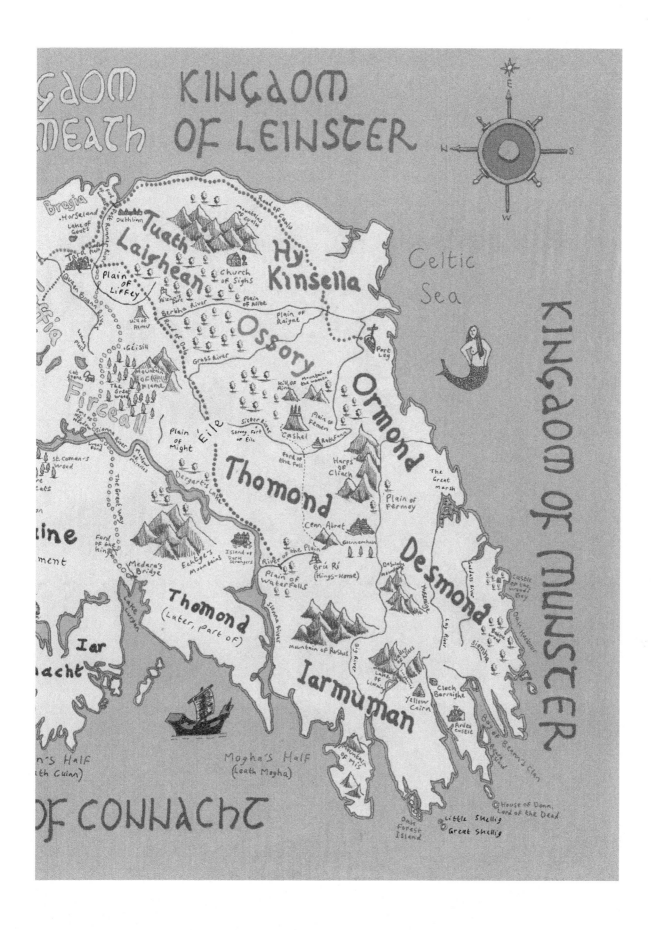

# KINGS OF MUNSTER

# THE ISLAND OF DESTINY

(Book 1 of 3)

# Jason Savin

**By the Same Author**

**Kings of Munster**

Book 1: The Island of Destiny

Book 2: Curse of the Aes Sídhe

Book 3: A Time of Heroes

**Other Books**

Beyond the Elven Gate          Mybook.to/Beyondtheelvengate

# Ríthe na Mumhan

## Óileán na Cinniúint

Ag

# Iasón Ó Sabháin

These three books are dedicated to the memory of my late wife, Tracy Savin, for without her love and support I couldn't have written any of this. I wish she had been here to see the books published, so she could have seen how much that she truly meant to me.

> *Her hands were always hot;*
> *Mine always cold.*
> *We were opposites in so many ways;*
> *But our compassionate hearts shone with the same values,*
> *And together we completed one another.*

And also, to my praiseworthy son, Cameron, whose absence from my life caused such a void that it urged me to engulf myself in such a momentous project to begin with.

To my nieces and nephews: Go forward with confidence my friends knowing that in your heart you descend from kings.

These books are also dedicated to the Irish storytellers, past, present and future.

# Acknowledgements

I would like to thank for their support, especially over the last tricky year and a half:

The fabulous Karen Clarke and Alison Barbour, whose amazing support and friendship has meant the world to me. Without your support I really don't know how I would have managed; as well as Sheryl Johnson, Helen Hardwick, Siobhan Dalton, Lynne Goldsborough, and the rest of the Blue Badgers, old and new. As well as the lovely Ruth Lund.

The Curry Boys: Steve Lough, Liam Gilfellon, Pete Fulham, John Frizzle, Eoghan Dyer, Craig Lough and Jamie Hope.

My old workmates: The incredibly talented songwriter, my very good friend and loyal drinking partner, Lee Howe, with Sharon Wilson, Iain Nicholson, Anthony Fovargue, David Leverett, Phil Ansell, Catherine Kemp, Michael Smith, Simon Peacock, Eddie Newbrook, Davy Jeffrey, David Alexander, Marc Bailey, Bob Baldwin, Ian 'the Chief' Charlton, Ian Johnson, Lewis Davidson, Paul Gray, Colin Milner, Paul White, John Sanderson, Warren Thompson, Curtis Davidson, Neil Armstrong, Craig Mackereth, Mandy Steele, Martin Stephenson and the impressive Sean Thompson. As well as John McDonald, Jordan Lee, Shaun Connelly, Rob Cowie, Craig Dunn, Terry Galbraith, Paul Hardy, Ken Harrison, Gary Hogg, Keith McNall, Bill Millican, Simon Rowles, Gemma Johnson, Richi Cunningham, Steven Trott, and even Ant Wood.

Actor Friends: Valerie Speed, Susan and Stan Barker-McGuire, Steven and Phil Toothill, Catherine and Robbie Murray, Mark and Mikey Hunter, Phil Docherty and Moira Doherty, Alison Walker, John Raine, Judith Doyle and Jonathan Richardson, Karen Bianco, Julie and Jarred, Adele Evitt, Kev Whittaker (who encouraged my writing in the early days, getting me to write plays which were all performed), and Bill and Diane Pickard.

And my family:

The Savins: my sister, Lisa Hoey for doing the amazing book covers; my brother, Scott, for spending many valuable days photoshopping the map of Ireland, and adding lettering to the world map and book covers; my late brother, Darren, who believed in me, and gave me invaluable advice and encouragement. It pains me that he also didn't get to see these books published; my mother, Joan Savin for early proof-reading and for giving me advice regarding the story, which greatly helped to improve the end result, as well as telling me that I needed to include a world map; and to my father, Derek Savin; sister-in-law, Donna; Alison and Bob Hutton-Keith; Elaine, Laura, Zoe, Sheila and Philip Hutton; Amanda and Peter Best; Sue Chippett; and Chloe Edwards: for all of your support. As well as my very good friend and affectionate, constant, loyal companion, my late dog, Mr. Tommy, otherwise known as Sir Tommy, and Tommy Tickle (the Lurcher), who gave me a well-needed routine and kept me busy over a very difficult period; you, my friend are greatly missed.

And the Robinsons: the incredible Danny and Betty Robinson; Dryden Hogg; Connor, Katie, Isaac and Laoghaire; Stuey Robson; June, Geoff and Dean Laidler; Neil and Bev Robinson; and Karen Manley for all being there in my corner over the last few years.

And also: Alan Dovaston; Lorraine Lunt; Audrey and Matthew; Maureen and Fred; and the friendly dog walkers: Reg's mam; the two Bichon's mam; as well as Paul and Max. The little conversations that I've had with you since my wife passed away have meant so very much.

As well as Leanne O'Sullivan; Reverend David, Jacqueline, David and Grace Atkinson; Tony Ward; Jack 'Badger' Greabes; Alec Watson; Marjorie Wright; Michael and Norma Falcus; Derek Beasley; Paul Wortley; Andy and Mary Blanchflower; and Michele Shield. The few, friendly conversations that I've had with you all have helped me get through a very difficult six months at work, before I ended up taking early retirement.

And a huge thank you to the extremely helpful staff at Murray Library, at the University of Sunderland, (my old alma mater) for their patience and kindness in helping me to access many of the old academic texts.

And to my editor, Guy Tindale.

And a big thank you to those previous managers whose personalities have been used to add detail to many of the villains in this book.

To you all I shall remain eternally grateful, for without you, this book wouldn't be what it is today. I humbly thank you all.

# Contents

# Introduction

I first came across the great Irish legends whilst researching my own family tree, beginning with my great-great-grandmother, Julia O'Sullivan. I was blown away by what I discovered, as I was literally reading about the legendary exploits of my very own ancestors. And some of these stories were well over a thousand years old.

As I began to write them down, piecing them together like bits of an old jigsaw, putting them into some kind of rough date order, to try to get a better understanding of my own ancestry, I slowly began to realise just how incredibly fascinating these stories were and how others might also enjoy them as much as I do myself. It was then that I decided to re-write them in a format that modern readers could appreciate, as many of the translations that I was working from were not overly easy to understand. In that way I could publish the stories for others to enjoy. What made it a little harder was that there were details in some of the stories that were contradicted by other information that I had researched. For example, accounts of people's deaths differed, as well as the meanings of place names. Therefore, these had to be written in whichever way was most logical for them to fit together.

This book trilogy isn't meant to be an academic study of the history of Ireland. That has already been done by more esteemed scholars than myself. These are a re-creation of the legendary tales that would have been told around the fireside by the ancient storytellers, so they'd be a combination of history and mythology designed to entertain and enthral the listener on those long, dark nights.

The stories contain accounts of powerful kings, beautiful princesses, druids and fairies; and yes, the fairies, known as the Tuatha Dé Danann (TOOR DEY DAHNUN), were well-documented in the ancient histories of Ireland. There's even the occasional mention of mermaids and werewolves.

By re-writing these stories, I've tried to do for the ancient tales of Ireland what Malory did for the tales of King Arthur, by bringing many separate adventures together to form one long coherent story, with my own invented storyteller being the 'glue' that holds them all together. I really hope that you enjoy the result, as it's been quite a lengthy endeavour.

Once you begin to read these stories, you'll find that they have a familiar feel, as these ancient tales have influenced the likes of J. R. R. Tolkien (who read them in their original language) and George R. R. Martin, as well as C. S. Lewis. These ancient Irish tales have many of the same fantasy elements that these great writers have themselves used, and the original stories are just as epic and equally as impressive as theirs.

I still find it incredible that these old tales aren't more well-known, and I hope that one day they'll equal in fame the legends of King Arthur and Robin Hood, and many others that I could mention, as the amazing characters of Irish myth truly deserve to be thought of amongst their peers. These old stories really do equal in importance the ancient history and folklore of other countries such as those of the Greeks, the Pharaohs of Egypt, the Viking sagas of Scandinavia, as well as the old tales of Europe, Russia, Japan, China, North and South America,

Africa, Australia, New Zealand, and all those other countries with a long tradition of oral storytelling.

In some ways, writing this has felt very much like I'm fulfilling my destiny, which might sound like a crazy thing to say, but I've been so driven to finish this, putting in an incredible number of hours, usually four hours per day, seven days per week, and then after my wife passed away, I increased this to about ten hours per day, seven days per week, constantly writing and re-writing, and only feeling ready for publication after I was a hundred percent happy with the work, which is why it has taken me over eleven years to complete. I've split the book into three parts: The first to be published on my 9th wedding anniversary on 19th October, 2022; the second part to be published on the 13th anniversary of meeting my late wife, on 28th October, 2022, and the third and final part to be published on what would have been my wife's fiftieth birthday, on the 17th November, 2022.

I've included maps, drawn by my own hand, one of them showing Ireland as it has never been seen before, to help the reader to follow the heroes' quests. (My brother, Scott helped to photoshop a few of my mistakes). And as an additional interest, in the third book: *Kings of Munster: A Time of Heroes*, I've included a genealogy section in the back so that many of those who come from Irish descent will be able to clearly see which of the heroes in these tales they are actually descended from. And for the rest, please enjoy these ancient tales of antiquity, and let them take you back to a time when life was very different from today, a time of real sword and sorcery.

On another note; in my lengthy research I came across the word 'Euhemerism'. It's defined in modern academic literature as the theory that myths originated from real historical events. Therefore, according to this definition, all legends must contain an element of truth. So, my friend, go seek your own truth within these pages.

I plan to use a percentage of the profits from the sale of these books to protect some of the ancient monuments of Ireland, such as the fairy-forts and castles. So, with the purchase of these three books, you are helping to protect a fragile history, for when it's gone, it will be lost forever.

If you are of Irish descent, then these are your ancestors.

And this is your origin story…

A strange, dense mist had eerily risen from the surrounding bogs. Throughout the fortress there were whispers of it being a Sídhe-mist*. But Sídhe-folk were rare these days. The mist quickly turned into a thick, impenetrable fog which engulfed our lofty little hill-fort, so very little could be seen beyond the strong wooden walls. It was in these conditions that the lone rider approached our stronghold on that cold Samhain** evening.

The sentinel on the wall nervously shouted down to see who dared desire entry on such a night. The strong, deep voice answered that it was the Chief-seanchaí*** of Munster. Another quick voice bounded down to the gatekeepers below, "Open the gates". And then louder, "OPEN THE DAMN GATES". The guards quickly responded to this second command and did as they were bid.

As the rider slowly rode out of the fog, framed within the large wooden gateway, we could see him clearly, illuminated by the flames from the two gatekeepers' torch-lights. He was indeed dressed as a Chief-seanchaí, wearing a tall pointed hat, with a six-coloured cloak wrapped around his strong shoulders; the cloak continued down his back, draped over the rear end of his horse and showed just how important he was, as only a king could wear more colours than this. Gently resting upon his back, covering much of the cloak, was a hero's circular shield. And beneath his cloak, being only visible at his front, was a white gown that exposed his bare knees to the night's air. Whilst at his side, hanging over his left thigh was a sword housed within a black scabbard, all adorned with silver, which glistened in the flickering torch-light.

One thing that struck us immediately was that this rider was alone; where was his entourage? Maybe they'd gotten lost in the fog!

We couldn't believe that such an important man had come to visit us on a grim night like this. We knew that we'd have to be on our best behaviour.

The visitor dismounted and his horse was stabled for the night.
As he strolled past us, our Chieftain met him, there in the courtyard. He graciously bid him, "A hundred-thousand welcomes", before leading him to the Great Hall for nourishment.

We followed a little way behind, not wanting to miss a thing.

Being a most-special guest, our attentive cupbearer handed him that most noble of welcoming drinks: mead, served in an exquisitely carved wooden-goblet that befitted a man of his station. How he seemed to enjoy sipping upon that warming elixir.

---

*Sídhe (pronounced SHEE) is an old Gaelic word and refers to the Irish Fairies or the mounds in which they live. Therefore, a Sídhe-mist is a magical mist created by the Fairies, and Sídhe-folk are the Fairies themselves.
** Samhain (pronounced SOW-INN) is the old pagan word for Halloween.
*** SHAH-NACK-EE

# The Island of Destiny

*May the warm lands of Iberia keep safe thy tribe,*
*To nourish and protect ye, all your days to abide.*
*But when nourishment ends and protects ye no longer,*
*then seaward bound head ye, for tarry no longer;*
*For the Island of Destiny shall be there awaiting ye,*
*To remain forevermore till the ends of eternity.*

There were many of us gathered in the Great Hall that evening with bellies stuffed from all the joyous feasting. There was much merriment and boasting and the roar of manly laughter engulfed the room like a cloud of smoke. This was indeed a happy gathering. Now came the moment that we'd all been waiting for; this was when the entertainment was to begin.

The seanchaí was handed a drinking-horn which was promptly filled with ale. We all patiently awaited his first words, daring not to stare at such an important man before he began. As the stranger cleared his throat, all eyes darted towards him. This gave us the opportunity to properly look him over. He appeared to be in his mid-thirties, and even though his clothing seemed a little worn and frayed at the cuffs, which was unusual for a man of his standing, he was still well turned out, with a large brooch of gold, whilst silver embellished every other item that he wore. He had dark brown hair, with a long, forked beard that looked like it contained every tincture of the colour brown, from a light golden ginger to a shade almost as black as tar. There was considerable wisdom in his eyes, for they appeared to have seen much during his lifetime, but still there was a touch of humour deep within. This well-respected man, who was well trained in the art of storytelling, was about to begin. He slowly raised his drinking-horn to wet his throat with a sip of ale. As he started speaking, in his warm, resonant voice, the room quickly fell silent as everyone stopped what they were doing and moved closer to hear his tale.

"Come closer…No my friends, really come closer; closer to the fireside. Gaze into the dancing flames and listen to my tales; tales that will transport you to a world of long ago.

Ten tales I shall tell, though I shall only abide with you for thrice three nights, before I embark upon my final quest; hence I shall tell you at least one tale each eventide. These tales will teach you the ways of the old code, when wars were fought justly so no man fought more than his equal and when sworn oaths couldn't be revoked without punishment from the gods. These lessons shall guide you nobly throughout your life, to the land beyond the grave.

The first two tales were told to me by the seanchaí of old.

Our first tale begins a long time ago, when the earth was much younger. It was so long ago that even I hadn't been born", he smiled, "This was one thousand and seven hundred years before the birth of the mighty Roman Empire, or so the holy clerics do reckon. Although some calculate this as being seven hundred years closer, in the days of Solomon. But whichever date is true, it matters not in our tale, for these are the facts told to me by the storytellers of old.

The first hero that I shall acquaint you with was the powerful Celtic King, Breoghan, son of Brath, son of Deag, son of Arcadh. He ruled over the vast kingdom of Iberia, on that great peninsula where the lands of Spain and Portugal stand today. Breoghan was a huge man, with a big bushy beard, a long, noble nose and a handsome brow. He was blessed with a loud manly voice which, when needed, could be heard for many leagues above the din of battle. He was the sort of warrior-king who commands easily due to the overwhelming respect that was felt for him, for beneath his powerfully confident exterior he held a strong desire for fairness whilst exhibiting such genuine charismatic warmth towards his people. In fact, such was the immense love that his people had for him, that they were only too eager to help him to achieve his considerable aims. This helped to make him a most significant figure upon the world's stage. Furthermore, it was from this one single foreign ruler that all the nobility and gentry of Ériu now find themselves to be descended.

Breoghan was the father of ten sons; and big strapping lads they were. His eldest was Bilé, who was being rigorously educated in the disciplines of kingship, so that one day he would follow in his father's footsteps and lead the kingdom. And what a magnificent kingdom it was. Although it was Breoghan's father, Brath, who'd originally tried to conquer the land, by landing upon the far north-eastern coast, just south of those majestic mountains, and there he launched a mighty, though unsuccessful campaign to gain control. Thereafter it fell to Breoghan to finish his father's work, with a lengthy all-out war that eventually won him that vast territory, which, as I've said, comprised of much of the Iberian Peninsula.

After the flames of war had subsided, Breoghan began anew by creating his own vision upon the landscape. This took the form of his royal capital of Galicia, which he raised in the north-western corner. It was indeed a great achievement, as that part of the country was all green hills and rocky cliffs, with a thousand rivers cutting through, all sheltered beneath an endless canopy of trees. Therefore, it was within this wilderness that Breoghan built his walled town; when completed it was named Breoghan's Fortress, or Brigantia, in his honour. And within the town walls children could be heard playing as nearby warriors noisily practised their warcraft, all within the safety of Brigantia. Above the town walls flew Breoghan's royal banner; its emblem being that of a majestic castle, which represented his mighty fortress and showed not only his strength, but also highlighted the protection that he offered his new subjects across the whole of his domain, for it was by using their unified strength that the fortress was built.

At the most westerly point of Galicia stood the cliffs known as *Cape Finisterre*: 'the edge of the world' as nothing was thought to exist beyond, except for the infinite Sea of Darkness. Therefore, with no threats being expected from the west, Breoghan's attention was drawn to the small peninsula that lay to the north where he built his magnificent, huge, hulking, watch-tower; it was a thing of beauty, being built entirely of stone, with a staircase running all around the outside. It was set high up upon a hill not far from his majestic fortress, in such a commanding position that it could be seen for many leagues around, which reinforced, to all of his people, that it was indeed he who ruled their land. It was so tall that watchmen standing atop the tower could see far into the distance, to the lands of Gaul to the east, and across the unending expanse of uninhabited ocean to the north and west, so that if anyone, or anything, dared to invade, they would certainly be seen coming.

(Some say, that Breoghan's Tower stood upon the very spot that the Lighthouse of Brigantia stands today. Whilst others say that those two buildings are one and the same).

King Breoghan had a noble young grandson; his name was Galamh (GALAV), son of Bilé, and at that time he was famous amongst his people for his incredible strength, as well as for his healthy and active pursuit of knowledge; but let us not forget also his natural, hereditary skills of leadership, for this too was important. Though it was these first two qualities that caused him to venture southwards, to explore the neighbouring lands of Africa, for he wanted to acquire knowledge from that mysterious land, as well as to put his own bravery to the test, in that wild, possibly hostile terrain.

Galamh was tall, rugged and handsome, slim of build, yet wide of shoulder and strong of arm like his father and grandfather before him. His brown hair was shoulder length and his youthful beard was just beginning to fill out. He wore the regal clothing of a man of noble birth, with a knee-length royal tunic beneath a red woollen-cloak that brushed the backs of his calves as he walked. Beyond his clothing, the one thing about him that was impossible to ignore was his boyish smile, which seemed to exude a most playful and kind-hearted sense of fun, along with that mischievous twinkle in his eyes that made you feel as though he was the king of joviality and you were going to have a wonderful time in his company. Many sought out his companionship because of this. Ah, that huge smile of his! It was always so generously welcoming, having a most disarming affect, instantly putting others at their ease. Whilst behind that fledgling beard was a heroic, manly square jaw, which was another admirable quality that inspired confidence in all those whom he met. Furthermore, Galamh was so driven and determined in each of his many endeavours that his highly infectious enthusiasm excited others, making them feel compelled to follow. And who wouldn't follow such a man? He was also a highly skilled sportsman who excelled at every event, from swordplay to riding. But his one flaw, which rarely was seen, except in the most exceptional of circumstances, was his stormy temper if ever he was crossed; but most people knew not to cross such a big, stout-hearted man.

Galamh's last days in Iberia had been memorably warm. During that time, he'd ridden down to the far south of his kingdom with a few trusted companions, where they feasted well each night around campfires and slept under the dark cloak of sky. Their conversations had been lively, in places, but there were periods of silence and apprehension, as none but the gods could know what truly lay ahead for young Galamh.

It was well past nightfall when Galamh found himself standing upon the deck of the galley, waving goodbye to his closest companions as his ship slowly sailed away from the safety of the port. The sound of the soft lapping waves adding to his feelings of unease. He knew that he wouldn't be away for more than the period of a moon, and even though he gave off the air of someone who is always in control, deep within his nerves had begun to show from the very moment that he had anxiously said goodbye to all those who were close to him, for he had never been away from home before.

Through the desperate darkness the glowing moonlight shone down, glistening upon the gentle waves, its faint yellow light accompanying the ship on its journey across the narrow strait that spanned the mouth of the Middle-of-the-Land Sea. Galamh planned to sleep as much as he could, for he wanted to feel refreshed when their ship arrived at the other side; but before dreams had entered his consciousness, he lay awake, gazing up at the stars, as he contemplated his own mortality, as youthful men so often do, during those seemingly endless and lonely periods of darkness.

As Galamh woke the following day, the ship was nearing the African harbour. The sun was only just beginning to show itself, glistening like a jewel, far off, along the watery horizon to the east. Its golden rays sparkled along the entire length of the Middle-of-the-Land Sea. Apart from the sea's entrance, which they'd just sailed across, the rest of that huge, enclosed expanse of water was surrounded by the shores of the Middle-Land, with little being known of the world beyond.

Once the ship had dropped anchor, Galamh jumped into the beautifully clear waters, landing knee-deep with a splash. The cool water helped to revive him, for he was not feeling fully alert just yet. The bottom edge of his scarlet-cloak floated behind him in the shallow water as his sandalled feet trudged from the sea towards the sandy beach. Splash! Splash! Splash!

He cautiously stepped ashore, feeling a little apprehensive about this foreign land, as strange beasts were known to roam the plains, the likes of which he couldn't begin to imagine. Tightly gripped in his strong right hand was a long spear which he used like a walking-staff, its shiny, polished bronze-tip glinting in the African sun, whilst upon his muscular back, a sturdy round-shield lightly rested. He was also armed with a princely sword that hung from his left hip, whilst a handsome dagger sat snugly by his right side.

It had been arranged for him to be met by two of the local natives. They waved to him as they watched him walking up the sand. These two African guides seemed pleasant enough, though only spoke a little of his language. They were both brown of skin, each beneath a large black bush of hair, whilst a small tuft of black beard stood out proudly from their chins like the nose from a face. They were of middling height, so the tops of their heads were level with Galamh's shoulders, as he was so unusually tall; they were almost naked except for loincloths, whilst their glistening torsos were adorned with belts and necklaces fashioned from pure gold. How different they looked to Galamh, whose clothes were so typical of his own kingdom.

'Twas hot that day upon the African mainland, so the bottoms of his sea-drenched clothing quickly dried.

The two guides led Galamh away from the sea, and away from the sound of the waves noisily breaking upon the shore. They took him along the well-trodden earthen footpath in the direction of those faraway green and grey coloured mountains that filled much of the distant horizon. The further from the sea they walked, the quieter it became, as there was nothing to replace the sound of the waves except for the occasional cry of a distant animal.

The desolate plains that they crossed were sun-scorched, which had bleached them yellow, making them seem barely fertile. Beneath their feet the hard, compacted trail was dry and cracked. To either side of them they could clearly see that the whole area was made-up of patches of the poorest grass, although there were still clumps of trees to be seen here and there.

During those daylight hours, the further they journeyed, the hotter it seemed to get, especially for poor Galamh, who was more used to the temperate climate of Galicia with its cool ocean breezes, so wasn't used to this stifling sort of heat. It was due to this exhaustive temperature that during his time in Africa it was only during the mornings and afternoons that they could travel, seeking shelter during the hot mid-day sun, as well as through those colder, chilly nights.

It was upon that very first day, when the blindingly hot sun was almost directly overhead, that Galamh saw the shape of a small village in the distance. It consisted of many square houses built from pale-yellow mud bricks. Although, if it hadn't been for the short, dark patches of shadow that lay at the top of their western walls, cast from the overhanging flat rooftops, then he might not have noticed them, for they blended so perfectly with the colour of the surrounding landscape. He'd never been so pleased to find shelter, as well as water, for so great was his thirst.

As he approached, the villagers rushed out to meet him, although some of the younger ones were ordered back indoors, out of the intense heat. There was much excitement in the village, as they rarely got visitors from overseas. They made him feel most welcome, though he couldn't understand a word that they said.

Galamh was quickly welcomed inside of the chief's hut. It was noticeably cooler within. Sitting inside was the Chieftain, dressed in a similar fashion to that of the two guides, wearing the customary loincloth, though his black wool-like hair extended further down his back, being much longer than that of the other tribesmen. A brown leather belt carrying a row of golden discs passed over each shoulder, running diagonally across his chest. Around his left bicep he wore a golden arm-ring. Underneath all of this regalia, his body was completely decorated with tribal tattoos, which were reserved purely for their nobility. The Chieftain cheerfully welcomed Galamh to their village, as one of the guides acted as translator to the best of his ability.

During their afternoon rest period, Galamh stayed with an accommodating young family. He was so pleased to take shelter in one of those small mud huts. They seemed to exude that magical quality that can only be found in nature, for during the burning temperatures of the mid-day sun the walls were cool to the touch, whereas later in the day, after the sun had gone down and the land had become chilly, the opposite seemed to happen. The colder those winds blew that night, the warmer the walls seemed to be. It was as if the sky gods and the land gods were working hand in hand to provide those hospitable tribesmen with a comfortable shelter.

Galamh woke in the late afternoon to the delicious smells of food simmering away in large bronze cauldrons; these once-shiny cooking-pots now dulled and blackened with continuous use. The fragrant, almost intoxicating smells drifted throughout the village. Due to the tribesmen being farmers, they had a few small herds of goat and sheep as well as plentiful supplies of grain, so Galamh ate well that day, enjoying much of their spicy lamb stew mopped up with fistfuls of bread.

Later that night during the hours of darkness, the sounds of the feasting hyenas, located somewhere near the outskirts of the village, made Galamh feel most uneasy. He'd never heard such unsettling noises, their unnerving chattering laughter and long, loud mournful howls lasting well into the early hours. Most disturbed was his sleep that first night.

The following morning they set off early. There was a cool start to the day, so Galamh tightly wrapped his bare arms inside of his thick woollen cloak, trying to keep the cold air at bay. Briskly they walked, in a bid to keep warm. Galamh couldn't help yawning throughout that whole morning, so tired did he feel. Looking far into the distance, he saw that some of the higher peaks had a coating of snow. How out of place that snow looked, for as cold as the morning wind was, there was no icy bite to its breath. By afternoon, the sun was back to its sweltering self, making walking all the more wearisome.

Many more villages offered them hospitality and comfortable lodging, as they walked through those hot, barren plains, and within days they had reached the foothills at the base of the mountains. These were heavily covered in trees, making the temperature more agreeable. Following the path beneath the leafy canopy reminded Galamh of home. Despite the climate being cooler, which should have made the travelling ideal, he still found the going to be extremely tough, as there were many rocks underfoot, and his sandalled feet were getting badly bruised from all the walking. His hardy guides walked barefoot, however, as their leathery soles were accustomed to the rough surface of the ground.

As they walked through the forests, strange sounds could be heard all around. But whatever creatures were making these noises, they were certainly well hidden within their vast wooded realm. Galamh would have been most unnerved had it not been for the reassuring calmness of his guides, for never had he heard such curious sounds as these before.

That first night up in the mountains, they slept in a clearing in the trees, his guides taking it in turns to guard the campsite, for dangerous beasts were known to hunt in the vicinity. A large fire was attended to throughout the night by each of those watchful guides in turn; its constant shifting, flickering flames, compelling and enthralling as they were to watch by the race of Man had the opposite effect on the various races of beasts, for it kept them all well away.

The following day, Galamh and his guides walked further south, the land before them slowly rising upwards. They followed the path through the trees. To either side of them, beneath the branches, lay impenetrable leafy undergrowth that forced them to remain on the path. The smell from the surrounding vegetation with its warm, pleasant, almost spicy odour kept their senses alert, as the path snaked its way up the slopes of the mountainside.

By now Galamh was becoming somewhat used to the different character of his two companions, even though long conversations were terribly trying on both sides due to the language difficulties: Both guides were fairly quiet and reserved, though one of them being more serious, keeping his thoughts to himself, whilst the other one was more tactile, smiling a lot, and often seeking some sort of approbation. They were both keen to show him the vast desert that lay beyond the wooded mountains, and the beasts who dwelt upon those sandy plains. So, southwards, up those mountains they slowly travelled. But still, there was a long way to go.

It was upon the second or third day, up in the mountains, on a particularly tiring ascent, that Galamh finally saw, in the distance, through the treelined footpath, another village, this one nestled high up on the mountainside. The area around the houses had been almost completely cleared of trees, meaning that outside of the huts there was no respite from the sun's burning rays. The noises of goats bleating, sounding almost like cries for help, could be heard before they even reached the village. There they rested with more of those friendly tribesmen, who were more than happy to share their food.

Galamh enjoyed his time with the different mountain tribesmen. And what feasts the three companions ate as they went from village to village. Some even roasted whole lambs within firepits, cooking them in his honour, before he was given the eyeballs to eat. Hearing from his guides that to refuse such an honour would insult his hosts, his dry throat swallowed hard before lifting his head and popping them deliberately into his mouth, such was the princely nature of the man.

Many more days passed, and many more villages did those three companions visit before their time within the mountains were over. Galamh had lost track of how many days had passed or villages they had visited, as they must have travelled over a hundred leagues, with many of the days feeling just like the one before. His tired and bruised feet ached from all of the continuous walking, although the last few days, with them now heading downhill most of the time, had felt a lot easier on his body. But the extraordinarily generous hospitality that they'd received from all of those friendly tribesmen along the way had made the hard journey seem all the more worthwhile.

It was upon the final day, during morningtide, as their journey took them down the final mountain slopes, that Galamh was going to be tested, more than any man has ever been tested before. It was still fairly dark in those majestic mountains, for the sun was only just beginning to raise its golden head. Galamh had risen early, for he needed to relieve himself at the outskirts of the village. He was still only half awake, wrapping his warm cloak around his broad shoulders to keep out the morning's chilly air. He knew not to stray too far from the village and was warned to take his shield and spear wherever he went. Walking quietly through the sleepy, twilit village, trying not to disturb any of the tribesmen, Galamh soon reached the shadowy trees. As he stepped just inside of the tree-line, he gently rested his spear against a tall cedar, whilst he went about his business. As his warm urine flowed, his sense of relief was clearly felt. Ahhh, bliss, he thought.

Suddenly, just behind him, he heard a mighty, heart-stopping roar that sent tremors throughout his whole body. His water stayed as his heart beat a quick rhythm of war. In one swift movement, he grabbed his spear as he pulled his oaken shield from his back. Quickly he turned, being confronted by the biggest beast that he'd ever saw. A huge lion, about nine feet long, stood before him, still shrouded within the shadows. Its skull alone would have spanned Galamh's waist to the top of his head. It snorted fiercely, moving slowly nearer. Whilst most people would have fled or been too scared to move, Galamh nervously retreated, slowly drawing the beast out into the twilight, and there he stood his ground. Galamh took a deep breath, slowly raising his head and widening his arms, taking a fierce battle-stance. He'd been training all through his young life in combat, but never against a monstrous beast like this. There was no way that he could escape, not now that the lion had seen him. If he tried to flee, it would surely pounce and its jaws would crush his young body.

As it stepped from the trees, he saw that its long flowing mane was the colour of midnight. Still snorting, to show its vast superiority, the lion stealthily and silently moved forward, carefully stalking its prey. Growling loudly, it suddenly began its charge. Galamh held his nerve, ready for the attack. The ground shook at every bound. Then suddenly, it pounced upon the prince. Using his wits, Galamh quickly stepped aside, to avoid the full impact of its weighty body, as he punched his shield hard at its jaw. Within a heartbeat, his right arm instinctively jabbed his spear, grazing its ribs. As the lion's front paws landed back on the ground, Galamh winced in pain; the skin of his left shoulder had been ripped by its massive dagger-like claws. The lion slowly walked away, turning for a second charge. Galamh still held his ground. The huge beast cautiously looked at its brave prey, smelling the flowing blood that trickled down his arm, glistening in the first rays of the morning's sunlight. Galamh slowly raised his shield and spear once more. The lion roared, charging again. It thundered towards him. This time Galamh quickly stepped forward, hammering his spear hard into its chest. The beast continued its forward momentum, pouncing as Galamh naturally raised his shield in a last bid to defend himself. Its paws smashed into him, throwing him backwards. It landed heavily on top of him as he groaned under the impact of its immense weight.

Hearing the ferocious growls from within the village, the wary natives ran out carrying blazing torches to ward off the beast. Their rapidly approaching torch-light getting nearer and nearer in the dim morning light. But it was too late. Galamh was found covered in blood beneath the lion's body. His large fist gripping a bloodied dagger, whose dark dripping ooze glimmered in the flickering torch-light. He had already slain the mighty beast.

The young prince's wounds were carefully taken care of by those attentive natives, and much reverence was given to him for the bravery of his battle. Feeling much too restless to go back to sleep after his ordeal, that morning he sat, watching the sunrise, as the sky just above the heavily-forested mountain-tops blushed with a beautiful, warm, comforting orange glow. After facing such a monstrous, demonic beast, and surviving, he felt as though he'd never been so happy to be alive. That morning he ate well, breaking his fast with that warm-hearted tribe. Wanting to head off early, whilst the day was still young, Galamh and his two guides made their way from that friendly village. It seemed warm that day, even beneath the shade of those tall shadowy trees. The sun still hung low in the eastern sky and the winding path was much more open to the elements here as onward they went. There was a strong aromatic scent coming from the green needles of those surrounding trees; it was warm and pleasant to the senses, making Galamh feel quite invigorated.

Far they travelled through those heavily-forested mountains, as the path gently sloped down before them, passing by an infinite number of towering cedars. The trees were shaped like wide arrow-heads that stretched so tall that some of them must surely have pierced the blue cloak of sky. Whilst contemplating this, Galamh suddenly noticed, sitting high up in the branches, small pink-faced monkeys curiously peering down at them, each one tinged with a mixture of brown, yellow and grey fur and probably measuring less than two feet tall. Galamh was as fascinated by those little men as they seemed to be with him. Now that he'd seen them, he couldn't stop looking upwards, to see if he could spot any more. It wasn't long before he noticed a few more family groups of those extraordinary little creatures, some with babies clinging to their backs. How mesmerising they were to watch.

Suddenly, all at once the little monkeys started becoming agitated, leaping about and squealing. Both the guides stiffened in their tracks. Then came a nearby roar. Being a warrior-prince, Galamh instinctively took charge. He urged them to leave the path, pushing their way into the leafy undergrowth to hide behind a large tree. Galamh ordered his guides to remain behind him as they crouched low amidst the greenery. They desperately hoped that the beast would walk by without spotting them. Galamh held his shield up to his chin, protecting his vulnerable neck. He closed his eyes for a second, wishing that he wasn't there. His right hand tightly gripped his spear, low by his waist.

Slowly the lion neared, coming around the bend in the path, steadily plodding onward; closer. The three companions' hearts beat faster. Galamh had killed one lion, partly by luck, partly by instinct; but fighting against two of those monstrous beasts in one day was really going to stretch his luck, right to its very limits. As the lion prowled closer, the three men held their breath, not daring to make a sound. The snorting beast was now less than two yards away.

The next few seconds seemed to last for hours as closer and closer it plodded. Galamh's heartbeat pounding in his chest. How much longer could he last before madness ensued. Could it be drawn towards them by the smell of Man-flesh, or maybe even by the dried bloodied wound upon his shoulder? Galamh prayed not. Now only an arm's length away, its huge head and black flowing mane came into view. Galamh involuntarily shrank on the spot. Suddenly the lion growled, turning its head towards him. Its large jaws surging towards the prince's face. Galamh shoved his shield firmly forward as he was knocked back into the undergrowth, his spear thrusting into the beast's side. The lion side-stepped away, shocked by the sudden spear attack, then quickly turned its massive body around to face its fallen prey and bounded forward. In a last bid to stay alive Galamh jumped to his feet, quicky lunging forward from behind the tree, jabbing his weapon into the monster's ribs. The enormous beast fought with all its might, its massive deadly claws slicing through his flesh. Yet Galamh did everything that he could to avoid its bone-crushing jaws, using the protection of the tree as much as possible. Eventually the hero overcame it, slaying the deadly creature.

Scratched and bleeding, he was lucky enough to limp away from that fight. The two guides were now deeply concerned for his health and weren't happy for him to keep going onward, for so severe were his injuries. They wanted him to return to the last village so that he could be cared for, and then to be escorted back to the Middle-of-the-Land Sea, where he could be shipped off back home to Iberia for his own safety. But Galamh, having such a scholarly mind was keen to explore further so refused to go back. With that firm, persuasive manner of his, matched with his likeable, calming smile and a reassuring wink, he insisted that before he ended such a momentous quest, he wanted first to see the desert. Such was the mettle of the man. So, following Galamh's instructions, one of the guides patched up his wounds with whatever remedies were at hand, for he had a basic knowledge of herblore. And onward they went, following the path down to the stony foothills at the south side of the mountains.

The soil down there was very poor, with a thousand tufts of lime-green grass sprouting up from amidst the thin layer of yellow sand. The trees were also much more spread-out in these lower hills, being dotted about the landscape, so there was no respite from the hot, late-morning sun; it blazed down upon them, high up in the eastern sky, casting short dark shadows upon the ground. The three men walked past those tall, slim wooden sentinels, which were topped with delicate wisps of green, as they headed towards the far edge of the hills. Sitting atop one of those trees was a lone vulture with a white head, long beak and shrouded in brown feathers. It screeched at their approach.

From their elevated viewpoint they could look out, across the vast sandy desert stretching out before them. It was the like of which Galamh had never seen before, being a pure yellow sea of sand, with immense hills and valleys carved within. The guides pointed out a friendly village nearby, not far into the desert. That was to be their next destination and they'd need to reach it before midday, as the sun would be far too hot for them to travel after that. Therefore, the three men would have to pick up their pace. But little did those men know that at that very moment they were being tracked.

As the three men finished gazing out upon that awe-inspiring view, behind them, down the mountain path from whence they had just walked, a lone lion was trailing them. It wouldn't normally seek out groups of men, but it knew that Galamh was wounded, for the smell of his blood was upon the wind. The lion knew that when it charged, there was a good chance that the two guides would flee, leaving the wounded Man-animal alone; for wounded animals were always easy prey.

As the men turned to continue their journey, they saw, heading towards them, the giant killer beast. The men stood there, staring in disbelief. The guides had never before encountered three lions upon one day, let alone three in one morning.

The lion roared in the distance. Its short mane was a golden yellow, yet it appeared to be of the same size as the previous two. It slowly plodded towards them. Galamh bravely asked the two guides to stand behind him, for still he wanted to protect those two trusted men. And as he still had that confident air of command, despite his wounds, both guides did as they were bid, not wanting to offend their charismatic companion.

The huge beast started to growl, then snorted as it silently lumbered towards them. The three men felt very exposed with there being no large trees there in which to offer them protection. Suddenly the lion began to charge forward, this way and that, in a zigzag pattern, growling all the time. Galamh stepped forward, readying his shield and spear. As the lion quickly bounded forward, getting closer and closer, it crashed hard against his shield. Galamh was knocked back a few steps by the impact. The lion slowly walked away. The three men then readied themselves, for they knew that the lion wasn't yet finished terrifying its prey. Again, the beast charged, zigzagging once more. This time, Galamh, with fury in his heart, boldly stepped forward, and in his manly voice roared back at the beast. The two guides took a strong battle-stance behind the prince, desperate to protect themselves in case it came after them. As the beast neared, Galamh thrust the blunt end of his spear into the firm sandy soil. Waiting for its approach, he lowered his spear-tip towards the bounding charge of the beast. Quickly it ran. Nearer by the second. As it pounced, leaping towards Galamh's neck, he quickly raised his spear-tip towards its chest. Bang, the lion impaled itself, its own weight forcing the spear into its huge body. Its roar was like the thunder in the heavens. The lion collapsed onto the ground. Lying on its side, panting heavily, with long, sorrowful groans of pain. It wasn't long before the lifeblood drained from that deadly beast. But it had been a noble enemy to defeat. The two guides hailed Galamh as a hero, for never before had anyone defeated three lions in one morning. Never after was Galamh afraid of anything. He truly had defeated all of his demons that day.

So, onward the three men went, down from those sparsely forested foothills, which relentlessly did their best to keep the desert at bay, and then onto that magnificent yellow, sandy plain. It was slow progress trudging through the desert, especially with the unmerciful sun burning down upon them, yet within a couple of hours, they had reached the sanctuary of the village.

For the next couple of weeks Galamh slept well, resting till his wounds were almost fully healed. Only then would his guides allow him to leave the safety of that refuge. They spent but little time exploring the surrounding desert, till the pull of his homeland told Galamh that he'd tarried in that place now for too long. So, northwards they travelled, on their return journey back towards the Middle-of-the-Land Sea, and home; home to Galicia. And on the way through the mountains, every village that they went, it was found that news of Galamh's heroism had reached those people long before he did. Those African tribesmen were truly amazed by his incredible bravery; so much so, that every villager wanted to meet this hero as he passed through their land.

By the time that Galamh had finally reached his homeland, news of his valour had already reached the ears of many of his countrymen, so that they joyfully welcomed him home as a hero. Galamh enjoyed the celebrity status that this brought. And to be acknowledged by his father and grandfather for his acts of bravery was something that he'd always longed for.

Within a few moons, tales of his awe-inspiring courage had spread to every corner of his glorious kingdom, so that everyone knew of his reputation. Hence, from those deadly encounters a man of legend was born.

As his fame grew, he decided to use as his sigil, the emblem of three lions to adorn his shield and banner. These were displayed in a circular pattern, as was the Galician way.

But unfortunately, not long after his homecoming the old, well-loved King, Breoghan, sadly passed away. It was a period of much sorrow for their people. Galamh's father, Bilé took over the running of the Kingdom and ruled with the same firm yet fair hand that his father had done before him; thereafter peace remained throughout the land.

By now Galamh's fame had spread throughout the Middle-land and beyond; this meant that occasionally he received messengers from far afield, asking him to go to the aid of the military tribes throughout those quarters of the globe. The Scythians, those nomadic horsemen who ruled over a vast area north of the Black Sea, were the first to ask for his support. Galamh was more than happy to go on this new adventure as he was getting bored with the quiet monotony of his homelife, especially as there was so little conflict within his own kingdom during his father's reign. And like many young men, he longed for the excitement of war and the possibility of attaining even more fame for his heroism, as that can be a truly addictive driving force. So, without too much ado, after receiving his father's blessing, he made plans to set sail with a small contingent of troops.

Before many suns had set, Galamh, with an army of loyal soldiers, were sailing from their beloved Iberian realm, heading eastwards across the glorious Middle-of-the-Land Sea, which flowed so majestically through the very centre of their known world. They passed by the lands of Rome, and the land of the Greeks with her many islands, before heading northwards, past the noble kingdom of Thrace.

From Thrace they sailed into the Inhospitable Sea, or the Black Sea as it was sometimes called, being named after the northern wind, for it was the most northerly of all the small seas around the Middle-land. It was here that the Spaniards moored their ships along the shore. Galamh sent messengers to the nearby tribesmen, to inform them of his party's presence. It wasn't long before they'd been summoned to the Scythian encampment.

With Galamh not only belonging to the ruling family of Iberia, but also with him being next in line to the throne, it meant that he'd travelled with a large number of concubines, as was the custom of the time, for the more you had, the more prestige was attached to you, therefore the more power you were deemed to have; and Galamh wanted to instantly demonstrate his noble position to the Scythians in that way he could build upon the advantage that his royal pedigree afforded him. And if the gods were kind, he might even return home as a conquering hero.

The Scythian camp was the like of which those good Gaelic-folk had never seen before. It was a make-shift town, comprised of hundreds of wagons, if not more, all of different sizes, strewn about the grassy plain. Some had two wheels, some four, whilst others, mainly for the noble families, had six. The wagons contained the wives and daughters of the horsemen, whilst the children had the choice of either playing indoors around their mothers' feet, or outside in the open. All the men were ahorse, playing a game, with bows across their chest, and quivers of arrows tied to their saddles. Their horses thundered past where Galamh and his men stood, riding as swiftly as the wind. Each man looked as if he was at one with his horse; those nimble stallions seemed to know instinctively where their riders wanted to go, so subtle were the warriors' movement to control their mounts. They truly were incredible horsemen.

When the Scythian king saw the visitors, he rode over to meet them. He was a huge man, even bigger than Galamh, and loud of voice he was, but friendly, although a little wary of strangers. His name was Reflor, son of Neman. What particularly struck him at first was the sigil upon Galamh's shield and banner, for long had he known of the feats of this impressive young man before him.

As the Spaniards looked around at the other approaching horsemen, they noticed the other weapons that they wielded. Although they clearly favoured the bow, most of the Scythians also wore scabbards upon their belts, which housed swords of bronze, whilst in their belts hung their famed axes, with that lethal pointed killing-edge. It was easy to see why they were considered to be such a superior warrior race.

At first, these extremely proud yet brave horsemen, were very untrusting of the strangers, especially with the Gaelic warriors being ground-walkers, as Reflor's men were rarely seen unhorsed. But, in time, both sides got to know each other well, and the Scythians began to trust their new allies. What helped to build this trust was in part down to Galamh's quiet authority that people naturally gravitated towards, together with his friendly, approachable nature, his mischievous smile and his obvious bravery in battle, which added up to a man who easily attracted a great deal of respect, just like his father and grandfather had before him.

And as time went by, Galamh was given more and more military responsibility, in which he greatly proved himself, until finally he was made general of all the Scythian armies. These extra charges of power would have corrupted many ordinary men, or else caused them to suffer from a nervous anxiety, as they constantly worried about every conceivable outcome, but not Galamh. It simply transformed him into an even greater version of himself, so that a steely spark of confidence had grown within him, more than he'd ever known before, which engulfed his whole persona, marking him out as an unsurpassed leader of men. It was during this period that Galamh seemed to physically grow too, looking even taller and more broad-shouldered than ever before, appearing much more like a powerful king, and less like a mere general.

Many hostile enemy tribes were defeated during that busy period as Galamh led the cavalry charges as a thousand horsemen stormed across the plains shooting arrows with deadly accuracy, and when they neared their terrified enemy, they hacked them down with those lethal axes.

And with Galamh's endless victories came the understandable adoration by the Scythian people; what could they not love about this Spanish hero who had brought such untold successes to their tribe. The king even gave Galamh the hand of his own daughter, Seng. Everything in Galamh's life was going so well. He was indeed a most fortunate man.

Within a year of their marriage, their first son was born. Due to his hair-colouring he was named Donn, which means brown-haired in Galamh's Gaelic tongue.

Whenever wars within the Scythian borders weren't dictating where they travelled, they would remain at each site until the grazing land had been overused. Then the horses were hitched to the wagons and the temporary town moved to another location. How noisy those times were, with hundreds of creaking, groaning wagons rumbling across the plains sounding like distant thunder rolling across the heavens. Galamh saw much of the Scythian kingdom this way. Once they even ventured to the shores of the Caspian Sea, where Sirens were known to dwell. Galamh learned a great deal during that time, gaining much wisdom from the horsemen, as well as from the tribesmen of each land that they encountered.

Before too long, a second son was born. This one being red of hair. He was given the Scythian name of Arech, meaning wise. Galamh added the second name of Februadh, which was Gaelic for red-brow. In colouring no two brothers looked more different.

But sadly, Galamh's wife, Seng, died shortly after giving birth. Galamh was heartbroken for he'd grown to love his beautiful wife. The Scythian King also mourned the death of his daughter. And having much time upon his hands, his thoughts began to darken.

Reflor had always treated Galamh like a son, and when they stood next to each other they were noticeably of that similar masculine build, although the Scythian King was slightly taller and broader of shoulder than the Gaelic prince. Their personalities were very different, however: Galamh was loved by everyone, so his warriors did his bidding out of respect, whilst the king ruled through fear, using his huge size and temper to keep his fearsome warriors under control.

This should have been a glorious period of mutual accord between the king and his general, after all the Scythian people had greatly benefitted from them working together. But regrettably, the more that Galamh's fame increased, the more worried that Reflor became; he was convinced that the young Spanish general would one day overpower him and take the throne for himself, as his Scythian horsemen were already treating Galamh with the same reverence that Reflor himself commanded. As the King's rage quietly simmered beneath the surface, he eventually felt that he'd no choice but to send Galamh away from his Kingdom, to be quietly assassinated away from the Scythian people. His plans were already being set in motion when, during a particularly dark evening, a friendly messenger sneaked into the presence of the young prince. He earnestly warned him of the King's murderous intentions. Galamh was quick to anger; his fury instantly reaching boiling point. He immediately sought out the King, and without hesitation he slew the mighty ruler.

Galamh knew that it was now time to leave the country; it had obviously become too dangerous for him to stay, for no matter how well-loved he was, he knew only too well what a vengeful race the Scythian people could be. So, he gathered together his men; they packed up their belongings and bade their farewells to the loyal friends that they'd made, before heading towards their ships. But Galamh didn't speedily run away, nor did he drag his feet, he simply kept his unshakeable sense of courage as he bravely marched his men through the make-shift town, before slowly sailing away, in his own time, and with great dignity. Some say that they sailed with a loyal fleet of three-score ships, whilst others say that their ships numbered one hundred strong. But no matter how many ships they had, aboard each single vessel, fifteen warrior-families did sail, with each ship also containing a small contingent of unmarried soldiers. So, in total, as you can imagine, the combined troops were quite a significant number, being well over two thousand warriors strong.

But where should they go? Galamh wasn't ready to travel home just yet. And what would his father say? For him killing Reflor, who'd been his trusted friend and ally, hadn't brought Galamh any honour. So, he decided to sail his fleet back across the Black Sea, to a small island which lay just off the coast of Thrace; Irena it was called.

There they moored their ships upon the northern side of the isle, to protect them from the blustery Red and Yellow Winds, which blew so strongly from the southeast. Upon this northern shore they were also kept hidden from any questing Scythians, for those horsemen were known as a resourceful race, able to travel light, and were most deadly with their bows. Here, they could collect their thoughts, and decide what their next course of action would be.

It truly was a rugged, mountainous isle that they had found, but many breathtakingly beautiful waterfalls made them believe that they were much closer to the gods than anywhere else on earth. It really was that beautiful. And due to its sheer scale, it easily dominated the Thracian Sea, giving rise to its poetical name of 'The Mountain of Thrace'. It has been said that it was upon this isle that the god, Poseidon, watched the events of the Trojan War unfold. For sitting atop its highest peak, with trident in hand, he could see old Priam's city before him, and watched it being sacked by the Achaean ships. Whether or not that history pre-dates ours, we shall leave to the scholars to conjecture. In the sky, high above, louder than the roar of the many waterfalls, could be heard the high-pitched squawks of soaring falcons and the shrieks of hawks in flight; for here those majestic birds-of-prey found their home.

And there those Spaniards remained upon that island paradise for the period of three most pleasant moons. It was whilst speaking to visiting traders, whom our heroes occasionally encountered, that they heard talk of an impending war in Egypt. They decided between them to go to the Egyptians aid, for if they could secure victory for the Pharaoh, then surely that would restore their own sense of honour. So, they busily set to, readying their ships with fresh supplies, and before long, they had set sail once more.

Believing that Africa was but a small country, as Galamh had already explored its northern regions, and not wanting to head directly towards the Nile, in case their armada was spotted by any merchants allied to Scythia, they sailed in a counter-sunwise direction around that continent, so that they could reach Egypt by way of the Red Sea. This course would put the greatest distance between themselves and the dangers which lay around the eastern shores of the Middle-of-the-Land Sea.

The journey, at least to begin with, was pleasant enough, but as they reached the rocky southern coastline of Africa, things began to change. Tempestuous storms tossed the ships around the sea, as the waves began to war with each other. And then the powerful Pale Wind blew from the west, aiding their progress by pushing their ships swiftly eastwards. And once this wind's usefulness had run its course, they managed to escape from its path by heading northwards, following the eastern coastline of Africa, rowing towards their journey's end.

Three moons it took, before our voyagers had reached the Red Sea. Like the Black Sea, as mentioned previously, this had also been named after the wind direction, for the wind which lay roughly south-south-east, was known to be red.

Our heroes were now able to take things a little easier, having finally arrived at the busy Egyptian port. Many merchant ships were moored there, some having come from the nearby Arabian lands, whilst others were from Persia, and even India and beyond. These trading vessels were loaded full of merchandise, which included bolts of colourful silks, as well as large quantities of rice and dry, pungent, aromatic leaves and ground spices all stored in tall earthenware jars; as well as stacks of fragile pottery tightly secured to the decks with strong hempen rope. Many different languages could be heard along the entire length of that busy quayside, each spoken with a serious urgency, making it feel unfriendly and strangely foreign to any unaccustomed traveller. All of these sights, sounds and smells overwhelmed their senses. There were merchants who frequented Spain, but not in these numbers.

Galamh sent a trusted messenger to the royal court to let the Pharaoh know of their arrival, and to inform him that they were part of an immense army of warriors who'd been hardened in the wars of Scythia and who'd come to aid them in the defence of their country.

It took only a few days of traveling through the desert before that brave, hardy messenger had reached the royal court. And the Pharaoh was indeed pleased to hear of this generous offer. He responded by sending a high-ranking ambassador to meet Galamh, to escort his army back to the City-of-the-White-Walls.

The ambassador looked different to any man that they had ever met before. His skin was the colour of red clay, his black hair was shorn short and he was beardless; he was bare armed and shouldered, with a long gown wrapped around his chest, which flowed down to his ankles, leaving his bare feet on show. Two strange lines of symbols ran down the front of his gown. The ambassador had that stoical bearing favoured by many of his countrymen, although it was obvious from the way that he constantly gazed up at Galamh, that he was in complete awe of him, not just by his monumental size, as he stood head and shoulders above everyone there, but also by that charming, handsome, rugged, masculinity that he had, along with his natural regal presence; though the ambassador tried his utmost to hide his ever-increasing admiration.

With them spending the next few days together, Galamh learnt much of the ambassador's character, finding him to be the sort of official who puts efficiency above all other traits; but with a little perseverance from the friendly and reassuring prince, some warmth from the Egyptian's personality could be teased out. And as Galamh engaged him in conversation he was found to be a man of considerable knowledge, who could speak the Gaelic language well, which made him the perfect guide to escort them back to the Egyptian court.

And so, under the ambassador's expert guidance, our army was led westwards through the stifling heat of the desert. They travelled mainly at night and in the evenings when it was cooler. During the daytime they camped either inside of large tents or for some of them, outside in the shadows of camels or behind makeshift shelters constructed from blankets. During those unpleasant daylight hours, the warm, dry air felt strangely unnatural to those adventurers, for whenever they breathed in, it was as though they were inhaling burning particles of sand. How it burned the backs of their dry throats, adding to their desperate thirst.

That uncomfortable feeling went on for the next few days until finally they reached land where vegetation could partially grow, and where the air was a little cooler. It was at least a little more fertile here, as tufts of green grass sprouted up through the sand, and where trees, though thin and weak-looking, were sparsely spread out before them. Digging amongst the roots of the trees gave the men much needed drinking water, as they couldn't possibly have carried enough supplies from the merchants at the Red Sea to quench the thirst of every man in their vast army. This tract of semi-fertile land was obviously where the sand of the desert and the grass of the plain were forever in a constant state of war, each one trying to gain control over the other.

And that was how it was until they reached the lush green plains which flanked both sides of the River Nile. Here, the ambassador had arranged for them to be met by servants with large glazed pots of cloudy beer to quench their terrible thirst, for the river's water wasn't considered overly drinkable as it was known to spread disease. The beer was thick and lumpy with the consistency of gruel, but it was nutritious and tasted so very good.

Gazing at the busy waterway the ambassador informed them that the majestic river before them was known as the 'Mother-of-All-Men'. It was indeed teeming with a good-many ships. And each one of those trading galleys that sailed to-and-fro, each had their own unique design which showed from which country that they hailed.

Across the other side of that enormous river, they couldn't help but notice the bustling port where hundreds of ships were moored. It was even busier than the one where their own ships lay anchored, back upon the Red Sea, although this seemed a little more organized. And gazing past the pale-limestone port towards its magnificent staircase that drew the eyes upwards, stood the huge, majestic, gleaming, white-painted walls of *Hut-Ka-Ptah*, which means the 'Temple-of-the-Spirit-of-Ptah'. It towered over all the other buildings and was why the capital was called the City-of-the-White-Walls. Standing to either side of the temple's main entrance were two giant, lifelike statues, probably depicting the images of earlier pharaohs, who now guarded the temple; they must have stood at least twenty feet tall. The white walls reflected in the gentle rippling waters of the river, making it look twice as tall, and even more impressive, if that was at all possible.

The ambassador had a ship waiting to ferry Galamh, and some of his chief advisors across the river. The remaining force of his men made their camp upon the water's edge, where they idly rested, watching the ships sailing back-and-forth across that incomparably tranquil scene.

It didn't take long for their small party to reach the other side. They'd sailed across in complete silence, so overawed were they by the sight before them. Being this close to the City-of-the-White-Walls filled those weary travellers with overwhelming admiration and complete wonderment, for they'd always believed that they'd come from a highly civilized country, but since seeing this place, they knew that they'd have to completely rethink those notions.

Galamh and his men stepped forth from the ferry, onto the busy stone-lined docks, full of lively merchants who were hustling and bustling whilst chattering away in foreign tongues: there were Egyptians, Africans, Greeks, Thracians, and a whole host of others.

Before them stood the huge limestone staircase, which as I've said naturally drew the eye upwards towards that noisy, restless city. But before they took the stairs their own curiosity urged them to get a closer look at what lay to either side of that magnificent landing; for lining the western banks of the river, stood rows of large mud-brick buildings, some being industriously used as workshops, whilst others were used for storage, housing large quantities of goods and merchandise. Long processions of sweaty, bare-chested workers were seen coming to and from those buildings, towards the awaiting ships, carrying furniture, grain, bales of cloth, in fact anything that could be traded or bartered.

Following the ambassador, Galamh's party walked up the grand staircase towards the temple entrance. At the top of the stairs, before they'd reached the main gates, they turned right, following the white-painted walls, that proudly stood in the very centre of that vast city. Emblazoned across those temple walls were colourful life-size friezes bearing the likeness of pharaohs, amidst animal-headed gods and warring heroes. The ambassador pointed out images of the green-skinned god, Ptah, who that magnificent temple was devoted to, for the Egyptians believed that it was him who had created our entire world. Ptah wore a blue skullcap, tightly fitting clothes, with a short beard gracing his chin, whilst in his right hand he carried a tall staff of authority. Next, the ambassador pointed out Sekhmet, the lion-headed goddess of war, dressed in a long crimson gown. She was an extremely powerful god, being the wife of Ptah, as well as the daughter of the falcon-headed sun god, Ra. Sekhmet was known by many names, including 'The Powerful One', 'Lady of Slaughter', 'Mistress of Dread', 'The Red Lady' as well as 'Protector of Pharaohs', for legends told how in earlier days she had led their armies into war. She was also a great healer and was known to bring balance whenever the world turned to chaos. The ambassador then pointed out the son of those two gods: Nefertem, who was depicted bare-chested, wearing a golden skirt, with a large blue lotus-flower sprouting from his head. He was known for his exceptional beauty. It was said that it was from his tears that the race of Man was born.

The travellers were led along streets lined with hundreds of mud-brick houses. These buildings were square in shape, most modestly sized, but there were grander houses dotted along the route. Strange, exotic cooking smells travelled on the wind from the houses, opposite, distracting our adventurers, making them realise how hungry they were. Sitting outside some of those houses, men were seen playing board games, whilst others looked on. Apart from an occasional glance at the heroic size of Galamh, there was but little interest in the party, as the local people were used to seeing visitors calling upon the Pharaoh from places as far afield as the islands of Greece.

Running around the street were young naked children; the girls were playing with stuffed dolls, whilst the boys either played with clay soldiers or were wrestling. Some of the wealthier children even had wooden toys that could actually move: There was a wooden dog, which, when its back was pressed and released, it would physically jump forward. Our warriors were astounded by this wonderful technology, but still they followed the ambassador onwards.

As these buildings stood within the royal quarter, every now and then they would come across more of those gigantic statues of pharaohs, painted in lifelike colours. Galamh's usually talkative elders were still speechless, struck so by everything that they saw, in this bustling, advanced city.

Other than this lengthy white-walled temple, there were a few other religious buildings thereabouts, but these were much smaller, and stood in their own natural colours, being built of either limestone or sandstone, although their walls were still emblazoned with the same colourful murals of gods and pharaohs. Red or sometimes black granite lined the high, narrow entranceways to these buildings. Whilst tall, slim towering obelisks stood in pairs to either side of the doorway, carved out of more of that same pale-red granite; these tapered upwards, topped by sharp points that were so tall that they almost pierced the sky. These red stones starkly contrasted against the sandy-yellow surroundings.

There was so much to take in, and Galamh's weary party were indeed bewitched by everything that they saw. But one thing that they noticed, yet didn't fully comprehend until much later, was that upon these buildings and monuments, was a system of recording their words. This was in an elaborate form of pictures. And when drawn upon sheets of papyrus, these words and thoughts could be transported around the world by messengers. This was indeed a high achievement. So, with mouths agape, our warriors walked past the magnificent buildings of the royal quarter, unable to believe what they were seeing, so fantastical it all seemed. It really was a beautiful and well planned-out city, which must have taken many years to complete. The gentle, yet majestic River Nile, serenely flowed past, for even though it contained a good-many ships, because of the slow speed in which they sailed, it added a tranquil contrast to the noisy, vibrant street scenes that they were now encountering.

The ambassador led the company into the grounds of the royal palace, where tall, leafy palm-trees lined the avenues, which led directly to the inner gates. They'd walked past many guards, who had naked torsos, being dressed in pale linen skirts, with striped linen helmets, armed with lengthy spears and hook-shaped swords by their sides, proudly protecting the palace grounds.

The ambassador ordered Galamh to bring his sword and shield, but for his men to leave theirs outside, and for them all to follow him into the palace. They did as they were bid, so intrigued were they at what they would find inside.

So, following the ambassador through the tall, slim granite-lined entrance, they stepped inside, and onto that pale, smooth, shiny tiled floor, which gave a muffled echo as they walked. It was so quiet and subdued within the palace that at first it was a shock to their senses as it had been the complete opposite outside. Thereafter, a wave of solemnity flooded over the party as they walked through the corridors, for so humbling was the whole experience. And reverential hushed tones were spoken, for louder voices noisily echoed off the solid stone walls. Even Galamh himself took upon a serious countenance, though still briskly he strode ahead of his men, with that majestic, commanding air that he always had, as they cautiously followed behind.

Within those thick, solid palace walls, which were lit by torchlight and candles, magnificently tall pillars held up vast stone ceilings, which were painted deep-blue and dotted with a myriad of glistening golden stars. The walls were decorated with strange murals, whilst colourful statues of the Pharaoh and his animal-headed gods, stood life-size and much, much bigger, around the rooms and corridors. Gold and silver glinted upon the many objects within the different rooms, making the whole place seem even more magical than the world outside.

Galamh was led towards the great throne-room. And there, seated high up, atop many stairs, appearing like a moving statue, was the Pharaoh himself. He was tall and slim of build. Like his fellow Egyptians his skin was the colour of red clay. Beads of sweat glistened upon his naked chest, shining like jewels in the bright amber glow of the candlelight. He wore a shiny-golden headdress which hung around his face like a lion's mane, the bottom of which rested at either side of his broad, manly chest. And upon his brow, an inquisitive golden snake peered forward from the regal headwear. His eyes were lined with black paint, giving him a more lion-like appearance. Whilst a long, thin black beard protruded downwards from his chin.

The mighty Pharaoh welcomed Galamh with great enthusiasm, as he'd heard much of his impressive victories. And whilst Galamh stood there, in that completely alien setting, surrounded by hordes of armed guards, he still managed to exude that same relaxed air of intelligent command that he always exhibited.

After seeing the three lions upon the Spaniard's shield, Galamh was asked to slowly draw his sword. The prince did as he was bid. The golden-bronze, leaf-shaped sword glinted in the candlelight as though it belonged in that strange world. As Galamh moved, the light flickered up and down the length of the blade. And with Galamh's huge, powerful stature being akin to that of a demigod and with his natural heroic stance, the Pharaoh couldn't contain his excitement.

"Indeed, by the lions upon your sun-shaped shield, you must have been sent by Sekhmet herself, to lead us into war, as she herself has been known to lead us in times gone by", the Pharaoh gleefully exclaimed. He was deeply superstitious, and took Galamh's arrival as a sign from the gods, believing that the Spanish prince hadn't arrived in their country by accident, but was an unwitting envoy sent by the goddess. And with Galamh's height and build it was easy to believe that he could have been sent by the gods at this auspicious time.

During this initial meeting, the Pharaoh had remained sitting proudly upright upon his throne, whilst his obvious excitement visibly bubbled beneath the surface. But as he became more used to speaking to this apparent representative of the gods, his demeanour changed to become more serious, gently resting his hands upon his knees and calmly gazing down upon Galamh. It was in this way that he informed the Spanish prince that Egypt had been invaded from the south, by the King of Ethiopia, at the head of an almighty army. The Ethiopians had already gained the upper hand and were now asking Egypt to surrender, offering them terms. The good Pharaoh believed that never before had they needed more an emissary of the gods, to lead their armies in defence of their country. The Pharaoh was already fully aware of Galamh's legendary prowess, having heard from his many dignitaries how the prince had led the Scythian armies to victory; with being convinced that the Spanish prince had been sent by Sekhmet to protect his realm, the proud ruler had no qualms about offering him the leadership of his whole Egyptian army. Galamh, in that confident, majestic manner of his, standing proudly tall, gave a slight bow of his head, "I gladly accept", he said in his manly voice, winking at the Pharaoh, as a grin broke out through his serious expression. The Pharaoh grinned back, caught up in the Spaniard's sense of fun, his eyes twinkling in the candlelight.

And thus, the Ethiopians were asked once more to meet upon the field of war. This time Galamh was at the front of the Egyptian lines. And as impressive as his sword was, the Pharaoh believed that the leader of his armies should have a far more advanced weapon, more befitting of Galamh's rank. Therefore, the Pharaoh presented him with a long dagger-like sword made of the wondrous new material known as *iron*. Galamh had never seen anything like it before; it was long and straight with a many-jewelled hilt. It was as if Galamh had been given an enchanted sword, so strong was it, and not as prone to bending as his old bronze one. Although it lacked the golden shine of a freshly-polished bronze-sword, for this was of a dark-grey, almost black hue, but nevertheless what a beautiful item it was.

The Egyptian nobles were lined-up in their two-wheeled chariots, armed with tall, composite bows, and with quivers bursting with lengthy arrows. Their charioteers were trusted men who would bravely drive them into shooting range, and once there, their arrows would fly, sending terror into the enemy lines. Each chariot was made of toughened ox-skin over a lightweight wooden frame. It was this simple construction that made those vehicles so extremely nimble on the battlefield. Each chariot was pulled by two swift horses, which were accompanied by their own team of foot-soldiers; these loyal warriors, who made up most of the army, were dressed similar to the palace guards, being almost naked, except for short linen skirts, and upon their heads they wore headdresses made of striped padded-linen. Their skin, like the Pharaoh, was of the customary Egyptian colour. They carried rectangular wooden shields, with the top edge rounded, and each man was armed with a gleaming bronze-sword, which was somewhat scythe-like in appearance.

Upon the other side of the battlefield, the Ethiopian army differed greatly from that of the Egyptians. Their skin was as black as ebony, whilst their heads were topped by a mass of black hair, with strands as thick as wool. They were dressed in animal skins, wearing colourful beads and rows of bracelets upon their arms and legs. They had neither horse nor sword, but favoured spears with large shields, whilst some were armed with bows and arrows. They truly were a brave race of warriors.

Just before the battle began, the Ethiopians started singing, their war-music being quite unnerving, causing a sense of unease to spread throughout the Egyptian ranks. But as the news circulated throughout our men, informing them that Galamh had been sent by the goddess, Sekhmet, a great calmness overcame them, for they only needed to glance upon the great man to be instantly put at ease; for with his height, he was clearly very visible, so they could see how relaxed he looked, yet still powerful and fully in control, with his shield of lions and looking as handsome as Sekhmet's son, Nefertem himself. Knowing that the gods were with them made them feel as though victory was already on their side.

Sergem was the Egyptian High-priest of Ptah. He was an important man and knew it. He stood out from his countrymen due to the leopard-skin pelt that he wore over his shoulder. He walked along the long corridor created by the line of chariots to his right and the endless rows of foot-soldiers to his left, shouting to the men on both sides, inciting them to battle with fury in their hearts.

Galamh carefully climbed aboard the leading chariot. This was a new type of warfare for the Spanish prince; it was also the single most advanced military weaponry that he'd ever seen, let alone being the most advanced piece of equestrian warfare that he'd ever used, and he'd ridden with the horse-warriors of Scythia. Now that all the men were inflamed with a righteous passion to repel the invaders, with his sword aloft, Galamh led his archers across the field. The chariots slowly rumbled forward, like the sound of distant thunder growling in the heavens. Above this deafening noise Galamh shouted encouraging words to his men; his loud manly voice, like his grandfather's before him, had been forged on the battlefield, "TO WAR", he roared.

When in position the charioteers stopped to allow their archers to unleash a storm of arrows upon the enemy. Many Ethiopians fell within the next few minutes. With seeing their comrades dying around them, it wasn't long before the Ethiopian troops began to falter on the field; it was then that Galamh led his men in a thunderous chariot charge, followed by their furious foot soldiers. The chariots threw dust high up into the ether.

And as the dust settled upon that field of war, it was Galamh's Egyptians who were now victorious. And the terms of peace, which the Ethiopian King had originally offered to the Pharaoh, were now being offered back to the defeated invaders.

The Pharaoh was indeed a generous man. To thank all of Galamh's Gaelic Chieftains, he gave them swords of a similar style to the one that he'd given their leader. Those were wonderfully happy times for the victors. To further show his appreciation to Galamh, knowing that he'd recently lost his wife, he offered him the hand of his own beautiful daughter, Scota. Galamh happily accepted the union, and so the young couple were married soon after.

Ah Scota! What a beautiful princess she was. She'd been but a young bride, for only a few summers earlier she'd been playing with her dolls. But now she was of age and had recently become a warrior-princess who was highly regarded as an archer. She was slim of build, extremely pretty and so full of life. With her red-clay skin, and her straight raven-hair, which gently rested upon her strong, yet feminine shoulders. A long white gown hugged her firm womanly contours, caressing her breasts as it ran downward over her slender hips. Above her gown she had a long, regal neck, a slightly pointed nose, and black paint around her eyes, giving her a more feline quality, like that of her father, for that was the fashion of the Egyptian nobility. The gentle purity of her white silk gown contrasted against the warm tones of her skin, as well as against the cold, shimmering brightness of the exquisite golden headdress that she wore, with its matching necklace and belt.

The royal couple were truly loved by the Egyptian people. Galamh himself was thought of with so much affection, that the Egyptians began calling him *Milethea Spaine*, which means 'Spanish hero'; from this endearing name, his own men began calling him 'Milesius of Spain', which is what we shall also call him, from now on, to show our admiration and respect for such a remarkable man.

After those joyful wedding celebrations were over, Milesius remained in Egypt for another eight contented years; his father-in-law wouldn't hear of him leaving before that time. And during this period, with Milesius being so in awe of that incredible civilization, for they had some of the greatest minds in the world, as well as some of the greatest spiritual sorcerers, that he instructed his twelve most learned youths to learn everything that they could of the arts and sciences from those esteemed people. For with this knowledge, they would be able to educate their own countrymen in those advanced magical arts. The Pharaoh happily encouraged this, for he believed that 'Sharing is the greatest of all callings'. Therefore, by the time that they were ready to leave that land, each one of those young men had become an accomplished expert in his own field.

It was during those years in Egypt, that Milesius and Scota had two sons together. Their first son was the blond-haired Heber Fionn. He grew up to become a fine young man, although he lacked the ambition of his two older brothers. But that was because he wasn't brought up to lead the tribe as they had been, for that could have led to bloodshed if all the brothers had craved the crown. Their second son together was called Amergin. He was a very wise and learned boy; so much so that he was taught the mysterious arts of enchantment, which fully prepared him to become their High-druid in years to come.

Milesius himself had learnt much during that time, for he constantly wanted to improve himself with any available knowledge that he could acquire. He even had a tour of the desert, where the ambassador took him, by camel train, to the nearby 'City-of-the-Dead'. This was about four leagues from the capital.

As they rode towards that great necropolis, Milesius couldn't believe what he was seeing. On the horizon a bright star appeared. It was uncomfortably warm in the desert that day, as the blazing sun warmed their backs as they rode westwards towards their own lengthy shadows in the sand, towards the glistening star ahead.

As they got closer it turned out that it wasn't a single star, but three separate ones, far off on the desert surface. So, onward they rode.

As they finally reached the deserted city, the first structure that they came across was a colossal sphinx lying in the sand. It was enormous, towering over them by at least twenty yards in height, and at least eighty yards long. It silently lay there, proud and noble, guarding the entrance to the great necropolis. Its paintwork now sadly fading, due to the corrosive nature of the sand upon the wind.

Milesius could now see that the three shining stars hadn't fallen from the heavens, like he at first believed; they were more spectacular than that. The dazzling white light had come from three large pyramids, all with highly-polished, white limestone faces that gleamed so unnaturally in the bright Egyptian sun. The contrast of the glorious light that shone from those white tombs against the dull, endless yellow desert showed just how advanced this magnificent civilization truly were. There were a great many other pyramids there, although those three stood out as being much taller than the rest. One of those pyramids seemed to be half the size of the other two, yet even that would have made Breoghan's watch-tower look small in comparison, had they stood side by side. Milesius looked up at those three pyramids in complete awe, feeling overwhelmed with admiration at their whole cultural vision, as well as their unmatched craftsmanship, for never before had he seen anything like this place before. He returned back to the palace feeling a much wiser man, unable to forget about his incredible visit to the 'City-of-the-Dead'.

Those eight years went by at a good steady pace, as there was so much wisdom to soak up from that country. And when it became time to leave, three huge royal-barges were built for the noble couple. These ships were like nothing that Milesius had ever seen before; they were like floating palaces, breathtakingly stunning, standing high and proud in the water, with the flagship being even taller and more impressive than the other two. Carved into each of their wooden hulls were brightly painted seafaring scenes, comprising of some of Egypt's most powerful deities, including obviously Ptah, Sekhmet and Nefertem, as well as Wadj-wer, with his watery body, as he was the god of the Middle-of-the-Land Sea. Rising from the decks above this, were gleaming white walls which housed many windowed apartments. The ships were all topped with red roof-tiles, whilst to the front and rear were tall, white square towers which rose majestically skywards. And to finish off these visions of perfection, every detail was complimented with hues of blue, red and gold.

Not only would they be travelling in some of the most magnificent ships ever built, but they would also be returning home as heroes, with a beautiful Egyptian bride, and with four good royal sons to boot.

Most of the court were there to wish them a safe journey, including Sergem, the High-priest, as well as the ambassador, who was by now a firm friend. The Pharaoh had said his goodbyes in private, not wanting to show any weakness in front of his men.

They slowly left the busy port, waving farewell to all those good friends that they'd made. And so, down the Mother-of-All-Men our adventurers sailed, gently travelling along that long, winding, yet beautifully calm river. Tall reeds lined much of the riverbank along the route, which swayed lazily in the warm breeze. A mix of emotions was felt by all: there was the feeling of calm tranquillity as they slowly sailed down that relaxing serpentine river, contrasted with the excitement of finally returning back home where they could joyfully reacquaint themselves with long-missed friends and much-cherished family; all this was mixed with the tearful, sorrowful farewells, that tightly tugged at their heartstrings, of having to say a final goodbye to all their new friends; this last emotion could even be seen upon the usually stoical face of Scota, as she tried hard to hide her pain; but to her, parting meant so much more, for she was leaving behind the only family that she had ever known, and who she might never see again.

In the weeks before their parting, the Pharaoh had sent the ambassador to speak to all the tribesmen along the length of the Nile; his firm, yet carefully chosen words had guaranteed our heroes a safe journey all the way to the 'Great-green', as the Egyptians called the Middle-of-the-Land Sea. Due to this one piece of well-conceived preparatory action, their lengthy voyage went, thankfully, without incident, until finally they found themselves sailing out from the river's mouth, back onto that familiar sea once more. They'd left behind the wonderful Egyptian kingdom, having taken with them many advanced scientific ideas, amongst which was the alchemistical knowledge of iron-smithery.

As Milesius had already told his wife, Scota, much of the wonderful island of Irena, which lay off the coast of Thrace, in a bid to cheer her up as her homesickness was already noticeably visible across her beautiful young face, he decided to show her that tranquil isle before they returned home to the Spanish kingdom of Iberia.

It wasn't too far to travel for those three magnificent ships, which swiftly cut through the water. And once they'd arrived, Scota found that it was just as Milesius had described, with its many natural pools and its high, thunderous waterfalls.

Though, it wasn't long before they realised that Scota's malady wasn't entirely due to her missing her homeland, she was actually feeling the effects of being with child once more. So, they decided to stay upon that peaceful island until their son, Ir was born; he took his name from that remarkable isle. That boy, what indeed can I tell you about him? It was often said, from the time that he was old enough to wield a sword, that his bravery was beyond compare. He was handsome, fair-haired, a real prince amongst men. But the one thing that really separated him from any of his brothers was his driving, competitive spirit, for he was always foremost in any battle or tournament, even when there was no prize to gain.

And so those travellers remained upon that beautiful isle for a good-many moons, until the young baby was considered old enough to sail.

When the happy day was upon them, that the baby, Ir, was felt to be strong enough to endure the lengthy voyage, they took to the sea once more, resuming their journey onwards towards Iberia. But during this stretch of their voyage, Scota realised that she was again with child. Looking for another suitably safe haven in which the Egyptian princess could rest for the last few months before giving birth, they decided to harbour their ships within the port of that land once known as Gothia. This long-forgotten territory was found somewhere within the Middle-land. It belonged to the nomadic tribe known as the Goths. This proud race knew of Milesius by reputation, and being in awe of his magnificent ships, they gave him and his warriors a safe refuge from the sea until they were once more able to travel. And that was where their next son, Colpa, was born. Of all the sons, I think that he was one of my favourites; that boy had not an ounce of cunning or deceit within him. And what a skilled swordsman he went on to become.

Eventually it was time for our adventurers to set sail, homeward bound once more, to the green, tree-covered rolling hills of Iberia, for they were all of one mind, feeling that they had tarried far too long abroad. Thankfully, this leg of their journey wasn't a long one.

When indeed those intrepid travellers finally did return home, obviously expecting to find the country as they had left it, they were truly shocked at what they found. Milesius' own father had since died, and his old Kingdom was now in turmoil. Many of his people still welcomed the prince back with open arms; he was their hero after all. They also gave an extremely warm welcome to his beautiful Egyptian bride. Her appearance was so very beguiling, being totally unlike anyone that they'd ever seen before. So much so, that they found it hard not to stare, which she found quite refreshing, as her own Egyptian people wouldn't have dared gaze upon her for so long.

To find out the full state of the country, Milesius sent out his advisors to the four corners of his kingdom, to question the Iberian people. What they found out was that since his father's death, some of the natives had begun to rebel against his family's government; not only that, but armies from abroad were now invading and were desperate to take over the empty throne. Milesius was furious; he had to take action fast to gain back control of his family's vast Kingdom.

The first thing that he did was to crown himself king. After all it was his hereditary right to take the throne, and he already felt like a king, having successfully led two powerful nations into war. Therefore, Scota was crowned as his queen, to rule by his side. By my reckoning, Milesius must have been aged about five-and-thirty by this time, so was still as strong as he ever was. Scota, I think, may have been as much as thrice-three years younger.

With his kingly position now secured, Milesius went to war. He'd learned much from his time leading the Scythian and Egyptian armies; he was now a seasoned general and knew exactly what needed to be done. He called his country to arms and led his kingdom's loyal warriors in four-and-fifty bloody battles. His wife, Scota, being an Egyptian warrior-queen, insisted on joining her husband on the field of war. So Scota, in a chariot, armed with a bow, whilst Milesius mounted on horse, holding his mighty iron-sword aloft, led their forces, as they charged across the bloodied plains. They fought a vicious campaign, completely routing the enemy. Those who didn't flee were killed. It took a while, but eventually their Kingdom was brought back under their control, and peace was brought back to their people.

It was during this much needed time of peace, that the royal couple's two youngest sons were born, although there were quite a few years between them. Their names were Heremon and Erenan. Heremon was always such a determined youth, wanting to make his mark upon the world. Whilst Erenan, being the baby of the family, whom everyone adored, was desperate to grow up, so he could be just like his brothers. (It has been said that in total, Milesius had two-and-thirty sons, with four-and-twenty being born of concubines, but of these their histories aren't known. But the eight sons born to his two wives, our seanchaí knew them well).

But anyway, I digress; during that time, after all the hostilities were over, which was due to their enforcement of peace, happiness should have been forthcoming, but sadly there was a more pressing problem, in that a severe drought had spread throughout the whole of Iberia. It hadn't rained in sufficient amounts for many a year. So, obviously, with the crops failing, a great many of their people were now dying of starvation. Milesius consulted his twelve most learned men, those who'd learned their arts from the wise Egyptian masters. But none of them knew how to repair the land. Not even Scota's trusted grey-cloaked druid, Ethiar, who'd travelled with her from Egypt, knew how to help... For year after year this went on. Milesius was seething with anger and deeply frustrated. For the first time in his life, he knew not what to do. His people had to endure this misery for six-and-twenty long, deplorable years.

Then one day, Milesius suddenly remembered an ancient prophecy, one that had been made by his tribe's High-druid, many generations before:

*Our tribe shall not rest till the Island of Destiny,*
*Though it be not our quest, but falls to our progeny.*
*It's three hundred years till the sound of the call,*
*So, listen up children, listen up all!*

This old prophecy had originally been foretold by Cachear the Druid, son of Ercha, as he'd been the trusted prophet of the tribe's leader, Lamhfionn the White-handed, son of Agnon, son of Tait, son of Ogaman; both Tait and Ogaman having been amongst the illustrious Kings of old Scythia. Milesius himself was the ten times great grandson of the warrior-king, Lamhfionn the White-handed, who'd gained his name during his tribe's seven years at sea, for his hands had shone with the brightness of candles, guiding their ships at night; during this bleak period, they only had three vessels so kept them tied securely together, lest their tribe be parted forever.

Cachear's prophesy had become part of Milesius' tribal history, so had been taught to them as children. But as childhood rhymes are seldom thought of in times of crisis, it had been all but forgotten by the tribe's most-learned elders. The recollection came to Milesius like a bolt from the blue. Suddenly he realised what needed to be done: for the prophecy stated that his people must seek out the Island of Destiny, for the gods had obviously planned that from there they must rule. This revelation really opened his eyes. The time had already passed, as the prophecy dictated, in which they should have left the safety of Iberia to look for this land, for the allotted three-hundred-year deadline must surely have passed during his grandfather's day. Milesius now knew that the gods were punishing them, by causing this famine and thus forcing them onward, towards their final quest... But where was the prophesied Island of Destiny? They desperately needed a sign.

Then, upon a cold winter's night, when the waves were calm, and the bright moonlight lit up the sea for a good two-hundred leagues, Ithe, son of Breoghan, the uncle of Milesius, was acting as lookout atop his father's legendary tower. He was gazing northwards, across the vast, empty Sea of Darkness. It was a cloudless night so the moonlight glistened upon the gently rippling water, so no shadows were cast upon the waves to hamper visibility.

Ithe was indeed a learned man, having craved the new knowledge that the Egyptian scholars were teaching; he also knew much of the old wisdom, which meant that he was well-versed in many of the tribe's ancient prophesies. And with having studied the stars, he knew of every constellation and their respective positions within the vast cloak of sky. His eyes were keen, for a man of his age, and he prided himself on this, as he looked upwards, pondering upon the bright, shining stars above.

As his gaze gently rested back upon the horizon, there to the far north, right in the very distance, he thought that he could see an island, shining as bright as a white cloud upon the glowing moonlit ocean; staggered by what he could see, because he knew that if he was right, that if it was indeed an island, then it was unknown to anyone from within his realm. Ithe was more than just a little excited. Could this truly be a sign from the gods? Could this really be the sacred, prophesied Island of Destiny? He squinted, desperately trying to make out the faint shape. Yes, he was sure that it was an island. He quickly ran down the winding outer staircase of the tower, to tell his nephew what he'd found.

Milesius was readying himself for bed, so was somewhat startled by the unexpected intrusion, but still he greeted Ithe's entrance with a bemused smile. When he heard what the excitement was all about, he couldn't contain his elation. He strode towards the Great Hall shouting for his messengers to wake his advisers so that he could ask for their wise counsel.

The sleepy elders came immediately when called, rubbing the sleep from their eyes. After hearing what Ithe had seen, they thought carefully before committing themselves to an answer. But after much discussion they were of one mind: if this was indeed a sign from the gods, then it obviously couldn't be ignored. And with Ithe being the first one to see the island, then surely the gods must be electing *him* to make that monumental voyage, so that with his wisdom he'd be able to discover for himself if this truly was the prophesied 'Island of Destiny'.

Due to Milesius being a battle-hardened general, he'd learned when to rush into action, and when to wait, to acquire more information; this had made him a wise and cautious ruler, so he heeded the advice of the elders, adding that Ithe's son, Lughaidh, should accompany his father with one-and-a-half-hundred brave warriors, as an exploratory force.

Ithe was actually an excellent choice to lead the mission, as he was a natural leader who'd already proven himself on the field of battle, being both brave as well as intelligent; he also had a calm firmness of command, which probably came from him spending so much time with his beloved horses, for they were undeniably his greatest passion. His natural calmness would help to soothe the tempers of the crew, if any of them became prone to mutiny, during that long, desperate voyage. And with Ithe being so well-educated in all the sciences, his knowledge of the positions of the sun and stars would help him to steer a straight navigational course, through day as well as night, whilst searching for that mysterious island.

A huge King's Galley was built for Ithe's journey, big enough to hold one-and-a-half-hundred men. The ship was the biggest that their tribe had ever built, for never before had such a lengthy voyage been undertaken. The tribe's greatest shipbuilders worked long into the night for a good-many months to create this advanced exploratory vessel. It was enormously long, the deck appearing leaf-shaped when seen from above. In the very centre proudly stood a tall, solitary mast, for this ship couldn't reach its destination by rowing alone.

When it became time for the warriors to leave, Ithe himself supervised the loading of that huge wooden vessel, making sure that there were enough supplies to last them for at least a couple of weeks. They also took with them a few goats, so there would be fresh meat, as well as milk, to help keep them sustained. Many of the men were armed with newly-forged swords of iron, given to them to help guard them against the unknown. And many tearful farewells were said, for they knew not if they would ever return, for so dangerous was their voyage. Ithe left his trusted household to care for his beloved steeds in his absence, for it was quite a wrench for him to leave them, but he made sure that he personally fed and said goodbye to each and every one of them before departing that morning.

Finally, those adventurers set off, heading northwards, into the far reaches of those uncharted waters.

Not long into their journey, the men started taking it in turns to clamber up the mast, to look out for dangers upon the sea, or to spot land, if any land actually existed that far out, upon that unending Sea of Darkness. There was an unspoken danger, one in which they were all extremely aware, and which never strayed too far from their thoughts: those crewmen on lookout duty needed to keep their eyes peeled for the edge of the world, for many sailors had been known to sail out, never to return, so were likely to have fallen over the water's edge.

As dangerous as the edge of the world seemed, we must be thankful that Biblical tales of the deadly Leviathan hadn't yet been heard, and how it is now known to live beneath the seas that circle all around the great land masses, twisting and turning, with its tail firmly gripped within its mouth, ready to wreak destruction upon the earth; for if they'd known that at any given moment that their ship could have been destroyed by its mighty tail, and all those crewmen eaten alive, or burnt to death by its fiery breath, then they would surely have refused to make such a perilous journey. Although what was known, at that time, was terrifying enough, as many tales were told of the enormous, grotesque sea-monsters who preyed upon those who dared to venture too far from shore. So how brave those warriors were, for even though they were leaving behind such small comfort within their foodless homes, they were setting forth on an adventure with barely enough food to sustain them, heading towards possible death.

As the days turned into weeks, and the mocking aquamarine sky took upon the colour of the sea, the adventurers could no longer see the horizon, so knew not where the water ended and the cloak's edge of the heavens began. This new danger completely unnerved the sailors, for now, more than ever before, did they truly feel that they may never return home. Even Ithe himself was starting to doubt the island's existence. Whispers of a mutiny must have abounded upon the winds around that ship.

Ithe's son, Lughaidh, was well-known for his bardic poetry, so was often called upon to help keep the men's spirits up, but even that became tiresome after a while. So, it was indeed fortunate for Lughaidh, with him not only being Milesius' cousin, but with him also being married to the King's beautiful young daughter, Fial, that meant that these familial ties would offer him some protection from the anger that was bound to come, as the ever-increasing hopeless feelings of despair were being felt by each and every one of those watchful crewmen.

Another unsettling thought that constantly preyed upon the mind of Lughaidh, which greatly added to his unease, was him having to leave behind his anxious, gentle young wife, Fial, as he knew that she wasn't anywhere near as strong as her worldly siblings. He hoped that she was coping without him.

Three weeks into that endless, insufferable journey, over that huge expanse of unexplored ocean, and still they hadn't caught sight of any land. The sailors aboard warily kept one eye always upon the waves, as they increasingly pondered upon childhood tales of sea-monsters, who they knew lived within those murky depths.

The lengthy planks of wood that made up the sides of that enormous ship eventually began to creak and groan, quite noisily, after they'd travelled far into their journey. So now they began to wonder if their galley would even make it to land, before the stress on the wood ripped the whole vessel apart.

As their last ounce of faith of ever finding land had ebbed away, the food had become so scarce that all but the last goat had been slaughtered. The remaining animal was being kept alive solely for her milk. It was then that those forlorn travellers finally saw seagulls above, meaning that there must be land somewhere nearby, and yes, there, unbelievably far in the distance, straight ahead of them, was indeed a vast green fertile island, completely covered with majestic trees. How those weary half-mad adventurers rejoiced, albeit filled with caution, for they knew not what they would find. Yet, with dry mouths and sweat on their brows, they manned the oars, and with a renewed strength of spirit, they slowly rowed onward towards the mysterious isle.

It was upon the southern coastline that they landed their ship. So relieved were the men to finally reach the shore, without coming to any harm, that once the men had dragged their ship in from the waves, Ithe ordered the last goat to be sacrificed, as an offering to the sea god, in thanks for granting them a safe journey.

As soon as the ceremony was over, Ithe was keen to explore the wooded isle. He took a hundred eager warriors with him, whilst Lughaidh was left to guard the ship, with the remaining half-a-hundred men.

It wasn't long before Ithe's party had found some of the island's inhabitants. They belonged to the elven race of Fairy, known in the old tongue as the *Tuatha-de-Danan*. Ithe hailed them in a most polite and pleasant manner. Hearing the Gaelic language, the Fairies gracefully bowed, courteously wishing them all, "A hundred-thousand welcomes". Thankfully, they could all speak the same tongue, although the Fairies spoke with an older, more poetical dialect. The faces of those creatures beamed with excitement, for they were so pleased to receive friendly visitors.

I feel that I should really describe the Fairies to you, at this point, as you may not be too familiar with their appearance. They were as tall as the race of Man, slim and graceful in appearance, yet stunningly attractive, with pale skin and large blue eyes; their foreheads were slightly higher than ours, whilst golden-blond or red hair cascaded down past their shoulders. Their clothing was without compare, being made of the most remarkable material, exquisitely tailored, which had produced beautiful, long flowing outfits. As to their personalities: They were usually found to be extremely charming, being a most wondrous and mirthful race.

"What is the name of this island?" asked Ithe, curiously.

"In truth, during this king's reign the land is called Ériu, for 'tis named after the queen of this isle".

"And who holds the sovereignty?"

"For thrice-ten years the three sons of Cearmad Honey-mouth, son of the Dagda, have governed this land. Each son dost rule in turn, but for a single year. During that time, the land is named after *that* king's wife. As regal titles, our goodly rulers have taken the names of the sons of the gods. The generous Kéthor is our king during this term. He is known as the son of Greine, god of the sun. Before him was the wise Ethor, known as the son of Cuill, god of the hazel-tree. And next shall once more be the industrious Téthor, known as the son of Ceacht, god of the plough. And if thou dost seek them, then verily thou shalt find them, together in counsel, within the fortress of *Aileach Neid*, which rests nobly upon a mountain to the far north of this land".

Ithe thanked those good and helpful people. Then, sending a messenger back to his son, he ordered him to take their ship northwards, to meet them upon the opposite side of the isle. And to show that he'd arrived, he asked him to light a fire, so the smoke could guide Ithe's party back towards the awaiting ship.

And then, with those preparations made, those Spanish adventurers ventured forth to find the rulers of this land.

The air was warm that first day under those majestic trees, yet a gentle, cool breeze made the walking seem quite pleasant. Nevertheless, it took many days of travelling across that dark wooded isle before they neared their destination. Fortunately, many of the trees were heavily laden with fruit as well as nuts, the rivers full of fish, whilst large herds of red-deer and wild-boar could often be seen just casually roaming through the forests, meaning that there was never a lack of food during their journey. This made Ithe smile, for he really was beginning to believe that this truly could be the prophesied Island of Destiny.

It must have been almost noon, as the end literally came into sight, as the travellers saw daylight through the shadowy trees ahead of them. And there, beyond the treeline, stretching out before them, was the majestic sloping banks of a mountain, completely cleared of trees. An earthen path snaked its way upward, over the contours of the grassy banks, towards the summit. And there, clearly standing atop, resting just beneath the clouds, was the mountain-top castle that they were seeking.

It was Ithe who first stepped forth from the trees, cautiously leading his men towards the mountain. With mouths agape, those men slowly followed behind their wise leader. Having spent so long at sea, they didn't expect to see any buildings at all, this far away from civilization.

Up that steep winding path they walked. Before long, their legs started to ache as their bodies became uncomfortably warm. As they reached halfway, many of them had already started to heavily pant, but no-one wanted to be the first to quit. Eagerly, they urged their tired bodies onward, up those terrible slopes, for they could see the grey, stone castle walls ahead, drawing them nearer.

A small number of armed guards could now be seen patrolling the grounds outside the outer walls.

Upwards, those weary travellers clambered. And as they neared the summit, they could see that the guards were now all briskly heading towards them. Those tired voyagers stopped in their tracks as they curiously looked back over their shoulders, to momentarily take in the beautiful, breath-taking views of the vast wooded land that completely surrounded the mountain. Then, hesitantly turning back, they greeted the approaching guards.

"A hundred-thousand welcomes", said the two parties. After a brief, but cordial exchange, the friendly guards led those men through the large gateway of the curtain wall, which circled their mighty keep. The brickwork was made from perfectly-cut grey stone, standing at least twenty feet tall. Those guards were very talkative, telling Ithe about the history of the castle, and how it was the first stone building ever to be constructed upon the island, being built upon the orders of the Dagda himself, who'd erected it over the grave of his gentle, young son, Aedh. (It was curiously built upon the very spot now occupied by the Grianán of Aileach. But more of that anon).

The adventurers followed the guards across the almost-empty courtyard, as only the occasional servant passed by. They headed towards the magnificent stone Keep which dominated the whole enclosure; this impressively tall building was fronted by two huge, ornately carved wooden gates.

The gates creaked open as the guards firmly leaned their weight against them. A sudden rush of light shone from within; it was a yellow, glowing torchlight which lit up the corridors ahead of them, but neither a flickering flame nor any smoke came from those magical lights, just a steady yellow glow. The guards stepped through the gateway leading the travellers inside, onto the flagstone floor and along the stone-lined corridors towards the nearby Great Hall. Their many footsteps echoing off the walls, alerting everyone to their presence.

Once inside of the Great Hall, more Fairies joyfully greeted the hundred-man force of strangers. And each man was made to feel at home by those good people. It was indeed a good-sized gathering, made up of all the nobles of the Fairy race. They were there to settle a long-running family dispute. There were princes and druids, as well as brehons who were there to make sure that all judgements were legal, and there were bards who were experts in all things relating to their tribe. With having guests, the Fairies graciously decided that they would listen to the arguments after the feast was over; in that way the banquet wouldn't be spoiled by angry words.

It truly was a delightful company, with all those good folk clearly wearing their finest clothing. Amongst them were the three kings, who couldn't be mistaken, as their jewellery and costume were some of the most exquisite ever made. They noticed King Kéthor first. He wore a shiny, golden lunula that hung from his neck, resting gently upon his chest like a large crescent-shaped moon. It was intricately engraved with otherworldly designs, showing that it was indeed he who ruled that year as king. Below this, upon his gown, emblazoned right across the front, was the image of a huge golden sun, for Kéthor was styled as the son of the Sun god. Behind him was Ethor, who was known as the son of the Hazel-tree god, which was the Fairy's symbol of wisdom, so he had a tunic with that emblem upon it. And then there was Téthor, who was known as the son of the Plough god, so had that item adorning his gown.

During the feast, there was joyful music adeptly played on both string instruments as well as flutes, whilst much food was eaten by all. Most of the food was served from a huge black cauldron, which never seemed to run dry, despite the large number of people there, much to the confusion of our warriors, but to the merriment of the Fairies. It turned out that the cauldron had magical qualities, and had once belonged to the Fairy-Kings' grandfather, the

Dagda, who was a powerful King-druid, otherwise known as the 'Good-God', the 'All-Father', and the 'Lord-of-Great-Wisdom'.

Ithe told them that bad weather had forced them to land upon the Fairy's island, and that as soon as the feast was over, they would be heading homeward, without delay, as their return journey was a long one. With this deception having put their hosts at their ease, and as the feast wore on, it didn't take long before talk turned to how the Fairies came to rule over that land. It turned out that they'd been inhabitants there for less than two hundred years, after taking the land from the primitive natives, who called themselves the Fir-bolg.

As the Fairies joyfully spoke of their past adventures, their eyes lit up and they became much more animated. I know I've said it before, but they really were a most mirthful and fun-loving race, seeming to radiate that same innocent excitement that children have, when telling playmates of their recent exploits. They told Ithe how they'd come to that land inside of huge ships, which they could only describe as looking like dark clouds that sailed high up in the sky, moving slowly against the wind. Magical mists then formed around those phantom clouds, so dense that the sun was blocked out for three whole days. Then, after surveying the land, the cloud-like ships descended upon the Iron Mountains that stand to the northwest. Ithe was having trouble picturing this scene, for due to his considerable knowledge, he knew that it was impossible to sail clouds; but he kept these thoughts firmly to himself.

When the Fir-bolg natives saw the clouds slowly descending, and the Fairies stepping forth, they were terrified, not knowing whether these strangers were gods or men.

The Fairies managed to find a way to communicate with the Fir-bolg, and asked to share their land equally, or else to go to war and fight for it. But the Fir-bolg had themselves won that land by right of conquest, after a hard-fought vicious war with the previous rulers; so, they couldn't just allow themselves to give away what they had so rightfully won. Therefore, war it was!

It was Nuadath, son of Ectach who led the Fairies back then; whilst Eocaidh, son of Erc was the Fir-bolg king.

Those Fir-bolg. What can I say about them? They were a brutal, primitive race, who were always so quick to anger. They lived in crude wooden hillforts, keeping sheep and farming the land, dressing primarily in sheep-skins back then. They were stockily built and shorter than the race of Man, but had powerfully strong limbs. In battle their huge hands would grip thick-shafted javelins, hefty war-clubs or large, heavy bronze-swords, and they would run into the fray behind stout lime-coated shields of wood. With great force they would break through the enemy lines, shattering shields, smashing bones and leaving their attackers with huge gaping wounds, dying in their wake. They were indeed a formidable foe. Whereas the Fairies liked to win using their magical arts, as well as their swift prowess on the battlefield, so fought with lighter, venomous-tipped spears, as well as bronze leaf-shaped swords; their shields were of an advanced design, plated and edged with bronze and emblazoned with their own personal motifs. And during warfare they were known to conjure up injurious enchantments upon their enemy.

As the war broke out, in that heavily forested land, that was how they fought. The Fairy-king, Nuadath led his army, armed with an amazing magical weapon which wielded such immense power. It was a white, glowing sword-of-light, known as *Claíomh Solais*. Everyone who saw it became entranced by its bright luminous blade, and once drawn, no one could escape. Nuadath led his troops onward, running through those shadowy forests, whilst his glowing sword lit up the trees around. They chased the Fir-bolg south-westerly, through Connacht, and there, within Uí Maine, upon a vast, cleared plain, the Fir-bolg made their stand. It was upon *Magh Tuired:* The Plain of Lament, where this epic battle took place.

During the battle, through powers of enchantment, the Fairies commanded thick, dense clouds to float above the enemy, and when in position, rained upon them showers of fire, followed by a drenching downpour of blood: cold, wet and crimson. Yet still the Fir-bolg wouldn't yield as they had been slaves before and didn't want to suffer that same fate again. So onward they fought.

Eventually the Fairies won, due to their far-advanced expertise in the arts of warfare, as well as in their obviously unmatched channelling of the powers of enchantment. By the end of the war, ten thousand of the Fir-bolg lay slain. And Nuadath himself had lost his hand, without which he couldn't remain as king.

This battle became known as 'The First Battle of the Plain of Lament' (or sometimes as 'The Southern Battle of the Plain of Lament'). Being an honourable and fair race, who believed in rewarding all valiant enemies, the Fairies gave a whole quarter of their newly-conquered land back to the proud Fir-bolg. Hence, from that time, many descendants of those defeated warriors have continued to live within the kingdom we now know as Connacht. Due to this generosity, the Fir-bolg kindly agreed to share their secret knowledge of the arts of farming, for the Fairies knew not those skills. And under the Fir-bolg's careful tuition, the Fairies learned how and when to plough, sow and reap. In this way the Fairies thrived within our land.

With it being an ancient law of the Fairies that a blemished king could no longer rule, Nuadath lost his kingship the moment that he lost his hand; the rule of power being transferred over to his next in command, which was Bres, son of Elathan, who was half-Fairy and half-Fomorian, which was an earlier conquered race of this isle. Of how Bres came to be, wasn't explained to Ithe, for in that part of the tale, the Fairies had only just arrived in this land, so how could anyone possibly be born as the progeny of both of these races, let alone someone old enough to lead their army?

Sadly, Bres turned out to be a cruel, hard-hearted and ruthless ruler, forcing even the most-learned Fairy into doing hard manual labour. Even the powerful King-druid, the Dagda himself, was forced into doing demeaning work, such as digging ramparts around Bres' lofty fortresses; whilst the Fairies' own Champion, the magnificently strong, Ogma of the Sunny-face, had to endure the daily humiliation of carrying enormous stacks of firewood to furnish all of Bres' many hearths.

For seven years that was how it was, until a highly skilled physician of the Fairies, constructed a silver hand for Nuadath. After which, he became forever known as Nuadath Silver-hand. The metal hand was the same size and shape as his original hand, with the same full range of movements. This was impressive enough. But it was the son of this doctor, who used his magical arts, over a period of thrice three days and nights, in which he grew real skin upon the hand; when finished, his hand had all his normal feelings and senses upon it. And so, with Nuadath now deemed as being whole, in that old sense of the word, so was thought to be 'without blemish', he was once more able to regain the kingship of the Fairies. Now that his power had been fully restored, Nuadath led his downtrodden people, warring hard against the tyrannical Bres and his Fomorian army, for the rule of our whole country was again at stake.

Lugh of the Long-arm, like Bres, was himself half-Fairy and half-Fomorian. He proved to Nuadath his worth, for he was highly skilled in many arts, especially those of warfare. So impressed was the Fairy-king, that he made Lugh his High-general, giving him the overall leadership of the whole Fairy army. Armed with the Fairies' magical 'Spear of Victory', which protected the wielder's army from ever losing in combat, he led his men onward, in what was to become known as 'The Second Battle of the Plain of Lament', (otherwise called 'The Northern Battle of the Plain of Lament'), which took place to the southeast of the Mountains of Gamh.

The Fairies won that war, although in its final moments, the Dagda realised that his magical harp had been stolen; it was a truly powerful instrument, able to control the seasons, as well as the moods of men, for it had the ability to make all those within its hearing laugh uncontrollably, wail with grief, or to sleep soundly. So, the Dagda, along with the High-general, Lugh of the Long-arm, and their Champion, Ogma of the Sunny-face, chased after the fleeing enemy for a good-many leagues, until finally they were able to reclaim their valuable magical instrument.

Ithe and his men were completely astounded by these fantastical tales. They clearly showed the Fairies' supremacy in warring, as well as in their unmatched skills of enchantment. And the way in which they'd replaced Nuadath's hand showed just how skilfully adept they were in the druidical arts of healing. Ithe had certainly learnt much, not only of their prowess on the battlefield, but also of their chivalrous generosity towards fallen enemies, by granting them large territories of land. But whether these tales were true or not, he couldn't quite yet tell.

As the feast continued, both sides got better acquainted. The Fairy-bards kept their guests well-entertained throughout, with music and the singing of heroic poems, whilst Ithe kept complimenting them on their island as he casually questioned them; he was determined to find out if this truly was the prophesied Island of Destiny, for if it was, he'd need to return with Milesius and their whole Gaelic army as an invading enemy force. With this thought constantly at the forefront of their minds, our warriors began comparing weapons with those of the Fairies. The golden-bronze leaf-shaped blades of the Fairy-swords were a world away from the hard, black, iron-swords carried by most of our men. As exquisitely made as the Fairy-swords were, and shining like the sun, they lacked the strength and balance of our iron-swords, making them unwieldy and much more prone to bend, or to even break.

The Fairies told Ithe about their skills of Foreknowledge, and how many of them were able to see future events, before they happened. But Ithe seemed even more sceptical of this claim, as they appeared to believe his story as to why they'd travelled there, when it was so clearly a falsehood; so maybe the Fairies couldn't quite see into the future as they so clearly tried to have him believe.

Throughout the meal, Ithe believed that he was really getting a good grasp of the different personalities of those three kings, for they each seemed to exude the same characteristics that belonged to their own personal god: Kéthor had a bright, friendly smile and was as generously welcoming as the sun's rays upon a summer's day; Téthor was muscularly built, and as strong as an ox, so managed to get much done, for he worked as hard as the farmer's plough; whilst Ethor believed himself to be as wise as the hazel-tree, so felt that he was far superior to all those around him, so looked down upon everyone that he met.

As the meal was coming to a close, the three leading Fairies had concluded, from their lengthy conversations with Ithe, that he really was a man of great depth and wisdom, for he had acquired a wealth of knowledge from many realms, including those of the advanced society of Egypt. They were all highly impressed. The Fairy-king, Kéthor, himself was particularly taken with him, not only due to his scholarly knowledge, but also with Ithe being descended from a powerful royal house of conquerors, as they themselves were. So Kéthor, with both of his brothers' consent, asked Ithe if he would give a ruling over their long-standing disagreement, and with him being a stranger there, he would undoubtedly be impartial. Ithe humbly agreed to preside over this important affair, which so many of those eminent Fairies had come to witness that day.

And so, shortly thereafter, the hearing began. Ithe listened carefully to all the matters of the dispute, which was, in essence, how best to divide their ancestral treasures, as well as their land. After carefully thinking it over, Ithe decided that the three ruling brothers should share the treasures equally between themselves, so that no one has more than the other. They should also do the same with the land. Ithe continued, "Be not in strife with one another, for you live in a land that surpasses all others. For 'tis abounding in honey, fish and milk, as well as fertile soil, which produces the most exceptional fruit, corn and vegetables. The weather is also ideal, being neither too hot nor too cold. So, in every way, you have the most perfect of all lands here". Ithe knew this to be true, for during his time on the island, he and his men had enjoyed much of its remarkable produce, as well as appreciating its perfectly temperate climate.

The Fairies thanked Ithe for his wise judgement. Even Ethor, son of the Hazel-tree god, who prided himself on his wisdom, couldn't find a flaw in what Ithe had said, even though he searched the depths of his soul trying to find some fault.

It was now time for the Spaniards to return home. Their quest had been a huge success, even though Ithe felt extremely guilty for having deceived the Fairies, especially after all the kindness that they had shown him and his men. But if this truly was the Island of Destiny, which he now believed in his heart that it was, then surely the gods would furnish a solution upon them, and maybe they could even share this glorious land with those kind-hearted Fairies.

King Kéthor, with his characteristic generosity, gave them plentiful supplies of food, so they'd have enough provisions to see them home. Neither side particularly wanted to part company, for so enjoyable had it all been.

As they stepped forth from the Keep, Ithe and his heavily laden men were greeted by the warm sunlight of a glorious blue afternoon sky. His hosts kindly accompanied them as far as the curtain wall, trying to prolong the merriment before the inevitable parting.

Walking through the large gateway, they could clearly see before them, far in the distance, beyond the heavily forested landscape, a thin grey thread of smoke drifting lazily upwards. Ithe smiled, and pointing towards it, told his hosts that his son was there waiting with their ship and the rest of their crew. Thereupon, a warm farewell was said by all, as Ithe and his men happily departed; each man as one smiled with that warm-hearted feeling of contentment that you can only get from eating good, hearty food whilst in the presence of a jovial, hospitable company.

So onward Ithe led his men, in the direction from whence the Dark Wind does blow, towards the forest, and beyond, to where his son was waiting. Lughaidh had moored their ship in the nearby lough, which was just over an hour's march away, in what is now known as Feabhal's Lake. A strong, cool breeze ruffled each one of those warriors' hair, as they slowly walked down the hillside; this being the most perfect condition for strolling towards their waiting ship on a day as warm as this.

But sadly, our tale now takes a dark turn: for it was only after they'd left, that the Fairies started making sense of the visit. For you see, it was our warriors' iron blades that had unwittingly befuddled the Fairy senses, blocking out their considerable skills of Foreknowledge. And thus, accordingly, with Ithe's men having now gone, the Fairies started to increasingly sense the true purpose of the Spaniards' intrusion upon their isle; for with their Foreknowledge now restored they could clearly visualise more of Ithe's warriors returning, as conquerors, bringing bloodshed to their peaceful isle. The sudden shock of this realization hit them with quite a blow. And with Ithe being so enthusiastic about their isle, stating that it was 'the most perfect of all lands', it all started to make sense. Those good people were furious, especially after all the hospitality and generosity that they'd naturally given.

Ethor, son of Cearmad Honey-mouth, had never really trusted the visitors. They weren't of his race, or of his breeding. So, he asked King Kéthor if he could lead an army against them. The Fairy-king reluctantly agreed; but what choice did he really have?

So Ethor quickly mustered an army of one-and-a-half-hundred of his nearby troops, and without delay, gave chase. Those Fairy-warriors were swift of foot, carrying only light arms, and oh so fast did they run.

Ithe's men hadn't even reached the trees at the bottom of the mountain before they spotted the angry Fairies giving chase. Ithe sent a messenger to flee through the forest with all haste, in the direction of the ship's smoke, to bring back reinforcements. Ithe's warriors weren't able to hurry, for they were heavily laden with large, cumbersome jars that brimmed full of food; they couldn't just drop these and escape, as without them, they knew that they'd starve on the long voyage home.

Ithe stood at the rear of his men and urged them onward, towards the trees. The golden leaf-shaped blades of the Fairy-swords flashing in the bright sunlight as they rushed down the mountain. With the banner of the hazel-tree now coming into view, Ithe knew that it was Ethor giving chase. In a way he was relieved, for he would have been deeply ashamed to have fought against King Kéthor, after all the kindness that good man had afforded him. And Téthor was another good man, but hugely strong, so Ithe wouldn't have liked to stand against his powerful sword blows either.

Just as our warriors entered the trees, the Fairies were almost at the foot of the mountain. Again, Ithe shouted to his men to hurry onward, as he did his best to protect their rear lines as they fled into the shadows of the forest. But as the Fairies caught up, an explosive battle broke out. Both sides fought with vicious blows. Our iron-swords ringing against their bronze-plated shields, whilst their bronze-swords chopping and thudding against our wooden ones.

Ithe's men struggled against this much larger force, for every two of his men had to fight against three of the enemy. And they desperately tried to avoid the sword and spear blows for they knew only too well that the Fairy-blades were likely to be poisoned. It truly was a violent battle. Our men fought hard, inching backwards through the trees. Whenever possible they used the trees as an extra shield, to dash behind for cover, from which they could lunge forward to devastating effect. With Ithe desperately trying to protect his men, he was taking the brunt of the battle's blows. Therefore, in such a lengthy barbaric attack, it wasn't long before Ithe himself was struck down.

Just at that very moment, running from behind, through the gloomy depths of the forest, came Lughaidh, heavily panting, leading half-a-hundred men. It was then that the battle broke apart, as both sides retreated to regroup. Mortally wounded, Ithe was helped through the trees, back towards the awaiting ship.

The supplies were quickly carried aboard, before the whole Fairy army had time to catch them. Hurriedly casting off, they journeyed southwards, around the island, and then out, into the open sea, and homeward bound.

It was a long voyage back to Galicia. The men did everything that they could for Ithe, but his wounds were far too deep. Whether or not those Fairy-blades had been venomously tipped, or not, we shall never know. But it was upon that return journey that Ithe succumbed to his mortal wounds, and sadly passed away. Some of the crewmen thought that upon the wind the sound of his beloved horses could be heard, neighing sorrowfully, as they cried for their master; but the wind sometimes plays tricks upon the minds of Men.

There were few dry eyes upon that voyage, so loved was that great man of learning. Thence it lay to Lughaidh to take command of the company, charging himself with the morbid task of returning to Galicia with his father's dead body. This was a long, deeply depressing journey, made all the worse with having a dead friend for company. Not just with the sorrow of his death, but also the real misery of those flies and the smell; I shall say no more.

Each day felt the same as the previous one, as one day merged into another. Every man on that ship just wanted the whole voyage to be over. Despair hung around that ship, clinging to the very souls of those poor tortured warriors.

Eventually, after three long weeks at sea, those heroes had made it back home. It had been the lookout atop Breoghan's Tower who'd spotted them first, as a black dot upon the northern horizon, between the deep-aquamarine sea and the pale-blue sky. He'd watched them slowly rowing nearer. So that by the time they'd reached the shore, Milesius, and many of the townsfolk were already there waiting. Rarely has any Man felt such a strong contrast of emotions as those crewmen did back then, feeling deep mournful sorrow, for the loss of the great Ithe, mixed with guilty waves of ecstatic relief, at being home and safe, once more. They knew not whether to laugh nor cry; some were seen to do both, uncontrollably.

By this time in our tale, King Milesius must have passed the age of three-score years, but was still a towering, virile figure of a man, keeping fit daily, often with lengthy bouts of swordplay, so that no one would ever think to question his authority. His beard was now ash-grey, and his slim muscular frame had widened, but the twinkle in those intelligent eyes, and the smile upon those lips, was still very much there, even though today there wasn't much to smile about. He'd always gone out of his way to be as friendly as possible, even as a child, often making witty quips to put others at their ease, but still it was true that there were many who were intimidated by his manly confidence, especially now, for due to his age, he seemed to be looked upon as very much a fatherly figure to each and every one in his tribe.

As the ship docked, Lughaidh had the unenviable task of carrying his father's dead body ashore. Milesius was obviously devastated to learn that his uncle had been so brutally murdered, in a seemingly unprovoked attack. The news spread throughout the town with the speed of a forest fire. Wails of grief seemed to come from every conceivable corner, for his gentle wisdom had touched so many lives.

Milesius questioned Lughaidh and his men, desperate to find out the events of the journey and of the mysterious island in which they'd explored. The warriors who'd accompanied Ithe as far as the grey stone-fortress of *Aileach Neid* were all convinced that it truly was the Island of Destiny; they tried to vividly describe it to the elders, for it did indeed seem like a paradise, with the lakes and forests being so abundant with food.

It was after this line of questioning that the conversation took a darker turn, as Milesius asked about the death of Ithe. Every one of those townsfolk who stood there, listening to that dreadful, woeful tale, were overcome with fury, craving revenge upon the Fairy race; but none more so than Ithe's mighty brothers, together with the brave sons of Milesius. With the air itself being so emotionally charged with feelings of vengeful rage, it wasn't long before the cry went out, which seemed to echo all around that corner of their kingdom, 'To the Island of Destiny', 'The Island of Destiny', 'The Island of Destiny', 'The Island of Destiny'.

Over the next few weeks, Milesius learnt everything that he could from those adventurers, speaking to them on many occasions, trying to wring out every bit of information that he could from their memories. And so respected was Milesius, that those warriors themselves each had a burning desire to impart every minute detail of their journey, no matter how trivial it seemed, for so desperate were they to please their king; Milesius seemed to absorb everything that was said. He learnt much about the Fairy-folk during those lengthy discussions, as each warrior described them as being naturally light-hearted and full of energy, though obviously powerful and fierce when needed. He heard how the Fairies had told them tales of how they were highly-accomplished sorcerers, but those returning warriors hadn't actually witnessed them performing any magic, so didn't know if this was actually true.

With all the information that he'd gathered, Milesius formed a Council-of-War; this comprised of himself and his three-and-forty Chieftains, many of whom were made up of his sons and Ithe's brothers, as well as his own brave cousin, Lughaidh, son of Ithe. They carefully planned out their strategies to fully revenge themselves upon the Fairies, and to conquer the land in the process.

On a different note: one piece of news that had joyfully greeted Lughaidh, son of Ithe, on his return home, was that his daughter, Téa, had married Milesius' son, Heremon. It was an important royal wedding, with them both being members of the same ruling family. The bride and groom were even related, being second cousins. Téa had always been known for being ruthlessly ambitious, but this wasn't unusual in her family, as the conquering spirit was so obviously flowing in all of their blood. At the time of their betrothal, Heremon was already married to his own sister, Odba, having had four young sons to her, but Téa, using her feminine machinations, had set out to ensnare him. Téa desperately wanted a man who embodied some of her own ambitions, who would be able to carve out a prosperous and rewarding life for her, and for any children that she might come to have; with this thought in mind, she set her eyes upon Heremon, as he was clearly one of the three most suitable men out of all of his powerful brothers. But another reason why she so desperately wanted Heremon, was because he had already unwittingly captured her heart, so she had made it her life's purpose to do the same to him. And with her plans set in motion, Heremon fell deeply in love with the beguiling Téa. Compelled by this love, he left his wife for her. For that was the way things were done back then.

Those two women, how different they both were. Téa was a little younger and prettier and really looked after her appearance, whilst Odba, with having four young sons to care for, was constantly kept busy, so obviously didn't have the time to make as much effort; but she had become more comfortable anyway, in presenting a distinctly more unkempt appearance than Téa ever would have dared. Even the way that they wore their hair partly summed up the personalities of the two wives: Téa's hair was very carefully prepared, trying out the latest fashions, whilst Odba's hair was loose, giving her a more maternal presence. But it wasn't just how they looked that separated the two women, for their temperaments were also very different: Téa was more assertive, constantly craving improvements, and deliberately taking steps to bring her plans to fruition, whilst Odba was more passive, kind-hearted and agreeable, leaving her fate in the hands of the gods; and it was for this last reason that Téa was able to so successfully steal Odba's husband away.

But now, back to our tale of revenge. Since Ithe's ship had been on such a lengthy voyage, it was thought best to retire it, as it was deemed unsafe to make any further journeys. So, an armada of thirty new galleys were built, but not quite to the same grand scale as that of Ithe's old ship, as it had often been mentioned by many of the previous crewmen that the creaking of the long planks had terrified all aboard, making them believe that the forces upon the vessel could have ripped it apart at any given moment. The largest of these new galleys was designed for Milesius and Scota, being just over two thirds the size of Ithe's original ship. The other vessels were to be smaller, probably measuring only about two thirds of the size of Milesius' new flagship. The shipbuilders worked tirelessly building these magnificent vessels. They would take a good-many months to build. The tribe's weavers were themselves equally as busy, creating a huge mast for each one of those thirty vessels. In fact, everyone seemed to be involved in some activity designed to furnish those ships with supplies, from the farmers trying to save whatever little crops they could, to the armourers forging new iron arms; indeed, the whole of Galicia was a hive of activity.

But whilst all this was happening, a deadly plague ravaged the land. It held no distinction between nobleman and commoner, nor between the worthy and the unjust. More victims were caught in its net every day. Friends eagerly listened for any gossip, to see if any of their loved ones had now been taken. And once news of this pestilence had reached foreign shores, even visiting merchants refused to step foot ashore. And anyone found to be suffering from its horrendous symptoms were forced to isolate themselves away, to avoid spreading the deadly virus on to others.

Then, just before the newly-built ships were ready to sail, the great Milesius himself, powerful king of our Gaelic tribe, started to feel the effects of the fever. Weakened by its grip, he had no choice but to take to his royal bed. His whole tribe patiently waited for his recovery, before they could set off on their final quest.

But the fever floored the great man. Never before had anyone seen him looking so weak, or in so much pain. Hourly reports from his bedchamber told of his ashen skin, his bedclothes drenched with sweat, yet his cold, clammy body shivering with cold. His marital bed was now becoming his grave. What made his final hours all the more painful was that his whole family were prevented from seeing him, their beloved liege, during that dreadful time, in case they too succumbed to the plague that he was carrying. Broken-hearted, each one of them wept that they couldn't keep a bedside vigil for that manly, all-powerful, larger-than-life heroic king that they were proud to call husband, father, and friend. Not even being able to say a final goodbye made his death all the more painful to bear.

When news of his death was announced around his fortress, after the initial disbelief had passed, it felt to each and every one in his tribe, that their own father had just died. How could a man that powerful be dead? A man who had always been so full of life. A man whose very presence had caused the Egyptians to believe him to be a divine emissary of the gods. The whole town wept for Milesius. The cries and wails of despair overshadowed even those of Ithe's passing. The great King's subjects were lost with overwhelming grief.

Upon that same terrible day, twelve loyal families of their tribe also died from that same ravaging plague, including two of Milesius' most trusted Chieftains.

With tears still fresh in their eyes, Milesius' brave family vowed to continue with his quest, and to fulfil the old prophesy made by the noble druid, Cachear, all those generations before. And so, it was arranged, within a few days of the great man's funeral, before they too succumbed to that deadly plague, that his wife, Scota and his eight loyal sons would set off, with their mighty army, heading northwards towards the Fairies' realm. It was Donn, the eldest son, who would lead them. He must have been aged almost ten-and-thirty by this time, so was no undisciplined youngling. Furthermore, he was an extremely capable man, having trained for a good-many years at the side of the great Milesius, in all the disciplines of kingship. He was tall and strong, brown-haired, dark-eyed, with a long, noble nose, and with that confident air that all kings seem to exhibit. He was the perfect man to lead the mission.

With Donn having spent some of his formative years in Egypt, he'd also taken a kindly disposition towards the matrimonial practices of the pharaohs, just like that of his younger brother, Heremon, and he too had married his own sister, Dil. And if all things were equal to that of those glorious Egyptian kings, then Donn's marriage would also mean that he too was destined for greater things.

Milesius had taken much pride in training Donn in the arts of warcraft, as well as readying him for his role as future king, which meant that he was now fully prepared, and battle-ready to lead the invasion. And such was Donn's power of command that no one dared to challenge him for the right of leadership. He hadn't yet been crowned, but that was just a formality, for at that moment he didn't exactly have a country to rule; but once they'd defeated the Fairies, then crowned he would be, and made king of the whole Island of Destiny. The prophesy must be right, and this must be the island. They were betting everything on that one assumption.

And so, they set sail. Donn had taken Milesius' own galley, which had the sigil of his father's three lions proudly painted across the mast. It was this ship that took the lead, at the head of a large convoy of some thirty ships. It has been said that, including his own siblings, a total of seven-and-forty families made that journey, as well as approximately thrice-three-hundred battle-hardened warriors, most of whom were at that point unmarried. Also, amongst their number were four-and-twenty strong labourers, as there would be much work to be done once their quest was over. Hence, not including their flagship which was able to hold more, that means that each vessel carried roughly half-a-hundred voyagers.

They weren't short of leaders either, for ten-and-thirty brave Chieftains led those warriors under the lawful command of Donn. These were:

Donn's seven most-capable brothers: Arech Red-brow, Heber Fionn, Amergin White-knee, Ir, Colpa of the Sword, Heremon, as well as young Erenan.

The four sons of Heber Fionn: Er, Orba, Feron and Fergna.

Heber Donn, son of Ir.

The four young sons of Heremon: Muimne, Luighne, Laighean and Palap the Lucky.

Lughaidh, son of Ithe.

The nine-remaining greybearded sons of Breoghan: Bréga, Cualu, Cualgni, the noble Bladh the Bland (who preferred being called 'Bladh the Rough and Strong'), Fuaid, Eiblinni, Nar, Lui, and the famed Murthemni of the Lake.

Four of Donn's most-trusted Chieftains: Bile son of Brighe, Buas of the Battle, Bres, as well as Buaighe, who all proudly sailed upon the lead flagship.

Also included amongst this number of Chieftains were ten of their most fearsome Champions: Fulman, Mantan, Caicher the Victorious, Suirge the Slender, Én, Ún, Eatan the Proud, Sobairce, Sedga of Spears, and Goisten the Champion.

(There were two other Chieftains who were meant to have taken that same journey, but sadly, as mentioned earlier, they'd died of the plague on the very same day as that of Milesius).

Those brave voyagers, who were leaving behind everything that was familiar to them, in their beloved capital of Galicia, were now heading uneasily towards an unknown land, and without the great Milesius to lead them. Whether or not this upheaval was any easier for those of Egyptian birth, as Scota, her druid, and a few of her more mature attendants had lived, after all, during their formative years in a very different world, so had obviously been uprooted once before; but many of the others, especially the younger ones, knew no real life outside of Iberia. But one thing that they all knew for sure, was that there would be plenty of blood spilled before this righteous quest was over.

There was much hardship aboard those timber galleys, even though they were most beautifully constructed, being very similar in design to that of Ithe's old ship, with a huge billowing mast right in the very centre; although it could only be unfurled when the White Wind, or one of its friendly neighbours, was blowing favourably. At other times the crewmen had to keep it tied up and take to the oars instead. There was but little space for movement in those cramped conditions, especially when almost every inch of space contained jars of food or water, as well as livestock, and even horses. Unfortunately, these ships weren't anything like the palatial galleys in which Scota had travelled from her homeland, but that was at least six-and-twenty years before; that now felt like a lifetime ago to Scota. Even their own personal, newly-forged weapons, which wouldn't usually take up too much space, were now bundled together, wrapped in a waxed cloth to help keep them dry, and secured to the deck lest they be washed overboard; and these took up another large section of valuable floor space.

It was undeniably chilly, journeying across that vast, open stretch of ocean. All eyes were on Donn to see how he was faring, for the more relaxed and in control he looked, the happier everyone felt. However, it wasn't too long into the voyage before he purposely lifted up the hood of his warm brown cloak, pulling the material further around his broad shoulders in a bid to keep that cold, blustery wind at bay, meaning that his face was rarely seen.

Donn's second-in-command was his brother, Arech Red-brow, who was known for having bright, coppery-red hair, with the same colour eyebrows, and that distinctively pale skin that freckles far too easily. He was of a similar build to that of his brown-haired brother, sharing a close bond with him, for after all, they both came from the same mother, being the only sons born from the union between Milesius and his first wife, Seng. Arech was well-known for his wisdom and had received much of the same training in warcraft and weaponry as his elder brother, making him the perfect second-in-command. So, if anything happened to Donn, then Arech would be the next obvious choice of leader. Both these brothers sailed in the same ship, along with four of Donn's most-trusted Chieftains, so that they could carefully devise their warring strategies together. Half-a-hundred youths also sailed with them, and practised with their weapons, almost daily, depending upon the calmness of the sea, for they were to be the highly-trained warriors of the future. But sometimes, due to the tight confinement of their ship, it made those young men forget themselves, and juvenile squabbles frequently made that ship a most tempestuous one.

Milesius' widow, the beautiful Scota seemed to have aged considerably since her husband's passing, so was now looking older than her two-score-years-and-twelve. But still she was a very fine-looking Egyptian Queen. She was still slim and physically fit but her once-jet black hair was now streaked with grey. Accompanying her was her youngest son, Erenan, for the two of them were very close. Also aboard were the two highly-respected grey-cloaked druids, Ethiar and Uar. Ethiar was the Queen's druid, and was her most trusted spiritual advisor, whom she relied upon greatly for his wisdom and guidance. The keeping of her two horses were left to the charge of both of those esteemed men, and whenever the sea was at its calmest, they would slowly walk them around the deck, for a limited amount of exercise. Tied firmly to the foremost part of the deck was Scota's small, lightweight war-chariot; it had been brought along in case it was needed for the coming war.

Over on Amergin White-knee's ship was his wife, Sgene. She was a feisty woman, known for being a highly-efficient satirist. Her curses could lead to certain death, so she was treated with as much reverence as that of her powerful husband, who was now our High-druid. How evenly matched that couple truly were!

Colpa of the Sword travelled with his younger brother, Heremon, although there were so many of Heremon's brood aboard, that Colpa felt like a bit of an outsider. For onboard were Heremon's new wife, Téa, with her tiny mewling baby, as well as Heremon's four young sons from his previous marriage to Odba; those young boys would end up becoming big strapping lads like their father, but at this point in our tale, hadn't yet reached the age of ten, though were still classed as Chieftains, having gained that role by hereditary right.

Colpa was by now six-and-twenty, being two years older than Heremon, though still hadn't been fortunate enough to find himself a bride. As a way to pass the time on that lengthy voyage he was forever practising with his sword, with whichever warriors were feeling brave enough to try their hand against such a skilled swordsman. With him being such a genuine and kind Chieftain, however, he attracted many offers from those who just wanted to spend time in his good-natured company. Aboard their ship was also Heremon's spirited stallion, Gaber. He'd named his horse after seeking advice from his mother's druid, who'd told him that 'Gaber' meant 'powerful' and 'independent' in the Arab tongue. He knew that his horse had a strange sense of haughty playfulness about it, for he'd often heard it humorously snorting at people, which further convinced him to call it by that name, as 'Gaber' was coincidentally also the old Gaelic word for 'mocking'. Both these meanings seemed to suit the lively animal.

Of all the hardships aboard those vessels, the one person who seemed to suffer the most was Odba. She travelled in a different ship to the one that carried her four young sons and previous husband. And she travelled alone, so very alone, in a ship full of people. And whenever her ship came alongside that of her former husband, Heremon always seemed to be in the arms of Téa, with both of them making such a huge fuss of their little baby; it was incredibly heart-breaking for poor Odba. The new couple were so obviously in love with each other, that it became unbearable for her to see. Many times, she thought about dropping beneath the waves, to put an end to her torturous and miserable life, but still she carried on, hoping that one day her husband would realise how much he still loved her, and would come running back. For that poor shunned woman that unmerciful sea-voyage seemed to be without end.

During the lengthy voyage, upon each one of those ships, the crewmen took it in turns to act as lookouts sitting atop the masts. Even the youngest of Milesius' sons, Erenan, enjoyed the responsibility that this work afforded him.

Across that desolate stretch of ocean, the spirited brothers enthusiastically raced each other, for few male siblings lack that most compelling and driving of urges to outdo each other in a bid to win, at any given task. And in that highly-determined, competitive way of his, it was Ir who seemed to be in the lead for much of the journey, to the great annoyance of Donn.

Eventually, after almost three weeks of hard seamanship they spotted land. They sailed silently onwards. Not wanting to land where Ithe had, in case there was an ambush waiting, they lowered their sails to make themselves less conspicuous, and rowed eastwards.

Just around the south-eastern corner, they found a good, protected harbour. Donn ordered the ships to head towards it. So, rowing slowly around the narrow mudbank, which extended out into the sea, being kept forever slippery by the hungry waves that endlessly lapped against it, they made their way into the wide channel. Carefully, and silently, they glided through the water, navigating around the tiny islets that guarded the harbour entrance, and then between the treacherous mudflats that lay to either side. Only when they were safely through, did they cautiously head towards the expansive, green, tree-lined shore. There was plenty of space in this natural harbour for all thirty of their ships to safely moor. This port became known as Loch Garman and stood in the south-east corner of the lands of Hy Kinsella.

But as those travellers neared, they saw that within those dense, shadowy trees that the entire Fairy army were there, awaiting their approach. They were dressed in pale, flowing garments, which contrasted sharply against the green, leafy backdrop. (We came to find out much later, that it was when the Fairies were in larger numbers, like this, that their magical powers were strongest).

As those brave Gaelic warriors neared, the only noise to be heard was the splashing of their many oars rhythmically slicing through the waves and the sea noisily lapping against the banks of the shore ahead. The crewmen dared not speak, nor breathe too noisily lest they break the tranquillity of the moment. The Fairies still hadn't moved; and this calm state of inactivity caused an increasing, and unnerving sense of dread to wash over those crewmen. Upon the faces of the Fairies, a strange look of concentration could be visibly seen, with an outward air of near-serenity, whilst deep within, especially around the eyes, glowed an intensity of rage, as they appeared to be mouthing strange, primeval words. As the ships closed in upon the shore, the sounds could be heard of the Fairy-druids, as the very air around them filled with the chanting of spells. Suddenly, from all around the galleys, huge, billowing enchanted mists erupted. So much so, that the island quickly lay hidden behind impenetrable, grey, swirling clouds. As the warriors continued to slowly, and cautiously, row shore-wards, they found that the tree-lined bank had now completely changed shape; it was as if the whole Island of Destiny had literally transformed before them, taking on the contours of what can only be described as an enormous wild-boar lying upon its side, with monumental sloping banks preventing any ships from landing.

As the Fairies' chanting increased, the mist thickened, so the sailors couldn't even see their own hands in front of their faces. The terrified invaders were now forced away from the shore, hoping that the mists would be thinner elsewhere. They were struck with terror, fearing that their ships would founder upon those deadly mudflats, or the hidden rocks, or upon the many islets within the harbour entrance. These were truly dangerous, unchartered waters surrounding this destined isle.

Thrice did they sail around the whole island, desperately trying to find a safe place in which to land, but that impenetrable fog, and the steep sloping banks created by that army of magicians, made their task an almost hopeless one. Frustrated with despair, harsh words were said amongst the crews, for they greatly feared drowning in this distant part of the world. Was there no place where they could land, for they certainly didn't have enough provisions left for a return journey back to Iberia?

But then a strange thing happened, for when all hope seemed to be lost, and finding themselves off the southwest corner, a small parting in the fog allowed them a clear passage towards the shore. Was this just good fortune, a flaw in the Fairies' magic, or was it all part of a much bigger, secret plan designed to force their ships to land on that particular part of the island for reasons known only to the enemy?

The crews of the armada uneasily rowed through the corridor, between two gigantic walls of fog that stretched upwards towards the tops of the masts. They sailed towards the beaming strip of sunlight that glistened upon the water ahead. Their hearts drumming noisily in their chests, though the turquoise sea before them was eerily calm.

Once through the fog, a bright day greeted them. They now found themselves in a huge sunlit bay. There were six rowers in each of those ships, although there were eight in Donn's flagship, with his being considerably larger. They slowly rowed onward, pleased to be finally heading anywhere that took them towards land, and away from the dangers of that fog-engulfed coastline. Large isles and treacherous rocks filled the length of that watery valley. Far ahead of them, at the head of the bay, they spotted the perfect place in which to land. So eagerly towards it they rowed.

That landing place in which they were heading, with it being located at the 'Head of the Sea', was thereafter called *Ceann Mara,* from which that whole bay now also takes its name. (Today it's overlooked by the impressive castle known as the Height of Aodh).

It has been written that it was upon the fifteenth day of April that those Milesians finally landed upon these shores; 'twas on a Thursday, as I recall.

With Ir being the most competitive, as well as the least cautious, it was his ship that landed first. He quickly jumped ashore, before they'd even time to anchor, armed only with a sharp sword of iron. Its drab, dark-coloured blade hiding the ferocity of its lethal bite. The other ships landed shortly after. And on the grassy banks along the waterfront, they hurriedly gathered their troops, leaving the women, and a small contingent of warriors to guard the moored galleys. Whilst in their absence those remaining guards could exercise the poor horses, for too long had they been cooped up upon those ships.

Those brave Gaelic warriors clambered up the slippery, green banks towards the dense forest. Before them the trees spread out in every direction. The wide trunks stretching far up into the sky, with branches, like arms trying to reach for the wisps of white clouds floating by. Within their shadowy depths, green, leafy bracken grew waist-high. But thankfully, there were a few timeworn paths that cut through this impenetrable landscape. These must have been made by either the Fairies or their predecessors and were the only practical and safe routes across the island.

In order to get a better view of the landscape, they chose a path that trailed northwards. If this path didn't lead them to a better vantage point up one of the mountainsides, then they trusted, that it might possibly lead them towards the army of sorcerers; for these they'd have to overcome, if they wanted to wreak vengeance upon those three sons of Cearmad Honey-mouth for the death of Ithe, as well as to fulfil their age-old prophecy, which could only be realised by seizing that magnificent island for themselves.

And so, they trailed northwards, marching with a solemn determination, for they knew not where this path would lead, nor of the dangers or disappointments at its end. This rough tree-lined passage had been axe-hewn in times of old, meaning that some parts were narrower than others, whilst other parts had since become overgrown, so branches scratched and cut at their bare arms and faces, adding to their growing frustration.

Fortunately for them, the path took them directly through the forests towards the foot of a nearby mountain, as they had partly hoped. The walking now became significantly harder as they followed the long, dark, shadowy path that snaked its way up the gently rising mountain. They were making good time though, as they felt that there was a pressing urgency to conclude their mission.

Before too long, to their complete amazement, they could see that just ahead of them, streaming through the trees, bright daylight was clearly visible. As they got nearer, they actually wandered out from the dense woodland, to find themselves out in the open, for the top of the mountain was completely barren of trees, being covered entirely by lush green grassland. Up there, on the exposed mountainside, the bright sunlight gently warmed their cold, clammy bodies; it felt good.

As they continued walking upwards, away from the line of trees, they each turned to gaze out over the landscape. It was an amazing view of a land of endless trees deeply engraved with veins of meandering rivers; the whole island surrounded by the bluest of oceans. And when they gazed hard enough, they could see that amidst those dense forests there were actually a few clearings, here and there: some plains had been cleared for their strange religious rituals, whilst some mountaintops were also cleared, like the one on which they stood, so that the Fairies could build their strongholds, so that they could live in safety overlooking the trees below. There were also plains that lay near to these strongholds that had been either cleared for farming or for the grazing of livestock.

As they turned away from that magnificent view, to continue their journey upwards, along the winding path of the green mountainside, heading towards the summit, they soon realised that there was no fortress upon this cleared mountaintop. But what they did see as they neared the peak, was a large banner with a hazel-tree emblazoned upon it. Beneath this the invaders found Queen Banbha, accompanied by her many female attendants and a handful of her most trusted druids. The women all wore loose, pale, flowing garments, with flowers in their hair. It was as if the Fairies knew in which direction our ancestors would be travelling, for they seemed to have been there a while, patiently awaiting their arrival. That important meeting place has since become known as *Slieve Mish*: The Mountain of Mis, being named after a later Gaelic princess.

Due to Amergin White-knee, son of Milesius, being our High-druid, he was dressed differently to that of his brothers, being cloaked in a grey mantle over a short white gown. He was a reasonable man, though greatly feared by anyone foolish enough to make him their enemy. He had a wide range of knowledge, being educated in every subject, like all those of his calling, and this acquired wisdom was the reason why he'd been such an influential adviser to his brother, Donn. And with him being fully versed in the skills of diplomacy, as well as being highly-schooled in the arts of necromancy, as the Fairies themselves surely were, it naturally fell to him to speak to that gathering of the elven race. As he approached the Fairy-queen, she was noticed to visibly tremble, yet still she held her regal head proudly aloft. She pointed to the mountains to the northeast, as being the place where the Fairy-kings were waiting. In payment for her good counsel, she asked for a boon, which was for the island to be forever named after her.

"It will be so", Amergin graciously replied, knowing that without her help they would have been marching around in circles for many weeks to come.

And so back down the mountain they walked, for many more leagues they headed, along the earthen paths that had been cut through those dense forests, to continue in their search for the three enemy kings.

At last, following the path in which Queen Banbha had directed them, which took them along the edge of the Sionna River, they finally reached the mountains which lay to the south of Dergart's Lake. These were later to be named the Mountains of Eiblinni, taking their name from one of Breoghan's worthy sons. Like the previous mountain, this also appeared to be half-shrouded by a cloak of trees, which left all the upper portion completely barren. Seeing a party of awaiting Fairies standing upon the higher ground, the Gaelic warriors slowly made their way up the sloping banks.

It was tough going, clambering up those mountain paths, but eventually they reached the bare ground that lay towards the summit. This time it was beneath the banner of the plough, that our warriors met their next guide: Fodhla, the second Fairy-queen. As strong and manly as her husband physically was, Fodhla was gentler and quite fearful. And even though she was awaiting their arrival, so nervous was she at seeing our armed invaders approaching, that she fainted as they neared. After she'd recovered from her initial shock, she was most helpful, telling Amergin to follow the river northwards, and when they'd reached the river's ford, travel not westward across the river, but eastward, along the raised, winding path there, and that would take them towards a sacred hill, which marked the very centre of the island. For her guidance, she also asked for a favour, which was for the whole island to always bear her name.

Amergin smiled, "It will be so", he answered, thinking that from that time hence, the island shall forever have two names.

And so those warriors carefully followed her instructions, walking back down the mountainside. Thankfully, those days were mild and dry, with birds singing high up in the trees, and with enough food, seemingly supplied by the gods, that there was never a shortage of fruit, meat or fish, as it was just there, ready for the taking. And with there being plenty of old, dry wood scattered about the forest floor, it was seemingly effortless for them to build fires to keep themselves warm throughout the colder nights. It must have taken about three days of travelling between meeting each one of those Fairy-queens. And if it hadn't been such an all-important mission that they were on, they would gladly have tarried longer, for they were secretly beginning to enjoy their adventure, not only with the delicious food, which was a big thing in itself after leaving behind such a famine-starved country, but they were also enjoying the mountain views and the beautiful scenery along that wide, magnificent, sea-like river, as well as taking much pleasure in their own manly company.

Eventually, and it had to happen, they reached the shallow river's ford, beyond which was a long, winding footpath that ran westwards along the tops of the low hills far into the distance. So, it was here, at this junction where the path crossed the river, that sadly, it was time for them to leave the beautiful broad waterway that had been their companion for a good-many leagues. Following Fodhla's explicit instructions, they now headed eastwards, up into the low gravel hills, to follow that long, sinuous, serpentine path, which in many generations to come would have widened significantly to become known as *An Slighe Mór*: The Great Way. When upon that raised pathway, with them being considerably higher than the surrounding land, they found themselves gazing into the branches of rows of trees, to either side of them, standing like soldiers in a disorderly, but continuous line as far as the eye can see. The warriors headed along the path that stretched out before them, gently winding their way through the wooded landscape.

Within five hours or so, of them leaving the side of the Sionna they'd reached the sacred hill of Uisneach, where the Cat-stone stands today. And there they met the third Fairy-queen, Ériu, beneath her husband's banner, showing the sign of the Sun god. She was very beautiful, with pale skin, and a cascade of long hair, the colour of spun gold, falling down over her shoulders. She wore a loose, pale dress, which almost seemed alive as the material rippled as the wind caressed its flowing contours. She was crowned with a garland of seasonal flowers, and stood, looking much more confident than the two previous Fairy-queens. Almost every man there felt in awe, as they lovingly gazed at the vision before them.

"Welcome ye, warriors", she said as they neared. "Tread ye with much reverence upon this hill, for buried deep within are some of the greatest kings of mine own tribe... It is long since ye coming was prophesied, O sons of Milesius. For it hath been said that this island shall be forever yours, and there is no better land within this world".

"Thank you for your courtesy", replied Amergin, feeling both surprised and humbled that she knew of their ancient prophesy.

His brother, Donn must have been aged about two-score years by this time, being about eight years older than Amergin. He was stern of face and lacked Amergin's easy charm and skills of diplomacy. He wasn't interested in Ériu's beauty, or in what he deemed to be her flowery language, he was only interested in power and duty, and the chance to avenge his uncle. He also felt that each and every day that his command was being scrutinised by his Chieftains, so he needed to constantly prove himself, because he hadn't yet had the opportunity to win his tribe's love and respect, like his father had so successfully done before him. Feeling indignant, he shouted, "It is not to her that we need to give thanks, but to our own powerful gods, as well as to our own might".

"It is naught to thee", returned Ériu. "For thou shalt have no gain of this island, nor will thy children".

Directing the rest of her conversation back to Amergin, she continued, "Return ye back to thy path and resume thy journey eastward, until ye find thyselves at *Liathdruim:* The Grey-ridge, for there the elders await thy arrival. For this prophecy and for my wisdom, O sons of Milesius and children of Breoghan, a gift to me that mine name mayest remain forever upon this isle".

"It will be its chief name forever", replied Amergin, courteously smiling before bowing his head gently.

The beautiful Ériu had truly captured every heart, bar one, during that tempestuous meeting. And after their encounter with that glorious elven vision of womanhood, they did indeed honour Amergin's agreement, for the land has forever since been known as Ériu. And in poetical works, of which our race is so justly proud, the names of Banbha and Fodhla are also frequently used, as the honourable druid had that rare characteristic quality of his, of unfailingly being a man of his word.

And so onwards our invaders continued their journey, along that natural pathway, which ran along the top of those hills between the two lines of towering trees. Ahead of them the path snaked its way eastwards, whilst looking behind momentarily, they could see that it also twisted and turned all the way back in the direction of the western sea.

As they finally neared their destination, they saw peering through the trees ahead of them, the low, dark-hued limestone hill known as the Grey-ridge. But they couldn't quite believe what they were seeing; for as holy as the last hill was, they could clearly see that what stood before them was indeed much more sacred. Some of our men even rubbed their eyes in disbelief, for this ridge was literally wearing a monumental wooden crown atop its grey treeless slopes.

Those men slowly continued their journey, many of them feeling a little overwhelmed, as though they'd just entered into a strange dream. It wasn't much further until the path split into two, with the higher road continuing eastwards towards the sea, whilst the other led northwards directly to that monumental hill. Following Donn down that well-trodden path, those warriors curiously made their way, feeling astonished and in complete awe at what stood before them. As they followed the path, they couldn't help but notice a few large turf-covered burial-mounds scattered around the bottom of the hill, obviously the last resting places for some of the more important Fairy-kings of old.

Once they'd reached the foot of that sacred hill, they found themselves speaking in hushed tones, so reverential did they feel. And as they walked up the worn earthen-path towards the crowned summit, they felt as though they were heading towards something important; something that they couldn't quite understand.

They were met upon the hilltop by the three sons of Cearmad Honey-mouth. The handsome Kéthor, whose turn it was to rule, whose wife they'd just left, was at their front, whilst Ethor and Téthor stood behind, near the stone altar. Accompanying those three elven kings was a mass gathering of their most powerful druids. All the Fairies stood within the wooden structure. This huge timber circle consisted of many tall wooden pillars, which towered over them. Within that circle was another ring of even taller wooden columns. (They found out later that the druids had built this sacred, ceremonial edifice as a solar calendar, in which to calculate the important dates of the upcoming solstices and equinoxes, for these advised them when best to sow and reap their crops; the druids alone were trained to read these signs from the gods, and any mistakes would indeed be costly, for a poor harvest undoubtedly led to widespread starvation).

With it being common practice for kings to speak to those of a similar rank, it was now left to Donn to speak. He came straight to the point in that abrupt manner of his, "Give us battle for the sovereignty of this land, or quietly resign your rights and we'll allow you to remain as our subjects, to live under our rule".

The Fairy-king, Kéthor, boldly stepped forward in order to reply. His usual warm smile was now replaced by a more serious bearing. His golden lunula seeming to flash angrily upon his chest. They'd obviously been planning their response for quite some time, as their reply was filled with well thought-out wisdom. "We shalt abide by the decision that thine own brother, the High-druid dost make. But if he dost make an unjust judgment, then by magic shall he die, upon this very spot".

Amergin White-knee was quite taken aback by the Fairy's terrifying proposal. He carefully stroked his bearded chin whilst giving his full attention to his reply. After all, his life depended upon the next words that he uttered. He briefly looked at Donn, who nodded his assent, agreeing that he was content to leave this serious matter to the highly-regarded wisdom of the good druid. Amergin was increasingly feeling that they'd walked into a trap, and he alone would be the first to die. All eyes now fell upon him to see how he would answer. He needed to preserve both his dignity, as well as his life, so he shrewdly made a decision that he thought would suit both sides. "We shall return back to the bay where our ships are moored. And we shall sail nine waves out to sea. And if we can land our vessels, in spite of your druidic magic trying to prevent us, then the war that follows will decide the victor. But if we cannot land, then we shall return home to Iberia, and never venture forth again".

The Fairies were satisfied with Amergin's judgment, as they knew just how powerful their skills of enchantment were. And as both sides had agreed upon the matter, the Milesians immediately returned back along the winding footpath, through the forests, and back to the harbour to where their ships were waiting.

As they slowly made their return journey, they discussed their plans of action, in detail, including their fighting strategies, but their first task was a simple matter really: they just needed to do everything in their power to make it back ashore.

Once back in the bay, the re-united Milesians ate a hearty meal, before they were to return back to their galleys, for they knew that they'd need much strength before this first ordeal was over. It wasn't a particularly hurried meal, and some of them weren't really in the mood to eat, for they worried about the uncertainty of what was to come, but for those who could manage to block out their fears of the impending future, by fully concentrating on the immense beauty around them, then there was some enjoyment to be taken from the sheer tranquillity of that place; for it was a cool spring day, as they sat upon those grassy banks, overlooking the calm, yet wide waters of the bay, with the surrounding lush green trees at the water's edge reflecting upon the gently shimmering surface. And all around, birds called out to their loved ones, singing sweet songs of love.

After they'd prepared themselves, both physically and spiritually, for whatever the Fairies were conjuring up against them, and they managed to tear themselves away from the calm sanctuary of *Ceann Mara,* they once more set out in their ships, heading out of the bay and back towards the open sea.

Once they'd reached the agreed distance of nine waves from shore, it was time for them to return, for one final landing. But just then the skies above darkened and upon those calm waters a great mist did once more appear. Then the heavy rains began.

Donn shouted across to Amergin's ship, "This storm has been raised by magic".

"It has that", agreed the wise druid.

The heavy rain started bouncing off the decks around them, as Donn pulled the hood of his thick, brown woollen cloak up over his wet hair, to protect himself from getting any more soaked than he already was. By now the mist was so thick that they could no longer see the shore.

Over on Scota's ship, both druids were patiently trying to soothe the two horses, for they knew that there would likely be much worse to come. Erenan was the youngest son of Milesius and Scota, being aged only about fifteen, give or take a couple of year. With him being the baby of the family, he was always shown such affection by his mother. His youthful good looks favoured her Egyptian side more than any of his brothers. How well loved he was by all. He had that joyful enthusiasm for life that is so enchanting, captivating everyone that he met. He greatly looked up to the bravery of his brothers, wanting to be more like them. And if any occasion arose when he could live up to their bravery, then he was more than willing to attempt it. It was upon that fateful journey that he came to be travelling upon the same ship as that of his mother. For anyone who knew him, or her come to that, they wouldn't have considered him travelling in any other vessel. Erenan believed at that time, that the mist might be thinner above the top of the ship. Being both strong and agile, his young slim body easily shimmied up the mast, as he'd so often done before when acting as look-out for his brothers. He was right, from that heightened position the air was clearer, so he was able to guide the ship slowly back towards the shore, back into the direction of the bay from whence they'd just come; back to *Ceann Mara.*

But now the Fairy-druids intensified their magic. They raised from the sea a destructive tempest. The waves increased, crashing against the sides of the boats. Icy hail violently hammered down upon the heads of the Milesians, leaving any exposed skin feeling frozen and raw. Erenan tried to protect his cheeks and ears from the burning onslaught, which felt like his flesh was being ripped from his bones with blades of ice. Then a sudden violent gust caught him atop the mast, tearing free his grip, throwing him downward. Erenan plummeted down, his young body slamming hard against the wooden deck. A loud crunching sound could be heard from the impact of his body, as he loudly groaned in considerable pain.

As the hail lessened, the mist increased, into a thick, dense fog of billowing, swirling clouds of grey, which engulfed all thirty of the ships. Then the heavens came alive with the roar of deafening thunder, as bolts of lightning blindly shot around the vessels. Amidst the raging storm, the broken, dying body of Erenan was laid in his mother's arms. Heartbroken, she cried out, above the sound of the storm, "I should have heeded the signs. I was warned that he'd die between two mouths. And he was caught betwixt the mother's mouth that did bear him, and the bay's mouth in which he did seek". (Songs have since been written about that young prince and his needless death).

The enchanted storm grew even more in intensity. The ships began crashing against each other. Then hail hit the crewmen like stones from a sling. Painfully did they endure this, whilst desperately trying to hold on to masts and rigging, lest they should all be swept away. The druids struggled with the horses, using every bit of their skills, in a bid to keep them calm, whilst all around them the weather raged like never before.

The rolling of the rough sea then violently threw the ships about the ocean, separating Donn's leading flagship from the others. Away from the land the storm took him and his valiant crew. Powerless, they could do nothing but hold on for dear life. Yet still, further away they were blown. Screams to their gods were shouted into the wind, but no reply was forthcoming. The whole crew looked to their leader for salvation, yet even a highly-trained warrior-king like himself, who liked to be always in control, was helpless in this dire situation. This nightmare was endured for longer than any of those people could stand. Till finally an end to their horror was looming, as huge waves, the size of mountains, drove Donn's ship south-westerly, towards the tall, majestic Sand-hills. It was upon that sandstone isle that their gallant flagship crashed against the rocks with such force that it split into two, drowning every single person aboard. Alongside that mighty leader, was his wife (and sister), Dil, their scholarly brother, Arech Red-brow, four Chieftains, four-and-twenty warriors, eleven women, four servants, eight rowers, and half-a-hundred youths. It truly was a terrible loss to behold. And with that, Donn's death, as foretold by Ériu, had come to pass.

Whilst this was happening, the ship commanded by the brave and handsome, Ir, son of Milesius, was also separated from the others. It was swept north-westerly, away from the shallows of the mainland. The violent windstorm drove the ship in the direction of Great Skellig, the largest of two islands that rose majestically from the sea like the jagged fangs of a wolf. To stop the ship from being driven aground, the Chieftains, including Ir himself, impulsively leapt to the oars, to help the rowers, for they were the strongest of the men aboard. Despite the storm, with their combined strength, they drove the ship forward, tearing through the waves with the speed of an arrow from a bow. Ir's son, Heber Donn, angrily shouted, condemning the galley, though his youthful age meant that he himself didn't yet wield enough strength to take an oar. The men, working as one, put their whole strength into rowing, desperately heaving back on those heavy oars, cutting through that fierce storm. Suddenly, Ir's oar snapped, throwing him backwards along the length of the ship; the broken shaft still tightly gripped in his hands as his back slammed hard against the corner of a wooden bench, breaking his spine in two. Heber Donn rushed to his father's side. Knowing that without a leader their ship would be lost, he instinctively took charge and with a heart full of anger, roared at the men, spurring them to keep going, onward towards the destined isle. Sadly, Ir, son of Milesius, who'd always prided himself on being first into the fray, found that on his final adventure, which sadly every Man must take, that three of his brothers had already just beaten him. Ir's body was later returned back to that large rocky isle to be buried near to where he'd died.

Upon Colpa's ship, Heremon took charge, for he greatly feared that they'd all be killed in that terrifying storm. He ordered some of his crew to hold tight his spirited horse. And then, in a bid to bring misfortune upon the Fairies, as well as to misdirect their magic, he ordered his men to row counter-sunwise around the island. Going in this direction, against the natural path of the sun, was known to invoke powerful sorcery that could curse those whom they circled around.

Half the remaining fleet, which at that very moment consisted of just fourteen ships, trailed behind them, desperate to have someone to follow, for they rightfully believed that Donn and Arech Red-brow must by now have perished, after seeing the flagship being so violently swept away, for so terrible was that fearful storm.

Heremon's plan, at least in part, worked, for with having reversed their course, they'd managed to trick the Fairies, so were able to sail halfway around the island without being spotted, thus avoiding any sorcery that could have been maliciously aimed towards them; yet still the storm raged on.

Just north of the Plain of Bregia, lay the mouth of the Queen Boann River. It was here, amidst that heavy rain, that Heremon managed to land their ship. The half fleet that followed behind securely moored their vessels next to his.

Being desperate to stand upon dry land once more, whilst also hungering to face the Fairies, so that they could attack them wholeheartedly with rightful vengeance, Heremon and Colpa led those crews, valiantly jumping from the decks, into the river mouth and shore-wards. There was much scrambling across the slippery rocks, with their wet, leather footwear and their clothing already soaked through to the skin, as they struggled under all the relentless rain. And the thick, swirling fog made it difficult to see where they were going, but still onward they went. Heremon was proud to have travelled with his elder brother, Colpa of the Sword. They weren't too dissimilar in age, whilst the noble Colpa, son of Milesius, was as honest as the day is long; and how artfully did he use his sword. If he didn't become their new leader, he would have made the most perfect adviser. But he slipped upon those wet stones, hitting his head, and drowning within the river's mouth.

Heremon, with his wife and baby, as well as his four young sons, managed to make it ashore, along with his spirited horse. The crews too, from their half of the fleet, also survived that dangerous landing. For all Heremon knew, he was now the leading Milesian left alive, and all the Chieftains and their warriors were certainly treating him like a king, looking to him for leadership. It felt good. So, he took command, ordering some of them to build shelters, some to make a fire, whilst others were sent to find food.

A burial party was formed for that honest swordsman, Colpa, so that he could be buried on the land near to where he'd fell. Since that time, to honour such a worthy warrior, that river's mouth has forever been known as *Inbher Colpa*: The Mouth of Colpa.

Whilst all this was happening, over on the opposite side of the island, the remaining fourteen ships had also managed to find their way ashore, following the guidance of brave Erenan, upon his mother's ship, whose efforts had cost him his life. Amergin White-knee had then managed to cast his own spells, conjuring a brief tunnel to appear through the raging storm, in the direction that had been pointed out by that youngest brother of his; this had allowed their half of the fleet to safely row through, back into the bay of *Ceann Mara,* where first their ships had moored. But the tide had now fallen, exposing treacherous mudflats where before there were none.

Queen Scota's galley led the way, followed closely behind by Amergin and Heber Fionn. They sailed as far as they could, until the ships were beached in the mud. Then, jumping overboard, they splashed into the knee-deep water, trudging landward through the swirling fog and the never-ending rain. It wasn't long before the splashing water diminished, to be replaced by the sound of the squelching mud, as each footstep had to be physically prized loose from the sticky bog-like terrain.

It must have taken a couple of hours to walk that short distance ashore, as their clothing stuck uncomfortably to their rain-drenched skin, so that by the time they'd reached the land, their bodies were so exhausted and their legs ached so much that they felt like they'd never be able to walk again.

Scota, as well as her two sons, Heber Fionn and Amergin White-knee were actually the most high-ranking of the Milesians to have survived the storms. It was indeed most fortunate for those two noteworthy sons to have made it, for Heber Fionn was known to be noble-hearted and honourable, whilst Amergin White-knee was fair-minded and completely impartial in his decisions; so that between them they both exuded a generous, kind-hearted nature, who tightly held within their breasts a good sense of fair play.

Heber Fionn's wife and four sons had also survived that dangerous landing. But unfortunately, Amergin's beautiful wife, Sgene the Satirist, hadn't been so lucky, for she drowned in that treacherous river's mouth. It was believed that she may have become trapped in those deadly mudflats. Her body was slowly and reverentially brought ashore to be buried in the mouth of the river, which has been called, since that terrible day, *Inbher Sgene*, the Mouth of Sgene. Her grave stands proudly next to that of young Erenan, son of Milesius. It had become a day of great sorrow for those worthy Milesians.

It had been a truly desperate battle, against those dark, magical elements, for so extremely powerful had been those Fairy enchantments. From the eight brothers who'd set out, only three of them had made it through that terrible storm; a storm so fierce that we have never seen it's like since. With Donn having been the eldest brother, he'd felt duty-bound to make a dying request to his gods: that was for him to be allowed to collect his deceased countrymen's souls after they'd departed from this life.

Since that time, it has indeed come to pass, or so the old tales do tell, that whenever anyone of Celtic blood dies upon the Island of Destiny, that Donn, Lord of the Dead, appears before them in his brown hooded-cloak, and collects their souls upon a magical white steed, taking them back to that sandstone isle where he himself did die. And there they await the arrival of the Fairy Sea god, Manannán, son of Lir, who ferries them in his boat, Wave-sweeper, across to the Land of Promise, where they stay forever young in a land of eternal summer.

Most of those survivors at *Ceann Mara* lay exhausted upon the muddy banks beneath the trees, whilst those who were able, mirrored what Heremon's crew were doing on the eastern shore, burying their fallen comrades, making shelter and finding food. That night they slept well beneath temporary shelters to the sound of the pouring rain which never let up all night.

The following day, the rain continued and still the grey mists swirled all around as the troops prepared themselves for war. Heber Fionn, being the oldest of the surviving sons of Milesius, took charge, with his mother's blessing, of the remainder of those troops who had landed upon the western shore.

With there being a shortage of Chieftains to lead their army as most of Scota's sons had by now perished, the Queen herself began making preparations to lead Erenan's troops. Being a highly-accomplished Egyptian warrior-queen she had come to the island fully prepared just in case she was needed on the field of war, although with her age she didn't need to fight, as her father certainly wouldn't have fought at a similar age, but she felt that it was her duty to exact vengeance upon those responsible for the deaths of her many children. She calmly dressed for the forthcoming battle, armed with her lengthy composite bow and with two quivers bursting with arrows. She wore a long white gown, and upon her head sat a tall, blue crown-of-war. Fastened to her belt, an iron Egyptian scythe-shaped sword hung gently by her side. All these items being highly-embellished with gold. Her black hair, now streaked with grey, hung loose, gently blowing in the cool breeze.

Her two-wheeled chariot had been carefully unloaded from her galley and carried ashore, and was now being prepared by her charioteer. He attached her two beautiful, proud-looking, brown horses to its front. What magnificent beasts they were, covered with blankets striped with blue, red and gold, whilst their heads were adorned with huge rare feathers, also striped with red and gold, but tipped with blue to match her crown.

As Scota was finishing getting ready, all the other warriors had already grouped themselves into their own individual war-bands. Each one being commanded by a Chieftain, which now obviously also included Scota, as well as her sons, Heber Fionn and Amergin. Their scouts had already informed them that a large armed force of Fairies had gathered upon the upper slopes of the Mountain of Mis. So that was the direction in which first they headed.

It was slow going, journeying through such heavily forested terrain, travelling in a long, thin procession due to the narrowness of the path before them. By the time they'd reached the mountain, it had been three days since last they'd set off; three days in which their anger had time to magnify, as they mournfully dwelled upon the memory of those once-proud comrades who had fallen, to be buried in this hostile land: So, they were now more than ready to exact their revenge upon the whole Fairy race.


Lughaidh, son of Ithe was worried about the safety of the women, especially that of his delicate young wife, so he'd been excused from fighting, to be tasked with guarding the women with a small contingent of his own warriors. This was a job that suited him well, as he could keep all those under his charge entertained with his many verses of bardic poetry.

In a further bid to keep the women safe, Lughaidh and his men had separated from the main party. In this way he could escort the women further north, through that foggy, rain-drenched forest, continuing along that same path, which would take them well-away from the fighting. The women were keen to find a secluded river in which to bathe. So, northwards they headed, for a couple of days, for a distance of nine leagues, or so, until they'd found the most perfect spot, away from any possible prying eyes.

The river that they found was cool and inviting. Running alongside the water was a sandy beach scattered with pebbles and small stones that stretched far into the distance. It was well within the river's mouth, so was far away from the raging ocean, yet still the misty storm swirled all around them, meaning that visibility was still severely limited. The warriors wandered further upriver to give the women some privacy, wanting to keep out of sight, but still within earshot, in case of danger. Fial, daughter of Milesius, was amongst those women, who as I've said was the beloved wife of Lughaidh, son of Ithe; she was a beautiful flower, young and shy. Naked she bathed, though the day was barely warm, but how hot she felt, and grimy, for long had it been since anyone had properly washed, and still mud coated her shapely legs from her ship's undignified landing. As she stepped forth from the river, feeling clean once more, she enjoyed the sensations of the cool breeze and heavy rain upon her naked skin. But suddenly she became aware of the shadowy figure of a naked warrior on the beach, watching her through the fog. The look of horror paled her face, for she instantly felt as though she'd betrayed her husband, and all that was sacred to her. The shooting pain in her chest hit her like a mortifying arrow of guilt. Clutching her chest, she collapsed to the ground, and there she died, of extreme shame. But it was only her husband, Lughaidh, who had himself just finished bathing, who was resting upon the strand after his swim. He was taking in the eerie atmosphere of the place, when he suddenly saw the faint form of his beautiful, naked wife emerging through the swirling grey clouds of fog.

Seeing his wife's lifeless body dropping before him, and knowing that she was certainly dead, Lughaidh fell to his knees, heartbroken, in shock and inconsolable with despair. The other women could now be heard through the veil of fog loudly weeping over her death.

Lughaidh sat upon that cold, windswept beach as the storm still raged around him, overwhelmed with sorrow, and racked with guilt, knowing that he'd never fully recover from her cruel death: a death that he'd unwittingly caused. He wailed uncontrollably, shaking with feelings of desperate hopelessness. His body suddenly cold and numb. This was his second great loss, for still he grieved over the murder of his father, Ithe, who'd been the first casualty of the Fairies.

And so, it was upon that very spot that Lughaidh composed a lay to the death of his beloved, Fial, as the tears streamed down his cheeks, his voice quivering with emotion:

> *Sit we here over the strand,*
> *Stormy the cold;*
> *chattering in my teeth, – a great tragedy*
> *is the tragedy that has reached me.*
>
> *I tell you a woman has died,*
> *whom fame magnifies;*
> *Fial her name, from a warrior's nakedness*
> *upon the clean gravel.*
>
> *A great death is the death that has reached me,*
> *harshly prostrated me;*
> *the nakedness of her husband, she looked upon him*
> *who had rested here.*

The river that flows past where that beautiful, innocent young woman fell is now named after her, being called the River Feale. Since that terrible day, Lughaidh has forever been known as the first poet of Ériu to hail from the race of Man. Let us now leave Lughaidh to mourn, as we return back to his warring party to see what they've been up to in his absence: Scota's chariot bounced up the muddy mountain slopes, leading her army onward. This was unfamiliar terrain for the queen, although she'd trained in chariot fighting ever since she was a little girl back home in Egypt. Due to that childhood training she now knew exactly what needed to be done, so for the first time since she'd left Iberia, she was able to take some control of her own destiny. This newly-regained confidence suited her well, so much so that, even though she was about to go to war, our Egyptian queen was once more radiating an intensity of beauty, with her face lighting up from within with a shining inner glow. With having lost most of her family, she hid her pain behind a stoical veil of leadership, as she knew that if she broke down in tears, like she did when Erenan died, that she'd lose the full respect of her command. This outer confidence and beauty, mixed with her own uncomplaining vulnerability, made her troops want to protect her even more, so much so that each and every one of them would have happily given up their life to protect hers.

Standing atop that windswept mountain, at the front of her entire force was Ériu, beneath the banner of the sun. Behind her, standing in rows, shoulder to shoulder, her huge elven army waited, greatly outnumbering ours. Their heavily armoured shields overlapping, emblazoned with strange designs, whilst their venomous-tipped spears were angled skywards. Their grey-haired veterans stood at their outer-flanks, whilst the whole of the mid-section was comprised of their young men of arms. At their rear stood their Champions and armed serving-men. Whilst dotted around the landscape, standing upon hills and other high vantage points, were their druids, who were busily conjuring up malicious spells against our army. Also, similarly situated, were their poets, observing the war that was to come, so that they could compose odes to the heroic acts that would undoubtably be accomplished before this day was over.

As the war began, Scota's chariot thundered across the mountain top; her charioteer striving to place her in a position of the greatest advantage. When they'd reached that favourable position, she shot almost a full quiver of arrows, killing a good-many of the enemy druids who'd been responsible for the deaths of all but three of her precious sons.

Her men then rushed forward, flooding past her, into the fray. And with great fury, the two armies clashed; the Fairies' broad swords of bronze looking like bolts of lightning in their hands, which flashed in the sunlight. Their huge army of warriors kept on attacking, forcing our men back.

As our brave warriors slowly withdrew, retreating from such overwhelming odds, they now found themselves in earshot of Scota; hearing her encouraging words reminding them of just how rightful our war was, and desperately not wanting to disappoint their own beloved Queen, their strength was renewed. So, forward they advanced, with Scota leading them, as they pushed back against the fairy forces, carrying the battle onward, and from the mountain downward they fought, to the desolate plain beyond.

It was only through the wilful determination and courage of those warriors that they won that day. But if they hadn't so resolutely believed that this land was prophesied for them to rule, then they would have been driven back into the sea, to return to the lands from whence they'd come. So strong was their belief, that they kept on fighting, against such great odds, that eventually they won that first battle.

But 'twas a fearful fight, as the old tales do tell, as Scota herself fell from her chariot, dying during that first bloody battle. Her death was hard on all of those men, as many had known her since she was a young princess, from that mysterious and magical land of the pharaohs. How greatly she would be missed by all. But her journey hadn't been wasted; for due to her fighting prowess that day, she'd saved a great many of our men from being slaughtered, as they would undoubtedly have fallen, by way of those deadly Fairy enchantments.

Not long after her death, upon that slim peninsula, in the shadow of the mountain, the day began to darken as night began. There would be no more fighting that day.

Those brave Milesians spent the full night upon that blood-soaked place of war, digging graves upon the plain, as well as upon the slopes of the mountain, to bury fallen comrades where they'd fell. Thrice a hundred of our men had sadly died that day, but that was only a fraction of the ten-hundred Fairies who themselves lay dead.

Amongst our newly-missed friends were the two cherished druids, Uar and the Queen's druid, Ethiar, who'd both fearlessly looked after Scota's horses amidst that dreaded storm. A simple grey flag, cut from each of their cloaks, marked the spot of their graves. Our great Queen, Scota, was also buried where she fell, her grave lying near the sea, at the north side of the valley; the land there was named after her, being called *Glenn Scoithin*: The Glen of Scota. At least the position of her tomb would make her feel closer to her childhood home of Egypt, and nearer to her beloved husband, Milesius, who himself lay alone in a cold Iberian grave. Many large, heavy stones were placed around her graveside, by her loyal subjects, as a mark of deep respect.

The sun rose too early the following day, as our men were feeling decidedly weary from conducting all of those moonlit burials. Their camp was clearly feeling the effects of lethargy, as they sluggishly broke their fast, whilst desperately struggling to keep their eyes open. Some had even fallen asleep in a sitting position, between mouthfuls of food.

But Heber Fionn was feeling a compelling, driving force pushing him onward, so urging his men into action, he led them forward once more; this time to fight for the memory of their dead comrades, as well as their own beloved queen.

Searching for the Fairy armies, they followed the Sionna River, back to the Mountains of Eiblinni, at the south of Dergart's Lake, but saw no enemies waiting there. Sleep overcame them whenever they stopped to eat, and that night many of them slept well, but for some, whether they were asleep or awake, the depraved nightmares of battle never ended.

From those mountains, onward they went, as Heber Fionn hungrily searched the land, in a desperate bid to wage war against those Fairy enchanters, for all the deaths that they'd brought upon his family. Tears were in his eyes as he longingly remembered his caring mother, knowing that he would never speak to her again, or hear her voice, full of strength and love, as she spoke of Egyptian wisdom with an accent borne from her father's land; hatred now ruled Heber Fionn's angry heart.

Northwards they went, still following the path of the great Sionna River. And then up onto that low ridged path that snaked eastwards towards the sacred hill, which marked the very centre of the island. It was upon this path that they came across one of their own countrymen, who was a messenger sent by Heremon to see if any other Milesians had survived the storm. Both Heber Fionn and Amergin now uncontrollably cried with a kind of nervous joy, so excited were they to find out that their little brother was still very much alive.

The pace of their whole army now quickened, so excited were they to meet up with their fellow Gaels, who they thought had long since perished in the enchanted storms.

It took a few long days of travelling, but eventually, at the Mouth of Colpa, on the eastern coast, that there they did meet. It was indeed a most joyful reunion, not just for the three brothers, but also for the rest of the tribe. That afternoon they feasted well on the plentiful supplies of food in which that land abounded.

Whilst they enjoyed their feast, messengers were once more sent out, this time to find the three sons of Cearmad Honey-mouth, to challenge them to one single all-out battle.

The Fairies were found at their fortress of *Aileach Neid*. They'd been expecting such a summons to war and had already decided where best to meet, for this final pitched battle; for if they were to stand any chance of winning, they would need to fight upon sacred ground, so that hopefully their gods would look upon them favourably and bless them with the strength to win. Therefore, they chose as the location, Talti, which was just four leagues northwest of their temple upon the Grey-ridge. It was a magnificent sloping green plain in the lands now known as Teffia. Talti had been the name of a powerful queen of the **Fir-bolg**, who was the first person to have been buried upon that meadow. It was said that she'd died of exhaustion, with axe in hand, after clearing a huge woodland, for her people had deforested many such plains, for they were always in need of good fertile land for farming.

It was certainly a beautiful, calm and tranquil place, overlooking the Blackwater River. This enormous tract of land was once spiritually important to the **Fir-bolg** as for centuries it was their sacred burial ground, as can be seen from the dozens of large grassy mounds that lay scattered across its surface. Near the centre of the plain was the monumental three-banked earthen tomb of Queen Talti herself; due to the sheer scale of the mound, she must indeed have been a most powerful ruler. The land gently rolled downhill where it met the calm waters of the river. Across the other side of the river, bordering the water's edge was an almighty forest, whose reflection could be clearly seen upon the water's dark, glass-like surface.

Three keen-eyed Milesian scouts had been sent to overlook the plain, to report back the positioning of the Fairies. They hid themselves upon the higher ground, within isolated bushes and within the shadows of the higher, more distant mounds. From there they had a good view of the lengthy route in which the Fairies would take, as they travelled from the Grey-ridge; those men were most diligent in their duties and keenly watched the unfolding events which took place before them on the morning of the battle.

It happened during those last hours of darkness, just before the land of Ériu had become illuminated with the first bright rays of the breaking dawn, when still the dim moonlight was casting its shadowy haze across the land. It was in this dull light that the shapes of the Fairies could be seen, as they travelled the long, four-hour walk from their most holy temple of *Liathdruim.* But if it hadn't been for the moonbeams faintly lighting up the elven faces, then they wouldn't have been so easy to see in the near darkness. But then, as the sky began to glow upon daybreak, during that eerie period of twilight, when it's neither night nor day, as their long procession reached the Plain of Queen Talti, a strange thing happened: for those Fairies with their long flowing gowns took on the appearance of ethereal angels, for the twilight seemed to shine through their bodies, as well as their clothing, making them glow like luminous, ghostly figures, as their lengthy raiment gently shimmered in the breeze, so that they appeared almost as though they were floating*.

* For more information on this description of their appearance please read the short article 'A Treatise on the Evolution of the Fairy' in my book 'Beyond the Elven Gate'.

As they reached the plain, the Fairy procession gathered together upon the higher ground and there they stood, waiting, whilst their druids continued strolling, unhurriedly, down towards the burial-mounds that lay scattered about the meadow, including the one belonging to the great Queen Talti herself.

Then, as the sun broke over the horizon, flooding the sky with its golden-yellow rays, the Fairies immediately transformed back to their usual appearance of flesh and bone.

Only then did those scouts creep back over the hills, returning once more to the sons of Milesius to report their observations of those astonishing events; though not everyone believed such outlandish tales. After considerable questioning by the gathered Chieftains, their whole army set off towards that nearby battle ground.

It was Heremon who arrived first at the Plain of Talti, travelling there on horseback, with a similar heroic bearing that reminded all those around him of his father, the great Milesius himself. He rode at the front of his own band of warriors. The other Chieftains reached the plain shortly after, leading their own men; amongst these Chieftains were obviously his last two remaining brothers, Heber Fionn and Amergin White-knee.

By now the Fairy-druids were busily creating their magic. Strange-sounding words were uttered from atop the mounds; but these words were aimed towards their own men, not ours. Suddenly a few of those Fairies began growing. Before long they'd turned into giants standing taller than the Mound of Talti itself. Their colossal bodies like towering oaks upon the field, armed with swords thrice-three feet long and faces full of fury. And thus, the battle began as the skies above darkened.

The Gaelic warriors, with vengeance in their hearts, grabbed hold of their feared iron weapons and gave a mighty battle against those ranks of Fairies and the magical giants who stood before them. The air buzzed and clicked around the field as enchanted lightning flashed from the sky, as the Fairy-druids used their powers to control the very elements. Our warriors' bodies tingled with the electricity in the air, as even their body-hair stood on end. Bolts of lightning lit up the darkened plain, killing many of our men as those terrifying blasts of light pierced the ground around them. Intermittent flashes of light lit up the faces of friends and foes, as well as the towering limbs of giants, flashing across swords as well as the crazed designs of Fairy-shields.

Amidst this madness, both sides charged forward. Heremon, still ahorse, with his two remaining brothers, led their troops up the field, whilst the three Fairy-kings led their men downward. And there they met in the middle of that once-tranquil plain. The giants did their best to cleave their swords downward, hacking deep trenches into the field, leaving dismembered body parts at either side. The sons of Milesius sought out the Fairy-kings, as it was important for them to fight their equal. And a most violent clash took place between them. The giants, as well as their druids, were particularly targeted by our Gaelic troops, for those deadly enemies had the power to destroy us all.

Sadly, Heremon's spirited horse, Gaber, was killed during those next moments of that terrible war.

Unfortunately, much of the details of this decisive battle have since been lost in time. But it was indeed those last three sons of Milesius who did slay those three magical Fairy-kings: for it was our High-druid, Amergin White-knee who slew King Kéthor, that heretofore generous son of the Sun god; it was the fair-minded Heber Fionn who slew the arrogant Ethor, son of the Hazel-tree god; whilst Heremon fought the stronger battle of the three, fighting against the powerfully-built Téthor, son of the Plough god, and how hard and relentless were his vicious, smiting blows.

The greater part of the Fairies were slain in that battle. The remainder fled northwards, towards *Aileach Neid*. Onward, our troops gave chase, over mountains and through valleys, stopping every now and then to fight. It was indeed a long drawn-out, and hard-fought battle. Two of Breoghan's worthy sons were slain during that lengthy pursuit. The mountains where they fell were named after them: Cualgni fell upon Sliabh Cualgni, three leagues north of what was to become known as Dalgan's Stronghold, and Fuaid died upon Sliabh Fuaid, the highest point of the mountains where Fiacha Broadcrown was later to make his camp.

It was during this retreat that the three Fairy-queens were also killed, being slayed by three of our most esteemed Champions, but it was by no means an easy task, for those three queens were deadly on the field of war. Fodhla was slain by the proud and unyielding, Eatan; Banbha was killed by Caicher the Victorious; whilst the beautiful and generous Ériu was slain by Suirge the Slender.

Finally, after much bloodshed, the brothers managed to defeat the remaining Fairies, taking away their magical hold of the land. The Fairies had no choice now but to agree to sharing the land with the Milesian invaders. They proudly walked out from their grey stone-fortress and asked which half the victors wanted, swearing a most sacred oath that they would abide by any decision that was made. After much careful deliberation, our forefathers said that they themselves would keep the upper half, the portion that lay above the ground.

The Fairies were furious, knowing that they'd been tricked, but being honour-bound by their oaths, had no choice but to keep their word; thenceforth, using their considerable powers of enchantment, they journeyed underground, to live forever hidden within the hills of our majestic land. The only benefit which that enchanted race gained from this matter, was that it protected them somewhat, from the more severe vices of the race of Man. It was then that our people began calling them the Aes Sídhe which means 'People-of-the-Mounds'. And inside those hills those magical creatures attained the power of immortality, for in those dark, hidden places they continued to practice their most secret arts.

Those three remaining Milesian brothers had managed to survive that terrible, violent war, along with ten of their most-fearsome Chieftains. So now, all of their Gaelic warriors were finally able to rest; this was their first moment of peace that they'd known, since last they'd left Galicia.

With the storms now being over, it was time to bury those who'd newly fallen, as well as those who needed to be buried upon the surrounding isles, for it was customary to build their graves where they'd fell. So Ir was buried upon Great Skellig. Whilst the entire occupants of Donn's ship were buried upon that most south-westerly isle where they had all perished. A large burial mound was made for Donn. Whilst all of his drowned Chieftains were buried in their own mounds nearby. But it was their sister, Dil, whose death affected those Milesian brothers the most. As the final touches to her grave were being put in place, Heremon, with tears in his eyes, placed a section of grass over her mound, saying, "I place this turf upon a loved one".

With the tall, blond-haired Heber Fionn being the oldest surviving son of Milesius, he should have been crowned as the sole king of this land, but with Heremon having had a taste of power, and being encouraged by his ambitious wife, he demanded to equally share the throne. Luckily for him, Heber Fionn was a fair-minded sort of fellow, so he generously agreed, and so he and Heremon became the first High-kings of Ériu, sharing the rule between them. By this time Heber Fionn must have been aged about three-and-thirty, whilst Heremon was about ten years his junior. The land was evenly split between both men, with Heremon taking all the land north of the Queen Boann River, whilst Heber Fionn took all the land to the south.

This seemed like a fair division of the island. Five of the surviving principal Chieftains went to live under the rule of Heremon. These were Amergin White-knee, and the Champions: Goisten, Sedga of Spears, Sobairce, as well as Suirge the Slender (who was the one who'd killed the beautiful Fairy-queen, Ériu). Heber Donn, son of Ir, having proven that he could lead his father's men, was put under the protection of his northern uncles, and treated almost like a son by them. Whilst in the southern half, the five remaining Chieftains went to live in the land of Heber Fionn. These were mostly Champions themselves, being: Mantan, Én, Ughi, Fulman, as well as Caicher the Victorious (who was the one who'd killed the once-fearful Fairy-queen, Banbha, beneath her husband's hazel-tree banner). And each one of those Chieftains swore fealty to their own liege.

And with all of these arrangements now in place, that was the start of what could have been an extremely rewarding and satisfying rule, but unfortunately, all good things must come to an end.

As to the famous sigil that once had belonged to their father, the much-loved old King, Milesius, the two newly-crowned High-kings decided to share his triple-lion emblem between themselves. Therefore, both Heber Fionn and Heremon took a lion each as their own symbol. They generously gave the third lion to Ir's young son, Heber Donn, for after all, he was also descended from Milesius, being the last remaining son of his father's House. (With Ir having been the first son of Milesius to actually set foot upon the island, in that characteristic way of his of always being first at any given task, there was even talk of naming the land after him, as in something like *Irland*. But no, the island had enough names already).

Thereafter, each one of those three princes proudly bore a single lion as their own sigil, to be carried upon their shields and banners, but each one being of a different colour to show the uniqueness of their own individual House. Their descendants used these symbols for many centuries to come.

You may be wondering why Amergin White-knee didn't take the third lion; he felt that he didn't need to be adorned with any hereditary emblems, as he was the High-druid, so only spiritual symbols were of interest to him.

From that time forward, peace was enjoyed throughout the land; but alas, 'twas only for a period of twelve moons. That was until pride seized hold of the wives of the two High-kings... Heber Fionn's wife was very loyal to her husband, and hated to see him being taken advantage of. Whenever she saw Téa, she knew that this wife of Heremon was behind him craving a share of the throne; it made her anger boil within. But their real disagreement began when the three remaining Milesian brothers were one night feasting together.

At that time, Heber Fionn's wife was heavily with child. (The baby that would later be called Conmaol). This had changed her usual calm temperament, so that it warred with itself, so that at any given moment, she could be prone to either tears or rage. One of the things that she found the most frustrating was that, in her heart, she knew that the island should have belonged solely to her husband, Heber Fionn, after all he was the oldest surviving son of the great Milesius. And after him the land would have naturally gone to their sons. But now she felt that it was all being furtively wrested away from them... But really, both women weren't too different, for the two of them only wanted what was best for their children, for they knew that whomsoever ruled the land at that time, would hand down that power to their children, and their children's children, and their children's children, until the end of time; or so they believed.

It was during that feast, when Téa began bragging about the views from three of the mountain tops, which were within her realm; she stated that these were the best views in the whole of Ériu. But those mountains, it has been said, were near the border between both of their kingdoms. Heber Fionn's wife started shouting, "Those mountains aren't part of the north, they rightly belong to the south".

As the heated conversation became more and more intense, Heber Fionn's wife, shaking with venom, screamed, "I shall not spend one more night in this land, until those mountains are mine".

More words were said in anger, by those two women, and then idle threats were made. The husbands became drawn into the argument, and real, violent threats ensued. And so, the die was cast.

I have seen it many times before, when hot-tempered wives have caused husbands to war. When the women are too angry to back down, and so the reluctant men have to carry out the spoken threats in blood. It is simply for the sake of harmony at home that many husbands have faced blood on the battlefield. But this was to be that most evil of wars, that which involved kin-slaying.

Shortly after this quarrel, upon a cold morning, an almighty battle took place between both of those ruling brothers; it was what the seanchaí of old called the Battle of Géisill. It was there, just south of that long, winding pathway that ran atop those gravel hills, east of the Great-wood and with the imposing Mountain of Flame in the near distance, that Heremon slew his elder brother, Heber Fionn, to become the sole ruler of the land.

Thereafter, many changes were introduced to our island; for much of the country was transformed when the race of Man began to create their own world upon, what once was, the Fairy-realm. The magnificent Fairy-temple upon the Grey-ridge was pulled down, to be replaced by a large stone-fortress. This was a gift from Heremon to Téa. It became known as Teamhair*, which means the 'House of Téa'. And from atop its high, majestic walls, upon a clear day, much of the island could be seen. This palatial stronghold became a sanctuary of peace and tranquillity for the newly-crowned queen.

Another very noticeable change, which transformed the land, involved the four-and-twenty strong labourers. Each one of whom, over a period of many weeks, cleared a whole plain entirely of trees. This gave the island a whole new, and distinctly different character to the one that it had always had before. They really were creating a new landscape, and in their wake were obliterating any of the notable achievements that had been made by any of the previous inhabitants.

It was during this hectic and unsettled period of industrious activity, when most people were too busy forging ahead with their own goals, that little time was spent thinking about those who really needed support. We can now look back upon that time in hindsight, to see that Heremon's previous wife, the perfect and good-natured Odba, that her health was itself falling into a steep decline. She felt that all was now lost in her life, and having little left to live for, she died from the overwhelming grief that she was feeling, amidst the humiliating public rejection that she so painfully had endured. All her pride had been so cruelly ripped from her, making her feel as though she was literally drowning in her own sea of despair. Her young sons alone, when they'd gone to visit her, had tried their hardest to help, but she single-mindedly wanted only one thing; and that was Heremon, the man who had shunned her so bitterly, so openly, for a woman who was younger, prettier and more devious than herself.

Her four young sons, visibly heartbroken at her wake, helped to raise a large burial mound for her, covered with white stones, making it clearly visible from the ramparts of Tara. It would be close enough for them to visit, for they were still children after all; in this way she would be closer to Heremon in death, than he had wanted to be, during those last painful years of her life.

There were still more turbulent times yet to come. For during the second year of Heremon's reign, the High-druid, Amergin White-knee, decided that he too wanted to share the throne, for he felt that his brother was singularly wielding far too much power. But Heremon wouldn't part with what he'd so forcibly won. Therefore, another almighty battle ensued, wherein this time, it was the turn of the High-druid to be violently slayed.

Over the coming years, many more of Heber Fionn's old Chieftains were also brutally slain, in various battles. Until finally, it came to pass that Amergin White-knee's prediction was proven to be true, for due to Heremon's unequalled power, with being the absolute monarch over the whole of Ériu, the land itself began to display its own signs of unhappiness; eight lakes burst their banks during those early years of his reign. Some flooded the surrounding plains, whilst others were more powerful, breaking through narrow stretches of land to unite with the nearby sea, which changed the shape of the coastline forever**.

To appease the gods, so that peace and stability could be brought back to our sorrowful land, Heremon divided the country into four smaller kingdoms, similar to the way in which the Fir-bolg had split the land into five when last they ruled; these territories were to be governed by four Chieftains who Heremon promoted to the role of a subservient king, on condition that they all swore fealty to him. These territories were as follows:

The southern kingdom, which we now call Munster, was given to Heber Fionn's four sons, as a murder-fine to compensate them for the killing of their father. A small portion of this territory was to be shared with Lughaidh, son of Ithe, for he had lost much since first his ship had discovered this isle, with the death of both his esteemed father, as well as his much-cherished wife, Fial. Lughaidh's territory was named after himself, becoming known as the land of the Corco Luigde, and remained within his family for the next two thousand years.

The northern kingdom, which we now call Ulster, was given to the brown-haired Heber Donn, son of Ir, who had now come of age, for he had more than proved himself as a loyal, Milesian warrior-chief, who was greatly respected by all. Furthermore, the young lad was eager to live up to the reputation of his father, who always prided himself on being first into battle, which made him the perfect ally to have in times of war. And so, it was the House of Heber Donn that ruled over those northern lands.

Two of Heremon's chief commanders were also similarly rewarded for the incredible loyalty that they'd shown to the High-king: hence, the eastern kingdom of Leinster was given to Crimthand Shield-mouth, whilst the western kingdom of Connacht was given to Un, son of Oigge. (Within the land of Connacht still dwelt members of the old, defeated Fir-bolg race, so they were obviously forced to swear fealty to their new king).

All of these new kings did their best to preserve peace within their new kingdoms, although there was still some insurrection, like the instance when Cualu the Hundred-strong, son of Breoghan, ransacked Leinster. Crimthand Shield-mouth had no choice but to suppress the rebellion, so he warred hard against Cualu. Both men were evenly matched with forces of hardened warriors. But Crimthand slayed his enemy, leaving his bloodied, mangled head upon a large stone on that mountain which for many centuries bore the name of that defeated Chieftain: it became known as the Mountains of Cualu. In years to come the Road of Cualu, which was one of the main roads of Ériu, was found within the shadows of this mountain; but more of that anon.

With all four kingdoms now being settled, and the land being once more at peace, yearly tributes were paid by each one of those territories to the High-king, which made Heremon a very wealthy and powerful man indeed.

After Heremon's reign, his three eldest sons jointly ruled. That was until the seed of Heber Fionn slew the seed of Heremon, to take the High-kingship for themselves. And in return the seed of Heremon slew the seed of Heber Fionn. And that was how things were, for many generations, as each family fought to control the entire island.

Now think back, all of you, to the beginning of this tale, and to the first king that I mentioned. That was to the esteemed Galician ruler, Breoghan, son of Brath, son of Deag. Through both his grandson, Milesius, as well as his wise son Ithe, all the noble Celtic families of Ériu, to this day do descend.

And that is how the race of Man came to rule over the kingdom of Ériu; such is the tale as it was told to me. So, this is where our first story ends and where all others begin. I shall tell you more on the morrow".

The seanchaí gazed around the room; he was trying to look into every eye that he saw. The room was still deadly silent. We wanted to hear more but we knew that we dare not push such a respected man. His throat must have become intensely dry, due to all of his talking, as he suddenly became very quiet, resting his voice as he reached for his drinking-horn, which was quickly refilled with ale. Now a low level of excited chatter started to fill that large room, as the storyteller began to smile to himself.

* Teamhair is pronounced TARA
** This included Waterford Harbour (Port Leg); Lough Rea, in County Galway; Belfast Lough; Lough Graney, in County Clare; and Lough Rhynn, in County Leitrim.

# Usurper to the Throne

The following day, just after the evening's feast was over, just like the night before, the seanchaí cleared his throat so that he could begin his second tale. The room immediately fell silent, as though a Fairy-blast had turned mute all those within. We crept closer, treading softly, not wanting to break the spell. When we were all suitably positioned in front of him, either sitting around the fire, or kneeling by his feet, he slowly looked up from his drink and began to speak.

"Tonight's tale shall be brief, for tales are like lives: some span many years, whilst others are shorter, but are no less in importance. There is not much known about this bleak period, but I shall tell you all that I know.

A long time ago, in a very different age to our previous story, our second tale begins. We leap forward seventeen hundred years, to see what might befall the descendants of our adventurers. To put this period into perspective, at that time across the sea, the mighty Roman Empire controlled most of the Middle-land, whilst at Nazareth, a young, nine-year-old boy, was yet to make his everlasting mark upon the world.

But back home in Ériu, in the great southern Kingdom of Munster, the mighty monarch, Eanna Brightneck did rule. He was the son of Loich the Great, and the grandson of Muireadach Muchna who was otherwise known as the Grey of Dairbre, who gained his gloomy epithet after his banishment to the Island of Dairbre, which turned his hair as grey as ash.

Eanna Brightneck was indeed a powerful King. After all, he was of the Heberian line, which means that he was descended from the noble Heber Fionn. The name 'Eanna' means 'Birdlike'. Whether he was so named due to a birdlike appearance, which could have been down to a lengthy nose, or the way in which he held out his arms, or just merely down to the free, spirited way that he swiftly soared across the battlefield, with his cloak streaming behind, looking very much like a bird in flight, sadly, we shall never know. But his second name 'Brightneck' came from the magnificent, large, golden torc that he always wore; it was heavy-looking and deeply patterned, with a beautiful swirling design of Celtic knotwork.

Eanna was a good and fair king, though vain and a little too trusting, but he tried his best to rule justly, being equally fair to all of his subjects; but then, after all, the gods wouldn't have allowed him to rule in any other way.

Back then, there were still only four kingdoms, with a High-king who reigned over them all. And upon each throne was a mighty king who could trace his noble lineage all the way back to the great Milesius of Spain: Munster and Ulster were still governed by the noble descendants of Heber Fionn and Heber Donn, respectively; whilst the kingdoms of Connacht and Leinster were no longer controlled by the descendants of Heremon's chief commanders, as that line had since been interrupted, to be replaced by other warring nobles, many of whom were known to be the progeny of the fearsome Heremon himself.

Due to all of these kings being directly descended from Milesius, it was therefore undoubtedly their hereditary right to rule. This arrangement was obviously very pleasing for the ruling classes, but the other Celtic tribesmen weren't happy; they were jealous and felt as though they'd been deeply wronged. Their ancestors had been amongst the race of Men who'd arrived in this land, having risked their lives fighting alongside Milesius' sons. And ever since then they'd been regarded as an inferior class of citizen, having to pay rent for land, which they believed should be jointly theirs, inherited from those ancestors, who'd helped to win it by right of conquest. Furthermore, they now felt as though they were being treated little better than slaves, being expected to blindly follow orders, whenever their master commanded. When would it be their turn to rule?

Looking back, those lowly tribesmen may have had a point. So, I do have some sympathy for them, of course. But what they did was downright villainous. Their ill-feeling bubbled away under the surface, for quite some time, until finally they could stand it no longer. So, in absolute secret, those treacherous Celtic tribesmen gathered together, meeting up with some of the earlier conquered races, including the Fir-bolg and the Aes Sídhe. These conspiratorial meetings were to discuss joining forces to destroy our Milesian nobility.

As you can imagine, these tribal gatherings were full of tense and heated arguments, as they were all natural enemies as the Celts had defeated the Aes Sídhe, who before them, had defeated the quarrelsome Fir-bolg. But after many lengthy negotiations these mutinous betrayers managed to settle their differences and were able to unite, calling themselves the Attacotti; which means 'rent-payers'.

These 'rent-payers' picked from amongst themselves, someone whom they felt could lead them against our noble Milesian rulers. Their choice wasn't a Man of Celtic stock, but was of the Fir-bolg race, so to appoint him as their leader helped to rally all of the different Attacotti tribes, for them to go to war against the unprepared Milesians.

The notorious Fir-bolg King who they elected was unlike any other of his race. He was taller than most of his people, but had that same large, robust body with those same strong, muscular limbs. His blond hair was long and flowing, but the characteristic which separated him from his men was that he had one very unusual feature. His name was Cairbre Cat-head. And to go with that strange, feline name of his, upon his head, both of his ears were shaped like those of a large cat, being completely covered with fur.

He was elected as leader due to his aggressive and ruthless plans to overthrow the monarchy and to kill anyone who stood in his way. He was thoroughly determined in these ambitions and the Attacotti knew that he would be relentlessly cruel in carrying them out.

So Cairbre Cat-head outlined his vicious schemes to the Chieftains of the Attacotti and together they started to plan the overthrow of our Milesian Kings, so that they could take over the rule of Ériu for themselves. They thought long and hard, eventually agreeing upon an evil conspiracy of revenge. This long drawn out, treasonous plot was going to take them three years to orchestrate, and during that time they put aside a third of their crops to be kept solely for a magnificent royal feast in which all of the powerful rulers of our land would be invited.

It was nearing the time of the feast and the High-king, Crimthann 'Nephew-of-Nár', had just returned home from an adventure abroad with his aunt, who was a powerful member of the Aes Sídhe. They'd had a successful journey, bringing back with them many rich spoils, which included a golden chariot; a golden chess-board inlaid with a hundred precious jewels; a beautiful cloak embroidered with thread of gold which became known as *Cedach Crimhthainn*; a conquering-sword covered with many golden-serpents; a spear from whose wounds no-one ever recovered; and a sling whose deadly shot never missed its mark.

Crimthann was obviously returning home as a conquering hero, grinning with the satisfaction of how much more powerful his newly-acquired wealth would make him. Further good news greeted him as he reached Tara, for his beautiful queen, Baine, told him that she was pregnant with his son. The High-king was indeed a most fortunate man. You could almost say that he'd been born lucky, with him being directly descended from the fearsome Heremon.

But shortly after that glorious homecoming, disaster struck when he was out riding, and his luck finally ran out when he fatally fell from his horse. The shock resonated throughout the land; the High-king was dead, meaning that war would surely follow as many would try to seize the vacant throne. I know not who the Tanist was, who had been chosen to replace Crimthann, but even his son was yet to be born. It was during this unsettled period that Cairbre Cat-head took his chance. He sent messengers to the four kingdoms to speak to their leaders, be they king, lord or chieftain, in fact anyone who was descended from the bloodline of Breoghan, inviting them all to a magnificent feast. Amongst those invited guests were the powerful kings of both Munster and Ulster.

This was how their shameful plan unfolded: it was a beautiful sunny day in the western Kingdom of Connacht and on a large, verdant plain, which overlooked the calm waters of the Lake-of-the-Hounds, a glorious welcoming feast was being organized. Chairs and tables were readied, being positioned in the very centre of the cleared plain; the Attacotti really had planned every conceivable detail. Surrounding both that immense plain as well as the clear waters of the lake was a large, thick, dense forest of yew.

There are no records of which season this treacherous feast was held, but in my mind's eye I've often imagined these events unfolding around the time of November's eve and the feast of Samhain, when food was at its most plentiful and most of the cattle would have been recently slaughtered in time for winter, and also the alcohol by then would be fully fermented; this feast date has always been thought of as a time of new beginnings.

As the sun was setting, the honoured guests were soon to arrive, walking through the evergreen forest that was so full of those sacred yews; these trees symbolized both death and resurrection in our old religion. The trees stood like ancient beings within the forest, each with their own individual character: their huge, magnificent trunks with their gigantic boughs, some arching overhead, whilst others drooping downward, snaking their way back into the soil beneath. The Attacotti had carefully picked this place, knowing that these trees would hide their cold-blooded, vengeful deeds from the outside world.

Each item of clothing of most of the hosts consisted of only one colour, as befitting their rank, many wearing garments of either green, black, blue, grey or dun-coloured, as no bright colours were allowed, which made them blend more into the natural surroundings, as the twilight crept over that once-tranquil plain. Amongst their number, however, as the light faded, the Aes Sídhe momentarily glowed like ghosts amidst the shadowy figures of the throng. Then, just before the last rays of sunlight plunged the plain into complete darkness, bonfires were methodically lit in time to welcome the approaching nobility.

It was at that moment that the guests stepped forth into the clearing, coming from the dark recesses of the trees, dressed in their finest of clothes. Eanna Brightneck's golden-hilted sword hung by his side. He favoured the fashionable handle that was shaped like a small outstretched warrior; what it lacked in comfort it more than made up for in style. This sword, along with his large jewelled brooch and shiny golden collar caught the very last of the sun's rays, as well as the first flickers of flame from the bonfires as they slowly roared into life. This illumination gave his golden torc, which nestled under his bearded chin, a glowing, bright, gleaming, almost-ethereal lustre, so that he stood out, even from a distance. And with his purple cloak and tall stature, it showed, without any conceivable doubt, that he truly was the Munster King.

Those worthy nobles felt so honoured to be invited to such an opulent celebration. They firmly believed that this would be a feast that would be talked about for many years to come; and tragically they were right.

Those excellent joyous festivities went on for nine long happy days. The esteemed guests were eating and drinking and watching the entertainment as poets, musicians, dancers and jugglers all performed their highly-skilled routines. It was a magnificent and very enjoyable occasion. But during the last two days those vengeful Attacotti barely drank, their anger carefully hidden, bubbling dangerously beneath the surface.

Those Milesians nobles had themselves been a most convivial company. But on that final, and darkest of days, they'd been served highly-intoxicating, but exquisitely-tasting drinks. They enjoyed them so much that they couldn't stop drinking. By the end of the night, they'd gotten so drunk that they could barely stand. Some of them sat, half slumped in their chairs, whilst others heavily rested upon elbows around the table, most of them slurring their words as the alcohol freely flowed. After spending nine pleasurable days feasting with their hosts, they had become very relaxed and far too trusting. By the glow of the surrounding bonfires, Cairbre Cat-head could now be seen grinning, with a devilish glint in his eye; suddenly, without warning, he gave the signal. It was then that those cowardly assassins, the Attacotti struck, quickly turning on our Milesian noblemen; they rushed at them with swords drawn, shouting, and recklessly, swiftly and without mercy, massacred each and every one of them. (To honour those slain nobles, that once pleasant meadow has ever since been called *Magh Cro*: the 'Plain of Blood').

And so, the Attacotti's plan had worked, and their cold-hearted leader, Cairbre Cat-head became the new High-king, ruling over all the four Kingdoms of Ériu. Tragically, for the kingdom of Munster, the 'birdlike' Eanna Brightneck lay dead. But it should have been obvious from the start that treachery lay afoot, for even small children know that 'the bird should never feast with the cat'.

> *Thus was Cairbre the cruel,*
> *Who seized Ériu to rule.*
> *On his fair head he had two cat's ears,*
> *And thro' those furry objects he hears.*

Three celebrated noblewomen who were lucky enough to escape the massacre, as they weren't present at the feast, were Cruife, wife of Eanna Brightneck; Aine, wife of the Ulster King; and Baine, who was the wife of the old High-king, Crimthann 'Nephew-of-Nár'. All three were pregnant with the sons of the recently fallen kings so knew that they would need to flee lest they be murdered next.

These three queens were most swift in their actions, for strong were their spirits, though their powers lay barely intact, as they left these shores. They escaped across the narrow sea to Alba where they sought refuge from that friendly land there. Baine happened to be the daughter of the King of Alba, so was able to grant a safe refuge to the other queens, who each had equally powerful fathers: Aine was the daughter of Cainneall, the King of

Saxony, whilst Cruife was the daughter of Goirtniad, who was a powerful king of the Britons. They remained in the land of Alba whilst the ruthless Attacotti ruled over theirs.

The first year of Cairbre Cat-head's reign was in 10 A.D. But the old gods weren't happy; the old gods who were at one with the land, who brought peace and balance to the island, were angered that such a cruel chieftain was now the High-king. The gods showed their displeasure and during his reign no crops grew in the fields, no trees held any fruit, no fish were caught and no cows carried any milk. The people were starving; they still worshipped the golden idol known as 'the crooked god', sacrificing their firstborn, as was the age-old custom, but nothing would appease the gods.

This went on for five long unhappy years; that was until the cruel Cairbre Cat-head finally let go of his tight, evil grip of the land when, with the will of the gods, he fortuitously became inflicted with the plague, dying a horrific and just death. His end came as a huge relief to the people.

But as his rule had been so disastrous, the elders of the Attacotti didn't know what to do regarding the now empty throne. They offered Cairbre Cat-head's son, Moran, the rule of High-king. But Moran was wise and learned. He told them that the Kingship wasn't his by hereditary right and the country's famine wouldn't stop until the old gods were appeased and the rightful heirs put back upon their fathers' thrones. The Attacotti agreed to Moran's sage advice; henceforth, they sent for the young Celtic princes, to ask for their family's forgiveness and to urge them to return.

One of these children was the son of Crimthann 'Nephew-of-Nár' and his wife, Baine. His name was Fearadach Fionn the Truthful. And rightly did he take his father's throne to become the new High-king, though he was still but a young child. Even from childhood, he was always thought of as a good King, who ruled with justice and honesty.

Another of the returning children was Corb, son of the Munster King, Eanna Brightneck and Queen Cruife. Like Cairbre Cat-head, he too had been born with a most unusual feature, being blessed with an astonishingly bright, shining glow all about his body; a glow as red as the embers of a blazing hearth. This gave rise to his nickname of *Dearg Theine*, meaning 'Red-fire'. But that wasn't the only curious thing about the boy: for where Cairbre had been born with two cat-like ears, poor Dearg Theine was sadly born without any ears, which is why he was also sometimes called *Corb Ólomm* which means Corb 'Bare-ear'. With the Attacotti truce now firmly in place, Dearg Theine was able to return to his hereditary kingdom of Munster to rule as king. To celebrate this new age of Ériu, Dearg Theine's descendants named themselves 'Dergthine', in his honour, though still they were often referred to as 'Heberians', as they were also descended from the noble warrior-king, Heber Fionn, son of Milesius.

Also returning was the son born of the matrimony between Aine and the Ulster King, though sadly we remember not his name.

When all of those three young Kings were back on their hereditary thrones the gods were at peace once more, and from that point onward the land began to be restored and renewed: the crops again started to grow, the trees could now bear fruit, fish became more numerous, and even the contented cows began producing milk once more.

The Attacotti couldn't believe what was happening to the land; they were so impressed by the new kings that they all swore fealty by reciting the sacred oath. This was an oath that they'd dare not break:

*By the Heaven and Earth, Sun, Moon and all the Elements,*
*We shalt yield obedience to ye and all of thy descendants,*
*And remain faithful for as long as the sea shall surround this great land.*

And Moran, the son of Cairbre Cat-head, due to his extreme wisdom, was given the prestigious title of High-brehon, making him the highest ranking legal-adviser in the land. The position suited Moran's skills very well. And what made his verdicts easier to arrive at, was with the use of his famous enchanted collar, for when placed around his own neck, it would tighten if ever he gave an ill-judgement and would only loosen when he made a just one; but equally as important, when placed around the neck of the accused, the collar would slowly tighten if ever they told a lie. Moran went on to aid Fearadach Fionn in his ruling of the country, which is why that honest king became known as 'the Truthful', for no man would dare to lie in his presence.

And our good, young, Munster King, Dearg Theine, he also turned out to be an honest and decent ruler himself. He did have a competitor for the Munster throne, however; it was his distant cousin, Dáire, son of Ferulnigh, leader of the Ithians, who was of the bloodline of Lughaidh, son of Ithe. With Dearg Theine being fair and just, he made an honourable agreement with Dáire: he ruled that both of their descendants would take it in turns to rule Munster. And when one of his descendants was king, then the descendant from Dáire's line would govern the civil affairs of the kingdom; and vice versa. And so, to celebrate the terms of this treaty, Dáire's descendants named themselves 'the Dáirine', in his honour. This important covenant, noble as it was in design, sadly only lasted for two generations, that was, until the time of Magha Neid; but more of that tragic event anon.

And that my friends, is where this adventure ends. Such is the tale as it was told to me. Tomorrow we shall have a lengthier tale, one which involves legendary Champions, powerful kings and godly premonitions".

# The King with Four Names

The night's feast was finally over. Some of us younger ones who were clearly more eager had rushed our food in the hope that the evening's entertainment would begin sooner. This was the time of night that we'd all been looking forward to. It was always exciting to have a stranger within our midst, but this was no ordinary stranger, being the Chief-seanchaí of Munster, and what he didn't know about the old historical tales wasn't worth knowing.

As he coughed to clear his throat, the room immediately fell silent as we all quickly moved to get a good place near him before he began.

"The land had changed much since our previous tale. The powerful would-be king, Tuathal the Legitimate, grandson of Fearadach Fionn the Truthful, had been exiled to Alba. On his return, he'd landed with a huge invading force intent on reclaiming his hereditary High-kingship. After successfully winning the inevitable war that followed, Tuathal stamped his mark upon his newly-conquered land by demanding a royal capital from which he could rule the four existing kingdoms; this would show those four ruling kings that he was a man not to be messed with, so he created his own fifth kingdom.

At that time, the four kingdoms all met at the very centre of the country at the sacred green hill of Uisneach, where sat a large, towering rock called the Stone of Divisions, which was commonly referred to as the Cat-stone due to its feline appearance when seen from one side. This extraordinary rock marked the burial place of the Fairy-queen, Ériu. It was here that Tuathal claimed vast portions of those four adjoining kingdoms, by taking land from each king, to form his own fifth territory, which he named *Meath*, which means 'middle' as it was the middle-kingdom. And this became the ruling territory for all the High-kings, most of whom reigned from its ancient capital of Tara, which was its seat for the next five hundred years. And that was the state of the land as we begin our next tale.

Leaping forward two generations, we look towards Conn of the Hundred-battles, who gained his warlike epitaph after defeating both Munster and Ulster in a hundred battles each; then, on top of that he went on to defeat Leinster in another three-score battles. Conn was descended from a long line of High-kings, which included his father, Fedhlimidh the Lawgiver, as well as his grandfather, Tuathal the Legitimate, who I've just previously mentioned.

So auspicious was Conn's birth, that upon that extraordinary day five important roads were discovered which all led to Tara. These roads were named the Great Way, which ran all the way from the western coast; the Road of Cualu, which hailed from Leinster, passing by the esteemed port at Dubhlinn; the Road of Dalo, which hailed from Munster; the Road of Assal, which came directly from the Fort of Cruachan in Connacht; and the Road of Midluachair, which hailed from the far north of Ulster. These five roads hadn't been seen before (or at least hadn't been noticed as significant roads) and were now suddenly wide enough for two chariots to easily pass each other. Their discovery was deemed to be a truly fortuitous omen to behold for any future king, so it wasn't totally unexpected when Conn himself became High-king, with the first year of his rule being in 123 A.D.

Let our eyes now gaze upon our own southern kingdom of Munster, and to Magha Neid, son of Dearg, son of Dearg Theine. From birth he was known as Oengus and as was common in those days, for young sons of nobles, he was brought up by foster-parents, whose courtly position befitted the boy's rank; it was their job to educate their young charge in the ways of the world. And fortunately for Oengus, he enjoyed a most pleasant childhood as his foster-father, Net, was a good and kindly man.

Even as a child, Oengus was uncommonly big and strong for his age. And he completely idolized Net, and was often seen devotedly following him around, as close as a shadow, using whatever strength he had to aid Net in any way that he could; therefore, it wasn't long before the helpful little boy earned the nickname of *Magha Neid*: meaning Net's slave.

Magha Neid grew up, like all royal children, with a life of great privilege mixed with that always ever-present threat of impending danger. Although when he was very young, the threat of danger was obviously more of a worry to his guards and to those whose charge he was under than to the boy himself.

Years later, when the prince had grown into a naturally tall and muscular young man, whose charm and easy smile had made him the most perfect of companions, he met a good-natured company of travellers who were visiting from Ormond, which was the eastern realm of Munster. Being escorted amongst their number was the beautiful princess, Síoda, daughter of the powerful, Lord of Ormond, Flann, son of Fiacra. It didn't take long before romance entered the hearts of the handsome young couple, meaning that a betrothal was shortly forthcoming.

As the years went by, Magha Neid's strength and build increased, and like his grandfather, Dearg Theine, before him, he was also crowned as King of Munster, which was due to the agreement between Dearg Theine and Dáire two generations before, for their descendants to rule in alternate succession. What a man Magha Neid had now become! Due to his height and build he could easily be described as a mountain of a man who commanded so much respect, without even trying. He wasn't just admired by his people; we all adored him. It was mainly down to his huge, manly frame that housed within such a friendly, calm, patient and pondering mind, who liked to mull over any big decisions before he ruled upon them. But once he'd made a decision his course was then set. He was also slow to anger, usually, but when he lost his temper, he'd act with explosive fury. But most of the time he was found to be utterly charming and generous. And the warmth of his personality, as well as his loud, manly voice filled every room that he entered. So, we all felt safe knowing that we were under the protection of such a kind, fatherly figure, although, amidst the war of the battlefield his personality changed and this bighearted Champion became fearlessly swift, violently ruthless and unyieldingly strong; many of our enemies had sleepless nights worrying about facing such a giant, bear-like man in battle.

But away from the battlefield Magha Neid and Síoda had a mostly-blissful married life. They were even blessed with the arrival of a beautiful baby boy. From birth the child was simply known as Eoghan, which can be said to mean 'of good birth', although it can also mean 'born of the yew', which was one of our seven most sacred trees. His doting parents adored him. And Queen Síoda couldn't have been a more perfect mother. The glint in her eye and that gentle smile upon her lips as she gazed into his little face said it all.

When Eoghan became old enough, he too was sent away to be educated by foster-parents. It was obviously a terribly sad time for any truly loving parent, so much so that Síoda openly cried. Fortunately for Eoghan, he was being sent to the neighbouring Kingdom of Leinster, to be raised by a good and noble man, named Dáire Barrach, Lord of Tuath Laighean. Dáire was the Chief of the rulers of North Leinster, standing out amongst his peers as being a true hero amongst heroes; he was handsome and courageous, spirited and intelligent, whose own father had bestowed upon him the blessing for him to be generous to poets and also to favour victory in battle. What other attributes could a king truly desire?

It was indeed a large and powerful realm in which Eoghan was being sent. With a lot of trade goods entering the country through its ports, bringing goods from nearby Wales, as well as lands as far away as Gaul, it made it a truly wealthy realm. And with Dáire having such a fine pedigree, being the son of the old High-king, Cathair Mór, it meant that the young ward would truly be in safe hands.

Under the watchful eye of his foster-father, young Eoghan grew into a kind and handsome Champion, just like Dáire himself, but with the same muscular physique akin to that of his own birth-father, which meant that he too was also exceptionally strong. Dáire was particularly keen for his foster-son to have a good education, for he knew that without wisdom there can be no great power.

Let me try to describe young Eoghan to you, if I can, when he was still but a youth. He was tall, broad of shoulder and powerfully built, with long, flowing, braided hair, as was the fashion, wearing the customary under-developed beard sported by many young men of his age. Obviously, his clothing was of the highest quality, being made of the finest materials, and the workmanship, especially the embroidery, was beyond compare, together with a scarlet, satin cloak that showed that he was truly the son of a king. But without even noticing his cloak, you could easily tell his regal rank, even from a distance, due to how he held himself. He certainly had that characteristically powerful presence of a man who was destined to rule a mighty Kingdom.

One day, the charismatic Dáire Barrach was overseeing the excavation of a trench which when complete would circle all around the top of the enormous royal hill-fort of Dún Ailinne, which sat within the western limits of his realm of Tuath Laighean. The soil that was dug from this deep ditch was piled-up just outside of the ditch to form a steep surrounding bank all around the hilltop; this earthen-wall would then be finished with a layer of turf and topped by a tall pilloried fence to form a strong defensive structure.

Building proved to be a mammoth task as it took the combined strength of three-thousand of the local people; it was their duty to work on the site as a form of tribute to the Leinster king, Crimthann Yellow-hair; although it was only the obvious power of Dáire, being one of the leading Lords of the eastern Kingdom, that had brought those people there to begin with. When finished, this magnificent hill-fort would truly demonstrate the power which Leinster wielded as it would be the largest in the land; even bigger than Tara as well as that great red-fortress of the Twins of Macha to the north.

Dáire was indeed fortunate to be helped by the famous Ráth-builder, Nuada Long-heel, who was extremely experienced in building such projects. Nuada knelt there, grappling in the mud, his undyed white-tunic covered with dirt and stained with sweat. The colour of his clothing showed that he was unmistakably a slave. Like Eoghan, he too was enormously strong; it was often said that Nuada had the strength of a hundred men. He also had an amazing appetite and could eat the food of half-a-hundred; I knew this to be true, as I'd witnessed it myself.

During the building work, some of the local men were down in the muddy trench, busily digging it out, when they came across a huge granite boulder. The youths, who'd come from near and far, including our own Eoghan, watched from both sides of the bank to see this white-clothed, giant of a man, Nuada, lift the mighty rock. He struggled and struggled, loudly groaning with the effort, but he just couldn't move it.

Finally, he shouted to the young men to come down and help him. But they all refused, not wanting to obey the orders of a slave. But Eoghan, who'd inherited a spirited desire to physically help, both from his father, as well as his foster-father, jumped down, eager to aid the struggling giant. Standing next to Nuada, the build of the two men wasn't too dissimilar, but their clothing couldn't have been more different, with one wearing basic, plain white garb, whilst the other had sumptuous colourful red robes embroidered to perfection. Eoghan happily knelt in the mud, instantly grabbing hold of the massive boulder with his two strong, muscular arms and lifting it up, single-handedly onto his shoulder, before slowly standing upright and hurling it, with all of his might, over the edge of the trench. It rolled to the southern edge of the fortress, where it still remains to this day.

The Chief-druid of Leinster, who'd been watching the progress of the work, was truly amazed at Eoghan's feat. "You have a noble slave there, Nuada", he jokingly observed. And the name stuck, for in the old tongue, *Mogha Nuadhad* means 'Nuada's Slave'; thus, that became the first name that he rightly earned.

His father was equally impressed with his son's feats of strength, and when he'd heard about the lad's new name he roared with laughter, as he'd been named for a similar reason himself, although at a much younger age.

And so, the young, newly-named Mogha Nuadhad, with already being blessed with the dignified bearing of a king, was now also gaining an equally wide reputation for his enormous feats of strength too. Therefore, it wasn't long before our Kingdom's elders naturally agreed that Mogha Nuadhad should become our kingdom's Tanist, so that after his father's reign, he would instantly step into his shoes to rule as our Munster King. This important decision went against the agreement made by Dearg Theine and Dáire; although, before that momentous agreement had taken place, it had always been the most senior eligible prince who'd been picked to be the tribe's Tanist. He needed to be well-educated and deemed wiser than his peers, to be the greatest leader who was unmatched in princely honour; and above all he needed to look like a true-born king, so that when he took the throne his subjects would follow without question. And only Mogha Nuadhad fully fitted that description. He was by far the most suitable candidate. If there was anything that he lacked, it was only confidence in his own abilities. But throughout history sons of great men have often had that same unfortunate problem.

During that time, throughout Ériu, there lived brave bands of warriors called the Fianna. These were the standing armies of the provincial kings, who'd been recruited from landless young highborns. Their recruitment depended upon them passing many dangerous trials, so that once initiated these young men could become part of that elite, highly-trained military fighting force. Just to be part of this regiment was considered to be a huge honour. In times of war these bold warriors would be frequently called upon to aid their king. Tara, from whence the High-king did rule, had its own loyal group of Fianna; these were led by the celebrated Chieftain, Cumhal, son of Trénmór, whose brave feats were known throughout the land. Not only was he ruggedly handsome, standing head and shoulders above his men, looking every inch the hero, but more importantly, he was virtually unbeatable in battle.

Cumhal also happened to be the uncle of the High-king, Conn of the Hundred-battles, as the Fianna Chieftain and Conn's father, Fedhlimidh the Lawgiver were both born of the same mother; this meant that in times of war, that Cumhal frequently found himself working for his powerful nephew.

One day, Cumhal was riding his chariot along the Road of Dalo. It was one of those ideal days when the sun is warm but the wind is pleasantly cool, making it feel as though the world is perfectly in balance. It was upon that day that Cumhal happened upon a beautiful young maiden. After stopping his chariot to speak to her for a couple of minutes the handsome Chieftain became instantly besotted; it was as if a thunderbolt had suddenly struck him. And she was as taken with him as he was with her. The pretty young woman was known as 'Muireann of the Fair Neck', as her gentle beauty was a thing to behold; and as you can imagine, with human nature being what it is, all the nobles from a good-many leagues around wanted her to be their bride. But Muireann was the daughter of the stern, cold, High-druid of Tara, Teige, son of Nuadat, and he wouldn't allow just anyone to marry his precious daughter.

As the weeks went by Cumhal and Muireann got to know each other well, always meeting in strictest secret so that her father wouldn't find out. Until finally the two lovers decided that Cumhal would have to visit her father to ask for her hand in marriage.

So, the following day, Cumhal took to his chariot, fearlessly riding once more, along that road that had been named after the green-shielded hero, Dalo. He was heading towards the volcanic Hill of Almu that stood so prominently on the landscape, being seen from many leagues away. The old wizard had made his home within the strong, fortified stronghold that sat atop the hill, which had once belonged to his father, Nuadat the Great, son of Achi. Nuadat had been the High-druid of Conn's predecessor, Cathair Mór, and had been rewarded with that magnificent hill due to his exemplary service, so he named it after his wilful wife, Almu daughter of Becan, after she urged him for that honour. After Nuadat had died, his celebrated son Teige, became the High-druid, inheriting the hill on which the fortress stood.

It was a pleasant enough ride, although slightly cold, and even though he was a fearless Chieftain he still must have had some reservations about meeting with the intimidating High-druid. It wasn't long before the hill came into view; it wasn't overly tall, but it was enormously wide, covered with a thick layer of trees. And there, standing proudly at the top was the white-walled fortress itself.

On reaching the foot of the hill, Cumhal slowly dismounted from his chariot, leaving it with a guard, before boldly striding up the hillside to ask for an audience with the powerful High-druid. Cumhal had met the wizard before, so knew that he was a man not to be messed with. In fact, many had fallen foul of the druid's temper, as he was such a strong, forceful character whose suspicious nature often meant that he could easily take a genuine misunderstanding as a gross personal assault, for so worried was he, that others were trying to steal his power away. I myself can verify this from my own personal encounters with him: on first meeting, the druid came across as a most charismatic fellow, full of confidence, with a loud, commanding voice, steely-blue eyes, with grey-hair and a long grey-beard. About his shoulders was a cloak checked with six colours and speckled with white, making him look like he'd been caught in a snowstorm, whilst bright gleaming golden ear-clasps adorned his ears. Many nobles sought his friendship, but upon getting better acquainted, his vindictive manner arose, together with him being so quick to take offense, which is a dangerous combination of traits. With him also liking to have power over others, it resulted in him having very few real friends, but many wary enemies. As a father, he was stern and strict, who expected much from himself, but much more from those around him, especially from his daughter... Sometimes, it has been said, that daughters seek out a future husband with similar qualities to that of their own father. So maybe Muireann saw in Cumhal that he too was a powerful man who also expected much from himself.

At the top of the hill there was a commanding view of the green surrounding plains and shadowy valleys below. Walking through the large gateway, two brawny guards led the Chieftain towards the wizard's roundhouse. As tall as those guards were, their heads barely reached the tops of Cumhal's shoulders.

Teige's large roundhouse was covered with an overhanging thatched roof made of colourful birds' wings. Cumhal ducked his head to enter the doorway. So tall and broad was he that he blocked out the daylight from entering the building. Once inside, he came face to face with the hard-hearted Teige. Cumhal obviously towered over all three of the men as the elderly wizard was himself shorter than his two guards. After the initial cordial welcomes had concluded, Cumhal, being a man of action, promptly asked for the hand of the druid's daughter. But Teige angrily refused. He'd already had a prediction that a union between the young couple would result in him losing his family-home forever. And that he couldn't bear, so he forbade them to ever see each other again. So that was the end of their short meeting.

The two young lovers were obviously beside themselves with grief. What could they do? What really could they do? Their love for each other was so intense that they'd no choice but to continue meeting in strictest secret. During one of their clandestine meetings, they held each other close, gazing into each other's equally moist eyes, and talked so sweetly of their future plans. They knew that their only hope to be together was to run away; nothing else mattered. So that's exactly what they did.

Obviously, when Teige found out, he was furious. He raced his chariot to Tara to demand help from the High-king. Conn sympathetically listened to Teige's woeful tale; he couldn't believe what Cumhal had done. He was outraged. This was an extremely serious matter as the High-druid was one of the most powerful, highly respected and undoubtedly one of the most feared men in the whole of Ériu. Conn immediately despatched his trusted messengers to find Cumhal and urge him to return home with Muireann.

After much exhaustive searching the royal messengers finally tracked down the errant Chieftain and informed him of Conn's urgent demands. Cumhal obviously refused most defiantly. What else could they expect? So, the failed messengers reluctantly rode back home empty handed.

With Cumhal's refusal, Conn was stuck on a path from which he could no longer veer; he had to wage war against his uncle. He had no choice; to steer from this path would have shown him to be a weak ruler.

It was a desperate war that broke out within the shadow of Cnucha's fortress, which stood within the realm of Tuath Laighean, just west of Dubhlinn. I can see it so clearly when I close my eyes. I was but a young man of fourteen back then, when first called to arms. I was but a green youth, not having the wisdom that a lifetime of experience has now given me, although at the time I felt that I knew more than most of my elders. They seemed so old and completely out of touch with our modern world. How much clearer I can see things now! Though the older I get the less certain I am of what I actually do know, but I do understand the human spirit more. Yes, that is something that I do understand more with each passing year. I understand the cruelty and the greed which men possess. And also, the compassion. And the kindness. These latter two are what keeps me going. I've had kind, witty friends whose company I can relax in. I've also been befriended by those with a treacherous wit whose friendship felt like I was wading through swamps of blood, not knowing when their cruel spears of humour would maliciously pierce me in the back when but out of earshot; they sought to murder my personality with their cruel taunts when in the company of my peers. Aye, I've known both sorts of men: The cruel and the kind.

But I digress. Back to that fateful episode. I'd always felt that war was what we were bred for, having trained in these skills since childhood. Therefore, I knew my studies would have to wait until this war was over. I'd never experienced a battle before. It certainly opened my eyes to the viciousness of the human spirit. My brotherhood of seanchaí called this the Battle of Cnucha, naming it after Conn's foster-mother, whose fortress, as I've said, overlooked the field of battle.

There were many Champions upon the field that day. And as not just anyone could become King, the same was also true for Champions. To be a member of that elite order meant that you had to be bigger, stronger, fiercer and braver than all of your comrades. Only a man who truly stood out on the battlefield could become a Champion. They were by far the mightiest warriors in the Kingdom. And when your ruler made you a Champion, you had to swear a noble oath in front of witnesses; amongst other things you had to vow to protect the just and avenge their wrongs, being polite in words and address, even to your greatest foes. And you were honour-bound to live by the words of your oath. Yes, our Champions of Ériu were truly thought of as our 'Knights of the Realm'. From amongst those Champions the Chieftains were picked, but they had to have a claim upon the tribe's throne by hereditary descent, so needed to be related to a previous Chieftain. Of course, there were always usurpers in every realm who had no claim upon the throne, but still craved the position, often backed by a mighty army. But whoever was the Chieftain, they still needed to keep their men in check, so didn't just require a strength of arms, but also needed to possess a great strength of character, enough to make them unbiased lawmakers whenever disputes arose amongst their ranks.

Fighting at the head of our army that day was our King, Magha Neid, purple-cloaked and massively built, standing alongside his heroic son Mogha Nuadhad, who I believe must have been nearly twenty, more or less. They'd led us onto the field at the head of our great Munster army. And there we proudly stood, beside our loyal, old friend, Cumhal, son of Trénmór. As tall as Magha Neid and his son were, they barely reached the shoulders of the impressive giant, Cumhal. Not far from them stood our fair-haired hero, Luchet of the Hundreds at the front of his own battalion.

I remember it being cold that day, though the sky was strangely quiet, as though the birds knew of the carnage that was about to unfold upon this field before us.

Across the other side of the plain was the High-king, Conn of the Hundred-battles with an equally impressive force of loyal supporters. Conn had given the temporary leadership of Cumhal's Fianna warriors to the ferocious Aedh, son of Morna Wry-neck. That fearless Champion was of the ancient race of Fir-bolg. Their name means 'Men of the Bags' as they were kept as work-slaves by the Greeks, who forced them to carry huge bags of rich soil over many leagues to spread across their barren plains in an effort to make their lands more fertile.

The Fir-bolg were a little shorter and much stockier than the race of Man, but they were enormously strong, although they didn't like to waste too much of their energy, tending to only work for short bursts, if needed, but never doing any more than was actually required, preferring lazier, more self-indulgent pursuits such as feasting and resting; although they were also known for their less peaceful traits, which may have been fuelled by their greed and envy, which brought their cunning and argumentative nature to the fore, especially in the company of strangers, who usually saw them as loudmouthed troublemakers. But Aedh was different; with him being a renowned Champion of his race meant that he was somewhat controlled by his oath, as well as by his own strong sense of honour. Aedh himself was of royal blood, being descended from the ancient kings of Connacht. He was a lot taller than most of his race; actually, he was almost as tall as the average Champion from the race of Man, which was remarkably tall in itself, although he was obviously much shorter than Cumhal, as everyone else was, for that previous Fianna Chieftain was so especially tall that he towered over all other Champions on the field. Like all of his people, Aedh had a prominent brow, large bulbous nose and a heavy jaw, with that same stout barrel-chest, muscular build and long, flowing hair; although his hair was unusually golden-blond, as his race were predominantly raven-haired. Like most of the Fir-bolg, he was also extremely loyal to his king; his loyalty, together with his ferocious cunning is what made him the perfect Chieftain to lead the Fianna into war. And upon any field of battle, he was indeed seen as a most fearsome creature, full of brooding menace, which I myself found quite chilling, although still mesmerizing to watch, preferably from a great distance.

Alongside Conn of the Hundred-battles and Aedh, son of Morna, were Aedh's thirty terrifying brothers, along with their powerful ginger-haired father, Morna Wry-neck, who was otherwise known as Dáire the Red, son of Eochaid the Fair.

The battle eventually began. It was a noisy and ferocious encounter. At the start of it all, I stood in my rightful place, at the back of our battle lines with the other younglings, waiting for the war-horns to sound.

After one horn called, the other side answered. BOOO-ROOOOH. BOOO-ROOOOOH. On hearing the second blast, we ran as fast as our legs would carry us. Before us, brave warriors clashed and heroes were cleaved down. We continued running to meet our equals: those rapidly advancing enemy younglings, whilst our hearts were thrumming noisily in our chests as the cold wind blew across our cheeks and ruffled our hair.

We soon reached those enemy striplings, tightly gripping our shields and two thin javelins in our left hands, whilst our single mighty war-spears were firmly held in our right; for the tighter we gripped, the safer we somehow felt. Coming to a standstill, we automatically stabbed our great-spears into the ground, just as we'd been trained, before taking a javelin into our prominent hand and nervously hurling each one towards the enemy, though few hit their mark. Pulling our war-spears from the ground we moved forward. Cautiously at first, then with much haste we rushed to within stabbing distance. And then jabbed away at those young enemy boys, whose serious faces showed that they too had been trained in death. The sounds that could be heard when they each received their death blows unnerved all of us surrounding younglings. Some screamed, some cried, some called to the gods and others to their mothers. When I close my eyes, I can still see their young, frightened faces and hear those horrific bloodcurdling screams.

Amidst the battle, when my own close-at-hand enemy were no more, I stopped to catch my breath as I watched our heroic ally, Luchet of the Hundreds, as he fearlessly came against Aedh, son of Morna. And how savage was each of their deadly blows as both those red-cloaked heroes fought with all their might. After many violently murderous jabs had been punched home from both Chieftains, Luchet, with intense fury in his heart, savagely rammed his great-spear straight into Aedh's face, blinding him in one eye, hoping that this would end his enemy's fierce attack. But alas, this cruel blow didn't stop Aedh, it just made him even angrier. After a few more frantic stabs had passed between them, Aedh struck Luchet with such force that he killed our fair-haired hero on the spot. But as tragically sad as his death was, may Luchet's spirit feel a little less aggrieved knowing that he will forever be remembered as the hero who dared to blind the terrifying Aedh, son of Morna.

It was then that Cumhal, son of Trénmór came against Aedh: the old Fianna Chieftain fighting against his deadly replacement. Cumhal towered high above the Fir-bolg Champion, but Aedh was considerably broader. Those two Champions warred hard against each other, both with spear and shield, dealing out blows as though they were invincible gods; each one putting their whole strength behind every stroke of their fiercely brutal attack. It was destined to be another short-lived battle as both men were known to deal out deadly killing-blows.

The blood poured from Aedh's empty eye socket over his cheek, staining his golden-blond beard as he gritted his teeth hard, desperate to block out the pain. This should have made Cumhal the favourite to win, especially as Aedh now had a blind side, but Cumhal was still, by far, the larger target of the two.

After many more viciously frantic blows, performed so brutally between those two knights, and each strike of their seemingly endless assault more forceful than the last, it was Aedh who went on to finally deal out the fatal blow against our heroic Cumhal. After the old Chieftain fell to his knee, Aedh finished off his barbaric attack by cleaving clean through his neck. He promptly stooped to pick up the fallen head, gleefully lifting it up for all to see. The crimson blood dripping from beneath the bloodied skull onto the muddy plain below, making the blood-drenched one-eyed Fianna Chieftain look like an evil ghoul transported from an all-too-real nightmare.

Yet all around, the fighting still waged on.

It was a furiously deadly battle. I can still hear the shouting and the weapons smashing against each other and feel my heart beating faster as I remember the terror of the battle-field and the horrifically gory sights that I witnessed far too close at hand.

Eventually we managed to win but there had been considerable deaths on both sides.

Just before the defeated Conn had left the corpse-ridden field, his men had led a sneak attack that had captured Cumhal's new widow, Muireann daughter of Teige. This was quite a blow as she'd been under the protection of the Munster flag.

We were the victors that day, even though our leading ally, Cumhal lay dead, along with a great many of our kingdom's finest heroes, and having also lost Muireann, meant that we'd paid a terrible price for our victory. But at least we had routed our formidable foes from the field, so it would be a long time before they would try their hand against us again.

Magha Neid was immensely proud of his young son, Mogha Nuadhad, having witnessed him first-hand defeating a torrent of deadly foes, although none were quite as ferocious as the terrifying Aedh, but still he'd performed so many courageous and valiant deeds, that his father gallantly allowed him to lead our victorious Munstermen back home.

As a result of Aedh losing an eye, he was nicknamed 'Goll', meaning 'one-eyed'; and due to his fighting prowess, this newly named Goll, son of Morna, was justly made the permanent leader of the Fianna. This impressive Chieftain had now become one of the High-king's most loyal and trusted captains.

As to 'Muireann of the Fair Neck': she was forcefully taken back to her furious father. The outraged High-druid on finding that she was now pregnant wanted to burn her alive, but the mighty Conn wouldn't allow it; he'd been forced into this battle against his nephew and a great many of his warriors had been brutally killed. That was all that he could take, so he certainly wasn't going to be pushed into killing an innocent woman, no matter how angry his refusal made the druid. So, Conn made his stand, and the enraged High-druid had no choice but to back down, trying hard to keep his temper in check.

To protect the heartbroken Muireann, Conn hastened her away, to stay with Cumhal's sister, Bodhmall, daughter of Trénmór, within the forests upon the Mountain of Flame, which lay to the far south of Firceall. Bodhmall was a powerful druidess back then and was therefore able to offer the pregnant Muireann considerable protection. And when the beautiful baby boy was born, for his own safety Muireann left him to be lovingly fostered by his aunt, Bodhmall, as well as her companion, Liath Luachra. Those two formidable women were both experts in their own field, one in spells and enchantment, whilst the other was in weapons and warcraft. He learnt much from them both, becoming a highly accomplished Champion, whilst still but a youngling. When he later earnt his warrior-name he became known as Fionn, son of Cumhal and was one of the most famous warriors in the whole of Ériu's rich tapestry of history. And when fully-grown he paid a visit to his grandfather, Teige to demand compensation for the death of his father. The High-druid, not wanting to go to war against this impressive young warrior, had no choice but to give him the Hill of Almu. And so, Teige's prophecy had come to pass. Fionn made this his home and years later, after he himself had become the leader of the Fianna, he trained his warriors upon the flat land lying at the bottom of that mighty volcanic hill. But more of him anon.


Now I must tell you about this other interesting part of the story. Many moons had passed since that fateful battle, and within the royal fortress of Munster, during one particularly dark and wet stormy night, whilst Queen Síoda was in the midst of a deep sleep, she suddenly received a startling vision: she saw seven cows that were the colour of snow upon the mountain tops. Red ears they had upon their heads. Their eyes shone like pure, clear crystals, whilst sharp iron-horns proudly adorned their heads. Their harmonious lowing was like the sweet sound of an expertly played harp. Beneath their bodies, their udders were so full that when they walked, milk leaked out creating huge white-puddles across the land. Behind them followed seven black cows with skins of a dismal hue. Their fiery-red eyes blazed within their heads. They also had sharp horns of iron. Their mournful bellowing was loud enough to wake the dead from their eternal slumber. Suddenly, the black cows attacked the white ones, goring them with their razor-sharp horns until all the white cows lay slaughtered and mutilated.

The following morning, the terror-struck Síoda awoke, thinly coated in a cold sheen of damp sweat, her feet tangled in the blankets as she'd tried to escape from her nightmare. It was so real and disturbing that she instantly knew that it was a prophecy. Waking her husband, she anxiously told him of her terrifying vision. Síoda had painted such a vivid picture that Magha Neid couldn't get the images out of his head. Pacing the floor, he immediately sent for his trusted druid, Dearg Damhsa to come to interpret what his wife had seen.

The dawn sky glowed orange above the grey mountains to the east that morning, yet within minutes of the call, the royal messengers were ahorse, heading towards the Chief-druid's nearby stronghold to inform him of the King's summons. Thankfully the night's heavy rain had ceased, yet still it was cold and windy that morning as the horses galloped across the sodden plain, their thundering hoofbeats throwing up mud in every direction.

It wasn't long before they'd reached the gates of the modest stronghold that proudly sat upon the green hilltop, circled by a tall, white pilloried fence. The druid's guards momentarily halted the messengers before allowing them inside to deliver their report.

On hearing the King's order, the druid quickly made-ready his chariot, leaving the comfort of his home within minutes, whilst still those messengers' horses visibly panted their warm cloudlike breaths into the cold morning air.

Dearg Damhsa drove his horses onward, alone, towards the fortress of the King. As he passed through the gates, the druid jumped from his chariot, striding purposefully across the flagstone-lined footpath towards the royal roundhouse, as his long white gown dragged behind him along the muddy path. His lively cloak, predominantly red in colour, billowing in the wind as though possessed by a spirit determined to leave its fastenings. And with his wild, unruly hair being the colour of new autumn leaves, dancing about like flames in the wind, matched in colour by his untrimmed beard, this wise sage was unmistakably Dearg Damhsa, whose name means 'Red-dance'.

Two green-cloaked gatekeepers greeted him at the royal door, wearing leather aprons and each armed with a heavy mace. One of them promptly led the druid inside for an audience with the royal couple.

Obeying all the usual protocols upon entry, the druid listened very carefully as Síoda repeated her disturbing dream. He quietly nodded, trying to fully comprehend all of the intricacies of her prediction. It was only after he'd fully understood every aspect, that the wise druid carefully started to explain it to them:

"There'll be seven wonderful years when there'll be ample food for all the kingdoms. No one will be hungry or thirsty as there'll be an abundance of meat, fruit, corn, milk and fish. These will be happy, plentiful times. But following these, there'll be seven poor, miserable, selfish years when no one will have enough food; fathers won't share their food with their sons, mothers won't share their food with their daughters, and friends won't share their food with each other. These will indeed be terrible, miserable, deplorable times".

The startling news obviously shocked Magha Neid; he immediately gave orders for strong storehouses to be built with huge underground cellars. And over those next seven plentiful years the wise Munster King wouldn't accept any of the usual tributes from his followers, but only accepted food and grain, until all of these enormous larders were brimming with goods.

To help conserve as much dry food as possible Magha Neid asked his people not to eat too much grain during those abundant times but to stick to a diet of mostly venison and fish. The tribes of Munster did as they were bid.

Unfortunately, whilst Magha Neid was busy organizing all of this extremely productive activity, there was grave treachery afoot. Three Munster princes, the highest ranking being of the Ithian line, were feeling rather incensed that the elders had given their blessing for Mogha Nuadhad to become our Tanist, so they'd forcefully taken control of some of Magha Neid's fortresses, thereby stealing much of our Kingdom away. Obviously, after Magha Neid and Mogha Nuadhad had heard of this treachery, they were understandably furious. This wouldn't have been possible before the Battle of Cnucha, but that terrible war had killed hundreds of our loyal troops.

Mogha Nuadhad needed to do something drastic to win back control of his family's Kingdom; with being the Tanist, it was in his own best interests after all. So, with his father's leave, he urgently went to see his foster-father, Dáire Barrach, in Tuath Laighean, to ask for help to wrestle back his father's territory away from those princely usurpers.

Dáire was pleased to see his heroic foster-son back within his realm once more and, without hesitation, he gave the young prince a large army of warriors to help him take back his father's mighty Kingdom.

And so, Mogha Nuadhad led his considerable Leinster army back towards the southern Munster territory of Desmond where the villainous Aengus was unlawfully ruling; it only took a minor battle before our heroes had driven him from the land.

The defeated Aengus went immediately to seek help from Munster's greatest foe, the High-king himself, Conn of the Hundred-battles. The High-king, feeling that he was making a new ally, obligingly gave Aengus fifteen thousand of his own trusted warriors.

With these, the dethroned usurper arrogantly rode back to the south of Munster; the thunderous footsteps of his mighty army being heard for a good-many leagues, travelling back with but one desire: to ruthlessly re-claim the Desmond throne.

But the gods were once more on young Mogha Nuadhad's side that day, and he triumphantly defeated Aengus again, this time killing him and a whole host of his men. Without their leader, there was no real reason for these enemy troops to continue fighting and so they fled, back from whence they'd come, scattering forth like a myriad of dandelion seeds caught up in a gale.

But still there were two other enemy princes left. Their names being MacNiadh, son of Lughaidh and Conaire, son of Mogha Laine; and long shall they be remembered in the annals of Ériu for their dark treachery. If it hadn't been for that all-important ruling by the elders, MacNiadh would have been our Tanist back then; but due to his warlike behaviour, there was no way that Magha Neid would ever allow that to happen now, not even if the elders were to change their mind and grant a share of the throne to the Ithian prince. Therefore, the old, cordial agreement between Dearg Theine and Dáire was truly over, never to be reinstated. Magha Neid wouldn't let anyone but his son rule after him now. To help bring this to fruition, he decided to make Mogha Nuadhad the King during his own lifetime, so that with the strength of his arm and the respect that he commanded, he could secure the throne for his son. And that was his noble aim. But how could he make this happen when MacNiadh and Conaire still ruled much of his Kingdom? He prayed to the gods for guidance.

By now those seven, prosperous years were coming to an end, and terrible evil was looming upon the horizon. This was the time of the deadly famine, as predicted by Síoda.

The first year brought poverty and a great scarcity of food.

The second year was worse; people were giving away their most prized possessions to pay for any food that they could lay their hands on.

And then the third year came. This was the worst yet. In those dark days the whole country was suffering, but none more so than Munster. The famine was at its worst and the good people were literally starving to death. They were so hungry that they'd even started to eat each other. Those were low, dark times when good people were compelled to carry out the most deplorable of deeds.

Back then, most kings were ritually slain when the harvests failed, as this killing appeased the land, and Magha Neid knew this only too well. His only saving grace was that his storehouses were brimming with food, so he knew that he needed to somehow use this fact to turn their horrifically cruel disaster into an advantageous opportunity for his son. So, he called an important meeting with all the highborn from our Kingdom. Obviously the treacherous MacNiadh and Conaire hadn't been invited. The nobles discussed the famine and how it was desolating our whole population. Magha Neid told them that his son would save them, on condition that they agreed to his one request. They were stunned to learn that they could actually be saved, as they'd previously felt that all hope was gone. They quickly agreed, only too willing to do anything that Magha Neid proposed. They knew that they couldn't survive much longer without a great deal of aid. So, they gave the sacred oath; an oath that no man would dare to revoke.

"Name your request?" they pleaded.

The old king knew that the land was requiring a new ruler, one that would unite their kingdom once more, and Magha Neid desperately wanted to control the situation whilst he still had the power to do something about it. He'd been a well-loved king and the people had always looked up to him for his thoughtful, well-reasoned guidance, so this would be his last great ruling, "My one condition is that you banish MacNiadh and Conaire from Munster so that my son can take the throne. And once that is done the great Mogha Nuadhad will save you all, with his great larders full of food".

"This will be done", they all loudly answered, firmly and in unison. And that night they ate and drank more than they'd done for many a long year.

Let me take a moment to describe MacNiadh and Conaire to you, before we go any further: MacNiadh was descended from Lughaidh, son of Ithe, son of Breoghan. He was tall, though a little quiet, although certainly not shy, which made him seem to us as though his quiet mind was full of deep deceitful thoughts. He was clearly the cleverer of the two men. And by using that sharp mind of his, it meant that he'd be the first one to calm an awkward situation with his intelligent verbal skills. He also had that astonishing skill of surprising people with his seemingly generous acts of kindness, which made us wonder if he wasn't all entirely bad. He liked to have a laugh with those closest to him, but whenever he was feeling overtaxed with the burden of his position, he could be an outright bully. He was clearly the more dangerous of the two, especially as he often came across as being honest and helpful, but much treachery lay within his wicked heart.

Conaire was descended from Heremon, son of Milesius. He was equally tall, as well as being broad of shoulder and noticeably the stronger of the two men, but with that cold look in his eye that you knew that you could never fully trust. He may have loved, and been loved back in return by those closest to him, but the man that we knew had no empathy or sympathy for anyone or anything around him. When commanding his men, the look of horror on his face showed how much he detested having to make any quick decisions, as he just wasn't as intelligent or as capable as MacNiadh. Although he was still able to browbeat his underlings, but only when quick thinking wasn't required. On the rare occasions that we had to actually speak to him, how we hated having to do so, for so deceitful and manipulative was his character.

The following day the brave nobles of Munster gathered together their considerable armies and fulfilling their oaths, chased the usurpers from our Kingdom. And that my friends, was how young Mogha Nuadhad became King of Munster. He was very reluctant to rule at first, as he didn't believe that he'd ever be as skilled or as capable as his father. And during those early days he really felt as though his rule was being greatly overshadowed by the very presence of the still-powerful Magha Neid, knowing that whatever orders that Mogha Nuadhad made, they would be forever scrutinized and compared with those of his father; but those wise, kindly elders, along with the old king himself, gave him their firm and very vocal support. What cemented his rule though, especially in the eyes of our people, was that as soon as he'd been crowned, and after myself and the rest of his subjects from every corner of the kingdom had sworn allegiance to him, he did indeed generously give us food from his family's full larders. And due to that unbelievable kindness, which lasted throughout that entire dark period, he began being called, *Eoghan Mór*, which means 'Eoghan the Great', because, due to his unmatched generosity, he saved many thousands of his grateful subjects from a slow, desperate and miserable death, as we would undoubtedly have wasted away from starvation.

To further demonstrate his power as our new Kking, Mogha Nuadhad built three royal fortresses; they were each named *Fidfecc*, which means wood-bending, as that was how they were built. Mogha had made the perimeter fences himself by bending and weaving the wood, using his enormous strength. And it was from this impressive feat that he gained his third name of *Eoghan Fidfeccach*: Eoghan the Wood-bender.

With him now being known by three different names, to avoid confusion, we shall mostly keep to the name that we are used to calling him: Mogha Nuadhad.

Now back to our story; those two enemy princes, who'd been chased from Munster, had gone straight to the High-king, who was at his white-walled fortress of Tara, which stood within the vast Plain of Bregia, overlooking the mighty Queen Boann River. After hearing their tale, Conn was happy to take in the two exiled princes and graciously allowed them to stay.

It was whilst those two traitors were there, enjoying whatever hospitality that the capital had to offer, that they met two of Conn's charming and highly-esteemed young daughters. The girls were still young so had not yet flowered. But the princes knew that they were onto a good thing, with them being the daughters of the High-king, and as relationships have a habit of blossoming, given the right amount of manure, it wasn't long before both of those girls each had their own suitor; for that was the way things were done back then. And with Conn's blessing, MacNiadh married the pretty Sabina, whilst Conaire married the pleasant Sara. Both the girls were warm, loving, intelligent and full of good-humour. As they entered into womanhood their attributes grew, which showed that Sabina had that striking beauty that got her pestered everywhere that she went, having also a natural, gentle, flirtatious nature and the wit and charm of a poet, whilst the nerves of the fabulous Sara caused her to talk much, mesmerizing everyone around with her charming and witty conversation, which she sometimes used as a shield to conceal the fact that she was actually quite shy, though equally as pretty as her sister.

But anyway, back to our tale. Bad news has a habit of travelling fast and so it wasn't long before these marital tidings had filtered back to the court of Munster. Obviously, Mogha Nuadhad and Magha Neid were beyond furious. Not only had Conn given sanctuary to their family's two most hated enemies but now Conn had further insulted them by allowing those traitors to marry his precious young daughters.

Enough was enough. Conn's behaviour could no longer be tolerated. Magha Neid spoke to his son; he counselled him in how to deal with this thorn in their side. Hence, the young king, taking his father's bold advice, now refused to acknowledge Conn as High-king. There would be no more tributes paid from our kingdom of Munster.

Now it was Conn's turn to be outraged. He couldn't believe that we were stopping our tributes. Not only did he rely on the large number of cattle, horses, weapons, clothing and everything else that we sent, but for us to suddenly stop would make him look like a weak king; and weak kings didn't last long in those days. Therefore, Conn didn't have any choice but to show his strength and wage war upon our southern kingdom one more.

So, another bloody war was carefully planned out between our two warring sides.

Conn sent messengers to his three closest allies: these were to his foster-father, Conall of Cruachan, the Fir-bolg King who ruled the Kingdom of Connacht; to his old teacher, Crimthann Yellow-hair, who was the formidable King of Leinster; to the one-eyed Goll, son of Morna, with his ferocious army of Fianna; as well as to the various tribes of Tara. They all came to join the battle, with the intention of driving our ruling family permanently out of Munster.

It wasn't long before Conn and his men were marching to the round plain of Firceall, in the southernmost region of Meath. MacNiadh and Conaire joined him there, along with a large number of their own loyal troops; these were traitorous Munster warriors who were ready to do battle against their own Munster king.

I remember that morning being decidedly chilly as the Purple Wind blew upon us. We stood there waiting and watching from the outskirts of our camp as the first battle began. This was the battle of the Household Cavalry. These impressive troops were our Champions and heroes, being the most senior and elite warriors from both sides; they fought in two-horse chariots, driven by highly-skilled charioteers. It was the sworn duty of the cavalry to protect their king. Our troops were led by Deaghadh the Proud, whilst Conn's were led by the impressive Asal the Great. We must have been at least thirty chariots strong. Squinting into the distance, it was hard to count the number which Asal had, but I presume his number equalled ours.

The proud Champions stood in the back of their chariots, looking huge and imposing. Their red cloaks gently shimmering in the cold wind, each fastened with a silver brooch, whilst beneath their beards a golden torc gently rested around their necks. A silver bracelet adorned their wrists: another all-important emblem which proved beyond doubt that they'd reached the proud rank of Champion. Not that any proof was needed, as their huge stature was proof enough. Standing in front of them were their charioteers, tightly gripping the reins. The two men looked so very different as one was so very powerfully-built whilst the other was much smaller, wearing a colourful four-cornered helm that curved back between the shoulder blades to protect them from any spear throws. Fastened to the front of this helm, sitting proudly over each of their brows, was a large golden disk that shone as brightly as the sun so that they could be seen coming, long before their horses were even visible.

In the distance, the long, bronze snake-like war-horns were held aloft, which momentarily caught a glimmer of sunlight. These were dutifully blown to herald the start of battle. Their low, booming sound, slightly echoing two long, haunting notes. Then suddenly the chariots eagerly raced towards each other. Upon the field, the wind blew through their hair as the Champions' red cloaks streamed behind, as the chariots got nearer and nearer. When in range, without stopping, the Champions hurled their spears towards their foes. And when near enough, those nimble carts halted to allow the Champions to jump down to furiously attack each other. As this was happening those lone charioteers would race away to a nearby distance for a quick rescue and retreat if needed. After this initial frantic fighting had diminished, to give the Champions time to recover, they each ran towards their chariot, jumping back in, to be whisked away, as replacement troops were brought to the field to take their place. Substitute waves of Household Cavalry continued to rotate, all fighting a hard and grisly battle, their sharp weapons slicing and chopping through flesh. This went on and on until this long, bloody battle was finally over. Of those who survived, many found themselves mutilated with the gruesome wounds of war that had been equally inflicted upon both sides, with many of their comrades lying dead, sprawled across the field, including our own illustrious Deaghadh the Proud.

In the aftermath of the battle, Mogha Nuadhad and Magha Neid, who'd been watching from a nearby hill, gazed down at the bloody scene below: cold bodies of both man and horse lay amongst the upturned chariots, resting forlornly upon the torn earth.

Mogha's legs started to shake, although only very slightly, but enough for a caring father to notice.

"Hold steady, boy", his father calmly said as he put his large, strong hand reassuringly onto his son's muscular shoulder. "All wise men fear war. But brave men know that this fear must be conquered, for bravery pushes us forward, yet wisdom shackles our ankles, commanding us to stay. So, to have both wisdom and bravery will always cause us inner conflict. Therefore, Eoghan, my boy, in such instances, let honour be the light that guides you".

The two men turned to gaze over the fearsome Champions within our own camp, below, who were all purposefully keeping themselves busy, lest they spent too much time dwelling upon their own anxieties of the forthcoming battle. The smell of bread and porridge cooking around the many campfires made some of those men think only of the emptiness of their bellies, which came as a most-welcome distraction.

"If the war wasn't just", Magha Neid continued, "the men wouldn't follow".

In the distance Conn could be seen gathering his men. He'd won the first round and with a noticeably arrogant and triumphant air, he left the field, marching his army southwards, heading towards the northern half of Éile. This was Munster territory that they were now invading.

It wasn't long before we'd received messengers from Conn, challenging us to do battle the following day. Obviously Mogha Nuadhad gladly accepted, keen to despatch Conn once and for all.

By now the light had started to fade, making it too dark to continue. Fighting in the dark wasn't considered honourable or just. So, both sides camped for the night, although there wasn't much sleep to be had in either camp.

During that long drawn-out night our Chief-druid, Dearg Damhsa had a startling vision. He dreamt that our enemy, Conn was going to win the forthcoming battle and things were going to end disastrously for our esteemed Munstermen.

The following morning eventually came, as all mornings seem to do, and the main battle was about to begin.

Dearg Damhsa was inside of Mogha Nuadhad's tent, pacing the floor, surrounded by myself and the other nobles. Glowing coals sat within a central brazier adding much needed warmth to the tent. All eyes were on the druid, whose long copper beard, equal in length to the loose curls of his wavy hair flowed abundantly over the folds of his many-coloured cloak, of which scarlet was the main hue. His long white gown brushed the ground as he walked. And with this being a formal occasion he wore the tall pointed hat of his profession, midnight-blue in colour, circled with rows of swirling, golden suns orbited by moons, with the base of the hat being red-brimmed and delicately edged with gold. The astrological symbols upon the body of his hat were frequently consulted, for they were the druid's calendar in which he could accurately calculate the seasons.

In the warmth of the tent the druid's stern face turned a shade of red, which matched the scarlet of his cloak, as he desperately pleaded with us to heed his warnings that terrible evil would befall us if we fought that day, but we wouldn't listen. We were far too excited and blood-crazed to even consider his advice; and besides, when your troops are already camped upon the battlefield it's gone past time to turn and run. We just hoped that our Chief-druid was wrong, and that this was one of those rare occasions where he'd misinterpreted his dreams.

After the meeting had concluded we stepped forth from the pavilion, suddenly noticing how fresh the air was away from the warmth of the tent's brazier. We slowly walked away, deep in thought to take our places amongst the ranks.

Then the war-horns were once more held aloft as those haunting notes sounded across the plain. Mogha Nuadhad had become noticeably silent, his face turning a single shade paler. He was reluctant to face such a superior force, especially after hearing the grave warnings of the Chief-druid, but he understood only too well that from the very moment that they'd reached the plain, it was already too late to leave. This meant that they'd no choice but to fight. And furthermore, it had often been drummed into him by his father since childhood, that sometimes you have to fight against overwhelming odds when the only alternative is submission and humiliation, and those two demons are frequently followed by pain, misery and death, sometimes even exacted at the hands of your own men. Magha Neid knew that his son needed to fully grasp this all-important lesson, but above all, he knew that his son needed to face Conn in open battle if he was ever to gain the confidence and respect that he truly needed to succeed as king.

With Conn's side being made up of Connacht, Leinster, as well as his own kingdom of Meath, he greatly outnumbered our own Munstermen. Our only saving grace was that our old king, Magha Neid, was there with us. He was dressed in a boiled-leather corslet that tightly encased his stout muscular torso, with a matching helmet that neatly framed his intense gaze. He'd removed his purple cloak so that it didn't slow him down in battle. On his left hip was his kingly-sword, upon his powerful left arm was his shield, and tightly gripped in that same hand was his great war-spear, whilst in his right hand was his heavy, iron-capped war-club: only a powerfully-built Champion had the strength to effectively wield that violent weapon. Such was our love for the old king that our whole army would have happily fought against all the warriors in the world, for so charismatic had he been as a leader that we would have gladly pushed ourselves to the very limits; which is exactly what we needed to do on such a day as this.

Mogha Nuadhad was dressed in a similar fashion to that of his father, but preferred the skill of using spear and sword to that of Magha Neid's hefty war-club.

As the warriors surged together, the fighting quickly broke out between both of our illustrious armies. Magha Neid and Mogha Nuadhad stood firmly together, father and son fighting side by side. With Dearg Damhsa's warnings ringing in his ears, Magha Neid, did everything that he could to protect his son by fighting the most ferocious opponents himself. Desperately trying to stand his ground so that he didn't get separated from his son, the old king faced a torrent of furious enemies, all urged on by Conn. Magha Neid smashed through skulls and chests, reducing that tide of foes with every single blow.

As to the rest of us, with our army being greatly outnumbered, it wasn't long before we were all stained crimson. Shields were smashed. Blood was spattered. Arms were hacked off. Scars were ripped through warriors' cheeks. It was an intensely gory, bloody, horrific battle. The sounds and images still haunt me today.

Then the fierce Fianna Chieftain, Goll, son of Morna headed towards young Mogha Nuadhad, like a lion approaching its prey. Our old king saw him approaching, so quickly stepped in between those two unequally matched Champions, for even if his son had been successful, he wouldn't have had the strength left to face Conn. Goll and Magha Neid ran into each other with a clattering of weapons. A furious exchange took place as they hacked into each other. Both men stood their ground, raining violently heavy blows upon their opponent. Arms were sliced open as shields were cracked, becoming gapped and border-shattered. The fighting was ferocious. Neither screamed out in pain, just hitting and hitting and hitting; each blow more-fierce than the one before; shields were further smashed, bodies were brutally hacked but still they didn't scream.

It wasn't long before the final death blow came. Recalling the image sends an icy-chill down my spine. Suddenly Goll hit the noble Magha Neid. The almighty blow was so quick, it couldn't be avoided. The old King's legs gave way. He fell to the ground in a heap; stone cold dead.

The whole of Munster just stood there, staring in disbelief. It felt as though the whole world was moving in slow motion.

It took Mogha Nuadhad a few seconds to come to his senses. Then a sudden sense of control overcame him. If he'd thought too much, it would probably have turned into panic. He quickly raised his shield high above his head so that we could all see that he was still alive. He started to round up our remaining warriors. The young King, furiously angry, was now wanting to lead an almighty charge against Conn himself, but first we'd need to disengage from the enemy so that we could safely regroup.

But, on seeing Mogha raising his shield, the formidable Conall of Cruachan could spot exactly where he was. The Fir-bolg King ran through the crowded battlefield, keeping his head low so that he wouldn't be spotted, hurrying towards him, using the tactical manoeuvre of the 'crouched rush of a Champion'.

Mogha's maternal grandfather, Flann, son of Fiacra, the heroic Lord of Ormond, saw exactly what Conall was doing. To quickly protect his grandson, he lowered his spear, levelling it with the ground, and sprinted towards Conall, before letting it fly. The spear flew fast, straight and true. Bang! It hit the Fir-bolg King right in his side with such force that the spear carried on straight through his body, until the tip stuck out the other side. Severely injured, Conall collapsed to the ground, being trampled under the feet of the many frantic battling warriors.

Whilst this was happening, Mogha continued to gather our men together, pulling us back, away from the melee so that we could regroup. But the enemy wouldn't stop; they chased us hard, not giving us a chance to get organized.

After many leagues of frantic running, being chased over the uneven terrain, our two treacherous enemies, MacNiadh and Conaire, at the head of their own Munster troops, managed to finally catch us. We now found ourselves in the south of Éile.

They fought hard against the courageous, young Mogha Nuadhad, concentrating most of their vicious assault against him. The wounds they inflicted were horrific. Luckily, we had some brave and valiant men with us that day, who managed to rescue our young king before he was too badly wounded, and hastened him away from our formidable foes.

The enemy forces now had to rest as they'd suffered too many wounds themselves to continue their pursuit.

Knowing that the chase was over for now, our injured young king ordered his trusted druid, Dearg Damhsa to return back to the field of battle. He wanted the druid to ask the High-king for some time to decide our next move; this was a courtesy that only honourable men would dare ask or could expect to receive.

Mogha Nuadhad took control once more, pushing us onward, heading towards the Cooling Stream that flowed across the Plain of Femen. Despite losing his father, our brave young king was still very much in command and was able to function well. That's what it looked like to us anyway. The full shock hadn't completely hit home.

When Dearg Damhsa arrived back at Conn's camp, accompanied by a small retinue, he asked for three days and three nights for Mogha Nuadhad to make his battle-plans. With Conn wanting the war to continue in an honourable fashion, he graciously agreed. Whilst there, the druid humbly asked for permission to bury Mogha's father in a King's grave. Conn kindly gave his consent to this as well.

So, the Munster Chief-druid ordered his men to build a large turf burial-mound around the fallen body of our beloved old King. And with the obvious dignified reverence that befitted such a deeply emotional and solemn occasion, the turf was piled up, burying Magha Neid inside, along with his trusted weapons and armour.

Due to the overwhelming might of Conn's men, Dearg Damhsa re-named that fateful meadow *Magh Tualaing*, which means the 'Plain of Might'.

The Chief-seanchaí was not there to recite the old king's pedigree, and our Chief-poet was not there to compose the funeral song. Therefore, that sad task fell to our faithful druid, who stood at the graveside, with a tear in his wise old eyes, as he sang a dirge to his beloved ruler:

*Magha Neid lies in a grave on the Plain of Might,*
*By his strong shoulder lies his spear;*
*With his club that was strong in combat and fight,*
*With helmet and sword which caus'd fear.*

*His life was not easily ended,*
*The true head of the Heberian tribe,*
*While ancestral lands he defended,*
*Equalled Eochaidh Mumha we said with pride.*

*Father and son together they fought,*
*Side by side in mortal strife.*
*Good was the cast of Flann who sought,*
*His spear through Conall, saved Eoghan's life.*

*Magha Neid marched into war on the Plain of Might*
*To save the life of his son, for fear.*
*Long he'll be grieved for after this night;*
*His death will cause dark sorrow and tear.*

*Long he'll be grieved for after this night;*
*The Munster King in his grave lies here.*

It must have taken us at least another five hours of solid marching before we reached the Cooling Stream. And as it was starting to get dark, there we rested, remaining there until we'd received word from Dearg Damhsa. The thin, meandering stream certainly lived up to its name as many of us rested upon its grassy banks cooling our tired feet and splashing water upon our warm brows. During that break in the fighting, many of the men were first gripped with that debilitating malady of grief, unable to do anything other than despair.

It was there, upon the Plain of Femen that we camped that night, posting trusted guards to help keep us safe. It was during the quiet darkness of that first night that the enormity of Magha Neid's death first hit the rest of us. We were all in a state of shock, although some handled it better than others. As the sun went down, I experienced one of the toughest nights of my life. It took a very long time to come to terms with the fact that we would never see or hear him again. The whole camp was in an overwhelming state of grief. Then the shock finally hit Mogha Nuadhad; and the poor lad turned mournfully silent trying to cope with his own personal unending sorrow.

There were many horrific wounds that needed urgent attention during nightfall and many grown men went to bed with tears in their eyes, thinking of their old King's bravery and his shocking death; the whole camp really was in complete disbelief. We each found ourselves trapped within our own personal solitary and wretched numbness. To think of a man that big who was always so full of life to be suddenly no more. It made me think how much pain those sons of Milesius must have endured after the death of their own legendary father. I still spend dark nights caught up in a melancholic daze, lamenting upon the intense misery of losing such a great man as Magha Neid.

The following evening the red druid returned, meeting us at our agreed rendezvous. He told us of Conn's gracious agreement to temporarily cease hostilities. This was the news that we'd all been hoping for. This meant that Conn wouldn't reach our plain for another three days. Taking another night's rest by the banks of that refreshingly cool water, we slept well, knowing that we were safe, for now.

The following morning, Mogha Nuadhad pushed us onward once more, heading westwards, leading us deep into the kingdom of Munster, towards the mountains on the border between Desmond and Iarmuman, and to the safety of the Valley of Horses. It must have taken nearly four days of travelling to reach our destination. What slowed us down considerably was that on our way we were joined by shepherds and cowherds who brought with them a great many sheep and cattle. These animals weren't the fastest of movers, but their meat was greatly required to feed our many men.

I still don't know how our young king was able to motivate us, as we were all like lifeless, apathetic beings back then. But thankfully Mogha Nuadhad was rapidly becoming a hardened leader, which was just what we all needed.

After Conn's three-day peace treaty had ended, he followed us south, along the Sister River and into Munster. On his way he plundered many territories, stealing as much as his army could carry, taking also hostages and cattle. Whilst the gravely injured Conall of Cruachan, along with his friend, Goll, at the head of Clan Morna, headed westwards, along the Road of Dalo, crossing the River of the Plain, over the Plain of Waterfalls and past the Mountain of Rushes, they marched into Iarmuman, completely ransacking that territory. They took hostages and any spoils that they could find. What they couldn't carry they destroyed with sword and flame. Those Fir-bolg leaders were a cruel breed.

By this time, we were completely hidden within the Valley of Horses. It was the perfect place to conceal ourselves within the wide glen that was cut so deep into the mountains that we were surrounded on three sides by steep, green and grey rocky slopes, one of which was the towering, majestic mountain of *An Mhangarta*: 'The Longhaired' Mountain.

With having the foresight to bring a whole herd of cattle and a full flock of sheep there was plenty to eat, and with three lakes hidden within the valley there was plenty to drink as well. We could have happily stayed there for a period of at least a good-many moons, if not for many years. No outsiders would have dreamt of looking for us there. Unfortunately, MacNiadh and Conaire weren't outsiders; they knew this kingdom like the back of their hand. And they also knew that this was the obvious place for us to hide. They led Conn straight to us. Those two traitors had been invaluable to Conn, not only as expert guides, but also as leaders of their own considerable army as well. They'd arrived at our destination within a relatively short time, despite their men being weighed down with so much heavy plunder. Conall of Cruachan and Clan Morna turned up shortly thereafter, carrying their own pillaged goods.

Our king had carefully picked this place, not only because we were completely hidden, but also because the paths were so narrow that only a small string of invaders could pass through at any one time. It gave us the only advantage we had. Thus, with a few archers and spearmen in place, along the banks, ready to pick off the first enemy warriors who dared to pass through we still had some advantage, although we knew that we couldn't hold them off indefinitely and we'd eventually be overrun as Conn's army greatly outnumbered ours.

But before the war could recommence the High-king wanted confirmation as to what dangers lay hidden within the valley, for he knew that as he would obviously be leading the attack, he would undoubtedly be the first one to face mortal danger. Therefore, with this thought in mind, at the head of a small retinue, he slowly made his way up *An Mhangarta* where he could safely overlook the scene below.

It took only a few hours of climbing for him to reach a suitable position where he could gaze down into the valley. As he stood there, high up upon the slopes of *An Mhangarta*, close to where the mountain met the sky, Conn could clearly see what lay below: the first thing that stood out were our many tents that stood near to those three large lakes, then he noticed the large number of animals, which looked like two small pale clouds within the green and grey coloured landscape. As his eyes began to focus on the shapes in the distance he began to notice where our troops were positioned and the numbers at our disposal, as he could see that we were all spread out busying ourselves, gathering firewood, foraging and exploring.

We were shocked to see him standing high up upon the mountainside. And then we heard the noisy clash of metal and the thunderous footsteps of his troops approaching, so we knew that our time was drawing to a close. We were completely cut off and greatly outnumbered, so we knew that as soon as the battle began there would be no escape and we would eventually all perish. It was then that Mogha Nuadhad made the incredibly generous and noble decision to allow any of our men who wanted to be spared from fighting, to leave his side and go over to our treacherous enemies, MacNiadh and Conaire. He couldn't bear the thought of any more of our esteemed warriors being needlessly killed.

Most of our men agreed, as they knew that staying with our king would almost certainly mean death, therefore they took the humiliating decision to join with Munster's two traitorous enemies. I thought at the time that they were cowards and I cursed them for leaving. But really it was without doubt the intelligent thing to do. I prayed to the gods later that night that I had been brave enough to go with them. But I don't know if I could have lived with myself for making such a decision, for sometimes honour is all we have.

As the daylight was now starting to fade, Conn decided to postpone his attack on us until the following day, so he asked the two traitors where best they could find sustenance for their army. Knowing that *Carn Buidhe*: the Yellow Cairn, which stood close to the bay of *Ceann Mara* was nearby, they led Conn and his men south-westerly towards that large, yellow thatched tavern. A small number of Conn's troops were left to guard the entrance to the valley, making sure that we didn't escape before the High-king's vast army returned.

The Yellow Cairn was a favourite haunt of all Munster travellers who found themselves anywhere near these parts; they were drawn to it like moths to a flame. The building was huge, housing many rooms within, with a magnificent thatched roof made of bright yellow reeds, which encompassed most of the building, almost down to the ground, whilst the doorway stood out proudly, being the shape of a man's pursed lips blowing upon a fire. In the surrounding grounds, many farmyard animals could be heard, as these were always needed to supply hungry travellers. It was there that Conn made camp for the night. Our own deserting troops had gone with them, being now part of Conn's vast army. But by the time that Conn's men had reached the inn, every one of our deserting warriors had already wandered off, deserting once more.

As night closed in, Conn's Fir-bolg began singing. They weren't all known as great singers but when they got together, and ale was freely flowing, their light voices would harmonize over the sound of their skilled flute playing, singing their ancient songs from times and lands long ago. These mesmerizing, otherworldly songs were always sung in their old tongue.

During that long night, with the Valley of Horses being so dark, our spies had managed to silently creep up the sides of the mountains, completely bypassing the guards at the entrance, to scout around to get a good lay of the land. On their return, they informed us that our own deserting troops had already abandoned the High-king and, hearing that Conn had picked such a vulnerable place in which to make his camp, Mogha realised that this would be our best chance to launch an attack. He knew that we were completely outnumbered by the enemy forces and we certainly didn't have enough men to fight another daytime battle, so he ordered our loyal, remaining warriors to surprise Conn in his camp just before first light. We knew that this wasn't an honourable action; but what choice did we have? Our honour lay in the fact that we were fighting against a much larger force; so, we hoped that the gods would understand and aid our cause and forgive us for attacking before daybreak.

So, clambering up the banks of that dim moonlit mountain, as silently as we could, making our way up the steep and treacherous slopes, as our spies now acted as our guides, leading us out of the hidden valley, and from there we made our escape.

We now headed towards the Yellow Cairn, even though our numbers were small. It felt good to escape Conn's guards, yet our freedom would likely be short-lived as we were heading towards an even greater danger and very possibly death. But at least we were fighting on our own terms and for what we greatly believed in: honour and freedom.

We quietly gathered on the outskirts of Conn's dimly lit campsite where most of his men were still soundly sleeping. And around the huge, hulking shadowy shape of the Yellow Cairn many tents stood, barely illuminated by the last rays of moonlight. It was a cloudless night and the stars above burned with an incredible intensity. The very air seemed so very still although the gentle sounds of snoring permeated throughout that vast campsite. The High-king's nobles, along with his Champions were still asleep within the Yellow Cairn, whilst before us lay the majority of his forces, abed in tents that were scattered around the surrounding plain; although some of the poorer soldiers were left to sleep under the stars, keeping warm beside the dying embers of the barely-glowing campfires.

We moved slowly from the shadows, trying not to make a sound. It was Conn's Night Watch who were the first to see us. Their loud cries raised the alarm. Hearing the commotion woke Conn inside the tavern; he immediately gave the order for his soldiers to rise up from all corners and attack our small group. The tides quickly turned, and our bold attack now became a desperate bid to defend ourselves against the furious, frenzied, onslaught.

It certainly wasn't a fair or just fight as a steady stream of Conn's men all targeted Mogha Nuadhad, and as we greatly lacked numbers, it meant that he had to fight them off almost single-handedly himself. We did our best to protect him, but couldn't get near, as the tide of enemy soldiers were far too dense to cut through.

Mogha knew that he couldn't retreat before he'd given them a full taste of his steel; his sense of honour was too great for that. And being compelled to get revenge for his father's death, and with the odds being so overwhelmingly against him, he took on a battle-fury, throwing himself forcefully at his enemy as he looked around wildly for Conn. Mogha furiously chopped through his enemies. He exploded through them like a galley bursting from her anchor, surging forward with all his might. An astonishing number of enemies were slaughtered within the next few minutes. Mogha Nuadhad was like a wild beast.

This went on and on relentlessly, until Mogha Nuadhad came face to face with the ruthless, savage Champion who'd killed his father: the mighty one-eyed Fir-bolg Chieftain, Goll, son of Morna. These two esteemed leaders, who each possessed an enormous inner strength, now faced each other; their brave warriors' eyes burning with hatred. So much so that a watchful bard noted that 'their eyes blazed within their heads like the sparkling of the stars on a frosty night'... whilst...'their breasts heaved like the bellows of a smith blowing upon a flame': so intense was each of their fury. They attacked with such viciousness, these two fierce warriors, ferociously wounding each other in this desperate, formidable battle. Yet all the while, as they fought, a steady stream of enemies still came against our King. So Mogha Nuadhad had to fight not just against the mighty Goll, but against the rest of Conn's unending tide of troops as well. It wasn't long before our last remaining men, including myself, had become so severely wounded, that we were barely able to defend ourselves, let alone aid our King.

By now the sun had risen, flooding the scene of battle with glorious daylight. Conn's men continued their furious attack, desperately trying to overpower our leader. But Mogha, with that nobleness of his blood, the strength of his heart and mind, the height of his spirit and that excessive bravery of power and will, just kept going. It was these attributes that kept Mogha on his feet and battling like a ferocious madman. Our enemies couldn't believe the number of warriors that he was slaying, even though we were all so greatly outnumbered. Mogha Nuadhad was fighting as though he were a hundred Champions. It was incredible to see.

Mogha luckily had, not far from that place, a much-loved and powerful Sídhe-mistress called Eadaoin of *Inis Crecraighe*. This beautiful, golden-haired Fairy sensed that Mogha was in mortal danger and quickly came to his aid.

Upon the beach of *Ceann Mara* stood a large limestone rock; it had been there since the beginning of time. It was known locally as *Cloch Barraighe* and was cube-shaped with each face measuring seven yards wide. Finding ourselves on the beach, Eadaoin magically transformed the rock to look like Mogha, whilst the stones strewn around were conjured to look like our own men, guarding him. Then she spirited us away, with her powerful skills of sorcery, though Mogha was anxious to remain. She took us to the safety of her Fairy-ships, which were moored further down the shore. Goll and his men ferociously carried on their attack, battering away at the rocks thinking that they were still attacking their enemy. The clattering of their weapons echoing around the hills, being heard for many leagues around. It wasn't long before they'd broken many good swords and spears, and what they hadn't broken had become seriously worn. When Conn realised what was happening, he roared, "Cease your striking; these are only rugged-headed rocks that you're fighting. Mogha Nuadhad's escaped".

Then the startled Goll looked up and was instantly brought back to reality. He realised the embarrassment of the situation. His foes had indeed escaped in the swift Fairy-ships. From that time, this encounter has forever been known as the Battle of *Cloch Barraighe*.

After Conn watched the ships swiftly sailing out of the bay, southwards, he ordered his men to pack away their camp and follow. The men quickly did as they were ordered. Before long, they too were heading southwards, to try to pursue us, and our fleeing Munster King, to see if they could find where we would resurface.

Far into Munster those enemy troops headed, travelling well into the day, until the light once more began to fade. It was then that they finally made camp, a league or two to the southeast of the Bay of Beann's Clan. But that nearby bay was where Eadaoin's island lay, just five leagues from the shore in the direction of the enemy camp. And being presented with such a close target, Mogha Nuadhad couldn't resist leading us back over to the mainland in those Fairy-ships, so we could once more attack Conn whilst he remained as a most unwelcome guest asleep within our noble kingdom.

After sailing along the bay and mooring our Fairy-ships beside the shore, Mogha Nuadhad led our small company of warriors silently across country on another clandestine attack upon Conn's new campsite.

It took just over an hour for us to walk there, but the time was not as late as our last attack so there were still some soldiers left awake and the low murmuring of voices and the warm smoky smell of recently cooked food warned us of the immediate danger just ahead. As we neared, we could see that the whole area was well-lit with the bright orange glow of large flickering campfires and wandering guards holding torches aloft lest they be surprised again. So as soon as we neared a watchful guard spotted us and the hue and cry went out. With having our surprise attack discovered, we just hacked away at everyone that we encountered. Astonishingly we managed to kill three-and-a-half-hundred of Conn's host. Then just as quickly as we'd entered the camp, we made our escape. Mogha swiftly led us out into the fields and away into the darkness. Conn's enraged army, ruthlessly seeking revenge soon followed behind.

A witch called Siomha, who was a heroine of Clan Morna, jumped into her chariot and gave chase. She tightly gripped a wand of ash, using it as a horse-switch to drive her two stallions faster. Her wand wasn't fashioned from any of the seven sacred trees but still it held her power. As quick as we were sprinting away, Siomha was steadily catching up. Conn's other pursuing warriors were a long way behind. We headed straight for the nearby ford. Everyone knows that witches can't cross running water, so that was our best chance of escape, and she knew it. She frantically drove her horses onward. By their pounding hoofbeats we could hear them nearing. The powerful witch was getting closer and closer by the second. I've never felt so frightened in my entire life. The rush of the river ahead added to the urgency of the situation. Suddenly her swift chariot rumbled past us, as if the devil himself was pulling it.

Turning her chariot, she barred our escape. High up she stood, shrouded in a shimmering grey-cloak, with eyes blazing and a large red mane billowing in the wind. The moonlight danced upon her lively hair as though it was aflame. She truly was a terrifying sight.

We were halted in our tracks, almost bent double, puffing and panting. Behind us our enemy were catching up fast, as their torchlight neared in the dark. I watched as our young hero wiped the glistening sweat from his brow. We stood there for what was probably seconds, but in our immediate danger it felt like an eternity. We knew that at any second the witch would destroy us, unless the rapidly approaching mob tore us apart first. Mogha stared at the witch, bravely standing his ground. A complete sheen of cold sweat now oiled my entire body. My heartbeat thundered faster and faster as the nearby river roared by.

Mogha knew that he needed to steer a clear, mental path through our frenzied plight. He needed to block out all the distracting images of failure, as well as the nearing enemy troops, and focus on what needed to be done. He'd been training to cast shots like this since childhood. Before the witch had time to use her magic, with Mogha's mighty strength he launched his spear. It flew through the air, flying true. Then BANG! It hit her dead centre; it hit her with such force that it knocked Siomha, her chariot, as well as her two horses into the river. SPLASH! Siomha died before she'd time to cast her spells. And her two horses and chariot were washed downstream where the chariot smashed to pieces in another ford, further down that violent river.

Mogha took Siomha's fallen wand and thrust it into the ground near the river where she'd fell; it suddenly sprang to life, magically taking root in the earth and from there it grew into a mighty ash. We didn't have time to gasp. Our urgent need to escape was far too compelling, as Conn's huge army were quickly closing in. We ran westward, splashing through that turbulent knee-high river and away.

Before long, a detachment of the Connacht army had neared. They were quickly catching us up, being almost spear-length away. Their lively, flickering torches were so close we could actually feel their heat warming our backs. Mogha suddenly turned. He swiftly despatched the Fir-bolg son of the Connacht King. We joined in the skirmish and killed one-and-a-half-hundred of his men. With this immediate danger now being over, we quickly made our escape, running as fast as our legs would carry us.

We headed into the nearby woodland, now known as Battle-wood. Passing by the moonlit trees, each brimming with their own unique character; some I could swear looked like they had faces, whilst others were twisted and gnarled. There were even some that resembled many-limbed sea-creatures. These sentinels of nature were so beautifully grotesque, appearing to be sculpted to a lunatic's design. In the daylight they wouldn't have looked half so intimidating. It was behind the wide oaks that we hid, there in the dark, crouching low, as the hems of our tunics became soaked from the sodden, spongy moss underfoot. We breathed in the pungent, almost smoky aroma of rotting oak leaves upon the forest floor, as we waited there, our own panting breaths and drumming heartbeats almost deafening us.

As the footsteps of Conn's swift-footed advance guard approached, their torches lighting up the area, we leapt out, in a surprise attack. Finding them unprepared for an ambush, we killed many more of them, before the remainder fled. Not stopping in the clearing, we crept away, further back into the shadows and there we waited.

Shortly after, when their comrades came upon their dead bodies, lying in the woods, barely lit by the discarded torches that now glowed with dying flames, they were too afraid to continue their pursuit, as behind any of these trees could hide an enemy. Thence they too cautiously retreated. Only then could we finally disappear into the darkness and vanish from out of their reach.

Now that our frantic nocturnal battling was over, Mogha saw us safely return back to Eadaoin's Fairy-ships. On boarding, we immediately set sail, at a slow but steady pace, escaping across the bay, powered by what seemed like a magical wind. As you can imagine, we were all totally exhausted and suffering from many bloodied and gaping wounds. We sailed over to Eadaoin's island of *Inis Crecraighe* that sat in the mouth of the Bay of Beann's Clan, and it was there that we were finally able to pause for breath within the safety of her tranquil stone ringfort, whilst our scars and wounds were carefully tended. And there we abided for nine restful days until we'd all fully recovered.

The battle on the mainland was over, for now. And so, to the victor belongs the spoils. When Conn realized that we weren't returning for an immediate rematch, as he guessed how wounded we must have been, he claimed our great Kingdom of Munster for himself, dividing it into two, so that his sons-in-law, MacNiadh and Conaire could rule one half each. Conn was now able to return home at his leisure. He ruled the land without any more trouble whilst our heroic king was away. His competent spies keeping a watch all the while, around the Munster coastline, waiting and watching for Mogha's unwelcome return.

Those nine days passed quickly enough, enjoying the comforts of the Fairy's isle. Mogha was now back to his full strength and desperately wanted to return to the mainland to continue his war against Conn. But Eadaoin had other plans for us, "If thou hadst stayed on this island for a single day, then a full year thou wouldst have to remain abroad. But as thou hast abided here for nine days, then a full term of nine years thou wilt have to keep thyself away from Ériu".

Obviously, we were all completely shocked at hearing what the Fairy had to say, but she'd never guided us wrong before. Mogha Nuadhad started shaking his head in disbelief.

Eadaoin continued, "Thou knowest my wisdom to be true. During thine exile a fateful quest shalt take thee beyond the sea, to the wondrous Kingdom of Castile". She paused once more to let us take in the magnitude of her words before continuing. "To aid thee, I've prepared a 'Path of Protection' that shalt keep thee from harm till thy safe return".

Mogha carefully took the note from his Sídhe-mistress; he glanced at the words of the magical verse before putting them safely away. He completely trusted Eadaoin and knew that by chanting the words of the charm their power would be released, thereby keeping us all safe. I could tell by looking at him, that he really didn't want to take the quest; but what choice did he have? Eadaoin would never let any harm come to Mogha Nuadhad, and she did have the power of Foreknowledge, as many of her people had, so he really had no choice but to follow her wise counsel; we all knew that disaster would strike if we dared to take any other course.

I feel that I really need to explain this mystical Art of Foreknowledge. It was also called 'Second Sight' and could be learned by humans as well as Sídhe-folk. In Man, it manifested itself in different ways. For example, if those who'd developed this art had seen the vision of a dead body within a dwelling, then they knew that they would encounter the corpse of that person within that same house sometime in the very near future. Or if they saw someone in the flesh with, for example, the apparition of an arrow sticking out of their leg, then they knew that that person was going to be shot in the very same place by a very real arrow. The Aes

Sídhe seem to have much stronger visions of Foreknowledge than the race of Man and all those wanting to make use of these skills, needed to desperately avoid iron as that metal alone had the power to completely inhibit their visions.

Eadaoin kindly gave us a good ship in which to travel, along with plentiful supplies.

As our small group of warriors slowly departed, she said to Mogha, "May the road succeed with thee, young King", before she wished us all a "Safe Journey".

So onwards we travelled, continuing our adventure, going back to sea. Mogha chanted the words of the charm before we'd lost sight of the land; the words going up into the air to offer protection to our ship.

For nine days we sailed, across the vast Sea of Darkness, heading southwards towards Castile.

Heber the Great, son of Midna, was king of that magnificent land; he was a mighty ruler, held in high esteem by his people. He was proud and strong with dark hair whose two long braids hung down to either side of his face, whilst a short, cropped beard graced his manly chin. He favoured a scarlet gown with a matching cloak whilst a large golden crown sat regally above his brow. There was no mistaking the rugged nobility of this man.

Heber had an affectionate, highly-honourable, yet maiden daughter, known as the princess Beara. Her long, brown hair always seemed to catch the light as she walked and with her fresh, radiant pale skin and wondrous brown eyes that anyone could easily get lost in, it made her, without doubt, one of the most beautiful women in the world. She was always exquisitely dressed, as befitted her noble station; even her shoes were made by master craftsmen, wrought from pure gold. The princess was forever accompanied by half-a-hundred obedient handmaidens, who took care of her every whim.

King Heber, worrying that very morning, that Beara hadn't yet met a man worthy enough to be her husband, had sent for his wise High-druid, Dadrona, to ask for his counsel.

The druid came immediately on hearing the summons, his white robes gently shimmering in the warm afternoon breeze.

"Who will my daughter marry?" Heber anxiously asked the druid.

"I can easily tell you that", answered Dadrona, without hesitation. "A nobleman, of royal blood, who has claim to a kingdom as large as your own, and whose ancestors are of our own Celtic blood will arrive on these shores at nightfall and he shall wed the princess".

Well, the king was quite taken aback at hearing this news and couldn't quite believe the druid's words, but Dadrona assured him that it was all completely true, and he went on to tell him all about Mogha Nuadhad and his many accomplishments in the lands of Ériu.

So, when we arrived at the port of Castile, later that same evening, we were astonished to be greeted with such enormous affection, as news of our fame, or should I say of Mogha Nuadhad's fame, and of all of his heroic adventures had filtered throughout the whole town. Everyone had heard of his amazing deeds. The streets were full of crowds cheering for him. And we, by our association with him, were very well met. The people had so much love for Mogha that before Beara had even seen him she'd already fallen in love; and as soon as Mogha had met the beautiful princess he too fell instantly and madly in love with her. Thence, it wasn't long before these two young paramours were rightfully betrothed.

What a beautiful, warm, welcoming place Castile turned out to be. And during our time there, what fabulous feasts we ate. The King's table was never empty, and the meals went on long into the evening. Two things that I shall forever remember from those royal tables was that hearty and comforting garlic soup filled so full of good stale bread and flavoured with spicy paprika, and those ornate glasses of good strong red wine. I enjoyed all the food, but those two things remain so strongly in my heart.

At that time in Spain, it was said that once a year a giant salmon would swim the length of the mighty River Ebro. The fish had long, dagger-like teeth and was covered in the most exquisite golden scales. Whilst we were there in Castile, King Heber went in search of this legendary creature: the Golden Salmon, as it was called. After a lengthy battle the king managed to land the fish upon the shore. Its leather-like skin was carefully stripped from the creature, cleaned and tanned and given to Beara, who made the most beautiful shiny-golden cloak, as a wedding gift, which she gave to her new husband on their handfasting day. The local Spaniards couldn't believe how beautiful the cloak was; it was almost as bright as the sun and its shiny, shimmering surface changed colours in the light, like a metallic rainbow turned to cloth; it lit up Mogha's face, glowing in different colours. Due to this extraordinary garment, the locals began calling him 'Eoghan the Splendid' and everyone for leagues around marvelled at his visual magnificence.

During those early joyful days, Mogha and Beara had three children together; their plump, belligerent little son was named *Mais*: meaning 'Mass' or 'Lump', whilst their two sweet-natured daughters were called *Caomheall:* meaning 'Beautiful' or 'Beloved' and *Scothniamh*: meaning 'Shining-blossom'.

Time passed both quickly and slowly for us, in equal measure, in that distant land with some days seeming to fly past quickly whilst others dragged, as we slept each afternoon to avoid the searing heat of the mid-day sun, before feasting throughout those pleasant cooler evenings, so it was obviously only a matter of time before we'd been away from our homeland for those full nine years. Knowing that the day had now come for us to return home brought back to us an ever-increasing number of pleasant memories, thinking of all those family and friends whom we'd been forced to abandon, and of the breath-taking landscape of Munster. The more we thought about returning, the more homesick we felt; the pain of our separation was really starting to take its toll. So Mogha approached the king and told him of our plans. Obviously, King Heber didn't want us to leave, as we were now such an integral part of his court, but seeing how desperate the young Ériu King was, he calmly told him, "I can see that you need to go. Take my son, Fraoch the Militant at the head of his army of two thousand troops; he'll back you with his strength and support you against your powerful enemies".

Mogha enthusiastically agreed. We were overjoyed to be taking such an impressive army of well-trained warriors back home with us. We pictured the looks on our enemy's faces as we marched home leading this vast army. We hoped that the shock alone would kill all those who'd chased us from our homes. The thought of it made us grin till our faces hurt.

Shortly after, we took the King's leave, taking with us our new army of Spanish allies from those warm-hearted lands of Iberia. But as we prepared to say our goodbyes, it suddenly hit us what we were leaving behind. We'd made so many good friends in Castile, and the fabulous Spanish hospitality that we'd enjoyed was something that we were dearly going to miss; it would leave me with an empty feeling for quite some time.

The king kindly gave us a whole fleet of galleys to transport our impressive army, as well as goats for each vessel, as well as hundreds of amphorae, some filled with good red wine, some filled with water, and to my great surprise, and delight, some were even filled with that hearty and comforting garlic soup that we had grown so accustomed to. There were many tearful farewells as we headed towards our awaiting ships. Many people came to see us leave, wishing us all a safe journey. King Heber was especially sad to see his sweet, beloved daughter leaving his Kingdom. We all took a long time to say our goodbyes as neither side were really wanting to part, but we all knew that it was the right thing to do.

As we sadly bid our last farewells, we reluctantly climbed into our ships before slowly rowing through the calm seas and past the safety of the Iberian harbour, towards the Sea of Darkness once more.

It was upon entering the open sea that Mogha Nuadhad began chanting the words of his Path of Protection. But even with this precaution in place and the fact that the safety of the harbour was still in sight, it didn't prevent our nightmare journey from beginning as the wind and sea suddenly began to war with each other, both of them flinging our ships away from the direction in which we were heading; it was a dreadful struggle to row through such a terrible storm. Some of the men even joked that the violent winds must be caused by Donn, Lord of the Dead, riding through the clouds, for so terrible it all was.

Then, after a few days, amidst the storm, grotesque Sea-monsters came up from the black depths, terrifying us all. Some were even bigger than our galleys, having many long, slender limbs, which tried to grab all those in sight; whilst other creatures with gigantic eyes looked up from beneath the waves, trying to gaze into our very souls. But still we rowed hard, escaping those horrific demons, all the time heading northwards. During a short lull in the storm, a brave lookout clambered up the mast to keep watch, gazing out towards the distant horizons upon all sides and the endless azure ocean that held no land in sight.

Then the storm resumed, with waves the size of a fortress smashing against our many vessels. We had no choice but to keep going. Mogha Nuadhad clutched his Path of Protection, loudly chanting out those few magical verses; his belief in the power of Eadaoin's words was unshakable.

Eventually, after many weeks of struggling through this nightmare journey, the sea and wind at last made peace. This calmness meant that we could finally raise our masts. Our spirits steadily grew as we felt that the worst of it was over and we sailed onwards, heading in the direction of the Fairy's island of *Inis Crecraighe*.

A few more weeks passed, thankfully quite peacefully, before we finally spotted land. And then the sudden, happy chattering of the crews filled the boats as a huge sense of relief flooded through us all. Enthusiastically, we sailed forward. Our lengthy sea voyage was at last coming to an end.

It wasn't long before we were safely ensconced within the shelter of the southern harbour of the faithful Fairy's enchanted island; and the gallant Munster King proudly renamed it *Oileán Béarra*, or Beara Island, after his wife, as it was the first part of his Kingdom on which she stood.

Eadaoin quietly beamed with excitement at seeing Mogha Nuadhad return, even though she had obviously sensed that he was coming. She warmly wished him and his bride, "A hundred-thousand welcomes".

After Mogha had fully rested, Eadaoin told him the important news that he desperately needed to hear: all three rulers of Munster were together under one roof and if he went straight there, he could capture them all.

"Slay them not", warned Eadaoin, "but allow them to yield, and demand hostages".

Mogha wisely agreed. But before he set his large army onto them, he first wanted to give them the chance to bend their knee and submit to his kingship, so he sent his trusted druid to the Yellow Cairn, as that was where they were feasting, to ask for their immediate surrender.

That very afternoon, inside the thatched yellow Munster tavern, sat MacNiadh, Conaire and Mogha Nuadhad's grandfather, Flann, son of Fiacra, the Lord of Ormond, who'd now allied himself with those two traitorous Lords. There were many other highborn there and the place was obviously well guarded.

As Dearg Damhsa approached the crowded building he could hear all the hilarity and mirthful conversations from within. He stood there for a moment listening, before approaching the yellow thatched entrance that stood out proudly from its walls. Two solidly-built doormen stood outside, barring the way, armed with maces, wearing leather aprons whilst grey speckled mantles draped across their large shoulders. From inside, the smell of beef slowly roasting along with the unmistakable odour of generously-flowing ale drifted through the doorway. The druid graciously asked to speak to the three princes within. A messenger was called to relay the request to those inside. A reply came back shortly thereafter that they didn't wish to speak to him.

The angry Chief-druid bravely stood at the doorway, his bright coppery hair, and his beard now subtly tinged with grey, still shone in the sunlight. He venomously shouted at the nobles inside, threatening to curse them all. MacNiadh quickly came to the door, lest he be damned by the famous red druid.

After the wrathful druid had calmed down, MacNiadh eagerly asked him, "What news of Mogha Nuadhad?"

"He's already in the Kingdom and if you freely submit hostages and prepare oaths of allegiance then you'll be spared. Otherwise, he'll attack; and with him is the warring prince, Fraoch the Militant, son of Heber the Great, along with two-thousand Spanish warriors".

MacNiadh replied, "In the numbers that they come, they shall not return".

Hearing Conaire's wife, Sara, speaking within, the Chief-druid urged, "If you'll not yield, then at least allow Sara, daughter of Conn to leave, so she will not perish". He went on, "You three Lords of Munster are brave men indeed, but Fraoch is a man of might and high repute; a man whom chains cannot stop".

No matter how much Dearg Damhsa insisted, MacNiadh still wouldn't see sense, so the disappointed druid returned back to Mogha Nuadhad to tell him of their blatant refusal.

On hearing these unwelcome tidings, our furious king immediately gathered all of us together and we quickly and silently sailed over to the Munster shore aboard our many ships. It felt good to be back on Munster soil but there was no time to dwell on this as there was much work to be done.

Eadaoin skilfully used her magic to confuse the guards so that they couldn't see us approaching. We then swiftly surrounded the inn so that no-one could leave without a fight.

When MacNiadh, Conaire and the elderly Flann realised the desperation of the situation and that they didn't have any choice, they reluctantly surrendered; they gave Mogha Nuadhad the hostages that he demanded and solemnly pledged their allegiance. To celebrate, Mogha took command of their night's feast, and we all ate well. This became our victory feast. It certainly felt good to be home. And much ale was drunk that night.

The following day we all arose from our well-earned slumber to find that we had many visitors, as everyone from leagues around were keen to bend their knee and pay homage to the rightful King of Munster who'd returned to reclaim his throne.

With Mogha having now regained control of his family's ancient seat, he knew that if he wanted to keep it, he would have to wage war against his old enemy, Conn of the Hundred-battles. And the only way to stand any chance of defeating the mighty High-king was to amass a much larger, more powerful army than he presently had. With this aim in mind, he sent a trusted messenger to his brave ally, Fiacha the Lame, the well-loved Lord of Hy Kinsella; who reigned over the large southernmost region of Leinster.

The messenger delivered Mogha's communication perfectly, reminding him that it was Conn who'd killed his father at the battle of Magh Agha; it was also during that terrible conflict that he'd received his disabling leg wound. And it was also Conn who'd come up with the humiliating nickname which described him as Fiacha 'the Lame'. Crippled he may have been, but the bearing and dignity of a Leinster prince he still had, commanding the full respect of all whom he encountered. Now that Mogha Nuadhad was back in Ériu, and with the full backing of his hereditary Kingdom, along with a new army of two thousand loyal Spanish warriors, it was time to exact revenge. The spirited Fiacha, who was the youngest brother of Mogha's foster-father, Dáire Barrach, didn't need any reminding of his family's loyalty to the Munster King, as he already thought of himself as a blood ally. So, with this thought in mind, he gladly agreed to join forces and rebel against the High-king, as well as his own unjust Leinster King, Crimthann Yellow-hair, who'd been put on the throne by Conn after that same fateful battle. Whilst the messenger was concluding his business in the east, Mogha Nuadhad's trusted Chief-druid was sent northwards to the King of Ulster, who ruled from the magnificent red fortress known as *Emain Macha*, the 'Twins of Macha', home of the Red Branch Knights.

Dearg Damhsa was excited to be visiting the northern stronghold as it had such an enormous reputation for its generous hospitality, but still his journey was filled with anxiety as he knew not how the meeting would conclude as affairs of war were often fraught with tension. I know not at which port he landed, or to be fair if he actually travelled there by ship or by land, but sea would have been the safer option. The Twins of Macha was famous for being the most opulent fortress in all the land. Their proud boast was that no other royal fort in Ériu could match it for either its extravagant hospitality or for its lavish wine-feasts, for its swift, graceful steeds or for its border-patrolling charioteers, for its poets or its brave men, for its servants or its stout-hearted messengers, for its silks, satins or cloths of gold, for its warriors friendly and fair, or for its drinking or its chess playing. And above all, no one was ever refused a request either for a present or for a fight; although fighting was never forced upon any visitor. The fortress proudly stood upon a hilltop but was unlike any other. Whereas many forts, including Tara, were coated with white-lime or chalk so that they stood out like a beacon, this fortress was completely stained red. And flying above the castle walls was a large white banner, imprinted with a red, bloodied hand: the symbol of their tribe.

So, when Dearg Damhsa approached those crimson walls from a distance, he could easily see two of the tall thatched rooftops that belonged to the inner roundhouses as they clearly peered proudly above the outer walls, for they stood upon the twin hills that gave the fortress its name.

Once inside, the whole layout of the fortress opened up before him. There were the two roundhouses that he'd already observed, plus a third one, each one having a different use, and a slightly different colour: there was a dull-red, many-roomed roundhouse built around a large oak from whence the king ruled; a bright-red building where trophies of battle were kept, which included the skulls of their defeated foes; and a speckled-red house, which held their vast array of weapons. Due to Dearg Damhsa being such a high-ranking noble, he was obviously granted an immediate audience with the Ulster King. The red druid looked very much at home within those crimson walls. It was during that crucial diplomatic meeting that the druid reminded the Ulster King that it was Conn's father, Fedhlimidh the Lawgiver, who had killed his father, whilst Conn himself had always treated him like a lowly slave, expecting his kingdom to come running every time that it's summoned. The proud and powerful northern king needed no other persuasion and thereupon eagerly agreed to join us.

And that was how the kingdoms of Ulster and Leinster joined forces with Munster to rise up against the mighty High-king. Now Mogha Nuadhad had his powerful army.

Hearing that most of the country had now united against Conn of the Hundred-battles, and fearing an attack from his own kingdom, as the whole of Leinster had now sided with Fiacha the Lame, Crimthann Yellow-hair led his last remaining troops into Tara to stand by his old pupil, Conn. The High-king greeted him warmly but dreaded the coming days, for except for Meath and Crimthann's small army from Leinster, as well as the never-failing Kingdom of Connacht, all of the country were now rising up against him. Therefore, whilst he still had time to escape, he quickly called his last remaining loyal clans together and abandoning Tara, headed straight into Connacht and as much safety as that kingdom could afford.

Conall of Cruachan, the Fir-bolg King of Connacht, was pleased to welcome his foster-son, Conn, as well as his old ally, Crimthann. He immediately called his Kingdom's warriors together as he knew that Mogha Nuadhad would soon be on his way. Conall was still in considerable pain from the injury that he'd sustained from the Lord of Ormond, all those years before, but that didn't stop him, it just made him hungry to exact his revenge. He was eagerly joined by his old ally, and Fir-bolg brother, Goll, son of Morna and his army of Fianna. They were all ready for a fight, even though the odds were completely against them.

Mogha led us towards the Kingdom of Meath. We were keen to engage the enemy. But we would have to find them first. Finding that most of the capital was deserted, we camped in the very centre of the kingdom, which was in the west of Teffia, feasting and carousing whilst listening to warring tales, until our eyes could stay open no longer.

The following day arrived soon enough. It was then that Mogha learned where Conn had fled, and he exclaimed triumphantly, "As Conn followed me throughout the whole noble Kingdom of Munster, I shall follow him right into the heart of Connacht".

As our Leinster allies were now under the command of Fiacha the Lame, they kindly agreed to guard the borders of Munster, which enabled Mogha Nuadhad to lead our entire army towards the western kingdom. We travelled across fields and plains southwards back through Meath until we reached the Great Way. We followed that raised gravel path westwards, heading towards Luan's Ford. We made as much noise as we could travelling, and with being higher than the surrounding countryside we could be seen for many leagues around, as our lengthy procession marched along that winding footpath.

It took about two days of hard marching until finally we reached the side of the magnificent Sionna. And there we camped on the east side of the river, loudly singing songs whilst merrily feasting. Luan's ford, beside where we now sat, used to be known as the Great Ford in times gone by due to the significance of its location as it was the main crossing point over the Sionna and there were no other fords for a good-many leagues. And there we rested for the night.

The following day was very much different. As Conn would have been expecting us to cross here, we determined to misdirect his forces as much as possible by rising early and quietly following the Sionna northwards. With this being the longest river in the land, I feel compelled to tell you the fascinating tale surrounding its name:

Back before the Sionna existed, there was a small pool, no more than seventeen yards wide, surrounded by nine towering Hazel-trees of Knowledge. The pool was known as Conla's Well and the Hazelnuts which hung from the trees were famously known to contain all the wisdom that was known in the world. Occasionally, from the overhanging branches, the tree's nuts would fall into the water. Splash! And there they would be eaten by a large salmon, who grew more intelligent with every nut that he ate; due to his newfound wisdom he became known as the Salmon of Knowledge. At that time, the Fairy Sea god, Manannán, son of Lir, had an inquisitive young grand-daughter named Sionna. Desperate to gain knowledge, the young woman visited the pool in strictest secret, lest she be found out, as Manannán had forbidden anyone to go. As she approached the pool, the wise water within, sensing her presence, angrily rose up into an almighty wave, and carried the poor girl over seventy-leagues southwards, down the country and far out into the sea. And thus, Sionna's River was formed, being named after her.

The mid-section of the river forms the boundary between the kingdoms of Meath and Connacht. And it was this part of the river that we now marched along, northwards for two long days, until we finally reached the Wood-of-the-Cairn which overlooked the Lake of the Cows. And there we secretly camped, ready to cross the nearby ford on the following morning. Quietly we slept that night, lighting neither fires, nor noisily feasting, trying not to attract any attention to our whereabouts.

The following morning, we rose early, silently breaking our fast by eating dried meat, nuts and fruit. We'd slept in our clothes, so there was very little to pack away. And then we saw them, coming towards us with the rising sun at their backs. There was no reason to remain quiet any longer. Their Champions were at their front, all in chariots wearing the red-cloaks of their rank. They came beneath the banner of the red hand. How happy we were to see them. It was obviously our allies, the King of Ulster with his impressive army of Ulstermen. Their number didn't quite match ours, but that didn't matter, as we were famous for having the largest kingdom in Ériu, so our army would always be significantly bigger, and obviously we were also accompanied by Fraoch the Militant's two-thousand warriors strong, but how welcome we made those Ulstermen feel as with their combined strength our army was almost twice the size of all of Conn's men put together. We slowly emerged from those shadowy oaks to greet our northern comrades.

It wasn't long before we'd set off, wading across the old ford, where the green-hued Road of Assal forded the mighty Sionna, full of a renewed sense of confidence. With wet feet we emerged on the other side, having finally reached Connacht. It felt strange to be stepping foot, uninvited, into the legendary Conall of Cruachan's kingdom.

The gentle Purple Wind blew softly at our backs as our mighty army followed the road westwards. We made our way across the far-reaching Plain of Magh Ai, which was named after the druid's son, who'd once cleared this vast plain. This sacred land, where we now stood, was the ancient cemetery of the Aes Sídhe and many of their turf-covered burial-mounds littered the green landscape, making it look quite hilly indeed. From here our gazes automatically settled upon the enormous timeworn hill-fort of the Connacht Kings: Cruachan. Its defences consisted of three large, brown earthen ramparts up the side of the hill, each topped by a tall white-stone wall, and each one preceded by a deep, dry moat. This meant that the only way to reach the hilltop was by walking up one of the heavily-guarded footpaths that passed through the defences. And crowning the summit of the hill, circled by yet another tall white wall was a magnificent stone roundhouse, topped by an almighty yellow thatched roof that stretched far up into the sky. We could feel the eyes of our enemy watching our approach as hundreds of heads peered above each one of those tall white walls.

A short distance to the southwest of Cruachan was the eerie, deep, dark, subterranean tunnel known as *Oweynagat*: The Cave of Cats. This was the closest I'd ever been to the notorious gateway that led all the way down into Hell. Many demonical creatures inhabited the tunnel's unearthly black depths. It certainly filled us all with a cold chill. Even our bravest Champions wouldn't dare approach its small, mouth-like entrance.

It may have been due to the proximity of the Cave of Cats, but Mogha Nuadhad was determined to have a hurried attack on the fort of Cruachan and to swiftly plunder the surrounding plain so that we could leave this place as quickly as we could. But as the treacherous MacNiadh and Conaire had been marching with us, at the head of their significant armies, they tried to do everything in their power to aid their father-in-law by preventing our attack. They'd been secretly communicating with Conn, telling him of our battle plans. And now these two villains, knowing that Conn was greatly outnumbered, so that he would certainly lose if he went to war, were trying to persuade Mogha Nuadhad to send him 'terms of peace' so that Ériu could be equally shared between both sides. They told Mogha that a battle without terms wasn't honourable; that it would offend the gods and bring chaos to his reign. They told him that as he was now the most powerful King, he could set down the conditions and the gods would deem it fair if he offered Conn a half share of the whole country. Mogha carefully thought it through and reluctantly agreed; he couldn't risk offending the gods because he knew that their anger could destroy us all. Whilst we were being clearly distracted by these lengthy discussions, Conn was leading his men out of Cruachan by the back door, and heading to a nearby well, not far from the Cave of Cats. From there his spies could sneak nearer to our positions to determine how many men that we actually had. Conn had already sent their women and cattle away to safety, well away from the forthcoming battle. He then led his forces, as they silently crept away from the well and around our formidable lines, to the shadowy depths of the nearby Rough-wood. Conn then ordered his men to spread out and for every second or third man to make a large campfire, so that from within the dark recesses, it would seem as though he had a much larger force than he actually had. Throughout history these simple acts of deception have often resulted in smaller armies winning decisive victories. And it really did deceive us into believing that his army was much bigger than it actually was, especially past nightfall, for the whole tree-line was lit-up from behind as the many campfires blazed from within, giving the entire woodland an eerie sense of life as the red, flickering flames intermingled with the dark shadows, dancing together in the night air. It was from these fires that the place became known as the Red-wood.

That night our faithful druid, Dearg Damhsa was sent to meet Conn of the Hundred-battles, to offer him our terms of peace. They met by torchlight just outside the woods, each accompanied by a handful of their closest attendants. As the two men stood near to each other, Conn's golden crown with matching brooch and sword-hilt glistened brightly in the flickering torchlight, matched by the shining, gold swirling suns and moons upon the druid's tall shadowy hat. Conn already had an idea of what Mogha Nuadhad's conditions would be, as he'd been secretly informed by a messenger sent from the two traitors within our camp; but when he heard the terms given as an ultimatum, he became furious. He needed time to think before he could reply.

Conn turned his back as his heavy purple cloak swirled behind him, before he slowly walked away back into the darkness, returning to his camp, deep in thought. Before long, he had gathered his nobles together around his campfire, wishing to consult them, desperate for a consensus on what to do regarding giving away half the land that he rightly ruled. But they were all of one mind: they couldn't bear the indignity of their beloved king losing so much of his power. And Conn really didn't want to share his country with anyone, especially not with the likes of Mogha Nuadhad. So finally, he asked his good friend, and foster-father, Conall of Cruachan for his trusted advice.

"Do as thou dost to others: arm thyself and drive out thine enemy by Right of Battle", replied the Fir-bolg King.

Conn knew that he was right. The alternative really was unthinkable. He had no choice but to go to war. And if the gods were truly on his side, as he hoped they were, then he would certainly win.

As usual, the fighting didn't begin until the sun rose the following day. And a most appalling and horrific war it was. To begin with, the treachery in our own camp was unforgivable: to aid their father-in-law, MacNiadh and Conaire swapped their allegiances early on, taking their huge armies with them. This was quite a blow for us all, especially for Mogha Nuadhad, to have so many of our own Munstermen once more warring against us. But still, with the aid of the gods, Mogha Nuadhad was able to lead us in ten victorious battles, each one more vicious and bloodier than the one before. The scenes of those battles stretched all the way from Connacht back into Meath. The last of the battlefields was named after the victor: it was called *Magh Nuadhad*, which means 'Nuadhad's Plain' and stood just north of the Fast-runner River, six leagues south of Tara. The treacherous MacNiadh was killed in one of those savage battles. After that, many of us raised our heads and shouted towards the Twelve Winds, "May his death appease the gods!" And that became the changing point which brought an end to that whole damned war.

Due to his devastating defeat Conn needed to change his tactics and he needed to do it fast if he was to stand any chance of surviving, so he called a large assembly, in which the last remnants of his entire army could attend, so that he could ask for their wise counsel; it went on for quite some time, the outcome being that Conn should agree to our terms to share the country equally. The hidden reasoning behind this decision was two-fold: the Ulstermen would obviously immediately return home once peace had been restored and our Spanish allies would also follow suit shortly thereafter; this would mean that Conn would be completely free to attack us once more, and without the army of Fraoch the Militant by our side, he'd stand a much better chance of defeating us. Conn obviously liked this evil, treacherous scheme so he sent his messengers to willingly agree to our terms.

An important condition which Mogha Nuadhad demanded as part of the peace treaty was that Conn's beautiful, newly-widowed daughter, Sabina, (who had been married to MacNiadh) should now marry the Munster King's son, Mais. This would be a matrimonial alliance that would fully cement the contract between both leaders. Conn reluctantly agreed. Shortly thereafter, a magnificent handfasting ceremony took place which bound their agreement. Sabina must have been in her early twenties by this time and had a baby already, whereas Mais was but a young plump child of eleven or so when this deal was struck. Due to the intrinsically honourable ideals behind the contract, which was basically to bring much-needed peace and stability back to the country, the pretty young widow, from that time forward, became known as Sabina of the Fair and Faultless Covenant.

After much discussion, on how to equally share the country, the land was split into two, with the southern half being ruled over by Mogha Nuadhad and being named *Leath Mogha*, 'Mogha's Half', whilst the northern half belonging to Conn of the Hundred-battles was called *Leath Cuinn*, 'Conn's Half'. These two formidable rulers now shared the High-kingship between them. The boundary which separated these two new Kingdoms was agreed to be the *Esker Riada*, which was the naturally-formed winding ridge, upon which sat most of the Great Way. This was deemed to be perfectly placed to evenly divide the country. Mogha's Half contained the whole of Munster and Leinster, as well as that southern part of Connacht that stretched down to the Sionna, which later became known as the western portion of Thomond, whilst Conn's Half contained the remainder of the three northern Kingdoms.

Mogha Nuadhad then sent for the nine-year-old Fionn, son of Cumhal; for his age the young boy was extremely tall and very well-built, like his father had been. In fact, you could almost say that he was equal in size to any warrior of twice his years. Having trained so hard from the moment that he could walk he was now a highly-accomplished and exceptionally disciplined warrior. He'd also eaten the legendary Salmon of Knowledge which had made him wise beyond his years. Due to the keen advice of Mogha's loyal ally, Fiacha the Lame, the young boy was named as the High-king's Champion of *Leath Mogha*; this wasn't some pretentious title for a young child, Fionn really was that good a warrior, as well as being a highly-skilled leader of men. Fionn was obviously exceptionally grateful to be awarded such an exalted position, especially at such an early age.

Thereafter peace remained throughout the land between Mogha and Conn for fourteen long years. It was during the early years of this peace that another son was born to Mogha and Beara. His name was Lugaid Lága and an honourable Champion he went on to become. It was also during this time that I became the Chief-seanchaí of not just Munster, but of the whole of *Leath Mogha*.

But anyway, back to our tale. All through those peaceful years, Mogha had felt highly satisfied with his rule; after all, the boundaries of his kingdom had surpassed even that of his own father. But he still had a niggling fear, which was borne of the precariousness of the situation that if his Spanish allies were ever to leave, he would be in serious trouble, as he wouldn't have the military might to keep Conn from taking back his half of Ériu. And that niggling worry seemed to be slowly turning into a reality, as Fraoch and his Spanish warriors were increasingly talking of returning home as there were no wars to keep them here, and furthermore they were also really missing the company of their own countrymen, along with the lifestyle and warmth of the Iberian sun. Mogha had to think fast; he had to think of a way to cause a war with Conn so that with the help of his Spanish warriors he'd be able to crush his enemy once and for all.

As Mogha Nuadhad was out riding with a small assembly, making his ritual circuit around the boundaries of *Leath Mogha*, he was continuously racking his brains trying to think of a way that he could force Conn into a war that his own subjects would believe was lawful, for he knew that if his people thought that his cause wasn't just, then they would likely not follow him into battle. And obviously the gods themselves wouldn't aid such an unworthy cause.

He'd ridden to the far northeast corner of his mighty Kingdom, where the *Esker Riada* divided the country in half. Nearby stood the two important ports that brought in goods from the east. Mogha had walked up to a hilltop to overlook the scene below, carefully observing all the merchant ships coming and going. He stood there with legs shoulder-width apart in a very powerful, commanding stature as his purple-cloak gently ruffled in the wind. Light rain began to fall down upon him, blowing in from the direction of the sea, gently dampening his shoulder-length hair and matching brown beard, but he worried not as his mind was deeply entrenched in his thoughts.

Our seaport was called *Dubhlinn*; it received its name from that strange, nearby phenomenon, as *dubh*, meaning dark or black, and *linn*, meaning pool, was a wider section on the otherwise slim Dirty River, and was where our trading ships were moored, having travelled there by sailing up the adjoining Fast-runner River. Conn's port stood a little further to the north, up the Fast-runner River, nearer to the Ford of Hurdles from where it took its name; this was a path of interwoven willow branches that spanned that wide, and sometimes treacherous river. This woven path was held in place with stakes to prevent it from being washed away and was the 'hurdle' in which the shallow ford could be crossed during low tide. It was the only safe crossing-point for a good-many leagues, being part of the famous Road of Cualu that proudly ran from Tara into Leinster.

Mogha's eyes settled on the *Esker Riada*, which rose gently from the ground, and his eyes ran along the lengthy, winding hilly causeway that stretched far into the distance, heading all the way towards the western sea. As Mogha's eyes gazed back towards the ships, he couldn't help but notice that most of the trading vessels were mooring across the border, on Conn's side, taking their valuable goods straight into *Leath Cuinn*. Mogha was a little angry when he saw this. Then he quickly started to smile. He'd just thought of the perfect plan that he'd been looking for. Without a second thought he despatched a messenger straight to Conn demanding that he receive a fair share of the goods that came into the country.

The trusted messenger quickly galloped north, as the gentle rain blew in his face covering both him and his mount. It wasn't long before he'd reached the magnificent gates of that huge, white-stoned metropolis of Tara. As he dismounted from his horse the guards looked him up and down suspiciously.

On hearing the demands that Mogha was making, Conn was obviously furious. He couldn't believe the sheer impudence of the southern king. He promptly sent the messenger back with a firmly worded reply that he would, "never share arms, clothing, nor armour under the same rule of division as territory". This was exactly what Mogha was hoping for. The peace treaty could now be revoked.

Mogha immediately returned home to tell Fraoch the good news. The Spaniard was excited by this unexpected outcome, as he knew that his warriors had been bored for too long.

The news quickly spread throughout the whole country: Ériu was now at war.

Within days, Mogha had assembled all of our fighting men from Munster at his fortress of *Brú Rí*: Home of Kings. Some had pitched tents at the bottom of the hillside whilst others were crowded inside. I've never known it to be so busy, or so noisy, with everyone having to shout to make themselves heard. That fortress looked so spectacular: it was a magnificent, comfortable timbered ringfort that sat high atop a large green hill of three deep earthen ramparts, each topped by tall wooden palisades. The whole pile overlooked the sluggish River of the Plain. It was sometimes known, due to its location, by the more descriptive title of *Dún Ochair Maige*: Fort on the Brink of the River of the Plain.

Amongst our number, that day, were obviously, Fraoch the Militant's two-thousand warriors strong. And also joining with us were a thousand brave and mighty Champions, sent by the son of the illustrious King of Asia. These looked like no-one that we'd ever seen before. The way the sunlight gleamed upon them made them look as though their bodies were made up of a thousand sunbeams. The leader himself wore a shiny golden mask beneath a tall silver helm. His whole body was fully-encased within thin metal strips of highly-polished armour riveted onto cloth; his legs and torso being covered by strips of gold, whilst his arms were enclosed within silver steel. By his side was a golden-hilted sword in a black scabbard and a long spear was firmly gripped in his right hand. His men wore long gowns, split from the crotch downwards, made of the same shiny silver-strips of splint-armour. They had dusky skin and black pointed-beards, which added to their unusual appearance, whilst their distinctive noses ran straight downwards, each one pointed like a spear-tip. Upon their heads they each wore gleaming steel-helms, which left their faces exposed, and they were each armed with a bow, arrows, sword and spear.

We set off with the intention of crossing over the Great Way and into *Leath Cuinn*, to finally give battle for the whole of Ériu. Northwards we marched across the Plain of Waterfalls. It was a long journey, but we were eager; we'd been at peace for far too long. The armour of the Asian army thunderously rattled metal against metal as we went; this journey certainly wouldn't be a quiet one. We followed the Road of Dalo, through Éile, and past the Mountain of the Flame, before heading north once more. And finally, after five days of travelling, we eventually reached that huge mound which stood to the east of the Great-wood of Firceall (where Tullamore now stands). This mound proudly stood within the far northern reaches of *Leath Mogha*. Before our country had been divided in half, this land where we now stood would have belonged to Conn, as it was part of his ruling Kingdom of Meath. And in the forthcoming battle we hoped that the rest of his land would be wrested away from him just as successfully.

There was a commanding view from atop the mound; from here we could see beyond the Great Way to a meadow just three leagues northwest. It was completely covered with the blush of pink heather. It gave that whole plain a most enchanted feel amidst the surrounding green landscape. Mogha was informed that the pink field was known as *Mag Léna*: the Plain of Leana and lay well-within Conn's Half. We knew immediately that this would be our final destination.

So Mogha Nuadhad boldly led us onward. We made our way upwards, onto the low-lying Great Way. How majestic it seemed as we stood upon it, not particularly in height, but definitely in length, as it stretched as far as the eye can see in both directions, east and west. From there we all gazed down upon *Leath Cuinn*. We took a moment to take in the whole magnitude of what we were about to do. There was something about our actions that seemed so very wrong. But still we felt compelled to do it anyway.

We all ran down the other side, following Mogha Nuadhad. Our huge army descending downwards into Conn's Half. There was no going back now, not even if we wanted; the force of change burned too brightly in our hearts. We continued northwards until we were standing amidst that vast purple plain. It was there that our old ally, Fiacha the Lame, from Hy Kinsella, met us with his whole army from Leinster. Altogether our army now numbered nine battalions strong. And a formidable sight we were.

And that was where we made our camp. Mogha Nuadhad's silken tent was the first structure to be erected; it was a towering royal pavilion with many-coloured walls. We didn't just pitch tents for ourselves; no, we built houses and streets, and even market squares from the nearby woods as we knew that this would further infuriate Conn. And rushes were gathered from the shallows of nearby marshes to thatch our newly built homes. When this was finished, we were amazed at our own accomplishments, at having so quickly built a small settlement.

Our next actions were absolutely imperative: we had to find out the druids' predictions for the forthcoming war to see if we would be victorious; if the predictions weren't favourable then we would have to quickly abandon our makeshift village and thus postpone our fight for another day.

Due to our holy men being in complete harmony with nature, they'd obviously carefully studied all of the prevalent signs. They knew that the land had its own rhythm, its own heartbeat. It can be seen in the rhythmic pattern of pounding rain; and the undulating, swirling, ever-changing formation of a flock of birds in flight; and the motion of a fluctuating breeze across a grassy plain; and the sea's pulsating waves against a sandy shore; and the path of the sun as it ritually changes direction upon each Solstice: they knew that all of this added up to the land being a powerful all-living force. And this force could communicate its likes and dislikes as well as its moods. The druids understood this, and they used their vast knowledge to predict what the future had in store for us.

So Dearg Damhsa, the High-druid of *Leath Mogha*, led the investigation himself. He'd carefully studied all the signs, paying particular attention to the positioning of the moon. He'd made many calculations regarding the secret clues that were hidden within nature. He'd studied the calendar looking for auspicious dates. He'd consulted at length with many of his subordinate druids. There was no room for mistakes; many lives depended upon it. Everything was leading the wise druid to conclude that this was indeed a most favourable time to war.

The omens were looking good, and our army were willing; what more could a king wish for. And so, with that knowledge firmly understood, the good people of *Leath Mogha* camped upon Mag Léna that very night.

But true knowledge had been concealed from Dearg Damhsa, and false omens had presented themselves to his army of scholarly priests. Pride also had a hand in deceiving their understanding, along with willed-destiny, which had blinded them to the real omens of fate. We were all equally to blame really, as much as the druids, for we all single-mindedly craved a just war and our rage had completely clouded our vision from seeing anything else. But whatever we felt, Mogha felt it more deeply. His anger with Conn had turned him almost into a trance-like state of fury, which had separated him from any rational thoughts.

This really was not a good time to war!

There were other enemy kingdoms that were pleased with Mogha Nuadhad's invasion though. The new King of Ulster was very appreciative; he too felt that his kingdom had been armed servants to Conn's cause for far too long. This would be another opportunity for his kingdom's long-awaited retribution, when he knew that the High-king would be at his weakest, as he would be fighting against enemies upon both sides. So, with his gruesome banner of the gory, blood-stained hand, he led his army southwards, into Meath, where they ravaged and plundered, burning much of Conn's cherished Kingdom.

Whilst this was happening Conn was standing upon one of the hills within the great white-stone metropolis of Tara, gazing down over the whole of his kingdom's warriors. He was undeniably dressed for war, wearing a long, heavy shirt of mail, whilst a king's sword lay proudly by his waist. A High-king's golden crown rested upon his brow, encrusted with jewels whilst a golden torc encircled his neck, both gleaming in the sunlight. He shouted to his men, passionately trying to incite them to war, completely unaware that the Ulstermen were attacking from the north:

"Oh brothers, my good royal brothers, cousins of my noble race. We know that Mogha Nuadhad unjustly took all of Connacht south of the Great Way. Though I've been in Tara a long time now, I've never felt in good spirits, not since the day that he wrested our whole southern half from my grip. Until we lead a mighty army against the powerful son of Magha Neid. Until we have fought hand to hand, never shall we have peace. When that strong-willed king fled to Castile, few were his ships, but by his exile he obtained a vast army to fight against *you*, my royal brothers. Now let us march onward to our own plain of Mag Léna and once there we shall take back the whole of our stolen land".

Thunderous cries echoed from all around Conn's troops; they were roused and ready to do battle.

Just then a worried-looking messenger rode briskly into Tara. A sheen of sweat covered his brow and he looked very agitated indeed. He quickly delivered his message to a nearby guard, who in turn, rushed over to Conn to pass on the urgent news, "The men of Ulster are near; they've invaded from the north and are attacking the royal kingdom".

Conn's gathered troops couldn't help but hear the alarming news; Conn angrily shouted, "What are we waiting for?"

His men loudly roared their approval and with that Conn led his men onward to take on those ferocious northern foes.

The Ulster warriors had wrenched many captives from their homes, and the all too familiar noise which monstrously permeated the very air (as only the sound of an appallingly heinous deed can) was of the high-pitched sound of frightened women screaming mixed with the low booming voices of exultant warriors cheering. Cattle were also forcibly taken as well as any spoils that those northern warriors could carry.

The skies of Meath were filled with flames and thick clouds of grey smoke could be seen for many a league. We could even see the distant smoke from our own campsite upon Mag Léna, so it must have been an effortless task for Conn to pinpoint the whereabouts of those enemy invaders, as he was considerably closer.

When Conn neared the enemy hordes and saw their barbarous acts before him, he rushed out in front, with his battalions close at his heels, their many-coloured banners flapping violently overhead with the rush of wind. So swift was their advance that they neared their enemy completely unobserved, like lions closing in for the kill; the Ulstermen were far too busy enjoying their victory to notice anything else. Now Conn's men were just an arm's length away. Suddenly the Ulster King noticed their approach. A shout went out and then all hell broke out.

The princes and heroes were sought out on both sides and deliberately slaughtered. There were screams and the din of thunderous smashing, as weapons cleaved through shields and limbs. Every muscle was frantically active, all senses were suddenly alert, no-one could stop, everything was happening all around them; the sound of pain, anger, violence and death filled the air.

And then Conn, raged with anger that the Ulstermen had turned against him, threw himself full-force into the battle, killing many, many, fearless enemy warriors; not stopping, his fury being so intense.

The Ulster King, desperately wanting to end this fierce attack, charged towards Conn; neither king knew how to back down and both men were filled with a battle-fury that drove them forward on a mighty killing spree. They both attacked each other, plunging their powerful battle-spears right through the other's body, shattering their handles, leaving huge gaping wounds; the blood poured out, oozing from the cavernous hollows like gushing red waterfalls.

Immediately, one hundred of the greatest Champions, from each side, rushed between the two brave Kings; they furiously stabbed and chopped at each other, until the whole battle-field around them was swamped with pools of blood.

The maimed bodies of many valiant knights now littered the field in lifeless heaps, whilst Conn eagerly searched once more for the Ulster King. Finding him, he angrily thrust another great war-spear towards him. The northern king put his mighty shield in the way to protect himself but Conn's spear pierced the boss with such force that it carried on straight through, into the King's arm-pit and right through his back; blood came gushing out. Before Conn had time to remove his spear, eighteen of his own Rear-guards rushed forward, like a flash of yellow-hair and blue gowns, thrusting their spears into the Ulster King, making his body look like it had a palisade of death running across it. They quickly beheaded him; and then, without stopping for breath, they hurriedly re-joined their comrades and savagely killed all the remaining warriors of the north.

Now that this hurried and short-lived encounter was over, there was time for people's natural humanity to surface; and this being the case, before he'd done anything else Conn had freed all of the Ulster army's captives. And every woman was reunited with her own family and all the rustled cattle were returned home by the freed cow-herders.

Before Conn had even thought about his own considerable pain, he had visited each of his royal villages, making sure that everything was peaceful, before he could finally make camp. That evening Conn of the Hundred-battles rested his aching body, which was full of the most horrific battle wounds.

Many powerful Aes Sídhe visited Conn that evening, before the hours of darkness had set in. A good-many of his old comrades, who'd come from his allied territories had also gone to see him. They'd all brought ointments to heal his warriors' wounds, curing plants for their lacerations, soothing salves for their cuts and minor injuries, as well as healing herbs for their sores. These were expertly applied without much ado.

Night came quickly and all the weary warriors rested from the day's gruelling combat.

The following day they all awoke, their bodies feeling stiff, as though they'd done nothing more than played a game of hurling the previous day. All their wounds were miraculously healed, and they were now ready for whatever activities the day threw at them.

Then three of Conn's favourite, and highly-celebrated, Sídhe-mistresses paid him a visit; their names were At, Lann and Lean and they were the daughters of Truaghan from the nearby brave Fir-bolg plains of Treagha. They urged Conn to march west, without haste, towards Mogha Nuadhad's camp. They implored him, "Let not Eoghan the Great escape from thee, but seekest thee out this furious lion upon the plain of Mag Léna, and there shalt lie his grave".

After hearing their encouraging words Conn commanded his brave warriors to make ready, and before long they were all marching westward. They travelled across many leagues, marching down unobstructed roads and over vast open plains until eventually they came to the rush-filled ford, known as *Ath Luachra*. As it was now starting to get dark that's where they made their camp.

Sadly, it was said, that after nightfall, the wide, royal Wave of Rudhraidhe, loudly roared. And the long, tall, whispering Wave at the Mouth of Tuagh, was heard to reply. This was followed by the high, curling, white-foamed Wave of Cliodhna, within Munster's Oak-harbour, who noisily joined in with her own response. The gods had truly spoken. And they were now backing Conn.

This last wave, when accompanied by Cliodhna's loud cry, as it was that night, foretold the death of a Munster King. This banshee wail echoed throughout the hills and glens of Munster, terrifying our countrymen. We were far from home when we heard this tragic sound, and an uncomfortable chill hit us, as a terrible sense of dread spread throughout our noble warriors.

Even though Conn knew that these signs meant that the gods were on his side, he also knew that he was still vastly outnumbered, especially after the savage battle against the Ulstermen, that had considerably reduced his numbers. With this thought in mind, Conn went into counsel with his foster-father to ask for his learned advice.

"Avoid not the battle. For I pledge my word", quipped Conall, "that unless the solid ground swallows us up, or the mighty waves rise up to drown us, or the bright, cloud-hilled mantle of sky above our heads dost fall upon us, then none of our number shall retreat a single step in this forthcoming war".

But still Conn wasn't convinced, "Those words are the ravings of a man who soon stands in mortal danger, and that is the argument of a clown. I fear, foster-father, that we'll be slain by the mighty forces of the fierce Spaniards; for obviously if a lack of followers is a sign of weakness, then surely it follows that a small army is the door of death: and both these are attached to me".

Conn further added, "I have no choice but to send messengers to Mogha Nuadhad to bargain for peace. I'll allow him to keep the three Kingdoms that he's already gained, without dispute; these being Munster, Leinster and a good portion of Meath and, to show my good faith, I'll even give him the Kingdom of Ulster, which I've always thought of as my 'sword supporting territory'. And as guarantee I swear by the Sun and Moon, dew and air, sea and great land, not to commit trespass, or persecution, or injustice upon Mogha Nuadhad; all I ask for in return is to keep the entire Kingdom of Connacht with the adjoining lands of Teffia, as well as Tara with her fair profits, for by those I was fed since birth". This vow showed that he was serious as it was the most holy oath that any man could give. This was an oath that no one would dare to break.

Conn's men were amazed at how generous he was being. But Conn told them that he didn't have enough warriors or Champions left to defeat Mogha Nuadhad. So, without delay, he sent two trusted members of his court to act as messengers so that they could deliver his important communication; these handsome messengers were well-respected Lords of Connacht, as well as being the sons of the Leinster King, Crimthann Yellow-hair, so Conn had known them since they were small children and counted on them as being two of his closest friends. Conn felt that by sending such important men that it would show to the world that he wasn't trying to persuade Mogha Nuadhad into accepting the agreement from a weak position, his high-ranking messengers would actually be adding a lot more weight to his firm demands.

And thus, anon, those two worthy messengers rode briskly away from Conn's lines towards our makeshift village.

As soon as they arrived, Mogha took an instant dislike to them, as Leinster was meant to be part of *Leath Mogha*, thereby their allegiance should have been to him, not to Conn. The indignant Mogha listened to them fully, though was quick to respond; he was angry but still in control, "Accepting that proposal would be as ridiculous as me desiring pleasure but not having the horses in which to seek it, or to have ale but no drinking-horns in which to drink it, or to have happiness but without the music in which to enjoy it, or to rule without my subjects' obedience, that I should be without the centre of Ériu, which is Tara with her plains and hills; for them to remain in the hands of my greatest enemies. I shall not be denied that portion of my happiness, nor have that part of my dignity severed. Nor shall I bequeath that disgrace to my children. I will not accept these terms".

The Lords of Connacht were shocked that Mogha was turning down such a generous offer. They firmly, yet cautiously replied, "An attack over an offer of peace isn't lawful, nor is a battle over terms of surrender. Conn has offered you generous terms of peace, but he won't allow you to take one extra farmland more than he's proposed".

Mogha Nuadhad was furious that these messengers had spoken to him like that so he ordered his guards to seize them. We obviously weren't happy for 'messengers of peace' to be taken captive. But Mogha Nuadhad, was the High-king of *Leath Mogha*, and he insisted. He then demanded that these sons of the eastern king be taken to a nearby hill and executed.

This dark task was sadly done, which caused a great air of despondency to hang heavily over our whole camp. This was the lowest part of Mogha Nuadhad's reign; he'd committed an unspeakable act of which the gods wouldn't forgive. And we all knew it.

It was the hour when day and night are equally dark when Conn heard that Crimthann's two sons had been murdered. He couldn't quite believe what he was hearing. It had become too late to march anywhere that evening, so he just had to sit and wait as the approaching darkness engulfed him.

Conn cried for much of that night; he was deeply heartbroken by those needless deaths of his two young friends. His uncontrollable, wailing cries eventually being replaced by his loud moans of despair that could be heard all around his camp.

Conall of Cruachan tried to console him, "Cease thy sadness, for thou shalt obtain victory; if brave thou art and avenge thy friends in noble spirit, then by right of sword thou shalt win".

"I will do that", replied Conn, and once more he swore the sacred oath, "By the Heavens and by the Earth, by the Moon, by the Wind and by the Sun, I shall not yield one single inch until I have defeated our enemies".

The Connacht King smiled and had a glint in his eye; he could obviously feel the immense pain suffered by his foster-son, but he did love the thought of a good fight.

The following morning Conn arose from his pavilion. He'd already fought this battle in his mind, many times, during those long hours of darkness. He knew exactly what needed to be done. And he felt that the gods must surely be on his side after the unjust deed that Mogha

Nuadhad had so cruelly committed. He prepared his mind as he dressed for battle, pulling over his head his baggy, dark-grey leather-skin shirt so that it hung loosely from his large shoulders over his muscular frame. Gathering up some of the slack material, he secured it with three ornate circular brooches. On top of this he put on his long, well-fitted regal coat, edged with pure red-gold, pausing momentarily whilst his attendants pulled the straps tight, securely fastening the buckles. Then, as he slowly raised his padded hood over his head, his attendants carefully went to work, lifting the heavy, hooded shirt of mail, and slowly easing it over his head and down over his body. His legs were then adorned with strong, but lightweight greaves, made with threads of golden-bronze. Whilst upon his hands were placed white, magical lacerating gloves, designed so that neither sword, nor spear-cast would ever miss their mark. Around his neck was fastened a shiny, golden torc, and upon his head a High-king's crown was firmly placed, studded with half-a-hundred rubies amongst other precious gems. His rich-hilted sword sat firmly within its scabbard, which hung proudly by his side.

Now dressed he felt ready to face the morning and everything that it had in store for him; with this thought in mind, he put his shield straps over his head so that his beautifully designed wooden shield could hang upon his muscular back. Filled with a controlled fury that was waiting to be unleashed, he grasped hold of his two wide-headed battle-spears, whose necks shone with rings of pure gold, before striding purposefully from his royal pavilion.

"Are you ready for battle", he roared at his awaiting troops, "or are you going to let your enemy trample you into dust?"

"We're ready", they shouted. "Wherever you lead we will follow. And when you command us to stand, we'll hold our ground like a fortress wall, so that nothing can go through us, round us, or under us. You will not die here today unless three-thousand of your strongest warriors die before you".

Conn strode forward, motioning his men to follow, feeling that the right of combat was all theirs. The strong, disciplined troops marched rapidly, like an unstoppable, devouring forest fire that was burning its way towards its final destruction.


Conn's battalions didn't stop until they reached Mag Léna. They were then finally able to rest. They would certainly come to appreciate this well-needed break before the battle began. The weary troops leant against their spears; the supple handles bending to take their weight, reducing some of the load from their tired feet. They silently listened to their commanders discussing the plans of the forthcoming battle.

"Where is Fionn, son of Cumhal?" enquired Conn, making sure that he dealt with his formidable ally first, lest he forgot.

Fionn was now aged three-and-twenty and was obviously a very capable Champion. Like his father, he stood head and shoulders above his men, wearing a red-cloak kept in place with a large silver brooch. He'd been our Champion of *Leath Mogha* until Conn had tempted him away by wisely offering him the leadership of the Fianna; this was after the young man had successfully proved himself by using his father's magical weapons to defeat the fire-breathing Fairy, Áillen the Burner, thus freeing Tara from its annual destruction.

Conn had desperately wanted Fionn as an ally as he was far too powerful a Champion to have as a foe. And obviously Fionn was proud to follow in his father's footsteps, as he'd always been so fascinated listening to tales of Cumhal's prowess; he'd even sought out his father's old comrades to hear more tales of his glorious exploits. So, being Chieftain of the Fianna had made him feel much closer to his legendary father than ever before. It also meant that he now had complete control of two-thousand of the fiercest troops in the land. And they were very well-trained and extremely loyal. He was now able to experience first-hand, the power that his father had once wielded.

"Here I am", replied the distinguished young hero.

"Take your Fianna to protect our ruling seat of Tara, as well as its surrounding lands. If I survive, you'll be well rewarded. But if I die, guard fair Tara with your life until you're relieved by one of the rightful princes who survive this war".

Fionn gently smiled at the thought of the responsibility afforded to him by this new adventure and nodded in acknowledgement. He swiftly left the camp, taking his loyal men with him. Conn didn't want to push the young knight into a direct confrontation with Mogha Nuadhad, just in case his loyalties wavered, so sending him to Tara to protect his capital against any marauding invaders seemed to be the most advantageous use for him.

Then the one-eyed Goll, son of Morna, slightly peeved at having the leadership of the Fianna taken away from him, but still having the dignity of a hardened Champion, asked Conn, "Dost thou intend a night-time battle?"

"I do", replied Conn, "as we don't have as many warriors as Mogha Nuadhad, so we need to take him by surprise".

"I made a vow", admitted Goll, "on the day in which I first took up the arms of a Champion, that I would never attack mine enemy, either after nightfall, by surprise, or under any kind of disadvantage; nor shall I, at this day, violate that vow. Besides, the vision in mine eye is not as sharp at night; but tell me, who is thy greatest foe?"

"That is Mogha Nuadhad himself", replied Conn.

"Well then, by morn he shall be mine", pronounced Goll.

Conn would have preferred an attack during the dark hours of night, but going into battle against Mogha Nuadhad without Goll really was unthinkable. So, he would need to amend his strategy to survive this war. Conn slowly continued, "And who will ward off Fraoch the Militant, son of Heber, with his two-thousand Spanish warriors?"

Eochaidh, the one-eyed Pictish prince from the Fortrenn lands of Alba loudly replied, in his strong brogue, "I am he".

With his two most deadly enemies now matched, Conn and his captains continued to do the same for the rest of the Champions on the field, so that the battle would be more just, making sure that everyone fought their equal. After all of these preparations were concluded they pitched their tents to rest for the night.

Now back to our own leader, Mogha Nuadhad; he'd picked a good spot on the field in which to speak, just as Conn had been doing with his men. We'd all gathered round. Mogha knew that because he'd recently killed Conn's 'messengers of peace' that he'd really have to stir us up into an angry mob, who could still believe that the gods were with us, if he was to stand any chance of winning this forthcoming war.

"Never before have your ancestors been allowed to rule over the whole island", Mogha Nuadhad loudly began, "as their joint rule was agreed upon in the early days by our first High-kings, Heber Fionn and Heremon. That honour has always been kept from us by the greed of Heremon's seed. They've always been a thorn in our side, made ever worse when their treacherous allies, that is two-thirds of *Leath Mogha* turned against us, fuelled by their own deep-hatred and spite, led by the Leinster King and our own two traitorous Lords. It would have been more honourable for us to have had three more battalions fighting against us than to have the malicious, treacherous advice that MacNiadh and Conaire had given us. And when their men blatantly went over to Conn to fight against their own brothers; that treachery killed

MacNiadh. To think that he abandoned us for Sabina's pretty smiles whilst Conaire threw away our alliance for Sara's witty conversation. For their treachery and desertion, I brought a large force of Spaniards back with me, for they are men that will not desert; they'll fight for our kingdom so that you, my friends, will neither end up as Conn's farmers nor his slaves. There will be no hereditary claim, nor slavish rent put upon my clan by any other clan, but if we succeed in this battle with our almighty army, we'll have complete unopposed freedom forever".

This speech was exactly what we needed. It really strengthened us, making us feel as though maybe right was on our side; so maybe the gods would protect us after all. And the might of the Spaniards would certainly help.

"Will you fight bravely?" shouted Mogha Nuadhad.

"We will, O High-king", we all loudly replied.

A voice from the crowd added, "You will gain Kingship over all the five kingdoms or we will die trying".

Mogha was happy; he'd won back our loyalty, along with our belief in Munster's true hope of victory.

Caught up in Mogha's euphoria, we watched him grinning as he started back to his pavilion, when his expression suddenly changed. Out of nowhere came Conn's three pretty, but impudently, venomous-tongued Sídhe-mistresses. They slowly strolled towards him, accompanied by an unnatural-looking entourage of thrice-three creatures; these grotesque followers were made up of three coarse-haired Sprites encumbered with the frail, thin bodies of wizened old men, each one croaking wildly like an angry frog which added to our whole sense of unease. Behind these were three large, brawny, hideous-looking sallow-skinned Goblins with blue beards and black-hearted souls; they were completely unknown in our land, so the very sight of them visibly disturbed Mogha Nuadhad, along with the rest of us. We anxiously became silent, mesmerized by their appearance, when behind the Goblins, at the rear of the group, stepped forth three horrifying, long-whiskered, gloom-provoking women of the valley; their arms, which were capable of doing the most-evil of deeds were bony at the elbows with underarm skin sagging loosely like a soiled undergarment, and their long, crooked legs were bone-thin and bent at the knee, which surprised us how they managed to hold these creatures upright. Each one had blue-grey hair down to their shoulders and upon their brows they each had one long, coarse-haired eyebrow that continued down over their dull yellow cheeks, giving them a most angry expression. Beneath these were deep-set, hateful eyes. Their large, cavernous noses, corroded by years of hate, hung over their rotten, shrieking mouths, which contained long, thick, black, sluggish tongues that helped to give out the most vicious, loud, piercing cries.

"Where have you women come from?" one of our elders nervously asked the three women of the Sídhe.

"We've travelled from afar using the art of our race".

"Explain to us these arts", asked Mogha Nuadhad, trying to keep control of the situation, even though their very presence unnerved him.

"We shall speak of them indeed, O High-king", they sneered. "'tis the dark art of Sídhe-craft: we cause seas to flood over land, we lay cold snow upon thy ground, we bring daggers of lightning to stab across thy far-reaching plains, we change bodies of Man into baser creatures, and bring Fairy-mutations upon thy distinguished families".

Feeling angry, yet still fearing the malicious evil that these Sídhe-witches could do, Mogha carefully replied, "Those skills are not fitting deeds of good women nor are they noble qualities to be justly proud".

The three women smiled at each other. Mogha cautiously continued, "What are your names?"

"We are At, Lean and Lann, daughters of Truaghan, from the mighty lands of Treagha; and we bringeth thee tidings of thine own death and short life as thou shalt die in battle upon the morrow".

"Let your predictions be cast upon yourselves, and upon Conn of the Hundred-battles", retorted Mogha Nuadhad angrily, "And let your evil intentions lie upon the rocks and within the sea's waves".

"'Tis true", they calmly replied, "that our prophesies neither have been, nor never shall be avoided. These aren't fortune-tellings for the sake of silver that we giveth thee; we are telling thee that the termination of thy life hast come and that every stroke shall be death upon thee: every spear-cast shalt hit home, every wound will be mortal, and thy severed head will be left with Conn's glorious troops. And the raven shall skip upon the blood-soaked plain".

The women of the Sídhe wandered off, knowing that they'd achieved their aim, as our heroes had no morale left to destroy. We were all left visibly shaken and completely speechless; what could we possibly say to each other that would rid us of the evil words ringing in our ears? 'And the raven shall skip upon the blood-soaked plain'; this phrase I couldn't get out of my head. What evil it had caused. They'd left in their wake a cloud of despair that hung over our whole noble encampment.

The witches hadn't yet finished their work, for they continued their evil, poisonous journey by taking a slow, purposeful walk to the nearby camp of our Spanish ally, Fraoch the Militant.

"Hark ye", they told his assembled troops, "Hear our prediction of battle: courts shall be erected over the grassy tombs of your princes when Conn is victorious tomorrow. Tales of his acclaim shall be sung throughout the land".

Then speaking directly to Fraoch they continued, "The hideous woman who gazes upon thy troops;" they gestured to one of the crones at the rear of their entourage, whose unnatural blue-grey hair and monstrous features were hard to ignore. "The force of her scream as she shrieketh at thee shalt chill thee to thy bone. Our wisdom is sound. Our arts are many. Fearful is thy morn".

Speaking again to the gathered troops they continued, "Hark ye: Fraoch shall be slain in close contest by the unavenged arms of Eochaidh of the One-eye, as well as by the sword of the mighty Conn".

Even the war-hungry Fraoch found himself to be uncharacteristically moved by these shocking, vicious claims. He roared, "Begone! Away with you witches! You can't possibly know the outcome of battle before the first blow has been struck".

The Sídhe-women sneered at the defiant Spanish prince as they casually wandered from his camp.

By now nightfall had crept upon us. And as both sides needed to rest before tomorrow's violent encounter, we went inside of our makeshift wooden buildings to camp for the night. Many of us went to bed dressed for battle, just in case things started early, taking our swords and other hand weapons with us. Throughout our campsite we all felt rather subdued after the intrusion of those malicious Sídhe-folk and that night we struggled to get much sleep, just as those unwelcome intruders had intended.

Night came and went as it has a habit of doing and the sun was just starting to peer above the distant horizon when the Sídhe-women appeared back at Conn's camp. His men were all sleeping when they entered Conn's royal pavilion.

"Arise, High-king", they said to him, "for victory is in thy hands".

And then Lean playfully announced, "Morning hath come, good are the tidings, as sayeth Lann and Lean. Morning bringeth happy greetings now that the death of Mogha Nuadhad is cast. It's time that they are attacked, O Goll, son of Morna of the heavy blows; the morning is beautiful with glorious light and now thine hour hast come".

When Conn saw the beautiful early morning sky with the delicate bright wisps of cloud overhead, he knew that his Sídhe-mistresses were right, and that it would be a good time indeed to begin their battle. They quickly dressed and gathered their men, who were naturally full of nervous anticipation, and boldly headed towards the encampment of Fraoch, where his two-thousand Spanish warriors were waiting, tucked up inside their beds. Their tents were a distance away from our wooden huts and the Spanish warriors were soundly sleeping when Conn and his troops crept upon them.

Conn wisely left Goll at the outskirts of the Spanish camp so that the Chieftain could save his strength for battling against Mogha Nuadhad. And then Conn, along with his remaining men silently surrounded the tents and when in position the first war-cry was softly called, followed by others from all sides. The startled Spanish warriors jumped to their feet in an alarmed state as Conn's ungallant soldiers sliced through their tents, hacking down the sleepy inhabitants and slaughtering them, unmercifully.

The bold Fraoch, hearing the noises outside, sprang furiously from his pavilion, with only a sword in hand and wearing a thin, gold-embroidered night-shirt; he quickly, and courageously, began striking and killing Conn's Champions, so that half-a-hundred foes were slain in that first violent rush. That was until Conn and the one-eyed Pictish prince, Eochaidh came together against him; they were dressed in full battle-armour, tirelessly smiting, with sword and spear, using the combined force of all their might. Fraoch put on a good show; but no matter how well he fought, those two fierce, iron-clad Champions were far too well protected. Finally, the Spaniard managed to rip their armour asunder, grievously wounding them in the process, but it was too late for our hero. With one last vicious push, Conn and Eochaidh plunged their heavy war-spears, with all their venomous strength into his badly wounded body. This harrowing assault caused the noble paladin to collapse to the ground, dying from his murderous wounds. This hadn't been a fair or just fight. The deplorable victors finished off their vicious assault by using their blood-stained swords, with one almighty strike each, they cleaved clean through Fraoch's body, before ruthlessly beheading him; his mutilated body being left in four grisly pieces.

Conn's army, being carried away with frenzied excitement, couldn't help themselves; they shouted and screamed in triumph. We heard the noise in the distance and quickly jumped to our feet. Luckily a good-many of us had slept in our battle-clothes, but for the others, there was no time to get ready before Conn's troops were upon us, and the bloody onslaught began. We quickly grabbed our shields and weapons for protection. It was then that our two proud, nobly-descended parties attacked each other with the full pleasure of hatred and with an ever-increasing rage.

The terrifying noise of battle that we suddenly found ourselves plunged into was further plagued by the startling sound of ravens, chattering and croaking, along with vultures with their unnerving, high-pitched screams, all readying themselves to feast upon the fallen.

We knew that we'd need to quickly regroup if we were to stand any chance of surviving; and our enemies were doing exactly that.

We slowly withdrew, reassembling further up the field next to our comrades, facing the enemy, shoulder to shoulder, many of us barefoot and still in our night-shirts, standing next to those who were already dressed for war. We firmly gripped our shields before us, pointing our weapons towards the ironclad enemy.

The two front ranks of our opposing number were steely-eyed, firmly holding overlapping walls of shield; from expensive golden-bordered ones to the old, battered, iron-rimmed variety and many types in between. Their spears pointing over the tops towards us like the spikes of a hedgehog.

Both High-kings were desperately inciting their men to battle, as the Champions, standing defiantly, shouted out cruel, piercing words, hoping that where their weapons couldn't reach their words might penetrate.

The first clash came, as the Champions from both sides violently hurled a shower of thin, deadly javelins towards the enemy, which noisily whizzed through the air. This first cast going hither and thither, though following casts brutally hitting home.

Then we moved towards each other with our stout handled spears, trying furiously to thrust them past the solid wall of shield, into the bodies of our enemies. Many of these murderous weapons violently struck home.

Blood oozed out onto the battlefield. Helmets were crushed by the heavy, quick blows and faces mutilated by the jabs of piercing spears and other deadly, razor-sharp weapons.

The spears were soon covered in a sticky layer of blood from the deep cavernous wounds, though those gaping, gore-ridden wounds only heightened the anger of the injured.

This was a quick, furious battle, the noise was deafening as the hard blows rained down on both sides.

Our broad, hard-edged shields violently punched against the ridges of many enemy faces, which were now cut and badly bruised.

The blood on the battlefield, which flowed from this deadly encounter, became clotted, cold, thick pools which filled up the hollows and furrows of the ground, so that red-mouthed, deep-black ravens, descended upon the bodies of Champions, and upon the carcasses of noble warriors, and upon the broad chests of the poor deceased soldiers; their pointy needle-like tweezer-beaks piercing and ripping apart soft flesh of the once-active heroes, now lying deathly still in those scarlet baths of blood. It was a truly sickening sight to behold and one that still sends chills throughout my body.

With Mogha Nuadhad seeing so many of his honourable men being so mercilessly slaughtered by Conn's fierce warriors, and watching as their warm lively faces turned a cold deathly pale, and witnessing many of his Champions being so cruelly beheaded, whilst his injured comrades who'd fallen onto the field had their mangled bodies thankfully dragged away from that surrounding vicious onslaught, meant that his brave ranks were now rapidly decreasing. The Munster King couldn't take this slaughter anymore; a huge wave of violence and fury began to boil up inside. He rushed towards the enemy with such anger and ferocity that he left a crumpled path of dead and dying in his wake. Bowels and bellies were viciously hacked open, bruised beheaded faces littered the ground by his feet, as he went through the enemy lines, searching intently for Conn, as only his death would put an end to the war. Mogha circled the battlefield nine times trying to find his mighty foe. But Conn knew the ferocity of the younger King, so wisely avoided him at all costs; desperately fearing for his life, he commanded his Champion, Goll, son of Morna to fight against Mogha Nuadhad and drive him from the field.

Mogha Nuadhad was furiously frustrated; he couldn't locate the enemy king anywhere in all the throng. He loudly roared his deadly vow, "If I ever find Conn of the Hundred-battles, all the warriors of *Leath Cuinn* couldn't delay his destruction".

As soon as Goll heard Mogha's murderous words, he was able to pinpoint where he was. He quickly rushed towards him. It was then that these two furious beasts violently attacked each other, thrusting their spears so hard that their shields smashed asunder, falling apart in their hands.

On seeing the immediate danger, to protect their Munster King, a thousand formidable Asian Champions rushed to his aid, slaying the surging tide of Clan Morna as well as any of Conn's men who stood in their way. Unfortunately, Conn's forces were so strong, and the Asian warriors were still mostly undressed, which meant that the majority of them were eventually hacked down and murderously slaughtered.

The courage of Mogha Nuadhad now rose high, and he was transformed into a noble, furious lion, so ferocious that even the angriest dog, or the hungriest wolf would have knelt before him. He sprang towards his enemy. Goll, now fearing for his life as he knew that he couldn't defeat such a mighty warrior, desperately shouted his rallying cry.

On hearing Goll's urgent call, the rest of Clan Morna forced their way through the throng, desperately trying to defend their Fir-bolg leader. And as each member of Goll's Clan inflicted a wound upon Mogha, he wounded each and every one of them in return, whilst still maintaining his ferocious fight against their leader.

The remaining Champions of Asia, as well as many more of Mogha's allies, were now mortally wounded, sadly collapsing on the slippery, corpse-ridden ground near to their worthy King. Witnessing this shocking destruction, two more allies rushed to their King's aid; these were his grandfather, the Lord of Ormond and the fierce Nuada the Red. These two distinguished leaders fought furiously, and valiantly, leaving a pile of dead bodies around them.

That was how it was until Asal the Great, Chieftain of Conn's Household Cavalry, and his ally, Ross, the loyal son of the red-armed King of Ulster, furiously strode across the field to meet our two Munster knights. They fought so violently and ferociously against each other; not one of them yielding an inch, until the four of them left the battle, just as quickly as they'd came, with smashed sides, chests, faces and ribs, in a crippled state, in considerable pain and barely able to stand.

Then, in a sudden lull from the desperate slaughter, Mogha Nuadhad looked around. Everyone seemed to be moving slowly, though he knew that this wasn't really the case. He watched the huge wave of enemy troops surging towards him, the first of them just yards away, all with clenched teeth, murderous eyes and with one overwhelming desire to violently end his life. He saw the bloodied corpses of his once valiant troops lying sprawled around his feet, along with all the foreign heroes who'd fought so fearlessly for his cause. Seeing that more of his esteemed warriors were now in imminent danger and from such unworthy foes and the thought that at any minute he himself could be killed by a mere Champion or some foreign mercenary made him feel so deeply ashamed, which caused his anger to furiously rise once more. His cheeks reddened like crimson, so that he felt neither hurt, nor pain, nor wounds, nor cuts, even though his body was covered by them. He vowed, "Until now it has been a battle of man against man, but now I must fight against the masses. I pledge my word that people will speak till the world's end, the manner in which I shall wreak my anger and vengeance upon my enemy here today".

These words bolstered his kingly pride, his fury boiled and his formidable courage came to the fore as he slowly circled the mighty Goll the way a hawk circles a small bird before attacking. Goll again, loudly cried for help. His thirty formidable brothers quickly rushed to his aid; these were all furious fighting men. They all inflicted wounds upon Mogha Nuadhad, and he, in return, wounded each and every one of them, whilst still maintaining his furious attack against Goll.

Then came the many tribes of Tara; they came with so much strength and hatred against Mogha, that each one of their Chieftains wounded our hero, and Mogha tempestuously returned each and every vicious wound, whilst still fighting the ferocious Goll, until these tribesmen retired from the field, too wounded to fight.

Then Conn's most-loyal companions from his court joined in the assault on Mogha Nuadhad, and each one of them inflicted a wound, whilst Mogha returned one wound or more to each of them, whilst still maintaining his vicious fight against Goll.

Desperately needing assistance, Goll once more gave his rallying cry; this time heard by the powerfully-built Conall of Cruachan, and he too came to his aid; that was until Mogha wounded him, double-wounded him and triple-wounded him to such an extent that the Fir-bolg King collapsed to the ground, mortally wounded, never to recover.

Then Conn of the Hundred-battles himself finally came against Mogha Nuadhad. Conn knew how much danger that his warriors were in from this deadly one-man force. Knowing that his foster-father had now been left for dead and his Champion, Goll, son of Morna, was in immediate mortal danger made him furiously angry; so that Conn and Mogha started heaving tremendously brutal, heavy blows against each other. This truly was a battle of the Titans. And with Conn's enchanted gloves every blow struck home.

Then most of Conn's troops rushed around them, completely surrounding those warring Champions. We tried to get near, to aid our King, but couldn't get anywhere close as we were all fighting for our own lives ourselves. Fiacha the Lame limped forward, at the head of his men, as he desperately tried to rescue Mogha Nuadhad from that mortal onslaught.

Whilst Mogha Nuadhad was using all of his might against both Conn and Goll, they furiously wielded a most despicable and viciously brutal assault upon him. Our king was still putting up a tremendous fight. That was until Conn violently thrust his great war-spear straight through Mogha's shoulder. Conn hadn't managed to pull his spear back out when Mogha, with intense fury, thrust his long broad-spear right through Conn's body so that it came out the other side. Conn's legs instantly buckled beneath him and he fell to the ground in a fainting fit; his body by now had half-a-hundred gaping wounds across it, each wound visibly weeping with the fatality of death.

Conn's warriors, seeing their beloved leader collapsing to the ground, filled them with such boiling, furious rage that they all, as one, violently thrust their spears into Mogha Nuadhad. This viciously, deadly assault from every side was sadly more than our King's body could take. His last noble breath leaving his lips as his soul departed his body; his ashen-faced, limp body yielded to the onslaught and crumpled to the ground, stone cold dead.

Falling next to him, at that very same moment was his old friend and ally, Fiacha the Lame.

Conn's loud, boastful warriors, feeling triumphant, immediately, ghoulishly and ungallantly, raised Mogha Nuadhad's body up in the air with their spears so that his warm corpse was shoulder height. They all shouted and jeered. Their long, hard-fought battle was finally over.

The instant we heard the shouting, we knew that our beloved king was dead. Our courage quickly turned into fear and dread and unsteadiness. We felt suddenly confused and didn't know what to do, but we all felt a burning desire to escape. We backed away from our enemy and fled in every direction, as fast as our tired and aching bodies could go. We took shelter, hiding anywhere that we could, so that Conn's men couldn't find us.

Back on the field, the battle-weary Goll shouted to his men, "Lay down the heroic warrior; his death was not the death of a coward".

Conn's men immediately did as they'd been bid.

We didn't find out till much later that Conn's men couldn't pursue our retreating army, even if they'd wanted, as most of them were lying on the ground themselves, mortally wounded, so that there weren't even nine of them fit for marching, let alone fighting. Nearly one thousand brave Champions died in that sad, detestable battle. Donn would have been busy that night on his white horse, gathering the dead. No-one has ever been able to calculate how many men Mogha Nuadhad slayed that day, but there were more men slain by him than by all the rest of the warriors on the field, in what was to become known as the *Battle of Mag Léna*.

When Conn arose from his trance, feeling weak and in terror, he made his camp that night upon Mag Léna, as his doctors painstakingly patched up his wounds in a desperate bid to save his life. Conn and his warriors sang aloud the praises of the heroic and mighty Mogha Nuadhad; and only the most-worthy of men have their praises sung by their deadliest foes.

We all cried that night; some openly, some in secret, but we all cried. We couldn't believe that our honourable leader Mogha Nuadhad was dead; he really had proved himself to be as great a king as his father. He may not have had all of the compassion and wisdom of his father, but as a skilled general and leader of men, those who truly knew him would have followed him anywhere.

Mogha Nuadhad, son of Magha Neid, along with his great Spanish ally, Fraoch the Militant, son of Heber the Great, were both buried within huge earthen mounds upon the field of battle; two worthy graves for two worthy men.

*Four names he had and proudly wore:*
*Famous was he as Eoghan Mór,*
*Eoghan the Wood-bender, he kindly gave,*
*Eoghan the Splendid, and Nuadhad's Slave".*

And with that the storyteller drank the last remaining drops from his drinking-horn. As he stood up, I could clearly see tears glinting in his eyes. He pulled his warm cloak around his cold body as he briskly walked out into the courtyard, discreetly wiping his watery eyes as he did.

He spent some time that night upon our fortress walls gazing out into the distance, at what I do not know, before finally retiring to bed.

# Principal Characters in the Stories

**Aedh, the Chieftain of the Múscraige**                                    Releaser of Hostages
A good and honest ruler.

**Aedh (Goll), son of Morna**                                    The King with Four Names
One-eyed new Fir-bolg Chieftain of the Fianna. Enemy of Munster.

**Aes Sídhe (AYS SHEE)**
Their name means 'People-of-the-Mounds'. These were the Fairy race.

**African Chieftain**                                    The Island of Destiny
His depiction comes from a faience tile, showing an ancient Libyan Chieftain.

**African Guides**                                    The Island of Destiny
Their description comes from early recorded records of the Berber people, along with a statuette of a Libyan Libu Berber in the Louvre, Paris.

**Ailill Bare-ear**                         Curse of the Aes Sídhe, The King's Betrayal
Fearsome and ruthless King of Munster with one missing ear & blackened teeth.

**Ailill, son of Dunlaing**                                    Church of Sighs
Wicked and powerful brother of Iollann from Leinster. He went on to become the Leinster King.

**Aimend**                                    Releaser of Hostages
Conall Corc's second wife, the daughter of the head of the Corco Luigde.

**Áine**                                    Curse of the Aes Sídhe
Sídhe-princess who is killed by Ailill Bare-ear.

**Amergin White-knee, fourth son of Milesius**                    The Island of Destiny
He was the High-druid of the Milesians. He was impartial.

**Aodh Bennan, Eoghanacht ruler of *Iarmuman***                    Fingin and Mór
Powerful & protective Lord of *Loch Léin*.

**Aodh Dubh (ADE DUFF)**                                    Fingin and Mór
Raven-haired Munster King. The father of Fingin of Femen and Failbhé Flann.

**Aongus, son of Nathfraoch**                                    Church of Sighs
Vainglorious but good prince & later, first Christian King of Munster.

**Arech Red-brow, second son of Milesius**                    The Island of Destiny
His first name means Wise. Born in Scythia. He was known for his wisdom. His full name in Irish Gaelic is Arech Februadh.

**Arthur, son of Uther Pendragon**                                    Church of Sighs
The legendary King of the Britons.

**Art the Solitary**                                    Curse of the Aes Sídhe
Son of Conn of the Hundred-battles. High-king of Ériu & a good, fair and noble man. He was warm, charismatic and witty.

**At, Lann & Lean.**                                    The King with Four Names
Conn of the Hundred-battles' favourite (& powerful) Sídhe-mistresses.

**Baiscinn**                                    A Time of Heroes
One of the two Chieftains of the Corca Baisgin. They were descended from Cairbre Bascaín, son of Munster's old enemy, Conaire, the High-king, son of Mogha Laine, who'd warred against Mogha Nuadhad and his father, Magha Neid. Baiscinn's descendants are the O'Baskin, of south County Clare. (Not to be confused with other O'Baskin families from other counties).

**Banbha, wife of Ethor.**                                    The Island of Destiny
She was a brave Fairy Queen, being the first one of them to meet the Milesian invaders.

**Beara, daughter of Heber the Great.**                                    The King with Four Names
Very beautiful and honourable princess from Castille. She married Mogha Nuadhad.

**Bebinn, daughter of Turgeis**                                    A Time of Heroes
Sitric's beautiful sister., who he used to lure Ceallachan into a trap.

**Béinne Britt**                                    Curse of the Aes Sídhe
King of the Britons. He aided MacCon in their invasion of Ériu.

**Brendan**                                    A Time of Heroes
Saint Brendan the Navigator, also called Brendan of Clonfert. He became known as Brendan the Navigator after his legendary sea voyage to find the Garden of Eden. He founded Clonfert Monastery in 553 A.D. He was the patron saint of Kerry and of Clonfert. He died in 576 A.D.

**Breoghan, son of Brath.**                                    The Island of Destiny
Powerful ruler of his tribe and conqueror of the Iberian Peninsula. Grandfather of Milesius. All the Irish Celts are said to descend from him. So well respected is he still that a huge statue to him has been erected beside the Tower of Hercules, in A Coruña.

**Brian Boru, son of Cineidi (Kennedy)**                                    A Time of Heroes

He later became the High-king. It was through a law that he passed that surnames were first introduced in Ireland.

**Cairbre Cat-head**      **Usurper to the Throne**

Fir-bolg king and cruel leader of the Attacotti who had furry cat's ears.

**Cairbre Cruithneachan**      **Releaser of Hostages**

One of the twin Scottish sons of Conall Corc and Mong-Fionn. After being banished from Cashel by his father, he returned home, back to his mother in Alba, after which he gained the name *Cruithneachan* which means 'son of the Pictish-woman'. The brothers were called 'The Two Cairbres' and were known for being angry and jealous of their father's success.

**Cairbre Luachra**      **Releaser of Hostages**

One of the twin Scottish sons of Conall Corc and Mong-Fionn. After his exile he was named after the clover-covered mountains of Sliabh Luachra that separated him from his father. The brothers were called 'The Two Cairbres' and were known for being angry and jealous of their father's success. Cairbre Luachra eventually died at Femen and was buried at Loch Cend, in what is now called Rockwell Lake, within the grounds of Rockwell College, Cashel.

**Cairbre of the Liffey**      **Druid War**

Son of Cormac Longbeard, High-king's Tanist. He was a weapons expert & Inciter for Leath Cuinn. He was a trusted man. He gained his second name as he spent much of his youth on the Plain of the Liffey, where the River Liffey (Fast-runner River) flows past.

**Cathal (CAHAL), son of Aodh, son of Cairbre Crom**      **Fingin and Mór**

Fingin's cousin, the Master of the Eoghanacht fortress, *Glennamhain*. A good man.

**Ceallachan (Callaghan)**      **A Time of Heroes**

New King of Munster. Ceallachan has been described as being more senior in age than Cineidi, and Cineidi has a grown-up son, so I assume that Ceallachan must be at least in his mid-thirties by the time that this tale begins.

**Ceann Mór**      **Druid War**

Clever apprentice to Mogh Ruith but timid fighter.

**Chief-seanchaí (SHAH-NACK-EE) of Munster.**      **A Time of Heroes**

He is the narrator of these stories. He would have been one of the most important men in the kingdom, and as part of his job he would have memorised hundreds of stories.

**Chieftain of Éile**      **Releaser of Hostages**

An honourable man, when not provoked.

**Ciarán (the elder)**      **Church of Sighs**

Priest & friend of Aongus. A seer, who became Patron Saint of Ossory. He was one of the 'Twelve Apostles of Ireland', having studied under St Finnian. He was the first saint to be born in Ériu, as well as being the patron saint of Ossory. His father, Lagneach Faoladh, whose second name means 'werewolf' was cursed so that he would change into a wolf. There's more information about him in 'Companion to the Kings of Munster'.

**Cineidi (Kennedy), son of Lorcan**      **A Time of Heroes**

Tanist of Munster. Head of the Dalcassians & father to Donchuan, as well as the famous Brian Boru who later became the High-king. Cineidi was the ancestor of the Munster Kennedy and O'Kennedy family (Not the Ulster family as they descend from the Scottish Kennedy).

**Chief-brehon of Munster**      **Druid War, Church of Sighs, A Time of Heroes**

The top legal advisor to the Munster King.

**Chief-steward of Munster**      **Releaser of Hostages, A Time of Heroes**

A man responsible for every aspect of the running of the royal fortress, from the production of food for the table to the placement of guests in the beds. He basically ran the royal household and was considered a very important man.

**Cith Rua, Ceathach, Cith Mór, Céacht, Crotha**      **Druid War**

The five druids of Tara who Cormac Longbear forced to wage war upon Munster. Cith Rua appears to be the High-druid.

**Clan Fingin (CLAN FINEEN)**      **Fingin and Mór, A Time of Heroes**

The descendants of Fingin of Femen are known as Clan Fingin. Suilebhain (Sullivan) of Cnoc Rathfann was the head of the clan in the final story.

**Cliodhna**      **The King with Four Names**

She was the powerful fair-haired Sídhe-queen of Desmond. She left the Land of Promise to be with her mortal lover in Ériu, but Manannán son of Lir's Fairy-minstrel played an enchanted tune which sent her to sleep. And as she slept upon the shore of Oak-harbour (Glandore Harbour), a large wave suddenly appeared and washed her out to sea. Some say that the wave wasn't at Oak-harbour but was at nearby Castle-of-the-woods Bay (Bay of Clonakilty).

**Cobthach Fionn, son of Dungal of the Corco Luigde**      **A Time of Heroes**

His tribe descend from the ancient Dáirine. Cobthach's descendants are the O'Coffey. All the O'Coffeys of Munster descend from him.

**Colpa of the Sword, sixth son of Milesius**      **The Island of Destiny**

Was known to be honest and sincere, and completely without guile.

**Colptha & Lurga**      **Druid War**

Two very powerful & wise Sídhe-druid brothers. Swords & spears can't harm them.

**Conaire, son of Mogha Laine**                                   The King with Four Names

Treacherous enemy prince of Munster.

**Conall Corc**                                                   Releaser of Hostages

Much loved & kind king of Munster. Conall Corc probably died about 453 AD. This is thought to be the year that Aongus son of Nathfraoch became King of Munster.

**Conall of Cruachan**                                            The King with Four Names

Foster-father of Conn of the Hundred-battles. Powerfully-built Fir-bolg King of Connacht. In the Battle of Mag Léna, Conall went to the assistance of Goll, to save him from Mogha. It was then that the Munster King wounded him, double-wounded him and triple-wounded him to such an extent that the Fir-bolg King collapsed to the ground, mortally wounded, being left as a 'death-invalid', to be looked after at his home at Cruachan, where he died a year later from his wounds.

**Conchobhar, son of Cathal, of the Ciarraige Luachra**          A Time of Heroes

County Kerry takes its name from this tribe. Conchobhar's descendants are the O'Conchobair, now called O'Connor. All the O'Connors of County Kerry descend from him. Their ancient territory stretched from the town of Tralee northwards up to the Sionna (River Shannon).

**Conchubar of the Corcamruad**                                   A Time of Heroes

From the House of Fergus Mór. The descendants of Conchubar are the O'Connor family, of Corcomroe, County Clare.

**Concraidh, Lord of Ossory**                                     Church of Sighs

Handsome ruler of Ossory & a good & noble man.

**Conghaile**                                                     A Time of Heroes

One of the three Chieftains of the Corco Duibne. Conghaile's descendants are the O' Connell. All the O'Connells of County Kerry descend from him.

**Conla**                                                         Druid War

Son of Teige, son of Cian; excellent student but self-centred. A naïve & cruel young man. He becomes the foster-son of Cormac Longbeard.

**Conn of the Hundred-battles**                                   The King with Four Names

High-king of Ériu and enemy of Munster.

**Corb Cacht**                                                    Curse of the Aes Sídhe

His name appears in 'The Battle of Mag Mucrama' but his name doesn't seem to appear in any other records. As Cormac-Cas' name doesn't appear in 'The Battle of Mag Mucrama' and he is meant to be one of the three greatest Champions of Ériu then there could be a mistake and maybe Cormac-Cas is the same person as Corb Cacht as their names sound similar. Alternatively, Corb Cacht could be the same person as Mogha of the Chariots (Mogh Corb) and therefore a son of Cormac-Cas, son of Sabina and Ailill. But as his name isn't mentioned elsewhere and he is a great fighter leading a large army I have come to the conclusion that he may have been one of Ailill Bare-ear's ten illegitimate sons. Also, as Corb Cacht appears to die in 'the Battle of Mag Mucrama' whilst Mogha of the Chariots, as well as Cormac-Cas live on to fight in other battles, this further strengthens my conclusion that he is an illegitimate son of Ailill Bare-ear.

**Cormac-Cas**                              Curse of the Aes Sídhe, Druid War, The King's Betrayal

Second son of Ailill Bare-ear & one of the three greatest Champions of Ériu during his lifetime. Tanist and then King of Munster.

**Cormac Longbeard**                        Curse of the Aes Sídhe, Druid War, The King's Betrayal

Powerful and handsome prince of Tara and later High-king. A very wise leader and foster-son of MacCon. Son of Art the Solitary. He waged war on Munster.

**Crimthann-Cas, son of Eanna of the Foul-smile**                Releaser of Hostages

Powerful and ruthless King of Leinster.

**Crimthann Mór**                                                Releaser of Hostages

Powerful & ruthless Chieftain who becomes High-king of Ériu. Uncle of Conall Corc.

**Crimthann 'Nephew-of-Nár'**                                    Usurper to the Throne

Also known as Crimthann Niadh-Nar. A High-king who served the land well.

**Crimthann Yellow-hair**                                        The King with Four Names

Powerful King of Leinster & Conn of the Hundred-battles' old teacher.

**Cruife**                                                       Usurper to the Throne

The pregnant wife of King Eanna Brightneck & daughter of a King of the Britons.

**Cuirirán, swineherd of the Múscraige tribe**                   Releaser of Hostages

One of the two swineherds who saw the vision of the angel, Victor.

**Cumhal (COOL), son of Trénmór**                                The King with Four Names

Old Chieftain of the Fianna (FEENA) & husband of Muireann. Father of the famous Fionn, son of Cumhal (Finn mac Cool). An ally of Munster.

**Dáire**                                                        Usurper to the Throne

Distant cousin of Dearg Theine & leader of the Dáirine.

**Dáire Barrach**                                                The King with Four Names

Handsome & heroic Lord of Tuath Laighean in the north of Leinster & Mogha Nuadhad's foster-father. An ally of Munster.

**Dame Lyonors**                                                 Church of Sighs

Lyonors is Tennyson's name for her, as Malory calls her Dame Lyonesse, which is confusing, as it makes it sound as if she is from Lyonesse, which she isn't. She is from the Castle Perilous in North Wales.

**Dearg Damhsa (DERG DOW-SA)**                                      The King with Four Names

The Chief-druid of Munster. A wise sorcerer whose name means Red Dance.

**Dearg Theine**                                                    Usurper to the Throne

Son of Eanna Brightneck & Cruife. A fair ruler, born without any ears and with a shining glow about his body.

**Déisi wife of Fingin, The**                                       Fingin and Mór

Queen of Munster. A cruel & nasty woman, and daughter of the Chief of the Déisi.

**Diarmaid**                                                        A Time of Heroes

One of the two Chieftains of the Corca Baisgin. Their tribe were descended from Cairbre Bascaín, son of Munster's old enemy, Conaire, the High-king, son of Mogha Laine, who'd warred against Mogha Nuadhad and his father, Magha Neid. Diarmaid's descendants are the MacDermot, from the south of County Clare. (Not to be confused with other MacDermot families from other counties).

**Dil the Great**                        Church of Sighs, Curse of the Aes Sídhe, Druid War

Fiacha Broadcrown's maternal grandfather. Aongus, son of Nathfraoch's 5X great-grandfather, Elderly and blind, Lord-druid of Ossory. A powerful and respected druid.

**Do Déra**                                                         Curse of the Aes Sídhe

Loyal Jester to MacCon, with the skills of a druid. He was buried upon Cenn Abrat. Some of the old records state that it was Cairbre Músc who killed Do Déra.

**Doncha, son of Flann Sionnach.**                                  A Time of Heroes

The High-king during the time of our last story, during the Viking Age. (Father-in-law of Tor & therefore ally of Vikings)

**Donchuan (Duncan), son of Cineidi (Kennedy)**                     A Time of Heroes

Good friend of Ceallachan & son of Cineidi. He was the brother to the future High-king, Brian Boru. Donchuan was a great leader, being wise & courageous. Many great families descend from Donchuan, including the Kennedy and O'Kennedys of Munster, the O'Conaing, now anglicised as O'Gunning and Gunning, who descend from Conaing, son of Cineadh son of this Donchuan, son of Cineidi.

**Donn, first son of Milesius**                                     The Island of Destiny

His name means Brown-Haired. He was born in Scythia and was well-trained by his father, Milesius to lead their tribe when the time was right.

**Donogh Ó Caomh (DUN-ACKA O'Keeffe)**                              A Time of Heroes

Master of *Glennamhain*. An esteemed general. He was the first O'Keeffe.

**Donogh, from the Battle of the Island of Dark Strangers**         A Time of Heroes

This man has been described as 'great' 'valiant' and 'famous in song'. There were many men named Donogh in those days; the name means 'brown-haired Chieftain'. I don't believe that this was Donogh Ó Caomh, as he was supposedly in his house at the time of the battle, which would make the next encounter with him make more sense. So I don't really know who this Chieftain is.

**Drott**                                                           A Time of Heroes

These were Viking warlords or Chieftains.

**Duach Iarfhlaith, Eoghanacht Lord of Loch Léin**                  Church of Sighs

Rebellious ruler of Iarmuman. His grandfather had been banished to this territory by Conall Corc.

**Dubdaboirenn, Chieftain of the Western Uí Echach**                A Time of Heroes

His tribe, the Uí Echach Muman, belonged to the Eoghanacht Rathlinn. The Uí Echach Muman were from the area around the town of Bandon, County Cork. The O'Mahonys of the Barony of Iveagh, County Cork and the O'Donoghues of Cashel, Ossory and County Kerry all descend from the House of Echu.

**Duinechad the Dun, son of Fiangus**                               A Time of Heroes

He was one of the Chieftains at the coronation of Ceallachan. He also played an important role in the sea-battle to rescue Ceallachan.

**Duirdriu, swineherd of Éile**                                     Releaser of Hostages

One of the two swineherds who saw the vision of the angel, Victor.

**Eadaoin (AY-DEEN) of *Inis Crecraighe***                          The King with Four Names

Mogha Nuadhad's golden haired, very powerful Sídhe-mistress.

**Eanna Brightneck**                                                Usurper to the Throne

King of Munster-famous for wearing a golden necklace. In the Gaelic language he is called Eanna Muncain. I have given him as a torc, one that fits the description of the Broighter Collar. I've also given him an anthropomorphic grip to his sword, as these were used by noblemen at this time, so it is possible that he may indeed have used one.

**Edersceal, son of Fionn of the Corco Luigde**                     A Time of Heroes

His tribe descend from the ancient Dáirine. Edersceal's descendants are the O'Driscoll. All the O'Driscoll of County Cork and County Kerry descend from him.

**Egyptian Ambassador**                                             The Island of Destiny

His description is based on a statue of Sobekemsaf, who was an important Egyptian official at this time, being the Reporter of Thebes and Overseer of Granaries.

**Eithne the Hateful**                                                    Church of Sighs

Daughter of the Leinster King, fostered by the Déisi; all boys hated her as she was fed on the bodies of young boys to help her to grow.

**Eocha Areamh, son of Aongus, son of Nathfraoch**          Church of Sighs, A Time of Heroes

He was the third Christian king of Munster. Also known as Eocha Fionn, he was the ancestor of the O'Keeffes-according to the Irish Pedigrees. See the O'Keeffe's family tree in 'Kings of Munster: A Time of Heroes'. He died in the year 523 AD.

**Eochaidh (OH-KIDH) Gunta**                                          The King's Betrayal

Ulster's greatest Champion & a powerful leader. He became High-king after Cormac Longbeard had died. He ruled for a year before being killed in battle. Then Cormac Longbeard's son, Cairbre of the Liffey took the throne.

**Eochaid (OH-KIDH) of Cnoc Rathfann.**                          A Time of Heroes

See 'Suilebhain'.

**Eochaidh the Slave-ruler**                                            Church of Sighs

Otherwise known as Eochaid Mugmedon. The father of Niall of the Nine-hostages.

**Eochaid (OH-KIDH) the Wounder (Eochaid Guineach)**          Church of Sighs

Leinster Chieftain & Eithne the Hateful's villainous nephew.

**Eochy Vivahain**                                                        Church of Sighs

This is another name for Eochaidh the Slave-ruler (Eochaid Mugmedon).

**Eoghan Mór (OWEN MORE)**                                          Curse of the Aes Sídhe

First son of Ailill Bare-ear & Sabina, Heroic prince & future king of Munster.

**Erenan, the eighth and youngest son of Milesius**          The Island of Destiny

Born in the Spanish lands of Iberia. He was lithe, athletic and brave.

**Ériu (AIR-REE), wife of Kéthor**                                  The Island of Destiny

Fairy-queen. She was beautiful and wise, bold, fearless and serene.

**Errgi, Eng & Engain**                                                Druid War

Three very powerful Sídhe-druidesses. They were sisters whom no mortal man can escape nor wound.

**Ethiar**                                                                The Island of Destiny

He was Scota's druid. I assume the druids wore grey, which would explain the colour of the flags which marked their graves.

**Ethor**                                                                The Island of Destiny

He was one of the Fairy-kings. He was the son of Cearmad Honey-mouth. He styled himself as the son of Cuill, god of the hazel tree. He was lordly and haughty, known for thinking himself as wise as the hazel-tree, so looked down upon everyone he met.) His wife was Banbha.

**Failbhe Fionn**                                                        A Time of Heroes

Golden-haired Chieftain of the Corco Duibne & 2-sworded swashbuckling hero. In Fiangal's poem he says the line 'Do you grieve for the body of Uí Conaire'. This refers to Failbhe Fionn being the descendant of Conaire, son of Mogha Laine, the 111th High-king, whose descendants were sometimes known as the Uí Conaire. In the same poem Fiangal also says the line 'Descendant of noble Aongus, withal'. This refers to Failbhe Fionn's ancestor, Aongus Turmeach-Teamreach, the 81st High-king. Failbhe Fionn's proud descendants are the O'Falvey. All the O'Falveys of County Kerry descend from him. The O'Falveys were the hereditary admirals of Desmond.

**Failbhé Flann, son of Aodh Dubh**                              Fingin and Mór

He was the brother of Fingin. His rule was a long one, being in total two-score years. From him descend the Cenél Failbhé Flann, or 'Clan Failbhé Flann'. The leading families of this House are the MacCarthys, O'Callaghans and MacAuliffes.

**Ferches**                                                              Curse of the Aes Sídhe

The Chief-poet of Munster. A loyal and trusted ally of Ailill Bare-ear. After Fionn, son of Cumhal, heard that Ferches had killed his friend, Maccon, he spent seven years tracking the Chief-poet so that he could revenge himself on the old warrior. Although, another account says that Ael son of Dergdubh, while out hunting, threw his spear at a stag, but unfortunately missed the stag, hitting Ferches and killing him instead. Whichever tale is true we shall sadly never know.

**Feredach Fionn**                                                      Releaser of Hostages

The powerful King of the Picts from the land of Alba.

**Fer Fi**                                                                Curse of the Aes Sídhe

Vengeful Sídhe-prince, brother of Áine.

**Fergus Blacktooth**                                                  The King's Betrayal

King of Ulster and enemy of Cormac Longbeard.

**Fergus Longhair & Fergus Fire-over-Bregia**                  The King's Betrayal

Two fierce brothers of the Ulster King, Fergus Blacktooth.

**Fergus Mór, son Ros Ruadh**                                      Druid War, A Time of Heroes

Believed by some to be the father of the King-druid, Mogh Ruith, although that would mean that the King-druid was several hundred years old. Fergus was the King of Ulster until he was deposed. His sword was the powerful weapon known as 'Caladbolg', which means 'hard-cleft'.

**Fiacha Broadcrown**                                                    **Druid War, The King's Betrayal**

Kind, caring, generous, warm and friendly prince of Munster, second in line to the Munster throne. After he becomes King, he leads his army against the Munster invasion by Cormac Longbeard.

**Fiacha the Lame**                                                      **The King with Four Names**

Lord of Hy Kinsella, brother of Dáire Barrach. A universally loved, brave & spirited Lord of southern Leinster. An ally of Munster.

**Fial**                                                                 **The Island of Destiny**

Beloved wife of Lughaidh, son of Ithe, and daughter of Milesius. She was anxious, young, gentle and fragile. Fial and her husband, Lughaidh, were first cousins once removed. Their lineage being: Fial, daughter of Milesius son of Bilé son of Breoghan; and Lughaidh son of Ithe son of Breoghan.

**Fiangal**                                                              **A Time of Heroes**

He was a handsome young warrior. He was a man of honour and foster-brother of Failbhe Fionn. He selflessly killed Sitric, in revenge for the Viking Lord killing Failbhe Fionn.

**Fianna (FEENA)**                                        **The King with Four Names, A Time of Heroes**

These were the standing armies of the provincial kings, who'd been recruited from landless young highborns. Their recruitment depended upon them passing many dangerous trials, so that once initiated these young men could become part of that elite, highly-trained military fighting force. Just to be part of this regiment was considered to be a huge honour.

**Fingin (FINEEN) of Femen**                                             **Fingin and Mór**

Wise, playful, romantic hero & brave, fierce warrior, well-loved by his people.

**Fionn, son of Cumhal (Finn mac Cool)**                                 **The King with Four Names**

Well-built, brave young hero. Champion of Leath Mogha & new Chieftain of the Fianna.

**Fir-bolg (FEER BOLG)**

An ancient race.

**Flann of the Corco Luigde**                                            **A Time of Heroes**

His tribe descend from the ancient Dáirine.

**Fodhla, wife of Téthor.**                                              **The Island of Destiny**

Fairy-queen. She was gentle and fearful of conflict and danger.

**Fraoch the Militant (Fraoch Mileasach)**                               **The King with Four Names**

Warrior-prince of Castile. Son of Heber the Great & leader of 2000 Spanish warriors. A good ally of Munster.

**Gadhra**                                                               **Druid War**

A powerful Sídhe-druid and ally of Mogh Ruith.

**Galamh (GALAV)/Milesius of Spain, son of Bilé**                        **The Island of Destiny**

Heroic leader of his tribe.

**Gentle Moncha of the Boats**                                           **Druid War**

Beautiful, intelligent and caring daughter of Dil the Great and brave mother of Fiacha Broadcrown.

**Gilla Ciarain**                                                        **A Time of Heroes**

He was the son of Eric, the old Viking King. This prince was killed in the Battle of Macha's Height.

**Goll, son of Morna**                                                   **The King with Four Names**

One-eyed Fir-bolg Chieftain of the Fianna. Works for Conn of the Hundred-battles.

**Gothi**                                                                **A Time of Heroes**

These were the Norse priests who, under Viking rule, administered over every Irish church.

**Gouvernail**                                                           **Church of Sighs**

An educated man who tutored Tristan in Gaul, before becoming his loyal Chief-attendant. He became Tristan's Squire after he'd attained his knighthood.

**Gruibne**                                                              **Releaser of Hostages**

Highland Chief-poet of Feredach Fionn, who Conall Corc set free. I have given him the Orkney Hood as a way to describe his clothing.

**Handsome Scandinavian.**                                               **A Time of Heroes**

He was a Drott (warlord/chieftain), being one of 'The three Guardians of the Great Marsh of Munster'. He must have been from Denmark, as his island fortress seemed to be full of Danes, so he would have had dark hair.

**Heber Donn, only son of Ir**                                           **The Island of Destiny**

He was still a youth when he invaded Ireland with the Milesians. He was brown-haired, proud and noble. After the island was divided into two, I assume that Heber Donn must have gone to live in the north as an ally of his Uncle Heremon, for later on, when Heremon becomes the sole High-king he gives his young nephew the whole of Ulster to rule.

**Heber Fionn, third son of Milesius**                                   **The Island of Destiny**

Kind-hearted and fair-minded. Born in Egypt. He had four sons: Er, Orba, Feron, Fergna

**Heber Fionn's wife**                                                   **The Island of Destiny**

She was loyal and protective of her husband and didn't like to see him being taken advantage of.

**Heber the Great, son of Midna**                                              **The King with Four Names**

King of Castile, in Iberia. Father-in-law of Mogha Nuadhad. Much of the Iberian Peninsula was under Roman rule at this time which meant that many of the inhabitants were Romanized, therefore as no pictures or descriptions of Heber the Great I've given him the beard of the Emperor Hadrian and with him being of the same Celtic blood as Mogha Nuadhad, I've given him the hair and stature of Chief Huevos Y Bacon from Asterix in Spain, with the red cloak and crown of Pelagius of Asturias, who ruled about 500 years later.

**Heremon, seventh son of Milesius**                                              **The Island of Destiny**

Born in the Spanish lands of Iberia. He was a determined leader, being ambitious and fearsome. He had four sons to Odba: Muimne, Luigne, Laighean, and Palap the Lucky.

**Housekarl**                                                                    **A Time of Heroes**

These were Viking stewards who, under Viking rule, had to run every village or settlement.

**Ilbrecht**                                                                     **A Time of Heroes**

See 'Prince Ilbrecht'

**Iollann, son of Dunlaing**                                                     **Church of Sighs**

Wicked and powerful brother of Ailill from Leinster.

**Ir, fifth son of Milesius**                                                    **The Island of Destiny**

Born on the island of Irena, near Thrace. He was always foremost in battle & was a prince amongst men.

**Irial Faidh, the prophet**                                                     **The Island of Destiny**

He was Heremon and Téa's baby, who went on to rule Ériu as the tenth High-king. Like his mother, he also liked change, and it was upon his command that the majority of the country was cleared of its ancient forests. He had a huge, powerful army, but was known to be a cold and unsympathetic ruler.

**Iseult**                                                                       **Church of Sighs**

Famous daughter of Aongus, son of Nathfraoch. She was in love with Tristan.

**Ithe, son of Breoghan**                                                        **The Island of Destiny**

He led first expedition to Ireland. He was a very learned, wise and brave leader.

**Kéthor**                                                                       **The Island of Destiny**

The Fairy-king who ruled the land that year. He was the son of Cearmad Honey-mouth. Kéthor He styled himself as being the son of Greine, god of the sun. He was handsome and as generous as the sun's rays on a warm day. His wife was Ériu.

**King Arthur**                                                                  **Church of Sighs**

See 'Arthur, son of Uther Pendragon'.

**King Mark, son of Felix**                                                      **Church of Sighs**

Infamous King of Cornwall. An insecure ruler.

**King of Iceland**                                                              **A Time of Heroes**

He would probably be blond-haired as he was from Norse stock. If the events of this story are to be believed then his name may be, Thorsteinn Ingólfsson (Þorsteinn Ingólfsson), son of the first Norse settler in Iceland, Ingólfur Arnarson. His first name *Thorsteinn* means 'Thunderstone' or 'Thor-stone', so I've armed him with a large, heavy, stone-headed war-hammer.

**King of Leinster**                                                             **A Time of Heroes**

The Leinster King during our final tale. The kingdoms of Leinster and Munster were often at war.

**Laigin (LAYEN)**                                                               **Church of Sighs**

A powerful tribe from Leinster.

**Laisrén, son of Nathfraoch**                                                   **Church of Sighs**

He was the younger brother of Aongus. He studied under Saint Finnian at Clonard Abbey, eventually becoming the highly respected abbot and patron saint of Ox Island, which lay upon the Lake of Érainn. Laisrén was otherwise known as Molaise (MOLASH'A) and was one of the 'Twelve Apostles of Ireland'.

**Laoghaire (LEARY)**                                                            **Releaser of Hostages**

A High-king & son of Niall of the Nine-hostages.

**Law-speaker**                                                                  **A Time of Heroes**

He was a kind of Scandinavian brehon. Macha's Height was governed by the one in our story.

**Lenn-Turmon of the Berserkers**                                                **A Time of Heroes**

He was the leader of a blood-crazed and violent bearskin-coated company of warriors.

**Lenn-Turmon of the Journey**                                                   **A Time of Heroes**

He was Sitric's Strongarm. He led a band of fearsome warriors who enjoyed the more dangerous missions of collecting taxes and murdering enemy Chieftains

**Lobhan Draoi (LAU-VAN DREE)**                                                  **A Time of Heroes**

He was a very powerful druid from the land of the Britons, although he had a cruel and evil streak. His eyes were able to mesmerise and entrance all whom he encountered.

**Lochlainn of the Corcamruad**                                                  **A Time of Heroes**

From the House of Fergus Mór. The descendants of Lochlainn are the O'Loghlin (O'Lochlainn) family, Chiefs of Burren, County Clare.

**Lord of Ormond (Flann, son of Fiacra)**                    The King with Four Names

Mogha Nuadhad's maternal grandfather-a fierce warrior.

**Lord of Tir Conaill.**                                      A Time of Heroes

**See** 'Muirchertach, son of Airnelach'.

**Lord of Tir Eoghain**                                       Church of Sighs

Mighty ruler & grandson of Niall of the Nine-hostages, ruled from his fortress of the Grianán of Aileach, Ulster. An enemy of Munster.

**Lughaidh, son of Ithe**                                     The Island of Destiny

Known as the First Bard of Ireland. He was on both the first and second expedition that first went to Ireland.

**Lughaidh, son of Laoghaire**                                Church of Sighs

He claimed the throne as High-king and ruled for 25 years, until he insulted Patrick. Then a lightning bolt came from the heavens and killed him.

**Lugaid Lága**                              Curse of the Aes Sídhe, The King's Betrayal

Ailill Bare-ear's enemy brother. One of the greatest Champions of Ériu. He was MacCon's foster-father and Champion. After that he was allied to no-one. He was a good and honourable man. An honourable man.

**MacCon, son of MacNiadh, son of Lughaidh**                  Curse of the Aes Sídhe

Son of Sabina & step-son of Ailill Bare-ear. Wages war against his half-brother, **Eoghan Mór and** his step-father. Some records say that it was Cairbre Músc who wounded MacCon in the leg with his spear.

**MacNiadh, son of Lughaidh**                                 The King with Four Names

Treacherous enemy prince of Munster

**Magha Neid**                                                The King with Four Names

Much loved King of Munster, wise & protective father.

**Maghlar Dearg the Witch**                                   Releaser of Hostages

Mid-wife & healer. Known as the Red Mare. A good woman. Conall Corc and Niall of the Nine-hostages' foster-mother.

**Magnus**                                                    A Time of Heroes

He was the grinning Viking Drott (warlord) who was killed by a brown-haired Chieftain, called Donogh in their first battle, 'The Battle of the Island of Dark Strangers'.

**Magnus son of Turgeis.**                                    A Time of Heroes

He was a huge, angry redheaded Viking who favoured the battle-axe. He was the brother of Sitric.

**Main, son of Conall Corc and Mong-Fionn**                   Releaser of Hostages

Main became known as Main Leamhna, which means Main of Leven, as he settled at Loch Leven. He remained in Alba and was the ancestor of the Great Stewards of Lennox, from whom are descended the royal line of Stewart/Stuart, making him ancestor of the present British Royal Family, as can be seen in John O'Hart's acclaimed 19th century book, 'Irish Pedigrees; or The Origin and Stem of the Irish Nation'. See also 'Companion to the Kings of Munster'.

**Milesius of Spain/Galamh, son of Bilé**                     The Island of Destiny

Heroic leader of his tribe.

**Mogha Nuadhad**                                             The King with Four Names

Son of Magha Neid. Prince, then King of Munster. Clever, powerfully strong & brave. In *The Battle of Magh Leana*, edited by Eugene O'Curry, it says that Mogha Nuadhad wasn't fostered by Dáire Barrach but by Nuadha Dearg (Nuada the Red), son of Dáire, and that is who Mogha Nuadhad was named after. It goes on to say that the Ráth that they built was on Mag Femen (Plain of Femen).

**Mogha of the Chariots**                                     Druid War

Son of Cormac-Cas and Tanist of Munster. A trusted man & Inciter for the kingdom of Munster.

**Mogh Ruith**                                                Druid War

The King-druid. The most powerful druid in the land, although blind. Mogh Ruith's father, it was said, was the noble Ulster King, Fergus Mór son Ros Ruadh, who ruled from his palace of the Twins of Macha. There are stories about him in the Ulster Cycle which puts his reign at about 1 A.D. Mogh Ruith was believed to have been buried under a cairn on Corrin Hill, within his territory of Fermoy. In 1832 half of the cairn was removed to build a boundary wall. Two earthenware burial urns were found within the cairn

**Mong-Fionn**                                                Releaser of Hostages

Beautiful daughter of Feredach Fionn & Conall Corc's Highland wife.

**Moran**                                                     Usurper to the Throne

Son of Cairbre Cat-head. He was a good, honest & wise man.

**Morann**                                                    A Time of Heroes

For the blond-haired son of the Isle of Lewis' Fleet-King, See **'Prince Morann'.**

**Morann, son of Connra,**                                    A Time of Heroes

He was a dark-haired Drott (warlord) from Denmark. Otherwise known as great Lochlann. He was killed by the merry poet, Ribordan, in their first battle, 'The Battle of the Island of Dark Strangers'.

**Mór, daughter of Aedh, son of Echu**                        A Time of Heroes

Spirited wife of Sitric, daughter of Aedh, King of Innse Gall (Hebrides), but in love with Ceallachan.

**Mór Mumhain**                                                          **Fingin and Mór**

Beautiful princess, daughter of Aodh Bennan.

**Muirchertach, son of Airnelach**                                       **A Time of Heroes**

He was the Lord of Tir Conaill at the time of our Viking tale. He told Sitric of the whereabouts of Ceallachan's rescue party.

**Muirceartach, son of Earca**                                           **Church of Sighs**

He became the High-king. The first year of his rule was in 504 AD. He ruled for 24 years until he was killed in a 'threefold death' by being drowned in a vat of wine, burnt in a house fire and crushed by a falling roof beam.

**Muireann of the Fair Neck**                                            **The King with Four Names**

Wife of Cumhal & mother of the famous Fionn, son of Cumhal (Finn mac Cool).

**Murcha, son of Bran Fionn**                                            **A Time of Heroes**

King of Leinster who wants to fight against Ceallachan after his army has rescued him and they've almost reached home after their wars against the Vikings.

**Niall of the Nine-hostages**                                           **Releaser of Hostages**

Next High-king & Conall Corc's foster-brother. A good man.

**Norseman of the Blades.**                                              **A Time of Heroes**

He was a Drott (warlord/chieftain), being one of 'The three Guardians of the Great Marsh of Munster'. He must have been from Denmark, as his island fortress seemed to be full of Danes, so he would have had dark hair.

**Odba (OVA), daughter of Milesius and first wife of Heremon**          **The Island of Destiny**

She was a good woman, being perfect and harmonious (kind, friendly and agreeable). The white surfaced hill south of Tara bears her name.

**Olaf**                                                                 **A Time of Heroes**

He was a fearsome Jarl from the Island of Dark Strangers, who Ceallachan killed in his first battle. He was from Denmark so would have had dark hair. His name can also be written as Amlaib. Not to be confused with Old Olaf.

**Old Olaf**                                                             **A Time of Heroes**

He was the eldest of all the Scandinavian nobles. He was a Drott (warlord/chieftain), being one of 'The three Guardians of the Great Marsh of Munster'. His name can be written as Amlaib. Not to be confused with Olaf, the Jarl from the Island of Dark Strangers.

**Ottarr the Black**                                                     **A Time of Heroes**

He was a prince from Denmark who was killed in the Battle of Macha's Height.

**Patrick, son of Calphurn**                                            **Church of Sighs, Releaser of Hostages**

Legendary, powerful holy man & wise Christian Missionary. The famous saint who brought Christianity to Ireland. He was a friend of Aongus, son of Nathfraoch.

**Pharaoh**                                                              **The Island of Destiny**

King of Egypt and father of Scota. Some say the Pharaoh was called Nectonibus, but I'm not totally convinced that this was his name. From my research I've been leaning towards him being Khaneferre Sobekhotep IV of the 13th Dynasty, so this is how I've written it, although I've recently come across some convincing information saying that it could have been Akhenaten of the 18th Dynasty.

**Prince Ilbrecht**                                                      **A Time of Heroes**

He was the son of the King of Norway.

**Prince Morann**                                                        **A Time of Heroes**

He was the long, blond-haired son of the Isle of Lewis' Fleet-King. He commanded 150 blond-haired warriors. He was killed by Suilebhain in their first battle.

**Riordan, son of Aissidha**                                            **A Time of Heroes**

A merry poet who was often one of the first into battle. The correct form of the name, Riordan, according to Alexander Bugge, was Rígbardán, which comes from ríg-bard, meaning Royal Bard. It is possible that Riordan was the Chief-poet of Munster, but I doubt it as there was at least one other known Chieftain with the same name, so it does sound like a name rather than a title. I haven't been able to pinpoint which tribe he was the Chieftain of, but my source material says 'the sportive Riordan before the valorous children of Donngal'. Which makes it sound as though he led a tribe of Donngal. Whether this tribe were descended from someone called Donngal or were from a place once called Donngal, I do not know. If his tribe were descended from a person called Dungal then I have three possible candidates: Dungal was the name of a Lord of Ossory from the mid-8th-mid-9th Century; there was also a Pict King of Alba (Scotland) called Giric, son of Dungal who supposedly conquered Ireland in the late 9th Century; and Ceallachan had an ancestor called Dungal.

**Ruadhan**                                                              **A Time of Heroes**

Saint Ruadhan was one of the famous Twelve Apostles of Ireland. Even though he died about 300 years before this tale, he is still mentioned in the story. Maybe, this was his spirit protecting Eochaid, or a mistake by the clergy adding his name in place of someone else. Or more likely, another holy man who had been given the same name as the famous apostle.

**Rudhraidhe, son of Partholan**                                        **The King with Four Names**

He was the leader of the early invaders of Ériu. In the age of the World 2545 (2655 BC) Rudhraidhe was drowned as a large lake erupted and washed over him. In his honour this body of water was named the Lake of Rudhraidhe. It is now known as Dundrum Bay.

**Ruithchern**                                              **Fingin and Mór**

Sister of Mór Mumhain and daughter of Aodh Bennan

**Sabina of the Fair and Faultless Covenant**     **Curse of the Aes Sídhe, The King with Four Names**

Beautiful daughter of Conn of the Hundred-battles. She marries MacNiadh, son of Lughaidh. After his death she marries Ailill Bare-ear and becomes mother of his nine children. Also, mother of MacCon.

**Samhair (SA-MEE-RA)**                                     **Curse of the Aes Sídhe**

She was the beautiful daughter of Fionn, son of Cumhal, and the first wife of Cormac-Cas. She is sometimes called Samer or Lamaria. Some sources say that she was the daughter of Ossian, who was the son of Fionn son of Cumhal, and therefore the grand-daughter of Fionn, and not his daughter.

**Sara**                                                     **The King with Four Names**

Charming & talkative daughter of Conn of the Hundred-battles. She marries Conaire, son of Mogha Laine.

**Saint Patrick**                                            **Church of Sighs, Releaser of Hostages**

See 'Patrick, son of Calphurn'.

**Scota, daughter of the Pharaoh**                           **The Island of Destiny**

A brave Warrior-queen who marries Milesius. Queen Scota is buried just south of the town of Tralee, on the path of a very ancient road which runs southwards over the Slieve Mish Mountains. The grave is under a large stone supposedly inscribed with Egyptian hieroglyphs. Note: Scota- that beautiful Egyptian 'little flower', as her name means; with her being the mother of most of our present-day countrymen, her name has been given to our people, in her honour. Which is why, when our countrymen settled in Alba, that great, rugged country took its name from her tribe, becoming Scota's Land, and thence 'Scotland'.

**Seaghdha**                                                 **A Time of Heroes**

One of the three Chieftains of the Corco Duibne. Seaghdha's descendants are the O'Seaghdha. All the O'Shee and O'Shea families of County Kerry descend from him.

**Seanchaí (SHAH-NACK-EE).**                                 **A Time of Heroes**

A seanchaí is a highly-accomplished storyteller. See 'Chief-seanchaí of Munster'.

**Senan**                                                    **A Time of Heroes**

Saint Senan arrived on Inis Cathaig, the Island of Cathach the Monster (Scattery Island), that stood in the mouth of the Sionna River. The creature who lived there had been terrorising the local population, so the brave Senan went to face it and defeated the monster. After that, Senan built a monastery upon that holy isle.

**Síoda (SHEE-O-DA)**                                        **The King with Four Names**

Queen of Munster. Wife of Magha Neid, mother of Mogha Nuadhad & seer of visions.

**Siomha (SHEE-VA)**                                         **The King with Four Names**

Clan Morna's witch.

**Sitric, son of Turgeis.**                                  **A Time of Heroes**

Viking Lord of Dubhlinn and King of all the Irish Vikings.

**Suilebhain (Sullivan) of Rathfann**                        **A Time of Heroes**

Head of Clan Fingin (CLAN FINEEN) Master of Cnoc Rathfann. His original name was Eochaid. He gained the eyes of Lobhan Draoi. He was in his thirties at the start of the tale, but was aged about seventy when Ceallachan became king. From him all of the Sullivan and O'Sullivan descend. Eochaid/Suilebhain was born sometime around 864 A.D. By the time this story begins he is already a Chieftain. So, I have set the first part of this tale to begin about 894 A.D., when he is about 30 years old, and still in his prime. So later on in the story, it is set in 934 A.D., when he is about 70 years old, and still a formidable fighter. This might sound hard to believe, that a 70-year-old is still a great fighter, but my father, who is descended from Suilebhain, at 84-years-old was still regularly able to beat me, at age 54, and my 18-year-old son, at table tennis, with scores usually of about 21 to 4. So, he too was still very active and able.

**Téa, daughter of Lughaidh, son of Ithe**                   **The Island of Destiny**

She was driven to achieve her goals. So, she liked change. And believed that all change was for the good. She had her sights fixed on Heremon.

**Teige, son of Cian**                                       **The King's Betrayal**

Strong Chieftain & cousin to both Fiacha Broadcrown & Cormac Longbeard. Third in line to the Munster throne.

**Teige, son of Nuadat**                                     **The King with Four Names**

Angry, High-druid of Tara & father of Muireann. Enemy of Cumhal.

**Téthor**                                                   **The Island of Destiny**

He was one of the Fairy-kings. He was the son of Cearmad Honey-mouth. He styled himself as the son of Ceacht, god of the plough. He was known for being as hard working as the farmer's plough. Strong and ruthlessly did he smite in battle. His wife was Fodhla.

**Torna Éices**                                              **Releaser of Hostages**

Famous Bard & High-poet of Ériu. Also, Conall Corc and Niall of the Nine-hostages' foster-father, teacher & adviser. Torna Éices was a member of the Ciarraige Luachra tribe from the north of Iarmuman. Due to his exceptional verses, he is now called 'the last great bard of Pagan Ireland'.

**Tor, son of Turgeis.**                                     **A Time of Heroes**

Brother of Sitric. Who favoured the spear.

**Tor's Wife/Widow.**                                                                      A Time of Heroes

Daughter of the High-king. Her name was actually Mór, daughter of Doncha, son of Flann Sionnach. Her name isn't mentioned in the story to avoid her being confused with Sitric's wife.

**Troiglethan**                                                                           Curse of the Aes Sídhe

His name is recorded in the record books as being the ráth builder of the Hill of Tara; he is also famous for making sculptured images and so I've assumed that as well as building the ráths, he quite possibly did carvings upon the walls as well.

**Tristan de Lyonesse**                                                                       Church of Sighs

Famous nephew of King Mark and Champion of Cornwall. In love with Iseult.

**Tuagh**                                                                           The King with Four Names

She was a beautiful princess who was fostered by Conaire Mór son of Edersceal, the High-king. So beautiful she was that no man was allowed near her, as she was destined to be married to a worthy King. But Manannán son of Lir heard of her beauty and desired her for himself. He sent his trusted druid to sing a magical lullaby to send her to sleep. The druid then carried the sleeping princess to the northern coast and the mouth of the Goddess River (River Bann). And whilst procuring a boat, a large wave surged up, washing the sleeping princess out to sea, where she drowned. Manannán, in anger, killed the druid. The Wave of the Mouth of Tuagh, (Tonn Tuaighe) is now forever connected to that bay.

**Tuatha Dé Danann (TOOR DEY DAHNUN)**

This is another name for the Fairy race. They were also called the *Aes Sídhe* which means 'People of the Mounds'.

**Uar, druid of the Milesians**                                                            The Island of Destiny

He was a prominent druid of the Milesians I assume the druids wore grey, which would explain the colour of the flags which marked their graves.

# Places Mentioned in the Stories

**Adair's Plain** is Magh Adhair, near Quin, County Clare.

**Aileach Neid** was supposedly the first stone building built in Ireland. See Grianán of Aileach.

**Alba** is Scotland.

**An Mhangarta**: 'The Longhaired' Mountain is Mangerton Mountain.

**Ash-tree River** is the River Funshion, Fermoy, County Cork.

**Áth Tuisil** is now Athassel. The name means 'Ford of the Fall'.

**Battle of Cnucha** was named after Conn's foster-mother, whose fortress overlooked the field of battle. The place of the battle is located in the grounds of Castleknock College near Phoenix Park, Dublin. Cumhal was buried there in a large burial mound, now called Windmill Hill, east of the college. His grave is still there, under the old water tower.

**Battle-wood** is west of Dromdaleague. In Irish Gaelic it is called *Treas Choill*.

**Bay of Beann's Clan** is Bantry Bay.

**Bay of Ceann Mara** is Kenmare Bay.

**Beara Island** (*Oiléan Béarra*). See Eadaoin's island.

**Bedegraine Castle** stood somewhere within the vast forest of Shire-wood (Sherwood Forest), in Nottinghamshire, England.

**Berbha River** is the River Barrow. It is the boundary between Leinster and Ossory. It is one of 'The Three Sister'. All three flow into the Celtic Sea near to the mouth of Port Leg (Waterford).

**Big River** is the River Blackwater or the Munster Blackwater. Its Irish Gaelic name is *An Abhainn Mhór*.

**Black River (northern)** is the Duff River, or Bunduff.

**Bregia.** See 'Plain of Bregia'.

**Breoghan's Tower** is now called the 'Tower of Hercules', at Corunna, Galicia, in Spain. Until the 20th Century it was called 'Farum Brigantium', which roughly translates as the 'Lighthouse of Brigantia'.

**Brittany** is a French peninsula just south of Cornwall, across the Ictian Sea (English Channel).

**Brú na Bóinne** is a valley of tombs which includes Newgrange. The name can be translated as 'Palace of the Boyne (Palace of Queen Boann's River).

**Brú Rí**. This means 'Home of Kings'. The nearby village of Bruree takes its name from this fortress.

**Cambenet** was a territory that bordered central Wales.

**Camulos**. See 'Fort of Camulos'.

**Cashel**. The fortress of the Munster Kings from the time of Conall Corc. Sometimes called the 'Fort of Heroes' and the 'Flagstone of Hundreds'. In 939 A.D. Cashel was described in the Annals of the Four Masters as 'The beautiful chalk-white Caiseal' so its walls were still white at this time. This fortress stood upon **Sídh-dhruim, which** means Fairy-ridge, which is now known as the Rock of Cashel. See **'Sídh-dhruim' and** 'Fairy-ridge'.

**Ceann Mara** is Kenmare. The name means 'Head of the Sea.

**Cenn Abrat** is now known as the Ballyhoura Mountains, and borders the Counties of Cork and Limerick.

**Chinn-tire** is Kintyre in Scotland. The name means 'Head-land'.

**Church of Sighs** is the translation of *Cell Osnadh*. It was a small church built by Saint Patrick, probably constructed from wood. And it would have had a wall around it. This place is now called Kellistown and is situated 7 ¼ km (4 ½ miles) southeast of Carlow.

**Ciarraige Luachra.** This tribe's ancient territory stretched from the town of Tralee northwards up to the Sionna (River Shannon). County Kerry takes its name from this tribe. *Ciarraige* means 'People of Ciar' as they descend from Ciar, son of the famous, deposed Ulster King, Fergus Mór and Maedhbh, Queen of Connacht.

**Clare's Height** is Duntryleague Hill. See 'Dún Tri Liag'.

**Clear Island** is Cape Clear Island. It's the most southerly inhabited island of Ireland.

**Cloch Barraighe** was in the townland of Gortolinny North, which is East South East of Kenmare; the huge, cubed limestone rock was situated just south of the river. It no longer appears to be here.

**Clonard Abbey**, in County Meath, was founded by Saint Finnian in the 6th century. Finnian taught many people, including the famous Twelve Apostles of Ireland.

**Cnoc-Áine** is Knockainey Hill, near Bruff, in County Limerick.

**Cnoc Luinge** can mean either 'Hill of Encampment' or 'Hill of Ships'. This is now known as Knocklong.

**Cnoc Rathfann** is Knockgraffon. The name means 'Hill of Rathfann'.

**Cnucha's Fortress.** This stronghold belonged to Conn of the Hundred-battles' foster-mother, so was named after her. See 'Battle of Cnucha'.

**Cornwall**, at this time, may have meant the whole territory of Dumnonia.

**Crinna** is thought to be on the Queen Boann River (River Boyne) near Stackallen Bridge, halfway between Navan and Slane. Although some say it is nearer Mellifont, County Louth.

**Crooked Glen** refers to the hills of Crumlin, Dublin.

**Crotta Cliach** means 'Harps of Cliach' is now known as the Galtee Mountains. It is sometimes written as 'Galty'. Apart from *Crotta Cliach*, they've also been called *Sliab Crot, Slieve Crot, Slieve Grud, Slieve Grod* and *Mount Grud.*

**Cruachan** is Rathcroghan: *Ráth Cruachan*, which means 'Fort of Cruachan', and is situated on a hill near Tulsk, at the north of County Roscommon.

**Dalgan's Stronghold** is Dundalk. Dundalk Bay is named after the ruins of this nearby fortress. The legendary Red Branch hero, Cuchulain, once had lived in this fortress.

**Dergart's Lake** is Lough Derg.

**Dirty River** is the River Poddle, in Dublin. It has had a couple of other names during its time which have been translated as 'puddle', 'mire' and 'muddy pool'.

**Drobais River** is the Drowes River.

**Dromiskin monastery**, in County Louth stood two leagues south of Dalgan's Stronghold (Dundalk).

**Druim Dil** is Drumdeel, in County Tipperary. The name means the 'Ridge of Dil'. I presume this must have been situated near the boundaries between Ossory and the Plain of Femen.

**Dubhlinn** is Dublin. The original settlement was approximately where the High Street/Cornmarket area is located.

**Dún Aengusa mac Nathfraoch**, which means the 'Fort of Aongus, son of Nathfraoch'. This large fortress had a monastery within its walls. It was built on land that is now known as Pottlerath, in County Kilkenny.

**Dún Clare** means 'Fort of Clare'. It was a hill-fort that sat upon the hill of *Uachtar Clári*: Clare's Height (Duntryleague Hill), which itself was a peak upon the mountains of *Cenn Abrat* (Ballyhoura Mountains).

**Dún Crott** means 'Fort of Harps'. It was a hill-fort that sat upon the mountains of *Crotta Cliach*: Harps of Cliach, which is now known as the Galtee Mountains.

**Dundory** means 'fort of oak'. It was another name for the fortified settlement of Port Leg (Waterford). See 'Port Leg'.

**Dún Laoghaire** (DOON LEARY), which means the 'Fort of Laoghaire', is on the east coast of Ireland, about six miles south of Dublin. It can also be seen written as *Dún Laoire*.

**Dún Tri Liag** is Duntryleague Hill. The name means 'Fort of Three Pillars'. See 'Clare's Height'.

**Eadaoin's island** is officially called *An tOileán Mór*, which means 'the big island' but it is known locally as Bere Island (or Bear Island). In my stories its first called *Inis Crecraighe*, but then becomes known as *Oileán Béarra*, or Beara Island and is situated in the mouth of the Bay of Beann's Clan (Bantry Bay), County Cork. Much later, the O'Sullivans had their castle of Dunboy on this island.

**Echtge's Mountains** are Slieve Aughty. A range of mountains between the counties of Clare and Galway. A Fairy-princess was once given these lands as a dowry.

**Éile** (ELY) is a territory located in the south of County Offaly and north Tipperary. This tribe descend from Cian, son of Ailill Bare-ear. The powerful Chieftain of Éile owned the Fairy-ridge (Rock of Cashel) before Conall Corc.

**Eoghanachta.** (OWEN-ACTA)

**Eoghanacht Áine.** This tribe belong to Cnoc-Áine. Now called Knockainey

**Eoghanacht Airthir Cliach.** Their name means 'East Cliach' as their territory is east of the Harps of Cliach, which are the Galty Mountains, in the east of County Limerick and the west of County Tipperary. They descend from Aongus, son of Nathfraoch.

**Eoghanacht Chaisil.** This tribe belong to the Rock of Cashel.

**Eoghanacht Glendamnach.** This tribe belong to Glennamhain, which has been replaced by Glanworth Castle.

**Eoghanacht Loch Léin.** This tribe belong to Iarmuman, which is West Munster.

**Eoghanacht Ninussa.** This tribe belong to the northwest of County Clare and the neighbouring Aran Islands.

**Eoghanacht Rathlinn.** This tribe belong to the parish of Templemartin, near Bandon, County Cork.

**Ériu** (AIR-REE) is now called Éire, and in these stories refers to the whole island of Ireland.

**Esdara River** is the Ballisodare River, with the Waterfall-of-the-Oak being the Ballisodare Falls, at Ballysadare in Sligo. The Ballisodare River comes from the Owenmore River.

**Esker Riada** was a naturally-formed gravel ridge upon which sat most of the Great Way. The Esker Riada wound its way across the country from Medara's Bridge (Clarinbridge) to Dubhlinn (Dublin).

**Fairy-ridge.** This place is now known as the Rock of Cashel.

**Fast-runner River** is River Liffey.

**Feabhal's Lake** is Lough Foyle.

**Femen** is a plain stretching roughly from Cashel to Clonmel. This plain was thought to control the power and wealth of Munster.

**Fews Mountains** runs through Fews Upper and Fews Lower, in County Armagh.

**Firceall** means 'Men of the Churches'.

**Ford of the King** is Athenry, in County Galway.

**Ford of Senach.** This river crossing is at Ballyshannon.

**Fort of Camulos** is now called Colchester in Essex, England. Many people believe, myself included, that this was the legendary castle of Camelot. (Although Malory believed Winchester was Camelot, probably due to the famous round-table being there, and Caxton believed Camelot to be in Wales). Camulos was the Britons' pagan god of war, and after the

Roman army invaded England, they captured the Fort of Camulos. After rebuilding it as a military walled town, it became the first capital of Roman Britain.

**Fortrenn lands** is the area between the Rivers Forth and Tay in Alba (Scotland).

**Gap of Heroes**. Unfortunately, I can't find this place anywhere.

**Garlot** was a territory in Alba (Scotland), possibly in the Lothian region.

**Gaul** is the vast territory that lay nestled between the Alps and the Ictian Sea (English Channel).

**Glennamhain** (GLENNOWIN) means 'Valley of the River'. This castle was nestled in the valley, south of Cenn Abrat and to the west of the Harps of Cliach. It overlooked the Ash-tree River (River Funshion). It has been replaced by a 13th Century Norman castle called Glanworth.

**Goddess River** is the River Bann, Ulster.

**Gore** was a territory, possibly within the Briton's kingdom of North Humber Land.

**Grass River** is the River Nore. It is one of the rivers known as 'The Three Sister'. All three flow into the Celtic Sea near to the mouth of Port Leg (Waterford).

**Great Marsh of Munster** was a long, slim island that stood near the mouth of the Lay River (River Lee) surrounded by marsh-covered isles. It could be reached either by boat, or on foot at low tide. The original crossing place can still be seen at low tide, to the left of the Mardyke Bridge. After the surrounding isles were eventually reclaimed from the marshland, it became known as the City of Cork.

**Great Skellig** is also known as Skellig Michael. The word *Skellig* means 'splinter of stone'. Later in our tales this island became a monastery.

**Great Spring** is believed to be Oranmore, in County Galway. It was originally called Fuarán Mór, which means 'Great Spring', due to a large natural spring that was found there.

**Great-wood of Firceall**. Kilmore was part of the Great-wood, which is situated in County Offaly. See 'Firceall'.

**Grey-ridge** is the Hill of Tara. See 'Tara', 'Teamhair' and 'Liathdruim'.

**Grianán of Aileach** is sometimes known as Greenan Ely or Greenan Fort. The word *Aileach* means 'stone-house' and *Grianán* can either mean 'sun room' or 'place with a view'. A *grianán* was sometimes the name of an opulently furnished dayroom used by noblewomen. The Grianán of Aileach was built upon the spot once inhabited by Aileach Neid.

**Height of Aodh** (*Ard-Aodha*) is now sometimes known as Ardea Castle. The description in my story has mostly been surmised from the three prints of Arday Castle by Thomas Walmsley, made in 1809/1810, as well as modern photographs of the remaining walls. The ruins of this once-great castle now stand near Tuosist, overlooking Kenmare Bay.

**Hill of Almu** is the Hill of Allen. A large volcanic hill in the west of County Kildare.

**Hill of Miracles**. I'm assuming, after much research, that *Ard Fothaig Brenaind*, was the place now known as Ardfert (*Ard Fhearta*), as Saint Brendan the Navigator founded a monastery there in the sixth century.

**Hill of Rathfann** is Knockgraffon. See 'Cnoc Rathfann'.

**Hy Kinsella** was where the present County Wexford lies, but it was slightly larger than the current county.

**Iarmuman** means west-Munster. This territory sits within a large portion of County Kerry.

**Ictian Sea** is the English Channel that lies between France and England.

**Ilnacullin** means 'Island of Holly'. It is also known as Garinish Island, and Garnish Island, and stands in the Bay of Beann's Clan (Bantry Bay), close to the mainland.

**Inis Crecraighe**. See 'Eadaoin's island'.

**Innse Gall** means 'Islands of (fair-haired) Foreigners'. These islands are now known as the Hebrides, which lie off the northwest coast of Scotland. Back in the Viking Age the population was mixed, consisting of both Norwegian and Celtic Races. It has been poetically called the lands 'from whence the storm winds do roar".

**Ionad Phuball Fhiacha** is the Fews Mountains. The name means the 'Place of Fiacha's Tent'. See 'Fews Mountains'.

**Irena** is now believed to be the Greek island, Samothrace. Due to the island's appearance, it was nicknamed 'The Mountain of Thrace'.

**Iron Mountain** is Sliabh an Iarainn, in County Leitrim.

**Island of Cathach the Monster** is Scattery Island in the Shannon Estuary. Its Irish name is *Inis Cathaig*.

**Island of Dark Strangers** is the original part of the city of Limerick. It is now known as King's Island and is on the Sionna River (River Shannon).

**Islands of (fair-haired) Foreigners**. See 'Innse Gall'.

**Isle of Lewis** is at the northwest corner of the islands that make up the Hebrides, in Scotland.

**Joyous Garde** means 'Fortress of Happiness'. It was believed by Malory, and others, to be situated on the site of Bamburgh Castle, in Northumberland, England.

**Lake Lurgan** is Galway Bay. At one time, probably over two thousand years ago, it was actually a lake.

**Lake of Érainn** is Lough Erne.

**Lake-of-the-Hounds** is Lough Conn, in County Mayo.

**Land of Promise** is believed to be the Isle of Man. This was believed to be the place of the Afterlife, where we all go after we've died. The Fairy Sea god, Manannán son of Lir, was believed to ferry the departed souls in his boat, Wave-sweeper, across to the Land of Promise, where they stay forever young in a land of eternal summer.

**Lay River** is the River Lee. Its Irish name is *An Laoi*.

**Liathdruim** is the Hill of Tara. *Liathdruim* was the original name for Tara. It means 'Grey-ridge'. See 'Tara', Teamhair' and 'Grey-ridge'.

**Lighthouse of Brigantia**. See 'Breoghan's Tower'.

**Linn Duachaill** stood on the southern bank of Dalgan's Stronghold (Dundalk Bay), near the village of Annagassan, County Louth. It was a sister Viking sea-base similar to that of Dubhlinn (Dublin). This sea-base was almost completely abandoned by the time of Ceallachan's rule. Linn Duachaill means Duachall's Pool.

**Lions** was believed to be the capital of Lyonesse, which stood to the south of Cornwall, England. It was a magnificent fortified-city filled with towers and domes. Like Rome, this governing seat was also built upon seven hills. See 'Lyonesse'.

**Loch Gabhair** means 'Lake of the Goats'. It is situated between the villages of Ratoath and Dunshaughlin, in County Meath.

**Loch Garman** is Wexford.

**Londinium** is London, England. Londinium is the old Roman name.

**Luan's Ford** is Athlone.

**Lyonesse** was a peninsula that stretched south from Cornwall, in England. The Isles of Scilly are believed to be all that is left of this great land.

**Macha's Height** is Armagh.

**Magh Nuadhad** is Maynooth. *Magh Nuadhad* means 'Nuadhad's Plain', although some people say that Maynooth was named after the father of Teige, son of Nuadat, who was the High-druid of Tara.

**Magh Slécht** (MAW SHLAYKHT) is Plain of Prostration.

**Mag Léna** is Kilbride, in County Offaly. See 'Plain of Leana'.

**Medara's Bridge** is Clarinbridge.

**Memphis**, in Egypt. This would have been the Egyptian capital at the time in which my first tale 'The Island of Destiny' is set.

**Middle-Land** is the Mediterranean Basin. See Middle-of-the-Land Sea.

**Middle-of-the-Land Sea** comes from the word 'Mediterranean'. This body of water is located within the Middle-Land (the Mediterranean). In Latin the word 'medius' means 'middle', and the word 'terra' means 'land', which is where the word 'Mediterranean' comes from. I thought it would be best to translate the word 'Mediterranean' into its English component parts, the same way as I've done for most of the Irish place-names; in this way the readers can also look upon this part of the story with fresh eyes.

**Mountain of the Women** is Slievenamon.

**Mountain of Thrace** was a nickname for Irena.

**Mountains of Cualu** is the Wicklow Mountains.

**Mountains of Eiblinni** is the Slieve Felim Mountains.

**Mountains of Flame** is the Slieve Bloom Mountains.

**Mountains of Gamh** is the Ox Mountains.

**Mountains of Mis** is Slieve Mish.

**Mountains of Rushes** is the Sliabh Luachra.

**Muireadheach's Island** is Inishmurray.

**Múscraige.** There were many Múscraige tribes whose small territories were scattered around Munster, though their main strongpoint was in what is now called Muskerry, in County Cork, which is the valley, north of the River Lee, with the Boggeragh Mountains to the north and the Shehy Mountains to the south.

**Norgales** was a kingdom in Wales.

**North Humber Land** was the land north of the river Humber, in England. This vast territory of land stretched up to the (Alba) Scottish border, more or less.

**Nuadhad's Plain.** See 'Magh Nuadhad'.

**Orkney** is a large group of islands situated off the north-eastern coast of Scotland.

**Ossory** originally belonged to Leinster but from roughly around 450 A.D. until roughly about 850 A.D. it formed part of Munster; after this time, it became independent from both Kingdoms.

**Ox Island** is Devenish Island on the Lake of Érainn (Lough Erne).

**Palace of Queen Boann's River.** See Brú na Bóinne.

**Place of the Elms** is the village of Lucan, Dublin.

**Plain of Ailbe** takes its name from an ancient war-hound that once guarded the Leinster-Ossory border. It stood next to the River Barrow at the junction where the Counties of Laois, Carlow and Kildare met.

**Plain of Bregia**. This was otherwise known as the Great Plain of Meath. This plain was named after Bréga, son of Breoghan, who either fell there, or who's tribe had once resided there. The plain consisted of most of the present County Meath, along with Dublin.

**Plain of Femen** was in County Tipperary and stretched between Cashel and Clonmel.

**Plain of Fermoy**. The name comes from *Mainistir Fhear Maí*, which means 'monastery of the Men of the Plain'.

**Plain of Lament**. This vast plain stretched from at least the village of Cong, in County Mayo, northwards to Sligo Abbey. The First Battle of the Plain of Lament was near the village of Cong. The Second Battle took place near Sligo Abbey.

**Plain of Leana** is Kilbride. It's in Westmeath, to the southeast of Lough Ennell. Leana found Datho's son's huge prize pig in an oakwood. He kept the pig for seven years until one day he fell asleep in a trench upon the plain. Whilst sleeping, the pig buried him alive. Thereafter the plain was named after him. See 'Mag Léna'.

**Plain of Prostration** is Magh Slécht (MAW SHLAYKHT).

**Plain of Raigne**. The wide-eyed Raigne Rosclethan was the son of Fionn, son of Cumhal. It is in County Kilkenny and was previously a wooded ridge called the Wood of Conflict. Clan Morna killed Raigne on this plain and thus the plain was named after him. Although some say that the plain was named after a Roman called Raigne the Mighty, who cleared the wood from the land.

**Plain-of-the-Darkness-of-the-Sea** was a large piece of land from Dalgan's Stronghold (Dundalk) to Drogheda, being as wide as the present County Louth. It gained its name as at one time the plain was submerged under the sea.

**Plain of Ene** is *Magh Ene*, Bundoran, County Donegal.

**Plain of Waterfalls** was halfway between Croom and Adare, in County Limerick. The waterfalls in question were within the River of the Plain (River Maigue).

**Port Leg** is Waterford harbour. Its name in Irish Gaelic is *Port Láirge*. It was sometimes referred to as *Dundory*, meaning 'fort of oak'.

**Port Righ** means the 'King's Harbour'. This is a bay which has a small sheltered beach on the eastern coast of the peninsula of Chinn-tire (Kintyre), in Scotland. See 'Chinn-tire'.

**Queen Boann River** is the River Boyne.

**Red-wood** is the translation of Coill Ruadh. Its original name was Coill Garbhruis which translates as Rough-wood. Unfortunately, after extensive searching I've been unable to find where this place would have been.

**Ridge of Dil.** See 'Druim Dil'.

**River of Érainn** is River Erne.

**River Feale** is in County Kerry.

**River Muaidhe** is the River Moy.

**River of the Plain** is the River Maigue. Its Irish name is *An Mháigh*.

**Roman Wall**, otherwise known as Hadrian's Wall was an 84 miles-long defensive structure built by the Roman army in England, between Bowness-on-Solway on the western coast to Wallsend, near the eastern coast. It was the most northerly and westerly frontier of the Roman empire, built to keep the marauding Scots from attacking the Roman-held territory. George R. R. Martin based his wall in 'Game of Thrones' on this historical British landmark. (I actually walked the route of Hadrian's Wall myself in July 2022).

**Ros na Rí** is Rosnaree. The name means 'Wood-of-the-Kings'. Teige, son of Cian, son of Ailill Bare-ear was killed by a stag in these woods. Coincidentally, the High-king, Cormac Longbeard, when he died, was reputedly buried here.

**Samhair** (SA-MEE-RA) is the Morningstar River. It is a small river which joins the River of the Plain (River Maigue), just north of Bruree. It is named after Cormac-Cas' wife.

**Sand-hills** is thought to be Bull Rock. Donn, son of Milesius was buried upon this isle.

**Sea of Darkness** was one of the old names for the Atlantic Ocean.

**Shire-wood** is the famous Sherwood Forest, in Nottinghamshire, England. At one time it covered a quarter of the county of Nottinghamshire.

**Sídh-dhruim** means Fairy-ridge. This place is now known as the Rock of Cashel.

**Siomha** (SHEE-VA) River is the Clodagh River that runs into the River Ilen. It is named after Clan Morna's witch.

**Sionna's** (SHA-NA) River is the River Shannon.

**Sister River** (Rivers Suir) is one of the rivers known as 'The Three Sister'. All three flow into the Celtic Sea near to the mouth of Port Leg (Waterford). Its Irish name is *Abhainn na Siúire*.

**Sliabh Cualgni** is Slieve Gullion.

**Sliabh Luachra** is a mountain range that contains seven glens. It is, very roughly, at the northern half of County Kerry, especially along the eastern border; and also, to the adjoining western half of the border between Counties Limerick and Cork.

**Sligo Harbour.** The sandy ridge that the Munster army crossed went from Finisklin to Ballincar.

**Stony River** is the Colne River, in Essex, England.

**Straits of Moyle** is the narrowest expanse of sea between Ériu (Ireland) and Alba (Scotland). At its shortest point it is only about 20 km (12 miles).

**Stranggore**. Nobody knows exactly where this territory was.

**Strong Fort of Éile** (ELY) is Thurles.

**Talti** is now known as Teltown.

**Tara** is the Hill of Tara. See also 'Teamhair', 'Grey-ridge' and 'Liathdruim'.

**Teamhair** (TARA) is the Hill of Tara. The name 'Teamhair' is thought to mean the 'House of Téa'; although there are many other translations that exist for the name of 'Teamhair'. See also 'Tara', 'Grey-ridge' and 'Liathdruim'.

**Tir Conaill** is Tirconnell and is roughly where present-day County Donegal stands today.

**Trespasser River** refers to the River Trent in England. 'Trespasser' is a possible rough meaning of 'Trent', coined due to its frequent flooding.

**Tuath Laighean** was in the north of the kingdom of Leinster, being part of the Counties of Wicklow and Dublin.

**Tuirrin Castle**. Now called 'The Kemp', 'Kemp Castle' or 'Camp Castle', which is on Turin Hill, Forfarshire, Scotland. An old record mentions that this was his stronghold. There would probably be many other fortresses belonging to Feredach Fionn but I can't find mention of any in the ancient records so I've set this one as his main base where Conall Corc meets him.

**Twins of Macha** is Navan Fort. It was the third biggest fort in Ireland (Ériu) and was home of the Red Branch Knights. Its Irish Gaelic name is *Emain Macha*.

**Tyntagyll** is Tintagel in Cornwall, England. This is believed to be the birthplace of the legendary King Arthur.

**Uí Echach Muman** belong to the Eoghanacht Rathlinn. The Uí Echach Muman were from the area around the town of Bandon, County Cork.

**Waterfall-of-Red-Aodh** is the Assaroe Falls on the River of Érainn (River Erne), near Ballyshannon, County Donegal. It was originally named after Aodh Ruadh, the 61st High-king, whose daughter, Macha Mongrua was the only woman ever to rule Ériu, and so was the only High Queen; she was the 64th ruler, reigning from 667 BC. Her husband built the Twins of Macha (Navan Fort).

**Waterfall-of-the-Oak** is the Ballisodare Falls, at Ballysadare in Sligo. See 'Esdara River'.

**Wood-of-the-Cairn** is Derrycarne.

**Wood-of-the-Kings**. See 'Ros na Rí'.

**Yellow Cairn** (Carn Buidhe) may have been built on or near a burial mound. This ale-house seemed very spacious inside and being the only inn properly mentioned in my book it was obviously a popular place for the nobles to get sustenance. The place can't be found on any modern map. Even Victorian experts who have found many of the ancient sites couldn't pinpoint this place. But it does seem to be somewhere near to Kenmare.

Thank you for taking the time to read this book. I really hope that you've enjoyed my work.

**It would mean so much to me if you would leave a review on Amazon.**

If you want to connect on social media to be kept up to date with any future releases, my sites are:

www.Twitter.com/kingsofmunster

www.Instagram.com/jasonsavin

www.Facebook.com/kingsofmunster

And if you enjoyed my book and want to read more, this is my entire catalogue to date:

**Kings of Munster**

Book 1: The Island of Destiny

Book 2: Curse of the Aes Sídhe

Book 3: A Time of Heroes

**Other Books**

Beyond the Elven Gate    Mybook.to/Beyondtheelvengate

172

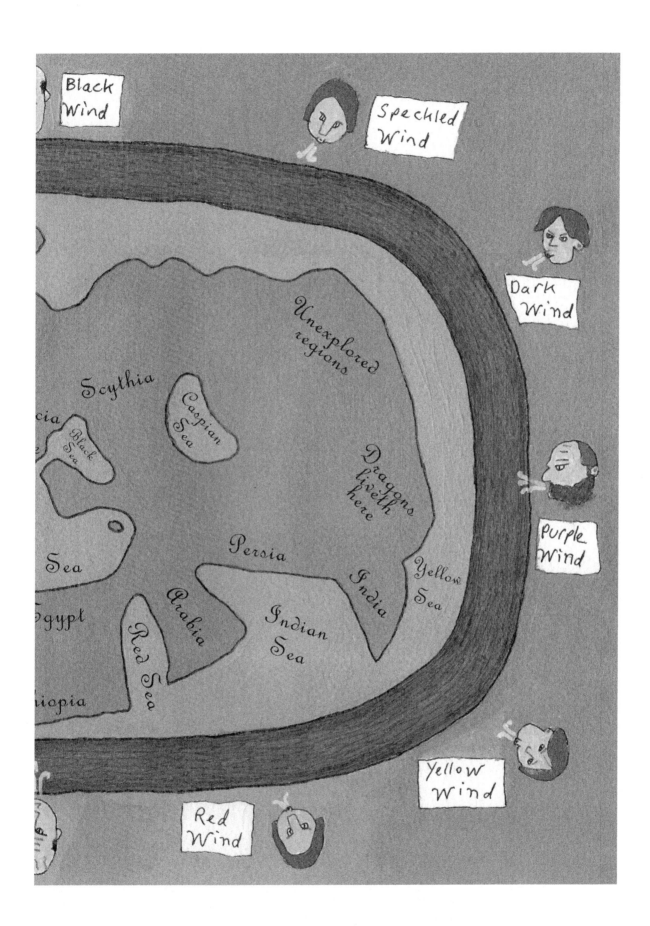

173

Printed in Great Britain
by Amazon

10330000R00099